RAINING SIDEWAYS

BY

ANDREW SHIELDS

WITH COLLABORATION BY BRETT CASTO AND LOGAN WATERMAN

A
BLADES
IN THE
DARK
NOVEL

RAINING SIDEWAYS

Copyright © 2021 by Andrew Shields

All rights reserved. This book or any portion thereof may not be reproduced or used in any manner whatsoever without the express written permission of the publisher except for the use of brief quotations in a book review or scholarly journal.

First Printing: 2021

ISBN: 978-1-7348074-5-5

Cover art by John Cliff Alvarez

https://shieldsuppublishing.wordpress.com/

IN MEMORIAM

Logan Watterman

CHAPTER ONE

Akoros is a study in failed transition.

The Emperor is himself immortal, and he outlaws any plan to shift authority to others. Within our cities, we distribute resources through civic and social structures designed to concentrate wealth and power with the ruling class. These structures shut out competition.

Transitioning from life to death is hardly peaceful. The Gates of Death shattered eight centuries ago, so when we die, our spirits linger. Almost all of them rapidly decay to starvation and insanity. As a result we must live in tightly-packed cities to protect us from the death storms in the wilderness. We scrupulously erase our own echoes, new generations of ghosts who would destroy us.

The living and the dead default to a transition plan amounting to this: "if you want power you must take it." Is it any surprise that a robust breed of law-breakers focuses on doing just that?

—From "Intrinsic Criminality: A Study"
by Retired Chief Inspector Darias

Bilt stepped into the alley, looking both ways down the filthy corridor. He took a deep breath, as though his expanding ribs could push back the buildings that loomed above.

Thirty paces would put him between the two bodyguards waiting by his carriage, out on the street. A moment of isolation was the price of his errand's privacy.

Three steps later, Bilt shrugged deeper into his coat as a shiver rippled across his ribs. Light reflected from the pooled water down the center of the alley. Dread welled up in his guts.

Ten steps along, he could not put one foot before the other. His breath steamed before him, and he heard the creak of ice riming along the water.

"B-blood and b-bone," he swore, his lips numb. He clutched at the spiritbane charm in his lapel pocket, over his heart. Just a bit of metal. He couldn't force it to resonate with his will.

Something was behind him. He could not turn, he could not run. Like a standing stone beneath the rising sun, he felt the energy of it roll along his flank. The presence moved in front of him, surfacing through the Mirror, taking shape in the air before him. Bilt was desperate to drag tiny sips of air into his clenched torso. He was drowning in fear as frost seethed along his cheeks.

"Y-you," he managed.

The apparition drifted in an invisible breeze that did not caress any physical sense. The ghost was an echo from the canals. Hollow eyes. A memory of skin, a memory of rot, a memory of rage, bundled into a feminine shape with a mane of weed-twined hair flexing in and out of view through the thinnest remaining membrane of the Mirror.

Her memory had claws.

"It's inefficient, what you did," a mild voice said, interrupting the intimate moment. Bilt recoiled, wound tight and trembling. He oriented on the doorway where a shadowy man stood quiet, observing. "Using the canals, that's sloppy," the man continued. "They are shallow, and the places where they aren't?" He gestured, vague. "Everyone knows them. Drags them for corpses."

"What—d'you—"

"Oh, I know you consider her to be... finished business," the shadow said reflectively. "They found her corpse after only one day, but... that drowning pool, just off the canal. So many fragments there. She printed on them, pulled them together. She was waiting for you, when I visited the drowning pool; she was right near the surface. She knew she'd get her chance. Somehow. Mysterious, how the spirits know things they can't know, yet other parts of their identity... gone." He cocked his head to the side. "Do you think you'll be a ghost, Bilt? When this is over?"

Bilt was speechless, his gaze lost in the ghost's empty eye sockets.

"This is about to be over," the shadowy man murmured. "Tell me where Lord Colsarch is hiding. Do that, and Giselle here leaves with me. She keeps suffering, of course, and your conscience carries that. Maybe you can extract additional payment from Lord Colsarch for your pain. She was his dalliance, after all; his plaything that you had to put away for him. Or, perhaps you care more about him. Perhaps you fear him more than you fear Giselle. Or you feel you owe him more than you owe her."

Bilt trembled, his tendons and muscles clenched so hard they hovered on the edge of tearing. His mouth worked, but no sound emerged. With a seething hiss, white flowed down a lock of his hair as death surged around him, touching through his fragile life force's caul.

The man in the doorway lifted his hand, ever so slightly, the black glove almost shiny in the dim light. The currents around the ghost shifted. She seemed to coil into herself, compacting, lips curling away from the crooked teeth of the skull beneath. A strange warmth was allowed out of Bilt's heart, threading into his limbs.

"Decide."

"C-Colsarch—aboard the Ripple Dame, moored on the Saverslick Canal Delta Third Arm," Bilt babbled, the words piling out.

The man in the shadows watched him for a long second, then nodded.

"Run."

The Mirror shifted, and the ghost receded away from the real world of breath and flesh. Adrenaline jolted through Bilt, who staggered into a sprint, flashing past his startled bodyguards, who scrambled in pursuit.

"Good girl," the man murmured to himself, flexing a perception layered somewhere between thought and meat. He held up the ice-rimed spirit bottle, limned with delicate sigils etched in the glass. Perhaps the ghost flowed into it, or perhaps its smooth walls swelled around her; the spirit was contained, and her captor let out a plume of too-hot breath into the chilly night.

He left another way.

THE PICKLED EEL. CROW'S FOOT
11ᵀᴴ MENDAR, 850. *THREE DAYS LATER*
HOUR OF SONG, 2 HOURS PAST DUSK

Wind gusted as the shadowed man hauled at the tavern door. He didn't let it slam. The night slithered in around him, bearing him into the dim room. The door clacked shut, and the man flexed at his coat, settling it.

"Uppercut, you sly dog, I was beginning to wonder if you'd even show!" pattered a server as he approached the newcomer, all smiles. "I do hope my hot tip paid off," he confided past the back of his hand with a smirk.

"You know I can't tell you that. For your own good, remember," Uppercut said absently. "I'm looking for Scarecrow."

"And he's looking for you," the server said in a stage whisper. "Right this way!"

Uppercut flexed his jaw as he followed the server past the long row of booths and through the door in the back. The air was thick, flavored with wet and dry rot. The server pushed a curtain aside, mock bowing and ushering Uppercut past.

"There you are," rasped the man seated with his back to the wall in the private room, his ornate crossbow tilted on the table in front of him. "'Bout time."

"No need to get testy, Scarecrow," Uppercut said, eyes lingering on several empty bottles arranged off to the side. "I trust you've been busy."

"*So* busy," Scarecrow agreed. He paused, staring directly at the server, who squinted into a servile grin and bobbed his head several times as he withdrew. "You sure he's not a problem?"

"No, I'm not sure," Uppercut said, seating himself opposite the Skov. "But if I stabbed everyone who might be a problem, I'd have no time to do anything else." He paused. "What did you find."

Scarecrow allowed a moment of silence, a smile growing on his face, and he settled back and crossed his arms over his chest. "You were right. Colsarch knows where to find the Merenkaynti Zemi. He's going to lead us right to it."

Uppercut let that sink in. "Alright, so far so good."

"He's burning through Coin fast, with the experts he's hired on," Scarecrow said. "The brains is Professor Grear, who lectures on Skov history and religion at Charterhall. Brains need eyes," Scarecrow continued. "You know Shimmer?"

"Snap the little bones," Uppercut swore.

"Right, thought you might have heard of her," Scarecrow said with a bleak grin. "She visited his boat. Several times. I'm pretty sure she's the one who will pull this together and direct it."

"And the muscle?" Uppercut said.

"Granite." Scarecrow paused. "Skovlander. Big," he added with a two-handed gesture for emphasis. "He once hurled a draft goat through a wall because it stepped on his foot."

"I can work with that," Uppercut said. He studied the bottles by Scarecrow, and tugged the stopper from one that was still half full.

"Then there's the Iruvian. A swordsman. I followed everybody else, found out more about them. All I could tell about this guy was that he's based out of a Red Sash hangout, and his pals are not too keen on curious Skovs."

"No adepts?" Uppercut said, studying the bottle. "No Whispers?"

"Not as far as I could tell," Scarecrow replied.

Uppercut looked him over for a long moment, and Scarecrow's smile faded.

"What," he demanded, the familiar scowl settling in once again.

"Sounds like you spent a lot of time around these people," Uppercut said. "You are sure they didn't spot you."

"Oh, I'm sure," Scarecrow said through his teeth. "Tracking the circulation? That's what I do. And I'm damn good at it. They didn't see me," he said, driving his finger into the tabletop for emphasis, "because I didn't want them to. And I didn't get close."

"I've been to the canal. The third arm. Not a lot of cover, not for multiple days." Uppercut cocked his head to the side. "How did you do it?"

Scarecrow leaned back, his frown deepening. For a long moment, he chewed his lip. Uppercut waited.

"There's a crane," Scarecrow muttered. "Overlooks the dock. Loading and unloading. But it's out of commission, damaged. So nobody notices if you take a sack of fishmix and a waterskin and snuggle in for a day or two."

"Lord Colsarch didn't move for days?" Uppercut pressed.

"Oh, he moved. Met with his crew at some bistro, hashed out the details away from his hideout—I don't think anyone but Shimmer knew where he was holed up at first. Since then they have met together and separately aboard the Ripple Dame."

"When they went to the bistro, they didn't spot you?"

Scarecrow locked his jaw. "They did not. I wasn't close by. I tracked them by feel."

Uppercut raised his eyebrows.

"I marked them," he ground out, touching his silk headband, widening his eyes meaningfully.

"Ah." Uppercut relaxed, leaning back. "You marked them. With your mysterious partner. And you think they're going to move soon."

"I know it," Scarecrow agreed. "They had instruments, telescopes, on the pier. Looking at the moon, and her dimmer sisters, measuring the refraction. Whatever defenses are around the zemi, they'll be weakest at low tide, and the day after tomorrow is the lowest tide in a month."

Uppercut savored a smile, then tilted some spore wine through it.

The curtain rattled aside, and the server bowed, energetic with suppressed stress. "Hey fellas, I got you a refill," he said through a smile. He put two bottles on the table and took a couple steps back.

"Why don't you join us," Uppercut said, inscrutable.

"I really can't," the server said, a caricature of apology.

"Walton, right?" Uppercut said. "I thought you wanted to have a drink with us."

"Normally yes, but—" Walton began.

"Tell me, or tell a ghost," Uppercut interrupted.

"—Bilt paid me to send word when you came back here," Walton said, "and I did, so maybe..."

"Maybe," Scarecrow agreed, grim. He rose to his feet and hefted his crossbow. "Goodbye, Walton."

"See you soon?" Walton squinted, flinching back from the possibility of an incoming blow.

Uppercut raised his eyebrows. "Unlikely," he murmured.

Then the scoundrels were gone, vanishing through one of the Pickled Eel's many back doors.

"Clock's ticking now," Scarecrow muttered, glaring across the street and down the block. Two coaches each disgorged half a dozen thugs who piled into the Pickled Eel. He leaned back further into the shadow of the alleyway. "Think they'll see us coming?"

"I think they'll be looking," Uppercut mused. He caught Scarecrow's eye. Let him see the hunger.

Scarecrow nodded. "Jumping at shadows," he agreed. "Shadows, deep and thick."

They turned away from the tavern and blended with the night.

Fog shrouded the docks, deadening sight and muffling sound. River traffic was sluggish and distant. Halos of light smeared in the mist. The few people who had not yet sought shelter avoided eye contact and kept their distance.

The Ripple Dame was moored to the quay, its pale hull glowing in the diffused moonlight. Workers hefted boxes from a pile on the dock, carrying them up the gangplank under the watchful eyes of half a dozen guards.

Uppercut gazed down at the activity, idly considering how ant-like the workers acted as they loaded cartons and boxes and sacks of supplies, steady lines draining the wagon's contents into the boat. Then he narrowed his eyes. That purple head scarf. He knew that scarf, and the man under it. Leaning away from the base of the crane, he followed the handrails down closer to the wagon.

Uppercut tugged a warded bottle from his coat pocket, ignoring the bitter cold radiating from the trapped ghost inside. He flicked the catch and shifted the stopper with his thumb, freeing a gout of energy.

"Behave," he murmured under his breath. "I give you patience." He concentrated the plasmic essence, his hand tightening to a fist as he commanded the ghost's complete attention.

"Now, the goat," he breathed. He shifted to look over at the bored draft goat standing in the traces of the wagon. "Go."

The driver stood in the back of the wagon bed, shoving the last of the supplies to where the workers could reach them. As he did, Giselle drifted into the goat's perceptions, and her teeth bared as she projected a whiff of her energy where the animal could sense it. The goat's eyes shot open, and it bawled as it scrambled backwards.

The driver swore as he tilted off balance, clattering in the wagon bed. The goat jumped forward, and a row of crates slid off and splintered on the cobbles. Bottles of oil bounced and rolled. A couple shattered.

Tugging his fist back, Uppercut drew the spirit's essence into his shadow, where it writhed for a moment before drifting around the confines of his visual echo. Uppercut approached the stalled out line of workers, ignoring their grumbling as he closed in on the worker with the purple scarf.

"Fackrell," Uppercut muttered. "A word?"

"Clears up the mystery of what spooked the goat," Fackrell replied under his breath with a quick grin. He glanced at the other workers and stepped out of easy earshot. "You want to board that boat, don't you."

Uppercut nodded. "Do you know where they're headed?"

"Set up a hideout somewhere. Furniture, lights, food," Fackrell muttered. He swiped Uppercut's hat and flicked it towards the shadows, expertly fixing a scarf to the Whisper's head. "With me."

Fackrell passed the driver, who was calming the wild-eyed goat, and hefted a pair of bags hanging from the side of the wagon. He draped one over Uppercut's shoulder as the Whisper ducked under it, then the pair of them were headed back down the shallow steps towards the gangplank.

"Just like old times," Fackrell said, his back to Uppercut. "The rich getting away with things, you trying to stop them. No coat this time, hey."

"No coat," Uppercut agreed. "You seem eager to help."

"Maybe later I'll tell you why," Fackrell said. "This window is closing. Tighten up." He passed the watchful guard by the gangplank. Uppercut followed him up the swaying ramp and over to the open hatch to below decks. They shrugged the bags down on the deck as a vigilant guard stood by the rail and watched the surrounding water.

Fackrell trudged back towards the gangplank, but diverted, Uppercut at his heels. As he passed the doorway to the cabin, he nodded to the side, and Uppercut peeled out of his shadow and stepped inside.

The compact luxury of the cabin was less apparent under the litter that recent planning had left strewn over its surfaces. Take-out containers from several meals had collected, as the cleaning staff was not allowed in the space. Unrolled floorplans, pages of notes, and a sheaf of correspondence confronted Uppercut with a landscape of clues to prioritize.

Giselle twitched in his shadow. As he refocused on his resting attunement, he felt the motionless energy shining out of the other end of the room. Uppercut tread lightly, crossing the room to see the stand with fireplace tools that was serving as a paper weight on the sideboard. A long-handled brush and a shovel hung from a hooked crosspiece. The elegant fireplace set was out of place on the yacht. Its burnished brass and curling ornamentation had been out of style for centuries.

Heavy steps approached the door, and stopped. "Be right there," a deep voice bellowed, and the knob turned.

Tugging back on his energy as he nested his fist by his ribs, Uppercut gathered Giselle in close as he felt her compressing essence spike. He fired his fist forward, and she gleefully rode the momentum, spreading her mantle as she burst through the door and shrieked in the big man's face.

Uppercut smiled as he heard the incoming guard's choking gasp. He saw the outline of the man's arms pinwheeling as he recoiled from the jump scare, banging into the railing and tilting over backwards. He smashed down into the filthy water below.

Cries of alarm followed. As the guards closed in on the site of the attack, Uppercut drew the spirit back and noted the other doorway out of the cabin on the other side of the boat.

Calculations raced through his mind. Uppercut weighed the value of taking material to study later against the value of surprise; it was still possible Colsarch and his scoundrels would be unsure their security had been breached.

There was really one thing he absolutely needed. He stared at the fireplace set, recognizing the exposed core of its energy. Colsarch's scoundrels had already stripped its defensive camouflage and exposed its unique energy print. A ghost key. The secret knock on a concealed door. Wherever they were going, they had found the impossibly specific access to a space behind the Mirror. Ghost doors were notoriously defended, and judging by the amount of research piled around the room, this crew had done some deep dives into what they might encounter.

Better to follow them in than abort their initiative.

If they still had the ghost key, they would remain confident; only a few experts could forge a ghost key. Even fewer could do it on demand, under pressure, without preparing.

Uppercut felt the seconds flake away. Approaching bootfalls drummed on the deck. Dipping into his pocket, he pulled out a cigarette case. It was rectangular, metal, and it opened—enough of an echo in function that it might hold the print. It had to. Touching the silver box to the base of the fireplace stand, Uppercut concentrated, his face drawn up in a tight wince.

His mind and soul gripped the key, clamping down around it, and the unmoved energy of the ghost key left painful impressions in his consciousness. Shaking, Uppercut refocused on the cigarette case, clutching at it with his mind. Air hissed out between his teeth as pain bloomed through him, but he forced his own life energy into the cigarette case, and it filled out to the mold of the ghost key.

Reeling back, Uppercut pocketed the case and crossed the cabin to slip out the door on the other side. Lights flared across the cabin windows from converging guards, drawn by the splashing and swearing of the man overboard.

There was too much activity on the gangplank to quietly slip away. However, the guard at the prow had relocated. The glassy black obsidian of the gentle swells below was anything but inviting, but he had already been noisy enough. Time to slip away.

Frowning, Uppercut straddled the rail and settled himself wholly on the other side, heels on the deck. Then he rolled his eyes, stowing his nerves, and stepped out into space. He plunged through the surface with an understated splash, ignoring the filth of dockside water as he kicked into a swim.

He had a copy of the ghost key, and the creased memory to go with it. Now they were a big step closer to the zemi.

Uppercut grunted as he hauled himself up out of the thick water, climbing away from the flotsam that nudged against the pilings on the low swells. He dragged his heavy coat off, too dispirited to wring it out. He was momentarily grateful he hadn't worn his hat aboard, and he made a mental note to swing by and pick it up before he left the area.

Reaching to the subtle pocket at the small of his back, the last one searchers would find, he pulled out his mask. It appeared to be simple porcelain, but he felt each of the thousands of cracks patterned across its face. Closing his eyes, he raised the mask and set it on his face. He breathed out, his noisy thoughts and feelings cooling into the night alongside his blood-fueled air. He inhaled, absorbing the filth and spice flowing off the city. Opening his eyes, he felt centered, inhabiting his chilly and rigid face.

He opened his senses to the night, gliding past the struggling knots of consciousness trapped behind the Mirror, looking for the bright echo of a freed spirit. There.

He caught Giselle's attention. She flickered, appearing before him, flexing her rotten jaw, corruption dribbling from her image as she floated in the etheric nothing.

"You still want your killer, right?" Uppercut murmured. "You'll never find him without me."

Tremors rippled through her form. Unearthly rage twisted her features; rage that she carried out of her death, yes, but that rage was a magnet for the hostility rolling through the city, concentrating in ghosts like Giselle.

Uppercut considered the merits of forcing her into the bottle to use again later. He could leave her here, to roam the docks until the Spirit Wardens or a freelance ghost hunter did something about her. He held up the bottle.

His mask granted a kind of depth perception that clarified the ghost before him. He knew the spirit's decision before it was made.

She flowed back into the bottle, and he snapped the stopper in place with a bleak smile.

Time to meet up with Scarecrow.

Uppercut swung his sodden coat over his shoulder, tucked his spirit mask away, and strolled off to find his hat.

WISHBOTTLE CANTINA. CROW'S FOOT
12TH MENDAR, 850. *ABOUT THE SAME TIME, ELSEWHERE*
HOUR OF THREAD, 4 HOURS PAST DUSK

"And I'm back!" Scarecrow said with a broad grin, sliding onto the stool at the end of the long bar.

"Scarecrow, hey," the bartender said with a forced grin. She tossed her hair and looked him in the eye. "Is the end of the week okay? I can get your payment, no question, but I need more time."

"Forget about that, Tanie, we're friends," Scarecrow retorted. "Good friends who tell each other things."

"Oh, good," Tanie said warily. She slid him a frothy mug she'd filled reflexively as soon as he caught her attention.

"You're from Six Towers," Scarecrow said. "I recently bumped into a Sash who might be from that area, and I was wondering if you could help me figure out who he is."

"Someone you plan to hurt?" she retorted, eyebrows raised.

"I hardly ever plan to hurt people," Scarecrow replied, hand on his chest. "I didn't hurt that sleazeball that was coming on to you, did I? You wanted that handled delicately. Quietly. With finesse. Has he been back?"

"He has not," Tanie replied, a smile warming the corner of her mouth. "What did you say to him?"

"Very little," Scarecrow said. "Now, this Sash. Belted on the left, looks like moonsilver in the pommel, wears his parrying dagger on the back of his belt. Dresses in white or silver, glove on the left hand. Cropped hair. Suspicious type. Maybe early thirties. Any ideas?"

Tanie leaned back, crossing her arms, her expression darkening. "I may have heard of him. But now I need to know what you want him for."

"He's working with some really sketchy types," Scarecrow confided in her. "Sloppy fellows who are likely to run into an accident or two. I don't want him to share their potential misfortune. Yeah?"

Tanie stared at him for a long moment. "You know my uncle runs the Red Sashes out of Blockmeet Corners in Six Towers," she said. "You know it's a family operation. I came to you with my other little problem because I didn't want to start a feud, and the Sashes—well, they might have overreacted. We take family seriously."

"Right," Scarecrow said.

"I have no idea who you're looking for," Tanie continued, "but if you want to come visit sometime, we're having a party in two weeks. My brother is about ready to take the mastery trials for the Setting Sun style, and we are all real proud of him. Just between us, he's also a Whisper, and one of my uncle's best agents. He helps in all kinds of ways. He's an observer, when outsiders want to run sensitive operations in our territory. He makes sure nothing gets out of hand, that the Red Sashes keep their promises. Because we keep our promises," she said, leaning forward, looking Scarecrow right in the eye.

"Your brother, huh," Scarecrow said over the sudden sour taste in his mouth.

"My brother," Tanie agreed.

"Whisper. Master of the Setting Sun." Scarecrow shook his head. "Sounds like it is going to be a great party. Thank you for inviting me. What are the gifts for the Setting Sun?"

"Masters get Sekka style daggers, jade ornaments for jewelry and trappings, and hawks. That's the tradition," Tanie said.

"That's amazing. Thank you so much," Scarecrow said, and he took a long drink from his mug.

"I'm glad you checked in," Tanie said, her smile growing as she relented. "I like having you around, Scarecrow. In bounds. Accessible. It would be a real shame if you couldn't come by anymore."

Scarecrow thought that over. "It really would be," he agreed. "Maybe we could have dinner sometime this week. I know a place, owner's a friend of mine, he's got a line on some pretty great sandshells. Those are your favorite, right?"

"Aw, you remembered," Tanie said. "Drink's on the house. You look like a busy man."

"So many irons, so many fires," Scarecrow agreed, standing. He touched his forehead and swept out a salute to her. "I'll be, you know, around. Like you said."

He turned and strolled out, mind racing. Reaching the street, he looked both ways.

Easier to dodge the incoming trample if you see it coming.

Scarecrow stepped under the overhanging second story, rain sluicing off him. He flapped his coat to shed the worst of it, and he turned to the barred metal door. He banged the door five times with his fist, and the viewport shot open.

"Password," the guard grunted.

"Seven beaches and eight rains, the captain's mast looms o'er against," Scarecrow said in Skovic with as little sarcasm as he could manage.

The bolt snapped back, and the door swung open on well-oiled hinges. Scarecrow passed the two door guards, entering into the curling smoke of the stuffy interior as the door clanged shut behind him.

Scarecrow nodded to the three guards, and headed down the claustrophobic hallway, ignoring the doors along the way. He paused to gather himself, then stepped through the arch into the storeroom.

"Well hello there Ulthar," said the portly elder seated with her back to the corner. She cocked her head to the side. "It's late for visitors."

"I don't believe you sleep," Scarecrow replied with his most winning smile, ignoring the smoldering pipe and intelligence reports covering her desk.

She sucked her tooth for a moment, then shook her head. "Out with it, what do you want. I'm very busy."

"I'm checking into some skullduggery in Six Towers and you came to mind."

"You know we don't do petty crime," the woman said, leaning back. "Not like what you're into."

"I'm not looking to involve you, I just want a bit of a summary," Scarecrow replied. "You've got contacts with most of the Skov labor in Six Towers. I'm looking to track some activity, get a sense of some Red Sash operations."

"I thought you were friendly with the Sashes," the woman said.

"Oh, I am. I think one of their agents might be in trouble," he said, not exactly lying. "Blockmeet Corners. Some scoundrels are planning a heist in their territory, and the Red Sashes are sure to assign somebody to make sure it doesn't get noisy. I want to know who the Sashes put on babysitting duty, and I want to figure out the target. I hear it's the boss's nephew running interference for the crew. He's a Whisper." He paused. "You know him?"

The woman watched him for a long moment, and Scarecrow stuffed his fists in his pockets and did not fidget.

"The Knotwork is all about Skov unity," the woman said slowly.

"And you know I'm all in," Scarecrow agreed. "In fact... I found someone who put me onto a symbol. Like we talked about."

The woman raised her eyebrows. "A symbol."

"Something the people could unite around," Scarecrow said, lowering his voice and glancing around. "This Akorosian is looking for it, and we're going to take it away from him."

"You are offering it to me?" the woman asked directly.

"No, I'm not," Scarecrow retorted. "You said it yourself, you're supporting Skov unity, and that means you don't want to be a competing faction. You're looking for the Skov leadership with the best chance of giving our people a boost. You're looking for someone to endorse. As opposed to me," he continued, "since I'm looking forward to when you're going to put your network at my service." He grinned to soften the arrogance of his statement. "Someday soon you can say you knew me before I was famous."

"You're cute, but you don't have a chance," the woman sighed. "No network, no following, no claim. None of the families will follow you. I still think you should join us officially. As a lone operator, you might succeed just enough to attract attention as a threat. Then you're done. At best, you're a spoiler." She indulged a wry grin. "But I like your spirit. You may not have a chance, but you've got some grit."

"Well, thanks for that," Scarecrow nodded. "Anyway, Blockmeet Corners. Red Sashes. Boss's nephew, the Whisper." He paused. "Your people work in kitchens and gardens all through Six Towers. Give me a hand here."

"You could figure this out easily enough on your own, so you must be in a hurry," she mused.

"Yes, I am," Scarecrow agreed. "If the Akorosian makes a move and we're behind him, or worse yet he moves out of our field of vision, then *he* gets what *we're* after. It moves into circulation with him. On the other hand, if we get to it first and take it from its hiding place, the theft stays quiet. It's unlikely our involvement will ever come to light."

"You think you can finesse this?" the woman said skeptically. "I've seen you work."

"You've seen *some* of my work," Scarecrow corrected. "I can keep a secret."

She studied him. "The Knotwork isn't going to help you out with the job, Scarecrow," she said. "But I'll give you a little update on one of the players. The Whisper you're after, he wears all white?"

"That's the guy."

"He goes by Riposte. He lives in the Dreskeul Court, a seriously protected community. He's babysitting some noble working out of a base in Crow's Foot. You won't be able to follow him, he's got a picket of watcher spirits. They look ahead and behind."

"That's all I need," Scarecrow said with a big smile. "Thanks, gramma."

"My best to your mother," the woman said with a dismissive wave. "Don't get yourself killed."

Scarecrow nodded, and headed out.

CASE OF BASKETS TAVERN. CROW'S FOOT
12TH MENDAR, 850. *TWO HOURS LATER*
HOUR OF WINE, 8 HOURS PAST DUSK

Scarecrow's eyes twitched, and he realized he had dozed off. Damn that soothing rain. He stretched, then settled back against the angle of the overhanging gable with a view of the run-down tavern across the street.

The uneven patchwork of tolling bells began to mark out the time, inexorably building towards the end of the night. Scarecrow grimaced. He was hours late for his meeting with Uppercut, but something was missing.

"You don't carry your wake," he murmured to himself, ignoring his own morning breath. His irritation grew as the watch bells kept on and on. Hours lost, hours passing.

He perked up as a long shadow interrupted the plasmic lamp light. A massive Skov trudged towards the tavern, his thatch of straw-like hair distinctive above the acreage of his shoulders.

A slim figure stepped out of the shadowed alley across from the big Skov. "There you are," she said. As she pushed the cowl of her cloak back, Scarecrow recognized her pale hair.

"Shimmer," growled the big Skov. "Make it quick, I've had a long day."

"Yes, I hear you had a mishap at the Ripple Dame tonight," Shimmer observed, barely audible from Uppercut's perch.

"Ghost," the big Skov agreed. "Came out of the cabin, pushed me overboard. We looked it over, nothing was disturbed. Probably just passing through. Rip said it was the moon phase, riles up the ghosts. That dock is a haunted area anyway."

"I don't like it," Shimmer clarified. "And I don't like you out of position. Replacing you before tomorrow night is a pressure I don't need."

The Skov's bearing shifted, showcasing his thinning patience. "You wanted me to set it up so nobody's watching the back gate tomorrow night. You didn't want me to give much notice, so I had to work it out with my contact tonight. At midnight, when he could check in without people watching. Then I took him out for a drink. Because we want it smooth tomorrow."

"You trust him?" Shimmer pressed.

"No," the Skov retorted. "But I don't trust you either. And we shouldn't be talking about this out here," he said with a furtive glance around.

"Please." Shimmer crossed her arms over her chest. "The walls in that tavern are so thin your buddies can overhear your dreams."

"I don't want to see you until tenth bell tomorrow," the Skov growled, barely audible. "We meet at the boat like we planned. Then—"

"*We* planned?" Shimmer scoffed. "You're lucky to remember what you're supposed to do. Leave the plans to us, just make sure you're ready."

"I'm ready right now," the Skov snapped. "But since my end is taken care of, I'm gonna get some sleep. Just as soon as you get out of my way."

"Don't forget to do the ritual with the new spirit charm," Shimmer said. "You have to sleep with it to make sure it's tuned up. You don't want to get lost under the Clavalian Seat."

Scarecrow sat up straight, breath frozen and eyes wide. The Clavalian Seat. One of the oldest piles in Six Towers, a manse with a history that echoed with atrocity and secrets.

"I won't get lost, and I don't forget anything," the big Skov muttered, uneasy. "Tomorrow." He shouldered past the slim intelligencer, and pushed his way into the tavern.

Shimmer seemed to focus intently for a moment, and Scarecrow felt the distressingly loud beat of his heart as though it would betray his hiding perch. On the street below, the slim woman glanced around, then vanished down a squalid side road.

"The Clavalian House, huh," Scarecrow muttered to himself.

He gave Shimmer time to get some distance before he dared slip away.

HOLDER'S HEIGHTS PUBLIC HOUSE. CROW'S FOOT
12TH MENDAR, 850. *ALMOST AN HOUR LATER*
HOUR OF ASH, 9 HOURS PAST DUSK

Uppercut interrupted his pacing, squaring off with the door as the handle rattled the bolt out of the way. The door creaked open, then Scarecrow quickly stepped in and closed it.

"You are three hours late," Uppercut hissed.

"But I know where we're going tomorrow," Scarecrow said. "Clavalian Seat."

For a long moment, the scoundrels let that stand between them.

"I'm going to make it worse," Uppercut said.

"Drama queen," Scarecrow sighed.

"They have a ghost key," Uppercut continued, ignoring him. "So not only are they going into that haunted pit, they're going somewhere sideways once they're on site."

Scarecrow let that sink in. "So I guess we hit them on the way out," he growled, doing the math as plans started pulling together in his mind.

"We have to," Uppercut agreed. "Unless we could somehow copy their ghost key."

Scarecrow blinked. "Don't tease," he said.

Uppercut raised the cigarette box into view.

"I didn't even know that was a thing," Scarecrow said. "You copied a ghost key?"

"Speaking of what you know, how solid is your lead? Are you positive it's the Clavalian Seat? We do *not* want to 'drop by' if it's a misdirect."

"I overheard Granite and Shimmer outside where Granite is staying. That's why I was late. I also found out who our Iruvian pal is. Riposte, a Red Sash...and a Whisper."

"That's not great," Uppercut said through his teeth.

"Plus we don't want anything bad to happen to him. He's along to make sure it doesn't get noisy, I really don't think he gives a damn about what they're after."

"Anything else?" Uppercut said. "Any other wrinkles to make this harder than it has to be?"

"Wait for it, I'm sure something will turn up," Scarecrow sighed. "We don't have much time. I figure we need a plan."

Uppercut squinted at the clock tower across the street. "Just a few hours until dawn," he murmured.

"I know I can't sleep until we've got some ideas," Scarecrow retorted. "What kind of dreams do you want to have?"

Uppercut considered that for a moment, then nodded. "I think I know a guy who can get us the basic layout of the place," he said. He turned up the light on the table lamp.

Lots to do.

CHAPTER TWO

Dynvus Clavalian's childhood was defined by shame. His family's noble lineage of Akorosian purity was besmirched by his mother's dalliance with a Skovlander—a dalliance that produced him. He saw himself as evil, and he weaponized his defects of character to murder his way to the top. He became the patriarch of the family and controlled its considerable fortune.

His secret hobby was delving into the mystery of what was wrong with Skovlanders. What essence were they missing, what disease drove them to indecency? Even as a youngster, he investigated and experimented, searching for answers. He studied religion, bloodlines, diet, history, necromancy, and art in his quest.

When he secured wealth and power, his experimentation and investigation took on atrocious proportions. By the time the law could no longer turn a blind eye, thousands of victims had succumbed to his horrific efforts. Even his family's wealth and influence could not suppress the consequences when Bluecoats raided his manse and uncovered endless dungeons and catacombs beneath.

Three centuries after his execution, the legend of Clavalian's gruesome inquiries reverberates through Skovland communities. The Clavalian name is shorthand for dangers immigrants face as they live among resentful hosts.

—From "Unwelcoming Shores: The Skovland Influx"
by Dr. Baltimus Freyn

STELMORIAN LANE. SIX TOWERS

13ᵀᴴ MENDAR, 850. *ABOUT EIGHTEEN HOURS LATER*

HOUR OF HONOR, 1 HOUR PAST DUSK

"What kind of nob builds a house with no doors?" Scarecrow groused as he squinted through the fog.

"There are doors a-plenty," Uppercut muttered, "but they are all above the ground floor. Daughran Clavalian designed the manse, and he disliked scoundrels sneaking around in the fog, so he built high walls. All the entries are on ramps and bridges, visible even during the Blind Hour." He paused. "You are sure we'll know when Colsarch and his people get close?"

"I've got eyes on them," Scarecrow replied, sour. "Don't you worry about that, they're still a ways off."

Quiet settled between them, as though carried in on the wafting drift of fog as the Blind Hour filled the alleyways and thoroughfares below. They perched on the side roof of a mostly deserted bakery.

"So you think the ghost door is in the Atrium of Stars," Scarecrow said, his face as expressionless as he could make it. His eyes traced the gantry that joined the bakery to the massive apartment block next door. From there, a bridge arched over the avenue to a city guard station that anchored a folding bridge connecting to a tower in the Clavalian Seat perimeter wall. That bridge was the closest thing to a back door the haunted estate possessed.

"Dynvus Clavalian was an astrologer," Uppercut said. "He felt like fate was shorthand for the interaction of blood and stars. The Atrium of Stars was built to project the appearance of an underwater scene, with important constellations mapped out with precious metals and gems inlaid in the walls and pillars and walkways, and multi-level paths so you could move around in three dimensions as the Leviathans do in the deeps."

"Drown it," Scarecrow grunted. "What's *wrong* with rich people?"

"Makes sense that he would focus his secrets in the star charts of his fortress," Uppercut mused. He looked down at the cigarette case he held, feeling a needling twinge in the back of his eyes as he felt the contours of his rigidly held memory, pressed into the shape. Soon he would be free of the need to hold it.

"And you're all set to get us there?" Scarecrow prompted.

"I pulled some strings," Uppercut nodded. "Got a look at the floorplans. I can find the atrium."

"Well first we have to get in. This guard tower is a good choice for insertion, Colsarch was smart to pick it. Granite is renting a guard's loyalty, probably distracting the incoming relief for a few minutes. Colsarch will stroll across undetected. We'll be right behind them." He frowned. "Looks awfully exposed."

"That's the point," Uppercut agreed. "This place was built to be hostile to infiltration. Still. If Colsarch doesn't know we're on to him, why would he pay attention to his back trail? It's far more likely they will focus on the barriers between them and the atrium."

Scarecrow shifted uncomfortably. "I would have liked to have seen the floorplan myself."

"I gave you a sketch," Uppercut said, mild. "Getting a look at it was one thing; taking it out of the archive would have been a *lot* more expensive. Besides, we just need the general idea." He paused. "Are you alright?"

"I'm fine," Scarecrow snapped, a warning glint in his eye. He hugged himself, and scowled over the fog. "Just thrilled to be here."

A shadow glided through the fog overhead, and Scarecrow squinted upwards. "Okay, they're—they're close," he said.

Uppercut also looked up, searching for what caught Scarecrow's attention. "Hang on," he breathed, "we may have a complication. That's a deathseeker crow."

"Right, he's with me," Scarecrow said, and he flashed a devilish grin. "My buddy Carc. Keeping an eye on Colsarch. That's how I know they're close."

Uppercut stared at him. "You never said your 'partner' was a deathseeker crow."

"It's fine," Scarecrow said, dismissive. "Let's get moving." Rising, he stretched out the stiffness from the vigil, and padded over to the bridge, fixing his eyes firmly on the tower across the way. Troubled, Uppercut heaved himself up off the rooftop and followed.

Scarecrow put one foot before the other, staying dead center on the wide stone bridge to the apartment building. By the time he skirted the balcony to the shadows at the corner across from the guard station, cold sweat trickled down his back. He leaned against the wall, eyes pressed shut, breathing heavily.

Uppercut swallowed his growing concern, and peered down at the street with interest.

"—take you for a drink," one guard concluded, slapping the other on the shoulder. Reluctant, the guard accompanied him across the street to a corner tavern. One quick drink couldn't hurt.

A huddle of cloaked figures crossed the avenue quietly and unlocked the door to the guard station. Uppercut saw Granite and Shimmer, they were obvious. The old man must be the professor. The elegant Whisper in pale garb was Riposte. The most featureless figure must be Colsarch himself.

"You see that?" Uppercut hissed.

"Looks great," Scarecrow replied through a locked jaw, looking straight across the avenue.

Uppercut turned back to the tower, waiting. It didn't take Colsarch's crew long to reach the third story, filtering out onto the walkway and heading across the folding bridge, connecting the House Guard tower to the perimeter wall of the Clavalian Seat.

"It's time to move," Uppercut said, restraining the urgency in his voice.

The rush of downstroking wings fanned the scoundrels as the death-seeker crow came in for a landing on the railing of the balcony, an arm-span away. He let out a triumphant croak, the echo of a thousand death rattles; the sound reverberated through the fog and sent chills rippling through the skin of all those who heard it.

Uppercut and Scarecrow stared at Colsarch's scoundrels, halfway across the bridge. The rival intruders froze, then dropped down to a low profile. They were far too distant to overhear, but they had to be speculating about what it could mean that someone may have just died, *very* nearby, with a deathseeker crow already onsite.

Not a great omen.

Still, could they turn back? Of course not. Freshly wary, eyes every-where, Colsarch's rogues crept across the bridge to the House Guard tower.

"You're right," Scarecrow murmured, his voice weak. "Time to move."

Scarecrow studied the space between Uppercut's shoulderblades as the Whisper led the way across the bridge to the guard tower. Scarecrow's face and hands were numb with strain, sweat beaded on his face in the cool night air. He reeled with a sense of dislocation by the time he sagged down to one knee, leaning against the wall of the tower and panting.

"Are you alright?" Uppercut muttered, kneeling beside him.

"I—may have—kind of a thing—heights," Scarecrow said with a tight gesture, struggling to breathe.

"Spectacular timing," Uppercut gritted out.

"I can handle it!" Scarecrow said through his teeth, and in that moment they were both keenly aware it was time to prove it. Scarecrow pushed himself up the wall, to his feet, stubbornly following Uppercut around the balcony.

Across the folding bridge, the last lights of the retreating scoundrels were vanishing as they continued into the Clavalian Seat. Colsarch and his team followed a walkway over the courtyard between the tower in the perimeter wall and the interior manse. Scarecrow hesitated as the image of the narrow bridge with spaced slats tilted wildly in his mind's eye.

"To clarify," Uppercut breathed, "you're a sniper. With a bird friend. Who doesn't like heights."

"Mockery later," Scarecrow said shortly. "Right now we gotta do this. Walkway is too exposed."

"No door at ground level," Uppercut reminded him. "What, you want to rope us together?"

"You think you're funny," Scarecrow growled, leaning heavily against the wall. He recoiled as a crusty switch slotted down.

With a screech, the long-neglected machinery of the folding bridge connecting the guard tower to the perimeter tower shuddered into motion.

Alarmed, Uppercut pivoted to stare down into the street. Sure enough, the door to the corner tavern flew open and the guards raced towards the tower.

Scarecrow could not tear his eyes away from the hinge and the creaking twinges of the cables pulling the gantry up towards the opposite wall, widening the gap. Somehow, the fog below made the drop even worse, as though there was no ground below it.

Uppercut rounded on Scarecrow, a terrible desperation in his eyes. "You're leaving this balcony," he snarled, "and you'll jump or you'll fall." He balled up the Skov's coat in his fists and slung him around towards the folding guard rail. Frantic, Scarecrow powered through the last of his will, banging a foot against the rail and launching to slam against the folding bridge.

Uppercut leaped, clattering against the retreating span. The Whisper grunted and swore as he hauled himself up, then snatched Scarecrow's collar and dragged him against the pitched metal. Scarecrow was dead weight, frozen; he was gripping the railing so hard he could not be pulled to relative safety.

"Come on!" Uppercut gritted out. It took all his strength to dislodge Scarecrow, and both scoundrels slid awkwardly down the supported side of the loudly creaking and bouncing walkway as it tilted up.

The dim light across the courtyard gantry winked out.

"Don worry I killem," Scarecrow gritted out, his face so bloodless it was almost translucent, his trembling hands straining to unclench.

The walkway and balcony offered clear sightlines. When an investigating scoundrel rounded the tower, they would be in plain view.

Poised on the wall, Uppercut saw the flowing fog in the avenue below on one side, and the bank of dark mist coiling within the estate walls on the other. He had already dismissed the idea of fighting off Colsarch's people; victory would be hollow and defeat was unthinkable. The choice was between scrubbing the whole effort and escaping into the city shadows... or going in anyway. Neither path was safe.

Scarecrow saw no good options, including freezing in place to be confronted. Rolling up to his knees, he scrambled over to the interior side of the wall, then hesitated as he looked across the arm span to the ladder cut into the rock. It seemed far beyond reach, as his hands were rooted to the stone.

Uppercut was past him to swing down onto the ladder. The Whisper tugged at him, pulling him out of position so his only recourse was to scrabble at the ladder and grip it tight. Then Uppercut swarmed down into the vague fog.

Practicing an old mind trick, Scarecrow gazed upwards and pretended he was ascending as he groped downward with his foot, finding the next rung down, and lowered. Lowered again. Strained against the paralysis that swelled through him.

He made it down four rungs, then hugged the wall tightly as Granite's shadow loomed above, stealthily rounding the tower and scouting around for signs of an intruder. The massive Skov ducked down as the guards across the way shone lamps at the perimeter wall. Behind the raised bridge, Granite was more or less out of sight.

"That quirky equipment," one guard said, too loud. "Acting up all the time. We'll have to get someone out tomorrow to take a look."

"Yes," the other guard agreed, also too loud. "Tomorrow we will look into it."

"Lightweights," Scarecrow thought to himself, sneering at their fear. Rather than confront the possibility of hypocrisy, he eased down the ladder into the shroud of the breathing night.

Glimmers and stains of light punctuated the fog, leaking from the pale crystals embedded in the roots of the bushes and trees. The glows layered the textures of the shadows in the depths, far below the lines of the wall and walkway above. A slow churn of breeze shifted the fog enough to give the sense that there was movement everywhere.

Scarecrow eased his crossbow around to a ready position. His muscles jumped into definition as he tugged the cable back to set it in firing position, and he slid a quarrel down the track, fixed in a killing posture. The crossbow was oddly cold in his grip, resonating with the uneasy energy of this place. A combination of solid ground beneath his feet and a trusty weapon in his hands breathed some life back into Scarecrow's limbs.

Beside him, Uppercut had the reverse experience. He felt the hatred and fury that saturated this place. Throbbing hostility drove into his senses, invisible and profoundly real. His breath shortened as his skin tightened. Uppercut felt the convergence, the attention that was drawing together, towards the warm blood that intruded into this haunted place.

"We can't stay here," Uppercut breathed.

Scarecrow gripped his forearm, staring up at a balcony on the manse that was just visible through the filmy mist. Dim lights grew as the door opened.

Scarecrow trained the crossbow on the archway, squinting through the scope. Shimmer stepped into view, gazing down into the fog, imperious. A smirk crossed her features, and she pulled something out of her coat.

She waved the hand-held object at the wall beside the balcony. Glittering energy traced the hidden outline of a glyph on the wall, activating with a scintillation of dormant power roused by the presence of its counterpart.

For a breathless moment, Uppercut was caught up in recalculation. Was that somehow the shielded ghost door, but out on the balcony— His eyes widened as he saw the glyph forming in the emerging radiant pattern.

Not a door. Not even close. The glyph was a failsafe control. An almost-mythical Spirit Warden technique rumored to be embedded in some of the Great Houses, allowing an agent of the Spirit Wardens to manipulate secret ethereal defenses. Uppercut had never seen anything like it before, and he was stunned as he saw Shimmer confidently flex her hand and plant it on the glyph, expertly twirling her wrist, sending the concentric rings of the control into a different configuration.

That should be impossible.

A Tycherosian intelligencer freelancing on a noble's heist, accessing ancient infrastructure of Spirit Warden defenses—there was no reasonable explanation for that.

No acceptable explanation, anyway. The awe snapped into fear and seamlessly pivoted into a familiar anger. Of course Colsarch's baffling desperation to get at some old Skov artifact wasn't wholly irrational. He was part of something bigger. Something *much* bigger.

A giddy terror swelled through Uppercut as his mind flashed through the stories—the connection of vampires to high court, and the church's mysterious tolerance of a handful of prominent occultists, contextualized by examining some seemingly innocuous and barely noticed policy shifts that were out of character with Ministry practices—

"Focus," Uppercut breathed, straining to push the jubilation of conspiracy out of the way before it unsettled him. "This is a chance to get some real answers."

"What?" Scarecrow hissed. "What is she doing? What are *you* doing?"

"I think she's opening some doors," Uppercut muttered. "And we better catch up before they close."

Shimmer glided back into the manse, taking the light with her, and the glyphwork on the wall faded as though it had never appeared.

"So how do you want to do this?" Scarecrow whispered. "Climb the ladder and back across, you know," he gestured at the walkway above.

Uppercut backed against the wall, then winced away from it as the zing of energy from an invisible embedded rune traced along his essence. This courtyard was warded, shielded, contained. He had a gut-dropping moment of suspense, flashing to a memory of crickets dumped into a lizard's terrarium. Free to wander. As long as they could.

"Yes, the ladder," he said. His voice was hoarse, his air clutched by stress. "Let's—go..."

For a moment, the scoundrels stared. The slots cut into the wall to serve as a ladder were gone. Smooth, blank, unclimbable stone seemed to mock them.

Just then a breeze slid by, drawing a soft hiss from the restless leaves, stirring fresh shapes into the fog. The crystals glowed like embers under a gentle breath.

"It's almost too late," Uppercut growled, his fists clenching.

Starvation and rage rippled the edge of invisibility, their currents on the other side of the Mirror swaying Uppercut. He glanced over to Scarecrow, who clutched Talon tight and stared around in the fog as his instincts thrilled with danger.

For a long moment, Uppercut envied Scarecrow. The hound's ignorance took the intellectual edge out of the dread swelling around the scoundrels. Scarecrow knew his gut feeling, and could see a strange mist. Scarecrow had a little experience with ghosts. He didn't know what Uppercut knew.

He didn't know about the pattern-bolstering crystals, about the roots of atrocity that vented an endless supply of suffering up into the contained garden where it could take shape. This was no untethered spirit adrift, no bound watchdog ghost. This critical mass of lethal corruption was an order of magnitude greater than one or two scoundrels could repel.

Scarecrow could not see the coalescing malice that was projecting through the Mirror with killing force, the shuffling bandaged echoes that gathered to crush the spark of life that intruded here.

Uppercut took a breath, then ducked into his spirit mask and prepared to throw up the best defense he could.

"I see you!" Scarecrow cried out in Skovic, a new depth to his voice. "Are you forgotten? If you were, no blood would stir your peace."

Stunned, Uppercut risked a glance at his partner. The short hound stood straight and proud, crossbow slung, shoulders back, fists planted on his hips. He stared right into the center of the gathering mass, locking eyes with a coiling spirit that was fouled with long saturation in suffering.

"You recognize me," Scarecrow continued. "You remember me. In my voice you hear the soaring words of times long gone, times when our people pronounced judgement on the lands where they were born and on the ships where they ruled. Would you strike that down?" he demanded. "Would you hear silence instead? Strike then!"

Scarecrow strode forward a handful of paces, right into the swirling fog. "The fear you send into me is the fear they sent into you. And the courage of my response comes from the past and the future of our people. You recognize this courage—it is yours as well! I see the echoes of what you were. But I know that you were more than the horror of your end. There are yet more tones in that echo than a dying scream. Remember, with me, your life—it has greater strength than your death."

Scarecrow let that pronouncement stand for a moment, waiting for more words. He dimly felt the blaze of sunlight on his shoulders and felt the flow of pride and euphoria he felt on that day so long ago, standing by the docks as his uncle gazed down at the gathered crowd. Scarecrow seemed to experience his mother's hand on his shoulder, as on that fateful day. The fine words from the clan speaker resonated with the fine words that punctuated his childhood.

The scoundrel, Scarecrow, was too petrified to speak. So he stepped back into another time, and in the haze of active memory, the essence of his uncle had yet more to say.

"We divide on every front as we face our oppressors," Scarecrow intoned. "Now the Mirror betwixt life and death separates us. Yet we choose—*you* choose. Will you turn on your own, as they intended? Or can you stand aside, and refuse to shield your tormentors from the vengeful hand of your own blood?"

Uppercut stared in awe as the turbulence behind the Mirror shifted and paled. A peculiar light filtered through, outshining the cruft of agony caking the energies of the dead.

The cloud of murder shifted into an honor guard that dimly lit the fog, clearly visible to the Whisper but clearly felt by the hound.

Scarecrow looked up to the catwalk above, and saw a hulking silhouette against the tortured clouds. Of course his speech was clearly audible above, and Granite was also his audience. He looked right into the massive Skov's eye somehow, even in the shadows. And his question stood to the living as well as the dead.

Granite nodded, ever so slightly, and stepped back out of view.

Uppercut stared at Scarecrow as the fog drifted clear of a corridor to the far wall. He saw the little Skov in a new light.

Scarecrow glanced back over his shoulder with a sketchy grin. "C'mon, let's go."

The beginning of a headache blossomed in the back of Uppercut's skull as he felt the tremendous pressure exerted by the Skov ghosts to allow the intruders to pass unharmed. He jogged alongside Scarecrow. Billows of fog fell in behind them.

"Neat trick," Uppercut muttered.

"How come Colsarch and his people didn't have to deal with the ghosts?" Scarecrow groused.

"They had amulets keyed to the frequency of the defenses. Probably took months and a fortune to pull it together. Still, I don't think these spirits will trouble us further, if we're quick," Uppercut said with a glance over his shoulder.

"So... how do we get in?" Scarecrow asked, squinting up the unbroken stone of the interior wall. "I guess we could try to climb up to a balcony maybe, if a tree grows too close somewhere along the edge."

Their only warning was a single gulping snarl, greedy with hostility. Scarecrow recoiled, yanking his crossbow up to deflect the snapping jaws that launched out of the foggy shadows; he was staggered, and Uppercut scrambled back, dipping his hand into his voluminous coat and tugging out a squat black jar.

"Where's the rest? You see the rest?" Uppercut gritted out as Scarecrow pivoted. Uppercut immediately saw the trap. The guardian mastiff growled between the wall and Scarecrow, so the scoundrel's back was exposed to the open courtyard. Too late.

A second mastiff leaped at Scarecrow's back, driving him off his feet. As the mastiff scrabbled, off balance from the hit, the first one darted forward and clamped its jaws around Scarecrow's forearm with bone-crushing force. Scarecrow released a strangled scream as the fog swirled; at least one more mastiff was closing in.

A glance revealed that the mastiffs were not just dogs. No flesh-and-blood animal would enter these haunted grounds willingly, much less hunt them. The ghost shine in the eyes, the radiant spittle, and the unreal multi-dimensional echo of the monster's growl were tells. These mastiffs were fangstriders, pack hunters from the Deathlands beyond the lightning walls. Their collars confirmed that they were not here by accident.

Flesh was hard to come by in the Deathlands, but the fangstriders also devoured ghosts. Uppercut hurled the black jar at one of the fangstriders, and the mastiff skipped to the side. The jar smashed on the wall, releasing a burst of ragged plasmic energy; a handful of half-formed spirits wailed, twisting, suffering as they smeared across the wrong side of the Mirror.

One of the mastiffs reared, snapping with its translucent black teeth, snagging the filmy gossamer of drifting energy and yanking it down into a ropy stream that the fangstrider gobbled up with distressing relish. The other fangstrider hesitated, torn between the killing in progress and cleaning up a past killing that was trying to twist away through the ether.

Uppercut flinched as the Mirror attuned to a powerful perception, and his world rippled for a moment. Both fangstriders jerked their attention towards a fixed point in the fog, as did Uppercut. A hooded figure loomed, rigid and imposing.

"Wait!" Uppercut hissed. "You are the Crolaange Houndmaster, right? Guardian of the grounds here, for generations—"

The hooded figure shifted posture slightly, and both hounds re-oriented on Uppercut. They did not need to growl to communicate menace.

"Okay—" Uppercut said, "but you don't want to kill me! I know your secret! And I can get you what you want!"

Somehow he knew he had seconds to make his best case. "Because you're a vampire—all the Crolaange limmers are—and you can only feast on the life essence of third generation adept daughters!" His tone was triumphant. "Allow us passage, and I can pass on some research I did, identifying targets that qualify. Some of *them* don't even know their potential!" Uppercut's eyes glittered with triumph.

The triumph had a few seconds to sour before the fangstriders leaped at the Whisper.

Uppercut took a long step back, reaching into his coat again and hauling out a pistol. He fired, blazing a plasmic shot into the first fangstrider. The blast tore at its flesh and its spirit. The mastiff was knocked aside, and the other scrambled in low, snagging Uppercut's boot and tugging him off his feet.

"Hey!" Scarecrow yelled, and the fangstrider glanced over at him in time to see him trigger Talon. A hissing quarrel leaped across the intervening space, driving into the fangstrider's ribcage at close range. Staggered, the fangstrider managed a pained retreat.

"Yeah, that's—" Scarecrow managed before something snatched his leg and dragged him into the curling fog.

The hooded figure strode towards Uppercut. The Whisper snapped off the pistol's second shot; the houndmaster leaned to the side, and the plasmic bolt burned past, searing up into the sky.

So the Houndmaster wasn't a vampire. If he was, Uppercut's specially prepared vial of quicksilver would have been really handy. It might still serve. He slid it out of his concealed sleeve pocket and squeezed the plunger, spraying the volatile substance at the houndmaster.

The houndmaster recoiled, and Uppercut didn't bother to rise as he snapped his pistol open, spent cartridges spinning out. By the time he slotted in another shot and looked up, the houndmaster had stepped out of sight.

Uppercut only had seconds until the next attack. "Scarecrow!" he hissed. No answer. No time to wait for one.

Uppercut ran towards where the houndmaster had appeared. Glancing around, he spotted a cable hanging from a post by a balcony, high overhead. Leaping at the cable, he struggled to climb hand over hand. Twisting hard as he strained, he managed to avoid the leaping fangstrider as it snapped at his heels.

Uppercut felt the yank on the cable as the houndmaster started climbing after him. He managed to slap one hand on the balcony, and he tore a knife from its sheath on his belt and sawed at the cable with abandon.

The houndmaster was almost within arm's reach of his feet when the cable parted and the hooded figure plummeted.

Uppercut groaned, his arms on fire, but he managed to drag himself up to roll over onto the balcony.

He only took a moment and a few shaky breaths before rising. He stepped through the door and closed it behind himself. Spotting a bar beside the door, he hefted it and slotted it across the doorway.

Well, at least he was inside.

He felt time slipping away. The gunshot was a last resort, as it alerted everyone to a fight nearby. Colsarch's crew would be looking for interference. They probably knew where they were going, and he did not. Now he was on his own.

Uppercut glanced around the spare quarters. Must be the houndmaster's living space. And there, a door leading further into the manse.

He prowled into the great house's shadows. No time to waste.

Branches whipped Scarecrow as he was dragged by the mastiff, agony streaking through him. The mighty creature hauled him into a thicket of bushes, underlit by filmy crystals.

The center of the brush mass had been forced apart to create a den. It stank of rot and filth. The fangstrider's last tug tore through the pants' fabric, and the fangstrider's quick snap caught Scarecrow's shin. Awash in new pain, Scarecrow desperately hammered a kick at the fangstrider's head. The monster was unfazed.

An ear-splitting screech outside startled the fangstrider; its jaws opened instantly, the muscle of its tongue pushing Scarecrow's leg out of its mouth. The fangstrider quivered, alert.

"Yeah, he's with me," Scarecrow managed. He rolled over and forced himself to crawl at the narrow gap he'd been dragged through. He couldn't think about the fangstrider pouncing on his unprotected back and neck.

His grip on consciousness was numbing away as he made it halfway out of the bush. His torn pants caught on the roots.

A gut-level certainty gripped him. This was it. He wasn't going to make it.

Behind him, in the bush lair, the fangstrider let out a peculiar hiss that had no business coming out of a dog-like shape. Before him, the deathseeker crow was majestic and poised.

Blood was leaving Scarecrow, but life wasn't. "Whu—whut are you doin," he slurred to the crow.

A figure emerged from the mist, oddly defined. It was as clear to Scarecrow as his own life pressed against the Mirror between the breathing world and the colder one on the other side. The spirit Skov's hair was braided back, fading to tendrils of mist, and his face bore a scowl that had hardened in the centuries since his death. The memory of blood slicked the torso of the apparition, and shimmering droplets and fans of viscera drifted around his shape.

I will take you out if you take me with you, the spirit focused at Scarecrow.

"Okay sure," Scarecrow gulped. "Where—how do we get out?"

We must go in to get out, the spirit hissed into Scarecrow. *Only flesh may go.*

Eyes bright, Scarecrow nodded. "Let's do this," he gritted out.

A torrent of cold sensation poured through him as the Skov spirit possessed his body. Scarecrow's agony was a hot and wet echo of pain that was so young it only registered as a novelty to the spirit stitched in centuries of suffering.

Scarecrow slowly climbed to his feet, and spared a glance back at the bush. The fangstrider within was oddly quiet. He turned to look at the deathseeker crow, and he saw it as a hole in the Mirror. The ghost riding him twitched away from the view—there was something in that hole, something they dared not see.

A tremor rolled through Scarecrow, and he stretched his neck; he was keenly aware of the blood trickling down his broken leg and welling out of the gashes in his broken arm. He had never felt intense pleasure wearing gore, but the borrowed sensation filled him.

Escape first, slithered through the back of his mind as the spirit drank all his pain and pushed stability into the frailty of his damaged limbs. *Then revenge.*

As Scarecrow strode through the fog, he felt other Skov ghosts pulled to him. As they flowed close, something in Scarecrow's passenger unfolded, opening to them to draw them in too—

Another ear-splitting call, and Carc landed on a branch before them. The call thrilled Scarecrow's bones, freezing his animating forces in place. The other spirits were driven back.

The message was clear. Just one passenger. Scarecrow could feel his guest's seething resentment, but the deathseeker crow left no room for disobedience. To push against the deathseeker was to fall into an unfathomable abyss.

Both Scarecrow and his passenger had far too much left to accomplish to squander their opportunity by picking a fight. Scarecrow felt himself nod, slowly. So be it.

There was only one mission they shared. To get past these walls.

Wind rushed past the Skov as he leaped, propelled by strange energies. He felt his body snatch the balcony railing and swing up over. The shocks of pain provoked by movement vanished into the starving ghost, who reveled in any new physical sensation.

As his body stalked into the dark manse, Scarecrow wondered if he would emerge sane.

CHAPTER THREE

How could the authorities fail to notice the atrocities unfolding at the Clavalian Manse? The answer is depressingly simple. They did not dare notice. The Clavalians were staunch defenders of the Barrowcleft dissidents in a protracted conflict with the Weatherwatch loyalists. The dissidents exerted themselves to protect Clavalian power from any threat, including justice.

The most intense conflicts between dissidents and loyalists unfolded around the middle of the Sixth Century. Contemporary sources suggest the strain of the struggle fueled the Clavalian madness. The fear and cruelty that flowed from high-stakes clashes to control the city's politics and culture needed an outlet.

There was no way the dissident houses would protect Skovlander victims from the predations of a mad aristocrat, because they needed the Clavalian family's support to defeat the loyalists. Every war has atrocities and civilian casualties, even civic power struggles. Especially civic power struggles.

It is easy to scoff at the cowardice of past authorities as they looked the other way and allowed this madness to continue. Yet empathy may temper your judgement. Do you have the courage to demand justice now, to halt the atrocities playing out in your own time, in the city where you live?

From "Sussing the Undercurrent: A Political Excavation of the Dusk's Mass Graves"

—By Tanvil Muros

Uppercut was armored by his spirit mask, and he held a freshly loaded pistol, but he didn't feel particularly safe as he stalked down the corridor in near-complete darkness. He paused to shake his frosted sphere with glowing algae inside, getting a little more light.

The hallway seemed twice as wide as it needed to be, with a shroud of dust over the ancient carpet underfoot. He saw footprints in the dust, and he followed them to the archway opening up to the balcony.

Well then. The Atrium of Stars.

The darkness was almost velveteen. The air was textured by layers of sediment from the glacial dissolution of the Great House. Mixed in was the heavy scent of the house trappings crumbling with exquisite slowness. The whole manse seemed to breathe very, very softly.

Dim light shone from below, sparkling in the gems of constellations embedded in the soaring walls and the improbable arching walkways. Cunning supports and odd angles crafted a whimsical sense of movement, suggesting undersea currents and the pressure of wind and stars. Glittering mosaics hinted at textures and patterns too distant to perceive.

The atrium resonated up six stories, and the stained glass of the skylights was reportedly mottled like the surface of the sea. No light penetrated the space from above tonight.

Uppercut crept over to the hardwood railing, peering between the slats at the scene below.

One end of the atrium had a walk-in fireplace. It was depressed below the level of the floor, and the stairs leading down to it were broad enough to also serve as bench seating in a semicircle facing the flames. Colsarch and his thieves finalized their preparations in front of the opening. The fireplace tool set was positioned by the grate. It did not match the fireplace. It must have come from another bedroom. After all, why keep the key next to the lock?

"Here we are at last," Colsarch said, barely audible from three stories above. "Are we ready?"

"Finished," Riposte said as he stepped back from a lantern. His ritual was bounded by lanterns set around the top of the stairs and along the mantle. "We shouldn't have any interruptions."

"Remember the plan," Grear said as he polished his spectacles. "Shimmer does the scouting, Riposte keeps us safe, and I get one item of my choosing."

"If you get us past the riddles," Colsarch retorted. "Do that, and we all get what we want."

"Indeed," Grear said. He looked sidelong at Shimmer. "You seem distracted, my dear."

"Granite isn't back," she observed. "We can't wait. Let's go."

"Let's go," Colsarch repeated, assuring no one was confused about who gave the orders.

Riposte knelt by the fireplace tools, concentrating. Reality twitched, and the Mirror swirled as the Whisper attuned to latent currents and pulled them closer to the surface. As the Mirror flexed, an opening joined some place beyond with the breathing world. Colsarch and his thieves vanished into the fireplace. Riposte took the key with him. The ghost door flowed shut.

Uppercut was on his feet and moving, along the balcony and down the confusing and improbable sweep of stairs. Several flights later, he reached the atrium floor, closing in on the giant fireplace.

He paused before crossing the line of lanterns. Yes, a ritual protection. He attuned to the barrier, and found it simple; he flicked a gesture to the side, opening a passageway without disrupting the ritual. It was only designed to snap around the unwary.

He stood before the gaping fireplace, allowing himself a moment to eye its more striking features. It was a face, of sorts; some undersea monster, gaping, its maw the seat of flame, clawing up from under the floor of the Void Sea. He shook his head, then produced the cigarette case from his pocket.

"Okay," he breathed. He sensed the shape he had copied from the fireplace tools. He pressed more detail into the rough copy in his hand, focusing on its shape on the Mirror as though sliding a block along a surface looking for a matching slot.

It didn't fit. A rough copy, after all.

Uppercut frowned, shifting the mask on his face. He concentrated harder, finessing the key. He widened his stance, and breathed deep, a column of air filling him and ordering his bones and organs, warmed by his blood.

A shock of force—he tightened his entire being, driving the key at the lock. Reluctant, the energies tried to squirm apart. But they could not.

Long cracks snapped through the case as it bore the strain, but Uppercut did not waver.

He stepped into the unstable swirl, and vanished.

For a moment of compression, the darkness was intolerable. Then it resolved.

Uppercut stepped out onto the thrumming deck. As the ghost door flowed back from his shoulders and ribs, depositing him on the aft deck, he felt the powerful currents under the hull resonating through the ship as though it was the body of a viol playing a low note.

The whole world was crooked. He stood on the memory of a massive Skov treasure barge, and it hung precariously on the glassy wall of a maelstrom. The rippling dark of the water's surface was robbed of surf by the current. Stars burned in the depths, visible through the slanting surfaces on all sides of the funnel. The pit below was obscured in eddies of fog.

Uppercut took a knee, balancing and wary. He studied the helm. A spirit lolled against the wood, chained with iron and rust and sinew, lashed to the wheel and obscured in a cobwebby cascade of beard and hair. The spirit's mad eyes stared at Uppercut, and the spectral mouth contorted in a futile effort to communicate. Uppercut hardened against pity as he understood that the ghost chamber was used as a treasure vault, and its shape and stability had been pinned in place with this ghost's essence centuries ago.

"One hell of a memory you've got," Uppercut murmured to the hapless spirit.

Peering past the railing, he saw the retreating glow of Colsarch and his people moving down the deck. They focused on a hatch, propped open to reveal stairs down into the hold.

Concentrating, Uppercut thought through the intersection of Whisper lore and Skov stories that might date back a few centuries. Clavalian would have sorted through his prisoners to find a spirit and memory strong enough to anchor his otherworldly vault. Oceanic vortexes like this maelstrom were tied to Leviathan sign, which was likely the demonic stain that lent stability to the memory so it would last reliably through the centuries. This ship was probably different from the vessel the spirit remembered, re-cast as a treasure barge as a matter of style.

Uppercut shied away from the thought of being forced to live in a stressful memory, a load-bearing consciousness for a created space, for all time. Giving up on locating a specific instance among the hundreds (maybe thousands) of Leviathan clashes with Skov ships across time, he focused on protocols. Spirits were keen on politeness, if you could get their attention.

"Permission to board, business before the helm," he said in clumsy Skovic.

The spirit stirred, and flexed. "Granted," the bound helmsman croaked.

Uppercut nodded, and passed the helm, down the stairs, crossing the broad deck. The clouds twisted upwards, dragged in a funnel that mirrored the maelstrom below.

A chortle drifted up from below, accompanied by the clank of bolts shooting back and the creak of hinges. Uppercut stealthed over towards the stairs, alert and thinking fast.

"There you are," Shimmer said, her tone silky. Uppercut pivoted to see her step out of the shadow of the stairs. He drew his pistol and lined it up on her, focusing down the barrel with a warning scowl.

"Let's review this plan," she said, examining her fingernails. "You take a shot at me, kill me dead, then shoot it out with the rest of the crew." She raised her eyebrows. "And then walk out with treasure, I suppose."

Uppercut said nothing, sidestepping around so his back was to the railing and he had both Shimmer and the treasure hold's hatch in his line of sight.

Shimmer smiled. "More likely you didn't have much of a plan at all. You must be our shadow. Asking questions about our plans. The little clatter at the bridge, the shot in the courtyard." Her smile grew. "Now you've caught up, so you'll bear with me as I do the same."

Uppercut's mind raced as he tried to think of something to say that would not sound stupid or give her leverage.

Shimmer took her time, considering Uppercut. His grip on the pistol. His stance. His boots, his mask, his gear harness under the coat.

"Homeschool Whisper, former Bluecoat. That mask looks like Irinaysee's work. You must be Uppercut," she concluded. "You still have that 'new Whisper' smell."

Uppercut cocked the pistol.

Shimmer chuckled. "I value both consistency and cunning, and you've got more of one than the other," she said. "Lord Bennington has killed twice since you were ejected from the Bluecoats. In case you were no longer close enough to spot the signs. I imagine that frustrates you," she said, condescending.

"How did you activate the failsafe control," Uppercut demanded.

"Very good," she observed, raising her eyebrows. "How indeed?" She looked him over again. "You probably think it's safe for me to tell you because I have no intention of letting you leave this place."

"And because secrets itch, or more people would keep them better," Uppercut growled as sweat gathered on the small of his back.

"You start," she said, something playful in her challenge.

"Spirit Wardens."

Her eyebrows raised. "Oh, very good. Then?"

Uppercut felt familiar vertigo, the spiraling interconnection of everything wrong with Doskvol, a disorientation that seemed to fit in this off-balance exile. "You want something else that's lost here. You found other people to get you in so you could collect something for your masters."

"We're running out of time for our private chat," she said, looking him in the eye. "Take it home."

Uppercut flashed through a thousand hours of sleepless searching, eyes burning over crabbed text, ears ringing with hoarse whispers. He could do this. He felt the answers, tantalizing, all present and sidling around just out of his line of sight. He knew this answer.

"Six Towers," he breathed. "The Spirit Wardens. Aristocracy. The Foundation. You want to rebuild the Residency Pattern." He reeled as the sheer scope of the plan weighed him down.

Arching an eyebrow, Shimmer raised a finger to her lips.

"We're breaching the defenses," the professor called out as he headed up the stairs. "Riposte says—"

The moment was past, and time was up. One against Colsarch's crew wasn't good odds. Uppercut hurled a flash-bang snapper at the deck, and as it crackled and gusted, he darted up the stairs to the aft deck.

Uppercut dove at the ghost door as he heard stinging curses in Tycherosian. The sharp crack of a pistol report echoed weirdly as he battered into the Mirror and it dilated around him. His ghost key crumbled to powder as he toppled through to land on the hearth, back on the breathing side of the Mirror once more.

Uppercut rolled over on his back, feeling the twinge in his ribs as they slid back into position; the grip of the otherworldly passage was brutal. He puffed out a couple breaths, then froze.

Out of the corner of his eye he saw the shape that stood on the other side of the defensive ritual. Waiting. He felt the cold shine of a powerful spirit. Uppercut propped himself up, facing the threat. His eyes widened as he saw Scarecrow's face, bloodied and slack.

Uppercut rolled to his feet, pain forgotten. "Get out of there," he hissed through his teeth, and with a sweeping gesture he gathered the energies flowing around the possessed scoundrel.

"No," the spirit and Scarecrow said together. The spirit continued. "We leave together or I take his air out with me."

Calculation fluttered through Uppercut's mind. Granite was likely nearby on this side of the Mirror. The ghost door could spit out threats any moment now. The possessing spirit was unusually strong, and on its own haunting ground. Getting out of the estate was not likely to be easy. Blood glistened all over Scarecrow, and his injuries were severe. Could Uppercut win a brute-force battle of grit and skill? Probably. Was it a good idea to provoke that kind of clash right now? Uppercut braced against a moment of dizziness in the thick gloom.

"You ride this body out, then you leave it. Yes?" Uppercut demanded.

"We all get out together," the spirit and Scarecrow agreed.

Uppercut flexed his jaw, then nodded. "Let's go." He swept the ritual defense out of the way, and the haunted scoundrels retreated.

Scarecrow felt the shadows glide by like the shoreline of a canal as he drifted in the motive force of the spirit. He focused to the fore, pushing the dark and murderous spirit aside for a moment.

"You're back through the door," he said, dismayed by the slur he heard in his voice. He concentrated on enunciation. "Where is the zemi?"

"If I didn't make it out at the moment I left, I am not sure I would have," Uppercut replied. "I was on my own against all of Colsarch's people. I would have lost a confrontation." He frowned. "We'll have to keep an eye on Colsarch. See where he stashes it. What his plan is."

Scarecrow was oddly self-conscious under the smoldering attention of his possessing spirit. He slid back down away from control, to the sloppy mudpit of the back of his mind.

"Hey," Scarecrow barked in the privacy of his own body. "You got a name?"

The possessing spirit focused, and formed a somewhat roomy stone cell with a high barred vent. The remembered stench from decades without a breeze compressed around Scarecrow's consciousness as he faced the lean spirit.

"Call me the Draper," the spirit murmured. His thoughts flickered, and for a moment Scarecrow glimpsed him screaming, slaying, in a rain of gore with intestines looped over his shoulders. Perhaps out of politeness, the spirit shifted, and once again the walls of the hushed cell pressed in all around.

Scarecrow grimaced. "Look, Draper—"

"*The* Draper," corrected the spirit.

"Right, this is real uncomfortable and I need to talk to Uppercut for a minute. Okay?"

The Draper stared at him for a long moment, and when he smiled it was a baring of teeth. "I'm made of patience," he rasped. "Call my name when you've had enough *comfort*."

Scarecrow grunted with pain and dropped to his hands and knees. He was back in the world, in his body, and the agony of his broken limbs knifed up through his consciousness.

"Whoa, you okay?" Uppercut said, pivoting too late to catch him.

"Oh, no, not so much," Scarecrow gritted out as he felt bone grating on bone in his broken leg. He slid down on his side, adjusting until the pain receded enough for him to speak, leaving him half-conscious. His eyes struggled in the shadow, but he made out a cave-like hallway, its gloom disturbed by their wan lights.

"What happened?" Uppercut demanded.

"My buddy gave me a minute—to have a chat. Oh, those bites water my blood."

"Yeah, you're running out," Uppercut replied, hushed. "Can you walk? This isn't a great time to stop."

"Inaminnit," Scarecrow managed. "Look, I knew we might not be able to pull this off. So I made a backup plan."

"A backup plan?" Uppercut echoed, wary.

Scarecrow nodded. "The professor. Grear. I got a cheap decorative zemi, gave it a coat of paint, handed it off to him to switch for the real thing. When they get out—if he can—he'll get me the *real* zemi."

Uppercut blinked. "Then why the hell are we here now?" he asked, muting his tone as best he could.

"I promised him a bunch of stuff I can't deliver," Scarecrow replied with half a grin. "It's a longshot. But we gotta—in case I don't—" He winced against the flood of pain.

Choosing from an array of ill-advised options, Uppercut shook his head. "Look, get the spirit back out here so we can get clear of the estate. Then we'll figure that out."

"Yeah. The Draper," Scarecrow grunted. Scarecrow's head lolled, then straightened on his neck. His eyes glinted with madness and death, and his broad smile revealed teeth that were pink with a film of blood.

"And we're back," Uppercut sighed, shrugging off the vital terror that squirmed in his blood.

The possessing spirit drew Scarecrow's body up to his feet. They continued towards one of the estate's doors.

"The canal gate is the only way to get me out. It has a more flexible defense." Scarecrow heard the Draper talking to Uppercut. His body's voice seemed muffled as he wavered, half-alive, adrift in his meat. Of course the Draper would have tested all the defenses looking for a way out. Of *course* he did.

First it felt like a breeze, like the wind blowing up out of an abyss and fanning those bold enough to approach the edge of the cliff. As they reached the boundary of the estate, scuttling along a broad stone walkway to the canal gate, Scarecrow became unsteady as glyph defenses pinched both sides of the Mirror together so spirits could not slip past.

"I think I can break one of these enough to slip out." Uppercut's distorted voice filtered back to where Scarecrow drifted. The Skov roused, pushing to the fore once again.

"Don't break it," Scarecrow gritted out. He shared vision with the Draper, and shared feelings too. While it was a relief to shunt the pain into the spirit, he got to experience the visceral need to open Uppercut, flaying him, getting a twisted satisfaction akin to that of peeling skin from a healing wound. The body's fingers twitched as Scarecrow restrained the killing urge.

"You want to stay here?" Uppercut retorted, eyebrows raised.

"Riposte—the only reason he's here—keep things quiet. You break this, that's... the Spirit Wardens. They'll know. That comes down on Riposte, I bet that's... you know, why he's here," Scarecrow said haltingly, feeling his life draining and the spirit increasingly taxed keeping the two of them moving.

"Seriously?"

Scarecrow didn't have time or energy to go into it, to dip into the late nights with Red Sash buddies to marshal evidence. Still, he knew. He paid attention to the stories about how the Red Sashes focused their business in Six Towers on managing the middle ground between aristocrat problems and Spirit Warden problems.

"You can do it, right? Just shift it enough for us to squeak through?" Scarecrow distantly wondered if his voice really sounded like that.

Uppercut spotted lights approaching from inside the manse. He shook his head. "I guess we'll find out."

Turning to the wall, he concentrated, sifting through the flavors of the glyph markers, visualizing their complexities. They were likely trapped. Guessing was dangerous. But it seemed they were built into a gate configuration here. Of course ghosts would sometimes need to come and go. And this is where the defenses could be... adjusted.

He took a deep breath, concentrated, then smiled. It was a bleak victory, but it would have to do.

"Go. Now, while we can," he ground out, his imagination locked into the meshing glyphwork. Scarecrow and his possessing spirit ducked past, forcing their way through an invisible door in an invisible gate. A moment later, a streak of blood ran from Uppercut's nose to his mustache, his sinuses trembling from the strain.

"I guess we live to fight another day," he muttered, and he followed the Skov into the tower.

They raced down the stairs, to the capstan by the door. It was virtually impossible to breach the canal gate from the outside, but from the inside? The scoundrels set to, pushing hard, and got the capstan grinding around. Two turns, three, four. They heard the door smack open up on the door to the wall, two levels up, but the gate had raised just enough. The two scoundrels rolled through, scrambled to their feet, and disappeared into the night.

An hour later they faced each other as they sat in a boat on the canal. Uppercut studied the Draper as the specter stared out of Scarecrow's eyes. Scarecrow's body was tucked back into the prow of the boat, shadowed. The Whisper leaned on the keel oar.

"We got out," Uppercut said quietly. "Leave."

A bloody grin writhed across Scarecrow's face. "For now," the Draper agreed. Scarecrow rose, pivoted, and knelt on the prow bench. Leaning over the side, he retched, and an ectoplasmic plume coursed out of his jaws, ramming down into the canal. Spent, the Skov collapsed, goo still oozing from his eyes, nose, and mouth.

"Let's get you patched up," Uppercut said, something distant in his eyes.

The Mirror reverberated, then stilled. The scoundrels drifted towards safety.

CHAPTER FOUR

An old Skov saying is coming to mind more and more these days. "You don't carry your wake." I think it's mainly a counter to indecision. Like a ship, you make ripples as you travel. You can't contain the consequences of taking action. Accept it.

In case that seems almost upbeat, there's another meaning too. You don't get to decide how you are remembered when you die. You get a drunken party funeral called "a wake" thrown by people who do not yet join you in the endless sleep. People celebrate when you're dead, not when you're alive. That last party is focused on your corpse. You don't have much to say about the memories people keep when you leave.

Trust the Skovs to coat their wisdom in a pithy little reflection on how death robs you of control.

—From personal correspondence,
By Lord Gemma Narsuli,
Captain of the Leviathan Hunter Coalheart

Uppercut shrugged to settle his new coat, and he frowned as he suppressed the urge to cast a furtive glance around.

"I belong here," he lied. "Blend."

Gripping his cane, he approximated a stroll as he headed for the library. Less than twenty minutes to go before his meeting with Professor Grear. Uppercut's new clothes didn't help him feel any more like a secretive aristocratic buyer. Still. This was his best shot to salvage the zemi right out from under the rival crew.

His stomach would not settle; it was poised, uneasy, and ready to bolt. Uppercut squared his shoulders and pretended it was too late to turn back now.

He mounted the stairs and pushed through the ornate double doors, crossing the foyer and passing the circulation desk. His footfalls were silent in the plush of the carpet as he followed the strip past the obelisks of end caps for long shelves stuffed with books, the scent of aging paper thick in the air. Passing the study tables polished to a mirror shine, he took an out-of-the-way staircase down to a sorting chamber for returned books awaiting reshelving.

"There you are," Shimmer said, cool. She was perched on a high stool, languorous as she relaxed against a pile of books on the table behind her. "Punctual. I like that."

A number of witty remarks struggled towards Uppercut's mind, but none made it past his cautions and alarm. He stood, unmoving, trying not to glare at the Tycherosian.

"I see this comes as a surprise," she observed. "The professor is not coming. Colsarch knows he had a side deal to steal the zemi. Seems likely Grear is dead by now." She raised an eyebrow. "But you're here."

"You think you'll kill me? That it?" Uppercut ground out.

"No no no," she said, flashing a too-white smile. "Nothing like that. I admire your initiative. I've got work for you."

"No thanks," he said, stiff. "I'll be going now."

"You misunderstand," she said, her smile fading but her teeth still visible. "We're having this talk because I did some checking into your background. I decided this discussion works best if you walked into it rather than me coming to you. And I could make that happen. I've got a broader field of view. And I know that steams your blood," she said, eyes glinting.

"Not everything can be bought or bent," Uppercut retorted.

"So touchy," she soothed. "You have a gift. A rare gift. I want to give you every chance to do something interesting with it. The zemi is nothing; there are far more interesting puzzles for someone with genuine Whisper talent." She cocked her head to the side. "You want your life to mean something. That's what I want too."

"I can spend my life however I like," Uppercut muttered, his heart racing.

"Were that true, you'd still be a Bluecoat," she said. "Your options narrowed when you moved outside the legal machinery of the city and into its shadows. I stand between you and death. I have chosen to do so because I have a use for you." She paused. "Shall I move out of the way?"

"What do you want?" Uppercut demanded.

"Mm. Like the kiss of sunshine, that question. I enjoy it every time it works its way out of the social niceties." She rose to her feet. "You squeezed together a forgery of a ghost key. I know of two other Whispers who can do that, and only one can do it on short notice under pressure. You're robust enough, for a mystic. Sure, you're still pretty raw, but I like the talent I see in you. I'm going to give you a chance to earn that backstage pass you want, and I'm going to put weapons in your hands to make the most of it. And, in exchange, you stay in my shadow." She looked him in the eye. "I am not asking. I am telling you about your best option. Work for me and you've got a chance."

"How long?" he said, unwillingly intrigued.

Her smile was a sheath for lethal thoughts. "Until you figure out a way to stop," she breathed.

"What about Riposte?" Uppercut said, desperate for a change of subject. "He's got experience, connections, resources. And he's apparently willing to work with you."

"He was willing to work for *Colsarch*," Shimmer corrected. "He didn't care much for me, so I made sure he didn't know I was involved until promises were made and blood exchanged. Anyway, don't you worry about Riposte. He's out of the picture now."

Uppercut sensed something in her tone. He didn't follow up... but he didn't let it slide. He considered her for a long moment, and she raised her eyebrows.

"He moved out of my shadow," Shimmer said, her lips and tongue shaping the words out past her gleaming teeth.

Something cold shivered in Uppercut's gut.

"I suppose you know where to find me," he growled. "For our next chat."

"Someone will approach you, wearing black silk gloves. The messenger will speak for me, and you will show respect and obedience," Shimmer said. Her lips pursed ever so slightly. "That's a nice jacket."

Uppercut turned his back and left the way he came.

LINKAGE ORRERY. CHARTERHALL
16ᵀᴴ MENDAR, 850. *ONE HOUR LATER*
SIXTH HOUR PAST DAWN

Granite descended the staircase, surprisingly light-footed for a man of his size. He reflectively wrapped a sash around one hand as he peered around the gloom of the algae-scented chamber awash in shadows.

A narrow catwalk led out to an island in the center of a dark and still pool. Ranked auditorium seating surrounded the pool. The dome above was invisible, out of reach of the small points of illumination from algae lamps at rest, inset as footlights.

"Professor Grear," Granite called out.

"He's not available," murmured a shadow, lost in the tide of dimness sifting through the space. Granite turned with a scowl, orienting on the small man seated on the usher bench next to the posh box seats.

"You must be Scarecrow," Granite said. "Fancy meeting you here."

"Today, Grear lives," Scarecrow stated.

Granite regarded him for a long moment, and slowly wound another layer of scarf around his hand. He closed to a fist. "Really."

"I'm taking him," Scarecrow said. "He will move in different circles. Take his time, do some research. Dig around Skov ruins. Field work. You can tell Colsarch you finished him. We both know this kill is to make a point. Colsarch doesn't really care." He paused. "And you don't really care about Colsarch."

"Except that he tends to disappear people who cross him," Granite observed. "Sometimes because he is petty. Most of the time, he makes an example. Encourages people to keep their promises. That's what I'm here to do today."

"He doesn't scare you," Scarecrow said. Granite's eyes had adjusted to the dim better, enough to see the paleness of Scarecrow's features.

"Maybe I kill you too," Granite reflected. "Colsarch was *not* happy that you got away."

"Drain Colsarch," Scarecrow swore with a dismissive gesture. "It's only a matter of time until somebody takes that zemi from him, and it might as well be me. Are you really going to stand in the way?"

"Yeah, the pay's good," Granite said.

"Scraps. You can do better."

"I can, huh," Granite echoed, dangerously mild.

"If you're working with me and my people, anybody who wants to disappear you has to factor some new consequences into their calculations," Scarecrow said quietly. "You want to kill somebody, sure. Easy. But if you want to get away with it, then it matters who stands with them in life. And in death."

"That's bold," Granite snorted. "Maybe desperate." He tugged on the scarf. It was all the garrote he needed to crush the life out of a victim's throat.

"Move against me and I put two bullets through your face," Scarecrow breathed. He did not need to shift position. Thumbing the hammer back on his pistol made his point. "If I wasn't wounded, I'd leave the gun out of this. I could smack your hammy slabs down without it. But I need this chat to stay civil today. So. Death threats." He allowed himself the barest of smiles.

A croaking call was shocking in the dim quiet of the chamber, reverberating against the stone walls and the water's surface. Granite startled, and spotted the imposing shadow of the deathseeker crow perched on the railing behind him.

"We're all just flying till our wings give out," Scarecrow murmured, recapturing Granite's attention. "Is today the day?"

Granite considered him for a long moment. "The professor leaves the city before the Blind Hour. Stays dead for at least a year."

"You got it," Scarecrow agreed.

Half a smile twisted Granite's face, and he shook his head. "Stay out of my way," he said. Turning, he headed back up the stairs without a backward glance. He unwound the sash from around his fist. Not today.

Scarecrow released a shuddering breath, his torn and broken limbs twitching.

Less than a minute passed before slippers whispered against the stone steps, and Grear approached bearing a glowing algae tube in one hand and one of Scarecrow's pistols in the other. "Is he gone?" Grear asked, the light painting his worried features in ghastly hues.

"He's gone for now," Scarecrow said, weary. "But if you aren't on a ship before dusk, you're a dead man." He looked Grear in the eye, serious. "Time to go on an expedition. Fast and quiet."

"Easy for you to say," Grear retorted. "I have a lifetime—"

"Stop," Scarecrow demanded. "If your career was worth a damn you wouldn't have freelanced for Colsarch. You wanted excitement and fortune. Go somewhere else and keep looking."

Grear bristled at his tone, but thought better of expressing himself. He flexed his sweaty grip on the pistol. It pointed at the floor. For now.

"Who *are* you?" he demanded.

"I'm the best luck you'll get today," Scarecrow said. "Nevermind who I am."

"How did you know," Grear mused. "The meet. My hiding place. Where I was going to rendezvous with Granite for... my payment." He frowned. "No one knew. *No one.*"

Scarecrow looked him in the eye. "I marked you," he said softly. "So I'd feel your life. Your death. And I felt your death coming. Raced it across the city to get here before it did. Snatch you up." His eyes were impossibly dark. "Keep you in here with me." He paused a beat. "In *this* world."

Unsettled, Grear struggled to manufacture a smile. "Lovely," he managed. He swallowed hard and put the pistol down on the arm of a seat. "If I'm going to make it out of town, I've got some favors to call in. Some packing to do."

"Skip the packing," Scarecrow advised, quiet and still. "Just go."

Grear stared at him for a long moment, then mumbled something; even he wasn't sure what. He backed away, stumbled, then turned and scuttled up the stairs and out of the shadowed chamber.

Heaving a sigh, Scarecrow levered himself up off the bench to balance upright, wavering on his good leg as he reached for his crutch.

A wind washed across him as Carc launched from the railing and flapped, then glided across the room to the island. The deathseeker crow perched atop the pillar at the center of the island, proud, an iridescent glimmer among less substantial shadows.

For an odd moment, Scarecrow felt pinned in place, fixed in position by pressures he did not recognize.

The crow screamed.

A jolt shivered the room, and the electroplasmic engine of the orrery glowed to life under the water. The armatures shifted. Points of light representing the constellations under the Void Sea blinked, then shone. Below the surface of the pool, the interlocked machine with its tracks and orbits slid into a slow churn, and the dance of the stars traced oblique paths under the water, casting strange lights up through the surface to pattern the dome.

As the gears meshed together, Scarecrow felt pulled into a pattern, caught between the teeth of what he knew and what he did not know.

He knew he did not mark Grear. He knew there was no one at the controls of the orrery right now. What else did he know? Hours ago, the visceral image of this place, and Grear, and the *sensation* of Grear's death slid through him with exquisite pain that left him thirsty for a taste of something like it. Somehow he knew he could prevent the death, and that he had to try.

He did not know how much of the Draper still curdled in his blood. He did not know how he could taste the back of the Mirror in the twinges of pain from his cracked bones, as though the cracks were in the Mirror and not his body. Worst of all, he had no idea what the triumph that radiated from Carc could mean, or what the crow was thinking or feeling.

Scarecrow stood shuddering in the tumbling patchwork of refracted light and resilient shadow as the orrery slowed, lights dimming until the only stars that still shone were the eyes of the crow.

"Gotta—gotta get back," he mumbled through nerveless lips.

He limped out of the darkness, but he carried the shadows with him.

CANTER PACE CLEANERS. CHARTERHALL
16TH MENDAR, 850. *TWO HOURS LATER*
EIGHTH HOUR PAST DAWN

Uppercut let himself in through the basement entry, glancing back past the obscuring stack of crates to assure no one watched his movements. Locking the heavy door behind himself, he sighed. Turning to the mold-printed washtubs that waited, still and silent in the darkness of the abandoned business, he reflexively opened his senses. No surprises. No obvious ones, anyway.

Shaking his head, he crossed to his workbench. Pulling the chilly jar from his coat, he regarded the imprisoned ghost. He could taste her frustration, her anger, the souring of her lust for revenge until it tilted her echo over an abyss of insensate madness.

"I know the feeling," he confided. Pulling a stone from the back wall, he tucked the jar in the shadows beyond, then levered the stone back in place. "We wait," he explained. "We watch. Another chance will come. We just have to stay alive long enough," he murmured. "Well... *I* do. And you? Don't give up." He thought about Colsarch for a long moment, and shook his head.

"Don't want Scarecrow to join you," he said to the wall. "Better check his bandages."

Weary, Uppercut trudged up the stairs to the shuttered scullery that they converted to an infirmary. Rubbing his hands on his trousers and thinking through his inventory of bandages, Uppercut approached the sick room and knocked.

"Time to wake up so you can get some rest on a schedule," he said, wry. Peering into the room, he felt a chill ripple through him.

The bed was empty. The crossbow was gone.

Uppercut swore, immediately flashing over all the places the injured Skov might hobble. He looked over to the cupboard, to be sure the food and supplies he procured were still there. What could possibly drive the Skov out? Or, more likely, who?

The front door creaked open, and Uppercut drew his pistol and stepped over to get some cover from the hallway arch. A shadow crossed the doorframe, followed by Scarecrow.

"What the hell," Uppercut demanded.

"Grear," Scarecrow said, pale and unsteady. "Saved him from Granite. He's on his way out of town."

Uppercut stepped into view, a fist on his hip, the pistol in his other hand. "How did you even find out about it? Who brought you the news? Did you tell an *informant* where we're hiding?"

"No. Too many people already know." Scarecrow managed before he lowered himself to rest on a dusty chair. "Sorry I scared you."

Uppercut crossed the room to close and lock the door, then he turned to Scarecrow."You are an idiot. Should have let Grear handle his own risks. Or waited for me. Now, who else knows we are here?"

"It was Carc. A little bird. Told me," Scarecrow explained, eyes serious even as he grimaced a little smile.

Uppercut's frown deepened. "What?"

"I don't know either. Look, maybe I'm delirious. But it worked. So… you know. Let's drop it."

"Yeah, I went to meet with Grear because you set it up. And he wasn't there, as you apparently knew."

"Seems you can still reach it," Scarecrow said mildly. "Drop it further."

"Had a nice chat with Shimmer. She is 'hiring' us. And apparently she had Riposte killed." He watched Scarecrow. "Grear seems to have escaped. Maybe Riposte did too."

Scarecrow looked thoughtful for a long moment, then his expression seemed to empty.

"He didn't." Scarecrow looked away.

"So... is this extra sense you seem to have picked up going to be a handy thing? Or a problem?" Uppercut asked as he saw the shadows dance and shiver behind Scarecrow's heartbeat.

"Like we'd even know the difference," Scarecrow replied, his grin almost boyish.

"Like helping you and hurting you, right?" Uppercut said, disliking the sense of relief that seeped into him. "On that note, let's change those bandages."

"You just don't give up, do you," Scarecrow grumbled.

The feeling was bittersweet, and Uppercut turned away. He tugged the cloth off his tray of medical tools.

"In it for the blood, thick or thin," he mused as he took up the scissors.

What followed was bloody. But at least they both survived.

CHAPTER FIVE

The peak of fashion 150 years ago was memorial tattoos. The result may or may not include your name; usually a symbol, and your death date. The idea was, as long as someone's living flesh wore your memory, you endured in the city.

Tattoo artists became genealogists and historians who could build picture structures and populate them with ancestor images. People sold their skin, and the skin of their children, to those desperate to be remembered.

Eventually the Church led an effort to banish the "shadow from our flesh." The Hierarchy encouraged the faithful to live pure, shattering all shackles to the ephemeral starvation of the withered dead. Predictably, the city's response was uneven.

—From "Tributaries to the Ink Sea"
by Amelia Skyless, PcR, E

Blood spattered down on the floor, and Uppercut let out a groan.

"You've been at this for a while now," murmured the shadowed figure leaning against the doorway. "Maybe it's time for a break."

"Maybe it's time to get furniture that doesn't wobble," groused Uppercut, slapping his hand flat on the table. He felt his heart race, speeding with the echo of the deadly feedback that missed him by the narrowest of margins. Staring at the swirls and warts of the stone zemi sitting in the bowl of his blood, he struggled with a number of simultaneous emotions all feeding into his frustration.

"You brought me in because of my religious background, yes? And my adept training? I may know something about this," the shadow said in subdued tones.

"I'm not questioning what you know about *this*," Uppercut growled with a gesture at the bowl and the zemi. "What you are *now* learning about is my *rhythm of operation*. You have no expertise with *that*."

Uppercut listened to his own uneven breath for a moment, ignoring the insight that he was being unfair to his new assistant. "Get me a drink and I'll try again."

"Certainly." His assistant crossed to the counter and poured out a stinking blend from the stoneware pitcher. "Shimmer will be here in about an hour. Would you like me to handle any preparation for your discussion with her?"

"It'll keep," Uppercut muttered. "I told Scarecrow I could figure out this damn rock, I want some progress before he gets back." He took the cup of potion from his assistant and poured about half into the bowl with his blood. He drank the rest.

His tongue and throat rebelled at the clotted substance. It was a sludge of oil and meat and herbal grit. Still, he swallowed hard, and aimed a stare at the zemi as he felt adrenaline flush his system, the poison opening his perceptions up as intended.

"I speak to my blood," he said in accented Skovic. "My blood speaks to stone. The stone hears the deep. Through surface and surface we meet."

His heart hammered, his breathing was still loud and unsteady. His instincts quivered; too soon to try again, cocky, unforced error. He ignored the plaintive chatter, concentrating harder at the bloody stone.

"I know you're in there," he muttered, frowning.

His mind flexed, like the lungs of a drowner, struggling.

Danger. His senses were saturated with it.

Explosively hissing out a sigh, Uppercut leaned back. "Okay. Okay. Fine."

The rusty hinges of the front door groaned, and Uppercut exchanged a look with his assistant. "You expecting anyone, Zekel?"

"No sir, I told no one about this place," Zekel whispered.

"Take it, go, go," Uppercut said with fluttering gestures as he yanked at his sleeve, pulling it down over the punctures in his forearm. He struggled to straighten his outfit as Zekel kicked a stained blanket over the bloody spot on the floor, sweeping the bowl off the table and withdrawing into the cluttered kitchen.

Uppercut took a deep, shaky breath, then focused on his heartbeat. He felt the swarming pulsation of the contrast potion in his blood, printing weirdly through the Mirror around him, and he frowned as though he could clench its influence out of his peripheral vision. He felt tiny cold hand-prints along his ribs and left leg, and he ignored them.

"Up here," he called out, drawing his pistol and laying it on the table as he faced the door. Casual. Act casual.

Shimmer glided up the stairs into the dirty box of the slum loft like a queen gracing the court with her presence. Her subtle and dark clothes were expensive, tailored, and durable, but her poise filtered through them so they seemed like formal wear. She raised one eyebrow at Uppercut as she took in the room.

"I do hope I'm not interrupting anything," she said.

"Impossible," Uppercut retorted, something defiant behind his tone. "It's too late to still be up to mischief, and too early to have started."

"I do hope you've managed the mischief I assigned you, to be completed by this morning," she mused.

"What, that business with the Chain Crossing and those arms dealers? Yes, that's done," Uppercut said. He rose to his feet, took a moment to settle his balance, and crossed to the tattered dresser with only one drawer left in it.

Reaching into a shadowed compartment, he fished out a stained box. "Here is some of their plasmic ammunition. I checked on it, like you asked. It's... fine," he said with a shrug. "I figure they made it with distillation pans, fishing the canals. That's a real slow way to refine electroplasm. But they should work okay."

"Nothing distinctive about the energy signature or craftsmanship?" Shimmer said.

"Basic, competent, nothing special. Probably military vets, based on the casing style. Definitely homemade." He put the box on the table, tugging it open, pulling out a round. It was chilly in his hand. He held it up to the light. "Right there, you can see this round was spent once and re-loaded with the custom accelerant. The tip of the bullet has a glyph carved in it, the coating on the round is probably makeshift. Takes a little time and a little workbench to pull it together, and the round is good for maybe a month before it degrades."

"And the other part? Their reserves?"

"I sent in a ghost, got them shooting. As instructed. I don't think any of them were killed, but they drew the attention of the Bluecoats like you wanted." Uppercut swallowed hard as his mouth bloomed with the flavors and sensations of cooked shrimp squirming through kelp.

Shimmer looked at the table thoughtfully, and hefted Uppercut's pistol. "Interesting," she said. "Did Scarecrow complete his mission as well? I expect a report on the Gutters."

"I know he intends to, and he may well have finished it. Still." Uppercut cleared his throat. "He's putting a brave face on it, but those injuries... he's really suffering. Slowing him down," he said with a solemn nod. "And you're early, almost a whole hour. He'll be in any minute now. I'll make sure we get you an update."

"Hm." Shimmer worked the hammer on the pistol, and frowned. "Needs cleaning, Uppercut."

"I'm living the good life," he muttered. "All focused on my chores. Hardly any danger anywhere. I may have gotten complacent." His heart was racing again.

"Tell me about Gadavant Circle." She sighted down the barrel, taking aim at the floor.

"Uh... I haven't gotten to that." Uppercut swallowed hard, feeling the blood loss. "Thought you didn't need that update yet. I was working on... the arms dealers, right? The ammo?" His smile was wan as he held up the round again.

The faintest shadow of a troubling thought drifted behind Shimmer's serenity. "I see." She pivoted the pistol and replaced it on the table. She looked Uppercut in the eye. "Two days. You come to me. Tell me everything I don't know, but should, about the Silver Nails in Gadavant Circle. Then I'll have a new job for you." She sucked a tooth. "And Scarecrow, of course."

"Of course," Uppercut said, his first sensation of relief undercut by a wary instinct. "No problem. Two days." He felt himself nodding like an idiot.

Shimmer picked up the creased box of plasmic ammunition. "Be careful out there," she said. "Bring me news and I'll have a bonus for you."

"Thanks," Uppercut said. He wondered if it was obvious to her that he was keen to end her visit. Of course it was. It had to be.

Shimmer turned, heading down the stairs, and the door screeched on its rusty hinges before clacking shut behind her. Uppercut sank back on the chair, rubbing his face.

Zekel stepped out of the side chamber. "She assigned you Gadavant Circle twelve days ago."

"I know," Uppercut muttered.

"Last week you told her you needed three more days," Zekel added.

"*I know*," Uppercut growled. "And I'll get to it."

"You are brave," Zekel said, shaking his head.

"I'm not worried about *her*," Uppercut retorted. "We have other priorities."

"You want the zemi?" Zekel asked quietly.

Uppercut listened to the thud of his heart, the swirl of blood through his flesh, the keening and hissing of his perception skirling against the flaws of the Mirror.

"Maybe... I need a rest," he mumbled.

Zekel handed him a cup of filmy water. Uppercut tried to smirk, then took a deep drink, trying to wash away the night's struggles.

CHALICE OF HORNS. NIGHTMARKET
32ᴺᴰ MENDAR, 850. *ABOUT THE SAME TIME, ELSEWHERE*
HOUR OF SMOKE, 11 HOURS PAST DUSK

The hollow thunk of boots on the rungs echoed down into the cellar long before Scarecrow arrived. Once his feet were on the ground, he sagged against the ladder, catching his breath.

"You need some stairs. Maybe a ground floor office," he observed, not yet bothering to turn towards the shadowed chamber.

"Good advice," breathed a sibilant voice, "for anyone who cared even a little for the convenience of the customer."

Scarecrow leaned to the side, still holding the ladder. He glanced across the counter that blocked off the room, and the pert young man behind it.

"That's not you," Scarecrow agreed. "I brought your payment." He held up a fist-sized box and shook it so it rattled. Limping to the counter, he tossed it down. "It's all there. Your intel was good. I retrieved the 'object' from one of Greer's assistants yesterday." He grinned.

"I'm so happy you're happy," the young man replied, casual. "You could have put the payment in the drop box."

"The drop box is for when our business is done. You've impressed me. I have more needs, and more treasure," Scarecrow said. "More business." He widened his smile further. "What do you say, Coinpurse?"

"I recommend backing off Colsarch," Coinpurse replied. "He's put a bounty on information about who is sniffing around Grear's various mysteries. Currently he thinks Grear took the secret of the stolen zemi to his shallow grave."

"That's what we want him to think," Scarecrow nodded. "Nobody needs to know I put a crossbow against Grear's assistant and persuaded him to give the real zemi to me. He's not likely to tell anyone he took the package then turned it over to some masked thief who broke into his bedroom. The only person that can connect me to him is you."

Coinpurse lost all trace of good humor. "Don't bore me. What's your new business."

"Frankly I'm surprised I even have to tell a connected spider like you," Scarecrow confessed. "I figured you would have looked into me when we started working together."

"I'm aware of your context," Coinpurse agreed, leaning his elbows on the counter. "But it is unproductive to guess at how people will react to their circumstances. There is a breathtaking quantity and quality of stupid out there. You've got your own share."

Scarecrow squinted at him. "I want to argue," he observed. "Anyway, my partner and I are somewhat under the thumb of Shimmer. I believe you are competitors."

"Turn this into a question," Coinpurse suggested.

"She wants us for something but she doesn't want us to know her plan. Or her objective. Or her boss. Or, you know, anything." Scarecrow cocked an eyebrow. "I want you to fill in some context for me."

"You jest." Coinpurse watched him for a long moment. "Three Coin to even have the rest of this conversation."

"I'm good for it," Scarecrow said immediately.

Coinpurse waited.

"What can I get for one?" Scarecrow asked, his smile eroding.

"An embarrassingly basic funeral," Coinpurse replied, eyebrows raised.

"You sell those?" Scarecrow replied with mock surprise.

"Let me see your Coin," the spider countered.

Scarecrow heaved a deep sigh, then made a big production of pulling up a leather bag. "I just have currency, not an actual Coin," he grumbled. "Drain it." He dumped the bag out and spent a minute pushing the thin coins stamped as scales or slugs around with a fingertip. "That's going to have to do," he said at last. He looked up at Coinpurse, who stared at him with distaste.

"Never do that on my counter again," Coinpurse said. "I'm not even sure we can do business."

"I think we can," Scarecrow retorted. "I found you, remember? You had me jump through a couple hoops before you took my money in the first place. You didn't think I had the finesse to get the zemi from the assistant. But here we are. Don't be distracted by all this charm," he said with a gesture at his face. "I'll get it done, and I'll do it quiet. Right?"

Coinpurse watched him for a long moment. "I suppose." He looked down at the coins. "But you must swear you'll never embarrass either of us with this sort of display. Ever again."

"Marrow and cord, so I swear," Scarecrow said. "Now what can you tell me?"

"You'll want to take a closer look at Thickwrist Patterns. It's an ink shop in the tailing of Ink Lane."

"Yeah?" Scarecrow said with a sage nod.

"One Coin," the spider reminded him. "Also. You are not one of my customers. Should anyone ask."

Scarecrow's smile slid back into place. "You are good people," he said.

"I'm really not."

"Right. I'll be back when I'm more wealthy," Scarecrow said.

Coinpurse said nothing. He watched Scarecrow return to the ladder and mount it with a laborious climb out of sight. Then, with a deep sigh, he swept the coins into a bin under the counter.

COAL AND CLAY STUDENT CELLS. CHARTERHALL
33RD MENDAR, 850. *THREE HOURS LATER*
SECOND HOUR PAST DAWN

Scarecrow paused outside the door, scowling at the scribbling sounds he heard on the other side.

Uppercut glanced up as Scarecrow pushed the door open. "There you are."

"Here I am," Scarecrow agreed, stepping in and closing the door behind himself. "I looked for you at Kettlebox Court. Zekel said you came back here." He paused. "He also said Shimmer stopped by."

"She did," Uppercut nodded. "And she's not happy with me. Much less you."

"Drain her," Scarecrow swore with a dismissive gesture. "I'm a step closer to figuring out what she's up to. I went back to Coinpurse."

"Already?" Uppercut said, surprised. "I thought we were low on funds."

"What are you up to here?" Scarecrow asked, gesturing at the table covered with papers and hasty scrawling.

"Oh, I looked into Colsarch. What he's been up to the last few months. What I could find out about other activity behind the scenes, what might be Tycherosian, or aristocracy, or... you know." He peered across the drift of writing under his nose. "I'm beginning to suspect she's not working with runic designs like the Residency Pattern at all. Mainly because of repeated instances of Spirit Warden contact show-ing up where I don't expect it."

"Speaking of patterns, I've got a new piece of the puzzle for you," Scarecrow said as he crossed his arms over his chest. "I got a hot tip from Coinpurse. A new place to look. Somewhere she won't *want* us to look." He paused for dramatic effect.

Uppercut stared at him.

"Thickwrist Patterns. It's a tattoo place, on the Docks. You can get some sleep, and we'll head out."

"Sleep?" Uppercut scoffed, rising and snatching his jacket from the back of the chair. "It can wait. Let's go have a look."

Ignoring the twinge in his barely-healed leg, Scarecrow stepped for-ward. He examined the dark circles under Uppercut's eyes, the tremor in his hand.

"I think maybe you better slow down," he suggested.

Uppercut squared off with him. "I have had lead after lead evaporate under my very nose," he growled. "We aren't going to wait. Let's take a look before this lead is gone too." He pushed past Scarecrow. "You coming?" he called back as he strode down the hall.

Scarecrow heaved a deep sigh, then turned and followed the Whis-per.

"You should probably let me do the talking," Scarecrow said. "I've got plenty of ink. I speak the lingo. These people get me. There's a whole subculture, you know."

"Sure," Uppercut said, weary past arguing the point. "Dazzle me."

The tattoo shop had a makeshift door, battered through a basement wall some time after the lane had sunk far enough to allow access. The one barred window was more of a vent. Uppercut shoved the creaking door open and led the way into the grimy shadows of the interior.

As Uppercut's eyes struggled to adjust to the dimness, Scarecrow stepped around him to glance across the back wall of the corridor-like shop.

The plaster started at waist height and stretched to the high ceiling. The pale surface was tightly packed with designs. Some were all black, others profusely colored. The wall behind each bench displayed the craft of the artist that worked there, providing samples and inspiration for customers.

"Fresh meat," smiled the big man behind the counter, his teeth shining in the dimness outside the pools of light over each bench.

"Yet kicking," agreed Scarecrow, echoing the response to the traditional Tycherosian greeting. "Nice shop you've got here."

"Truth." The big man cocked his head to the side, crossing his ink-sleeved arms over his chest. "Are you both customers? Looking for matching designs?"

"I'm just curious," Uppercut said quickly. "This one has the thirsty skin."

"We've got pain and ink to satisfy. I'm Getch. You looking for an appointment with an artist, or some right-now work?"

"So far I'm just looking," Scarecrow said, eyes roaming the art wall. "My ink advertises where I'm from. I want to sketch out where I'm going, too."

"I might risk a guess you're a Skov," Getch said, his tone dry as he glanced over the visible skin on Scarecrow's arm and the bold geometric knotwork inked on it.

"Nothing slips past you," Scarecrow grinned.

"What are you after?"

Scarecrow let the question simmer for a long moment, studying patterns and lines advertised over the benches. "I'm thinking about a Tycherosian flavor. A deathseeker crow, with some southern styling and colors—like that one," he said, pointing at a stark profile in black over a mirage of delicate tints.

"Illustration or heraldry?" Getch asked quietly.

"Ink's not a game and I'm not a decoration," Scarecrow said. He looked Getch in the eye. "Maybe I need this ink to paper over the cracks."

"So who would you pick?" Getch retorted, a note of challenge behind his tone.

Scarecrow took his time, crossing to get a closer look at the walls. He paced down the line. Only one bench was currently in use. A woman lay face down, a bony man intent on his work as he stitched a black line on the small of her back. He embellished a tentacle on the devilfish sprawled across her flesh.

Scarecrow stopped, and a bleak smile failed to warm his features. "We have a winner," he said. "Fourth row, she's got the lexicon of Ironhook's criminal resume. That's basic stuff, except in her hands."

"You assume the artist is female?" Getch replied, eyebrows raised.

"Please," Scarecrow said, eyes still tracing the wall. "I've never seen a man who could do that," he said as he pointed at the seventh row. "That's Iruvian brushwork, it's interpretations of the Six Codes. If she can make it look like that on skin then it's clear she's spent some time in the desert forts. Men don't last out there."

"No they do not," said the woman stepping out of the alcove behind the front door's wide frame. "You have a good eye."

Scarecrow turned to face her, and stopped, eyes wide.

"Take your time," she said with a smirk.

Her head was shaved, and she wore no shirt on her lean torso. She was so pale that the threadwork of her veins interwove with the complex patterns of ink that flowed over her skin, giving her a coloration that directed and confused the eye as it reinterpreted her shapes with complimentary patterns.

"I need a week," Scarecrow replied, his voice soft with awe.

She tapped two fingers on the side of her neck, and her ribs, and her abs just above her low-cut loincloth. "Can you read these?"

"The first one is 'teacher student lover,' only they can ink you," Scarecrow replied. "That second one says you've sworn to keep the secrets of the Twelve Codes, you're a Confessor. And... no. You are too young!" he protested, eyes on the third tattoo.

"Too young for what, schoolboy?" she retorted.

"Three Sisters. Radiant master. You can illustrate Whispers." He shook his head. "I'm in the presence of royalty. You must be Jafrain."

"Guilty," she agreed, crossing her arms over her chest. As she relaxed, designs on one forearm aligned with designs on the forearm below, forming a larger pattern. "You know enough to be dangerous. Maybe we can do business. Strip."

Scarecrow only hesitated a moment. Wincing, he flexed at his straps and fabrics, working his way out of his clothes. He glanced around, noticing Uppercut had relocated already. Scarecrow's breathing was shallow as he stood wearing nothing but his socks and his ink, looking Jafrain in the eye.

"Socks," she said, her eyes drifting across his narrow hairy chest.

Scarecrow hissed with aches and effort as he struggled out of his socks, then he stood trembling slightly in the cool of the shop, unencumbered by clothing or modesty.

Jafrain walked around him in a slow circle. "Isle of Storms," she murmured. "The Line of Elms. Oh, a skull cluster," she said in a tone normally directed towards a playful puppy. "And such a string of heartbreaks."

"Didn't want to forget, didn't want to repeat mistakes," Scarecrow agreed. "I had my share of edgy teen promises and romantic adventures."

Jafrain squared off with him, and looked him in the eye. "Not bad," she said. "You must know I only work through referrals."

"I've got one. Coinpurse," Scarecrow said.

"That referral is qualified," Jafrain said. "We've done business with him, but our needles never passed his pretty skin. So you must be here about something besides art."

"Maybe so, but I'd still be—honored—if you'd mark me," Scarecrow murmured.

"I won't," she replied, her gaze boring into his eye. "Kinlay already did."

"Kinlay—I mean, he did," Scarecrow confessed, momentarily confused.

"Kinlay's needle and mine will never taste the same canvas," Jafrain said, cool. "You have his work, so you won't have mine."

Scarecrow looked away. "I see." He cleared his throat. "I'm going to put my clothes back on."

"Suit yourself," Jafrain replied, amused. "Why are you really here."

"I'm wrangling a goat in the dark, and that's a sure way to get pancaked," Scarecrow replied. He considered the clothes at his feet, and weighed the relative discomfort of all the bending and stretching and struggle, against the ongoing nudity. Casual, he leaned against the end of one of the bench stalls. "I can trust you, right?"

"Absolutely not," Jafrain retorted.

"My partner and I have a handler, and I think we're losing our charm with her. I want to figure out what she's up to and get around it before she cashes us in. Shot in the dark," he said, shaking his head. "Maybe you know more."

"Goats, now shooting," Jafrain replied, bland. "Sounds like the dark is busy."

"It's Shimmer. She's a spy, an agent, she's up to something. Something she wants my pal Uppercut for, and I'm not sure I'm going to live long enough to find out what. So I'm asking around. Quiet like."

Jafrain rolled her eyes. "I know better than to get involved," she said.

"I don't want you to get involved," Scarecrow said quickly. "Just—you know, share some context."

"Here's all you get," Jafrain replied. "You might want to let it go. Shimmer is my sister."

*

Uppercut didn't wait to see how Scarecrow's conversation turned out. As soon as the Skov got the staff talking, Uppercut sidled along the side of the shop rails, keeping an eye out for doors or hallways.

"That'll do," he muttered under his breath, quickly mounting a ladder tucked into the shadow of an alcove. Pushing his way through the trapdoor at the top as quietly as he could, he hauled himself up into the stuffy back room.

Uppercut reached into his coat and pulled out an algae globe, vigorously shaking it until a wan light glowed out.

The triangular room was tucked under the steeply raked roof. The tallest wall, against the interior, was lined with book spines. A single round window high up on the side caught some of the light from outside. He froze as his eyes crossed the interior face of the roof.

The sloping multi-textured angle of the roof supported a frame that had a canvas stretched on it. Close-packed scrawl covered the canvas in a strange flow chart. The symbols were familiar, but their meaning was not immediately clear.

Uppercut stepped closer, carefully moving on the groaning floorboards. He squinted at the symbols, and they seemed to squirm against his mind as he studied them over. Something old, something dimly remembered.

"Over and below, resheath," he murmured to himself. Yes, the symbol above, then the symbol below the center of the sigil. Top left to bottom right. Heraldry, an old heraldry, an occult genealogy.

"Oh," he murmured to himself. His eyes locked on a symbol near the center. "Oh no." Reluctant, his eyes traced the connection, the bloodline, all the way out to the end.

"I see," he breathed. And he wiped his mouth with a trembling hand.

A low groan drifted through the gloom. Uppercut crouched, squinting, and picked out a bundled figure laying amid a jumble of empty bottles. Cautious, he stepped back, reaching the ladder and easing himself down. He left the hidden library.

*

"Yeah, the crest knotwork to the right reflects the ocean, and the peak knotwork to the left reflects the mountain. You can see them blend towards each other, that symbol in the middle is my name," Scarecrow said. He was still naked. He flexed his shoulderblade out, stretching the skin, tightening the picture. "I will always live between them. It's a blessing from my grandfather, like a prophecy."

"That's some fine work!" the gawky man said, examining the tattoo. "It's aged really well, too. You said you got that ten years ago?"

"Give or take," Scarecrow nodded, turning to face the other customers that had come in a few minutes ago. He smiled at one of the two ladies. "I'm pretty safe from amnesia. Anything that matters gets a note," he said as he slapped his tattooed bicep.

"You've got a lot of notes," the other woman said, arching her eyebrows as she considered the embroidered shapes with name sigils in them. "You have a trophy for every woman? Kind of obsessive."

"It's not like that," Scarecrow replied. "These are just the ones that hurt me so bad I had to wash the wounds out with ink." He grinned. Then he looked over the woman's shoulder. "There you are, ready to go?" he said to Uppercut.

"Yeah. Ready," Uppercut muttered, frowning. "Maybe put some clothes on."

"Does this happen a lot?" one of the customers asked with a smirk.

"What, him getting naked? Constantly," Uppercut sighed, shaking his head.

Scarecrow lowered himself to sit on a bench, slowly bending, pulling his heavy clothes over. Belts, buckles, weapons, layers. He started dragging a sock on, then flinched with a sharp gasp.

Jafrain swiveled around, eyes wide, breaking from her quiet conversation with Getch. "That was *you*?" she demanded, fixing her attention on Scarecrow.

"What—what was me," Scarecrow winced as his mending bones twinged.

"By the Ripped Cuff, you'll get out now," Jafrain swore. "Now I know why *you're* with him," she said directly to Uppercut. "Now!" She didn't raise her voice, but her tone chilled their marrow.

"At least let him dress," Uppercut said, muted.

Jafrain raised her eyebrows. Getch drew a long knife from his belt and took a menacing step forward. The other customers retreated several paces, watching with awe.

"Right," Scarecrow gritted out, hefting an arm full of clothes, straightening with a wince. "Come on."

Uppercut gathered up the rest of Scarecrow's effects and followed the limping scoundrel out of the shop. Getch followed them out.

"We left," Uppercut said, turning to confront the big man. "Are we done?"

"Just making sure you go on your way," Getch growled. "Not here," he said to Scarecrow as the Skov once again adjusted, balancing to dress. Scarecrow staggered, and cocked an eyebrow at the big man.

"At least tell me what this is about," he said.

Getch stared at him.

"Alright," Scarecrow muttered, tightening down on his frustration as he pivoted and shuffled towards the alley. "Fine."

Uppercut followed, keeping a wary eye on Getch until they turned the corner.

"Maybe *you* know what that was about," Scarecrow said through his teeth, dumping his clothes on a rickety chair patterned with mildew.

"I sure don't," Uppercut replied, heaping the rest of Scarecrow's clothes on the chair then posting sentry at the mouth of the alley. "What set her off?"

Scarecrow hissed in pain once more as he struggled with his pants.

"How are you doing?" Uppercut asked, suddenly thoughtful.

"How does it *look* like I'm doing?" Scarecrow snapped.

"You are a mess," Uppercut replied.

"Good talk," Scarecrow growled, pulling his coat on.

"Well she's a piece of work," Uppercut mused, still watching the front of the shop and the big man that stood outside gathering his composure. "I just got a quick look at that woman, but she isn't a Whisper."

"Maybe not," Scarecrow sighed as he leaned against the wall, spent. "But she's an adept in her own tradition. She's touched both sides of the Mirror. She is a master of radiant tats. She may not know what you know, but she knows some weird stuff that I'm pretty sure you don't."

"You have a very odd and uneven expertise," Uppercut frowned.

"I know ink," Scarecrow replied. "Not like she knows ink, but enough to know that she's the real deal. And something upset her." He paused. "I wonder if we're cursed."

"She reacted when your injuries flared," Uppercut said with a dismissive wave. "She was picking up on your bond with the deathseeker crow. It's not healthy, and I don't know what's going on there. Whatever it is, I know it's not good, and she does too. She's just positioning what she saw between different bits of lore than I've got. She recognizes something I haven't seen."

Scarecrow blinked. "Well—that's *great*!" he said. "She can tell me what's going on. I'll dig up a present for her and try again. If she knows what's up with my bond, then—"

"No," Uppercut said, forceful. "Leave her alone. She's wary of whatever it is that's going on with you, and maybe that will buy us some time. In any case, we have more pressing issues."

"Don't you think we could—"

"That's behind us now, what's done is done," Uppercut insisted. "We got out without violence, and considering you've lost a step to your injuries, we better keep things civil. I don't want to have to shoot your new hero," he said, nettled.

"Are you *jealous* now?" Scarecrow demanded.

"No. No. Listen to me, I got a look at their hidden library. We have a problem."

"I guess we do," Scarecrow retorted.

"Drop it," Uppercut growled. "You know ink. So tell me what you know about the Reliquary Scrip."

"Hah!" Scarecrow scoffed, caught between emotions. "We're back to conspiracy theories so soon? I thought you said we had 'pressing issues' to handle."

"I did," Uppercut said quietly. "We do." He straightened, turning away from the street. "I saw the Tyvissi Bloodmap."

"You can't *see* a bloodmap," Scarecrow said quickly. "The artists that did the signs swore to pass on the knowledge of patterns and carriers from master to apprentice with no written record."

"Right," Uppercut agreed. "That was over a century ago, when the practice was at its height, before the crack-down that made it illegal. You can talk about honor among thieves, but there are a lot of powerful pressures out there—and don't forget the Spirit Wardens are involved." He paused. "They hit hard."

"Even if there *was* a bloodmap," Scarecrow said under his breath, "what would it even look like? I mean, how would you read it?"

"Six years ago I was a special for an Inspector who was tracking down memorial tattoos. Knowledge of bloodmaps was the single factor connecting a string of gruesome murders. I was in the room for some sensitive discussions with deeply unpleasant Spirit Wardens. I picked up on how to read memorial markings so I could help the Inspector track patterns." Uppercut brushed at the sleeve of his coat. "That's where I first saw the Tyvissi sigils. You don't forget something like that in a hurry."

He looked Scarecrow in the eye. "I recognized several of the sigils on the canvas in *that building*," he said, jabbing his finger towards the tattoo shop. "From there it was straightforward to realize I was looking at a blood map. Tracking the shadow carriers and their minders, the sigils that are permutations of the mark of the individual immortalized on their flesh."

"And you think the Reliquary Scrip is real," Scarecrow prompted.

"I know it is." Uppercut took a deep breath. "Of all the people immortalized on the skin of shadow carriers, there are five that the Spirit Wardens will pay to eradicate. If you can provide a blood map and account for each shadow carrier, proving that the inked memory of the deceased has been erased from living flesh, then the Spirit Wardens pay you in Reliquary Scrip. It's not money." He paused. "It's whatever you want," he said softly.

Scarecrow stared at him, processing.

"I... I thought there were eight," he said in a small voice. "Eight people to erase."

"There were," Uppercut replied. "Now there are five." He watched his partner for a moment. "I saw somebody get paid, Scarecrow. It's real."

Scarecrow squinted, trying to force his thoughts into focus. "But—what does the Clavalian heist have to do with any of this?"

"That house holds secrets. Especially secrets about what happened to a lot of people who met a gruesome end. Documented, the kind of proof the Spirit Wardens would need."

"But that house was shut up like three centuries ago, before memorial tattoos were even popular," Scarecrow said.

"Right, it was," Uppercut muttered. He glanced around the street. "But it also has a lot of hiding places, and we don't know that those places are no longer used by surviving members of the Clavalian family." He straightened. "It's a damn good place to store trophies that the authorities would kill you for possessing."

"So to be clear," Scarecrow said, "you are suggesting Shimmer is filling in a blood map and making sure every shadow carrier for Tyvissi's sigil meets a documented end. That his memory is no longer washed in living blood. So she, or her boss, can get whatever they want from the Spirit Wardens."

"That's about the size of it," Uppercut agreed.

"Okay that's just…" Scarecrow shook his head, at a loss. "How do we even follow up on this?"

"We talk to experts," Uppercut replied. A mirthless smile adjusted his features. "I just happen to know one."

"Then why did you say we had a problem?" Scarecrow said. "We can get the jump on this. It's the break we've been looking for."

"The problem," Uppercut said with forced patience, "is that I know a little about the sigils. I could read some of the meanings. Most of the shadow carriers are marked out. There was a cluster that wasn't. If I read the chart right, there are three left. And they're all Skovs." He cocked his head to the side. "It's a safe bet Shimmer is going to send us to kill some of your people."

CHAPTER SIX

The Sedeesy Warren sums it up. Dandy fops and cinch-girdled ladies preen and strut before the glass walls of the restaurant. They play out their intrigues in the expensive lounges and parlors. They pride themselves on their palate and sample the exotic Sedeesy cuisine, famous across Akoros.

Meanwhile, that restaurant is built over the entry to the caves stretching into the dark below. Unfortunate debtors are locked into contracts, toiling among the vermin and the fungus. Those exclusive cultivation projects require the sacrificial efforts of fifty humans to support a single noble customer's needs. Debtors suffer and die in the darkness, and their bodies go into the planter beds to nourish exotic appetizers. The lucky few get a better life as servants.

We have decided it is acceptable for aristocrats to rest on the support of fifty other lives each to make their luxuries possible. It takes a whole lot of ugly caves to make a few beautiful rooms.

—From "Infectious Unrest"
by Dame Brightpenny

"I'm hungry," Uppercut muttered as he squinted at the bustle of the late morning traffic. "Let's get some stew and figure this out."

"It's your turn to buy," Scarecrow lied, matter-of-fact as he limped along.

"Right," Uppercut scowled. "So you've spent all the money again."

"Well you were supposed to work out more permanent quarters," Scarecrow said. "Remember that conversation? I mean, I can look out for the money, but carrying around all that wealth makes me a target. And the weight pulls my ensemble askew," he said with a defensive tug at his belt.

"At least tell me you settled up with our tavern circuit," Uppercut said through his teeth.

"I covered all the *important* creditors," Scarecrow said. "We are back to coasting on credit and our good looks. "

"And our brains," Uppercut added. He straddled a bench and lowered himself, gazing out at the wavering forest of masts and rigging. "I may have something."

"Well don't keep me in suspense." Scarecrow settled on the bench facing away from him, leaning back on the railing and watching the street traffic.

"Haunted paintings," Uppercut muttered. "The Spirit Wardens are collecting them from an estate auction house. The owner of a private gallery died, and the artwork was inherited by somebody who didn't want a bunch of ghosts soaked up in the decorations. Apparently the gallery was stocked with a dynastic set."

"Dynastic set? You mean generations of ghosts? Come on," Scarecrow scoffed.

"Right. Infusing ghosts into paintings was a hobby passed down through the aristocratic bloodline of the Vans family. The gallery passed to Aldric Vans, and he doesn't have any interest in art, but he's got enemies and bills. He's looking to bank some favors with the Spirit Wardens by turning the collection over."

"So why is an auction house involved?" Scarecrow asked, his mind already sifting through the possibilities.

"Because Vans is a fool, but not an idiot," Uppercut sighed. "He wants the art categorized, appraised, and documented. He thinks the Spirit Wardens are likely to double-cross him when they get what they want."

"And appraisal will take a little time," Scarecrow nodded. "Also adepts, experts, secure facilities; a real headache."

"Not to mention fending off the others who are interested," Uppercut said. "You ever hear of a scholar named Wildthorn?"

"He's a medium, right? Something about the Reconciled. Oh," Scarecrow said, a bleak grin creasing his features.

"Oh indeed," Uppercut nodded. "He's got ghost friends, he thinks ghosts are the next breakthrough in transmitting learning, right after books. This collection of paintings is something I know he'd pay for, and he's got resources."

Scarecrow squinted over at him. "So how did you hear about this?" he demanded as his instincts tingled with danger unseen.

"Wildthorn brought it to me two days ago," Uppercut said. "He said he heard I was working for Shimmer, and he wanted me to take her a message. I read it, of course."

"Of course," Scarecrow sighed. "And did you deliver the message to her?"

"I sure did," Uppercut nodded. "She didn't seem to take him seriously. She may not even read it."

"And you didn't mention it to me," Scarecrow clarified.

"You have your own business to look after," Uppercut retorted. "Remember the Gutters? She asked for a report on how that's going. And she brought up the Silver Nails in Gadavant Circle. Any progress on either of those?"

"I'll get to it," Scarecrow said with a dismissive wave. "This is on the clock. How long before the Spirit Wardens take the paintings from the auction house?"

"Probably three more days," Uppercut said. "Seems pretty open and shut. Get the paintings, turn them over, get paid. Then don't worry about where you'll get breakfast." His stomach gurgled.

"So you have some ideas for how we pull this off?" Scarecrow said.

"Some," Uppercut nodded. "You think this sounds good for our next move?"

"Good enough," Scarecrow sighed. "Did Shimmer say when she wanted Gadavant Circle checked out?"

"Two days," Uppercut said, subdued. "And she wants us to bring her a report. She's not going to come looking for it."

"So we do both," Scarecrow mused. "And with the leftover time I'll check out the Gutters. Who needs sleep."

"This art heist can be part of the bigger plan," Uppercut said. "We work for Shimmer. So we're going to use her name to secure equipment and access. Hint that she's involved. People know she's got us running errands for her, so we should be able to get at some resources that would be a challenge for us as independent operators."

"We gotta get a crew together," Scarecrow grumbled.

"Business first, then the rest of the business," Uppercut quoted. "Maybe we can figure that out at the end of the week if we're still alive. It's a risk dropping Shimmer's name, but it will be interesting to see how she reacts when she finds out."

Scarecrow wrinkled his nose. "We need leverage on that woman," he muttered.

"Yes we do," Uppercut agreed.

"And while we're at it," Scarecrow said, "I only heard of Wildthorn because he's got some notable Skov ghosts, both in his collection and among the Reconciled. We get him on our side, maybe we could build up our endorsement, get more Skovs interested in my leadership."

"Leviathan hunters, maybe some Whispers," Uppercut mused. "He might have lore on how to make the zemi functional. How to communicate with it." He paused. "What it can do."

A shadow passed over them, chilling the moment.

"That's what I thought," Scarecrow said through his teeth. Uppercut glanced up, spotting the deathseeker crow that glided between them and the arc lights on the warehouse across the street.

"What did you think?" Uppercut demanded, his hand resting on the butt of his pistol.

"I marked Getch. Figured that whole *thing*," he said with a gesture "wasn't over. Sure enough, he's getting closer. I think we need to have another conversation."

"So you lure him into an alley and I back you up?" Uppercut said quietly.

"No, I really don't think he'll hurt me. Whether he wants to or not," Scarecrow said as he settled the baldric holding the crossbow at his back.

"Have you forgotten you are still healing up?" Uppercut wondered aloud.

"Hey, if they wanted to kill us, they had their chance," Scarecrow said. "Either they're curious or they're desperate. I think I can find out more." He looked over at Uppercut. "We have less than three days to get a hell of a lot done. You chat with Wildthorn. Make sure he's on board, see what resources he may pitch in. I'll deal with Getch."

Uppercut hesitated a moment longer, then rose and clapped Scarecrow on the shoulder. He turned, merging with the morning street traffic, drifting out of reach.

Scarecrow painfully levered himself up to his feet, and limped onward. He crossed the street, his stomach rumbling as he passed the vendor with strings of fried mushrooms and ratmeat. Leaning against a green door with his shoulder, he followed its creaking arc and headed down the stairs on the other side.

He followed the corridor at the base of the stairs, going left, and taking the first staircase back up to street level. He unlatched the door and pushed it open, surprising the merchant whose stall was built across the doorway. Scarecrow managed to squeeze out.

"Just taking a shortcut," he explained apologetically, and the merchant eyed him warily as Scarecrow limped out of the tent and back to the street.

Squinting up, Scarecrow felt the skin bunch on his forehead, around his scar, and he felt the simmering burn of Carc's awareness. He felt the intent gaze pinned on Getch by the deathseeker crow. Scarecrow crossed the street, down some rickety stairs to the boardwalk. He followed it, sensing the heat of Getch's presence drift along the left-hand side.

Scarecrow clumsily mounted the steps back up to street level, easing himself down onto a crate discarded by the waist-high wall next to the stairs. He frowned at the broad shoulders of the man leaning against one of the merchant stalls, waiting, his back to the docks.

Scarecrow pulled his crossbow out and around. He cranked the bowstring into position and loaded a quarrel before resting the weapon on the wall.

"Getch," he said quietly. The big man flinched and pivoted, startled to see him.

"Not possible," Getch objected. "No way you saw me." He was positioned across the alley from the green door.

"Maybe this is just a standard little loop I do to throw off pursuit," Scarecrow suggested. "The point is we're here now, and we're going to have a chat."

"Are we," Getch retorted, eyebrows raised.

"Talon here can pin you to that wall. No noisy gunshots. And nobody here cares if you scream," Scarecrow observed in a deceptively pleasant tone. "So let's keep it civil and informative. Why are you following me?"

"I don't really know," Getch said through his teeth.

"Ooh, try harder," Scarecrow muttered as he squinted down the sight at Getch's bulky shoulder.

"I really don't," Getch protested, raising his hands. "Jafrain was shaken. I've never seen her like that. She tapped a bottle of Severosian Red that she's had under the counter for a decade. Drank half of it without taking a breath." He shook his head. "When she told me to find out about you, I thought maybe *you* could give *me* answers."

"Speculate," Scarecrow suggested.

"Jafrain is... sensitive," Getch said. "She feels things on both sides of the Mirror. Things she's seen, things she's done, things she's studied...

I don't know her very well, not really. But I respect her," he said, his voice deepening as he straightened. "She is *important*. Serving her is an honor, and it's worth my life. So when she reacts like that, I pay attention." He cocked his head to the side. "What did you do?" he demanded.

"Tell you what," Scarecrow muttered. "I'll work with you if you'll work with me. You figure out what this mystery is really about, and maybe we can do something to clear it up together. I don't want to hurt Jafrain. Are you kidding me?" he said with a wry grin. "But this whole thing, whatever happened, it's got me nervous. I want to know more. So do you." He tilted the crossbow up, away from Getch. "So let's find out," he suggested. "I want to know why she got upset. My partner thinks it's because my broken bone gave me a pang. I almost died recently."

"Yeah?" Getch said, wary.

"Yeah. I'm still kind of broken up. And I only survived because I was possessed by a ghost, walked me out of danger."

"Okay," Getch nodded. He waited.

"Maybe that's significant," Scarecrow prodded.

"I may not be steeped in occult lore, not like Jafrain," Getch said. "But I do know people. You aren't telling me everything. What's the rest?"

Scarecrow hung in the balance for a long moment, but trust wouldn't come. "Find out more," he said quietly, "and maybe I can fill in the blank parts. You want me, you leave a message for Quarrel at the front desk at Kettlebox Court. That's *not* where I'm staying," he clarified. "Still. I'll get the message."

"I guess that will do," Getch said. "Watch yourself."

"Sides and back," Scarecrow agreed.

Getch flexed his jaw, then deliberately turned and walked away.

Scarecrow let out a breath, and leaned forward, resting the crossbow. "Now we're getting somewhere."

Silent, adrift between lights and clouds, a deathseeker crow wheeled overhead.

"I can't believe I let you talk me into wearing eyeliner," Uppercut grumbled.

"You've got bags under your eyes, but you're not haggard enough to be Father Glut-Root of the Third Vine without some theater," Scarecrow muttered, his voice muffled by a mask. "Besides. *Everyone* here is fancied up."

Uppercut frowned at the deep cowl concealing Scarecrow's face. "Even the Executor?"

"Hey, you think this thing is *comfortable*?" Scarecrow retorted, leaning back so the spike studs over the muzzle glinted in the light. "My breath isn't all I'm smelling. My buddy Kinsolly must have lost most of his teeth, it's rotten in here. Whew." His grimace was invisible behind the impassive mask. "As long as nobody here saw the production of 'Sodden Nights in an Obsidian Spire' then we can get away with this 'Forgotten Gods cultist' act."

They leaned to the side, gripping the stability straps as the carriage clattered around a sharp corner.

"I guess I'm glad *you* saw the play," Uppercut said, unconvinced.

"You got that right," Scarecrow agreed. "Research," he said with a sage nod. "Both into portraying cultists, and into the bizarre culture of theater gangs in the underbelly of The Dusk's deviant subcultures." His grin was audible.

"You must have made quite an impression on the stage manager," Uppercut muttered, raising an eyebrow, determined not to think about it.

"An impression I'm not done making, so let's make sure all this stuff gets back in good shape," Scarecrow said. "Now look all mysterious. We're here."

The coach rattled to a halt, and Scarecrow hefted himself forward to open the door and step out, turning so Uppercut could plant a hand on his shoulder for support as he levered himself down to the sidewalk. Scarecrow gestured imperiously to the coach driver, who rose on the buckboard and bowed deeply before resuming his seat and driving away.

Scarecrow hefted his two-handed axe, gripping it upright before him as he treaded out a dignified gait towards the glass and stone entry to Sedeesy Plaza. Behind him, Uppercut brandished his scepter, then held it to his chest as he strutted after his herald.

The doorman coolly evaluated the pair as they approached the podium recessed in the stone arch. The scene was illuminated by the radiant vines that tumbled down from the arch to form a neat curtain, trimmed daily.

"Welcome to the Sedeesy Plaza," the doorman said. "May I have the honor of your credentials?"

"Father Glut-Root of the Third Vine, and guest," Scarecrow intoned. "Here by invitation of Sir Galthara." He paused. "We should be on the list."

"Indeed," the doorman said with a slight nod. "Aria will guide you and provide for your needs while you are with us. Do enjoy," he said, his polite smile pulling his lips back far enough to reveal the glint of teeth. He gestured, and a young woman in a sheer sleeve of fabric stepped into view and bowed to them. She opened the door and held it open, her smile plastic. Scarecrow stepped in, with Uppercut behind him.

Aria crossed the mirror-polished floor, and the scoundrels following her deliberately ignored the delicately scented air, the soaring glass and lanterns illuminating the exquisite space, the complex carvings and rare plants accenting the entry. Knots of gaily dressed aristocrats conducted social and economic business in the rarefied environs, untroubled by irritating distractions.

They mounted the sweeping staircase of bone and marble, following one of the three arterial corridors leading to different themed playgrounds for the wealthy. Bones and jewelry were embedded in resin building materials, the lanterns were hooded and wrapped in stained glass, and the overall somber tone was deliciously spooky. Delicate scents of exotic cuisine wafted through the air, and their footfalls were silent in deep-pile carpet.

There was so much to take in, the scoundrels almost didn't notice the alcoves with massive sculptures at rest inside. Security hulls. It was not necessary for either to remind the other that this was not an ideal place to start trouble.

Uppercut gripped his scepter tighter, irritated at the sweat oozing from his palms. He felt the cheapness of the fabric he wore, and forcibly suppressed the panic struggling up inside. The audacity of their intrusion, the paupers slipping into this playground of the wealthy, was a visceral sensation.

Grim, he reminded himself he should be furious that he, or anyone, would feel this response. Aristocrats were only people. He frowned, disgusted by how muted that idea was in the face of his more primal reaction.

"Ah, there you are," said a clipped and educated voice, cultivating beauty and boredom in the same intellectual garden. A trim young man barely out of his teens glided from one of the dining nooks adjacent to the corridor, all smiles. He wore a black lacquered coat with glittering skull and bone patterning and a stiffly upright collar, cream and crimson accents. His smooth face and professionally coiffed hair set him apart, appearing almost artificial compared to the pitted skin and visible flaws of real people. Aria curtsied to him, then joined the other assistant guides in the side chamber.

"Lord Galthara," Scarecrow intoned with a deep bow. "Thank you for your invitation."

"Oh, indeed, thank *you* for attending," Galthara said to Uppercut. "Tonight is special for my sister." He ushered them into the dining nook, a long chamber featuring a table that could seat two dozen people. A cavernous fireplace muttered and crackled with bales of dried kelp seasoned to release incense. About half of the diners were present, standing around in small groups, many breathing in flavored smoke with a variety of pipe designs and paper wrappings.

Galthara led the way to an elderly man with a silky beard down to his waist, dressed elegantly in black silk with bone accents, including phalanges wired together to form epaulettes.

"Master Ten Holes, may I introduce Father Glut-Root of the Third Vine?" Galthara said. "He has come for Sileska's Awakening."

Master Ten Holes arched one eyebrow. "Father Glut-Root, it is an honor," he said, his tone dry. He turned to Galthara. "Thank you, young sir, for the introduction. I believe the Father and I have business to discuss, about the many signs and portents permeating these recent nights."

Sweat beaded up on Uppercut's lower back as he sensed the sarcasm. The pistol hanging between his shoulderblades seemed heavy, weighing his ribs, pressing his lungs.

Still, Galthara bowed to Master Ten Holes, smiling as he stepped away. Master Ten Holes turned to the scoundrels. "Really. That's the best you could do."

"Short notice," Scarecrow shrugged.

"You better hope nobody here goes to cheap theater," Master Ten Holes mused, shaking his head. "How the hell did you get invited to this thing?"

"I know a guy, he knows a guy, you know," Scarecrow said airily.

"I want an answer," Master Ten Holes growled. "You'll give it to me, or you'll give it to the Galtharas."

"Zekel," Uppercut said. "He's a scholar who is working with us on a project. He knows the Galtharas, helped tutor some of them before his disgrace. He recommended us as local occultists."

"What do you want with the Galtharas?" Master Ten Holes demanded, eyebrows knitting.

"Nothing," Scarecrow protested quickly. "We just need to get into the Warren, and we thought we'd slip in through the front door." He swallowed hard.

"That's fast and sloppy work," Master Ten Holes said, his lip curling derisively. "Do you even know the way from here to the Warren entrance?"

"More or less," Scarecrow said defensively. "Sometimes you don't have the luxury of time to figure things out. We're on a deadline."

"No surprise there," Master Ten Holes sniffed. "Alright, I don't know or care who you are. I want this night to go smooth. I'm in charge of the Awakening ceremony for Sileska, she's turning eight tomorrow." He looked over to the girl in a silken robe at the head of the table, surrounded by elegant weirdos. "When the Awakening ceremony starts, the guides wait outside and we have the room. You can go through the passage built into the side wall of the fireplace, down to the main kitchens. You will have three hours," he said, his tone stern. "If you're not back by the Hour of Ash, there will be consequences. Do you agree to my terms?"

"Have we heard all your terms?" Uppercut asked, suspicious.

"You'll owe me one," Master Ten Holes gritted out. "And I'll put you beneath the Gaze of the Rapturous Chord. If you don't make it back, we may just have to strike the chord. You won't like that," he said with a shake of his head.

Uppercut and Scarecrow exchanged a quick glance.

"Yeah, okay," Scarecrow said. "Let's do it."

"Very well," Master Ten Holes growled. He planted his surprisingly-strong grip on Scarecrow's shoulder, and Uppercut's shoulder. Leaning in towards each other, they could feel Master Ten Holes releasing a long, hissing breath.

At the end of the breath, he whispered. "**Come back.**"

Scarecrow felt his guts buck as his throat flexed, as though struck by a wave of nausea. His mind twirled on a pivot, he felt the mark score him Behind the Mirror as the cultist wrapped a ritual around them. He also felt that ritual summons go through him. Past him.

Somewhere Behind the Mirror, in the misty night, the Draper turned his baleful gaze. Summoned.

Carc let out a screech, audible on both sides of the Mirror. Revelry? Disgust? Fury? The harsh sound was impossible for Scarecrow to interpret.

Scarecrow swallowed hard.

Uppercut glanced over at him, feeling the reverberation, then returned his attention to Master Ten Holes. "The passage," he prompted.

"Just attune to it. Now, I'm going to finish setting up this ritual, then I'm going to run it for my patrons. You aren't going to cause a *ripple* of trouble." He frowned. "Are you."

"No sir," they both said, more or less in unison.

Master Ten Holes nodded, satisfied, and turned away.

"Something I need to know about?" Uppercut muttered to Scarecrow.

"I'm sure it will be fine," Scarecrow lied.

The scoundrels stepped off to the side, retreating into their air of mystery. The other occultists were content to leave them alone, as there was other networking to do and good impressions to make among potential patrons. Uppercut was occupied breathing steadily and calming his nerves, and Scarecrow struggled against the dazed feeling that reverberated in him. He felt the Draper moving.

"This place is warded, right?" he said quietly to Uppercut.

"Profoundly," Uppercut agreed.

"So no ghosts get in," Scarecrow clarified.

"Right," Uppercut said. "That's why we had to set this operation up the way we did. What are you thinking?"

"Tell you later," Scarecrow said.

The evening seemed timeless, with the minutes racing and crawling at the same time. Eventually a gong was struck, the guides cleared out, and the guests shuffled into place at the table.

Midnight. The Hour of Pearls.

Before the invocation began, the scoundrels stepped into the corner of the fireplace, some distance from its center where the kelp blocks smoldered. Uppercut touched the wall and frowned, feeling the etheric switch, and he flexed his perceptions at it. The stone croaked ever so faintly, and the hidden door pivoted open. They were through, the door closed behind him.

"I'm having second thoughts," Scarecrow said in a small voice.

"I'm not," Uppercut retorted. "You're following through on this. We're too deep to pull out now. Remember the plan, and we'll make it through just fine." He paused. "What's the matter with you?"

"I'm just feeling it," Scarecrow admitted. "I'm not—not healed. And." He swallowed hard. "There's some... some weirdness going on. I'm just, all of a sudden..." He shrugged. "I'm not feeling it."

"Then maybe you better remember you're hungry, and get mad," Uppercut said under his breath. "Save one of your inspirational speeches for yourself. Because we're doing this. We've planned it, we're in position, and it's time to go."

"Yeah," Scarecrow nodded, avoiding eye contact. He felt saliva coat his tongue, as though he was about to throw up. "Time to go."

Uppercut watched him for a long moment, then nodded. "Alright then. We're almost to the kitchen. From there?"

"From there we follow the red track," Scarecrow repeated, remembering the diagrams they pored over in the flickering candle light. "The red track takes us to the old loading bay where we left our stuff."

"And if we get separated?"

"The green line to the Fist Junction, and the purple line swings close enough if you cross the pool," Scarecrow said with a decisive nod.

"Alright, let's go." Uppercut hefted his scepter and pivoted, following the narrow finished corridor. Scarecrow was right behind him.

In no time, they stood by the interior of the secret door that let out into the kitchen. They could hear the clatter and barked orders on the other side.

"Remember, they won't stop us, but they *will* report us. So we need to move fast," Uppercut said.

"Right," Scarecrow agreed. They both took a deep breath, then Uppercut toggled the switch, and the door slid open.

The costumed scoundrels strode into the kitchen, ignoring the surprised expressions on the cooks and servants. They took a sharp left and followed the hallway to the back coolers, confidently opening the third one in line and entering, closing it behind themselves.

Scarecrow tugged at a bracket on the back shelf, and with a croak, the secret passage opened. The scoundrels ducked through, and pushed it shut behind themselves with a loud click.

"Looks like Lumby was right so far," Scarecrow observed.

"Lucky for us," Uppercut agreed. "Now let's go get him."

The rough tunnel was foggy, but at least half the particles in the air were spores rather than moisture. Scarecrow suppressed a cough, and Uppercut stared at him.

"But you're the one in a mask," he muttered.

"Can—we just?" Scarecrow managed with an exasperated gesture.

Uppercut turned to follow the rough-hewn tunnel with planter boxes knee high along the sides. Clusters of glowing fungus were set in mesh baskets on chains, hanging over the center path, providing just enough light to wear out the eyes with strain.

"Shift change," Uppercut muttered. The tunnel opened to an exchange, with a loading dock and processing center as well as a cart rail head. A few workers stood around, dazed, but most were off down another tunnel where the workers were processed in and out from their dormitory area.

The scoundrels followed the crude red paint in a stripe along the wall, and in a stripe beside the tracks on the ground. The taller corridor had multiple ranks of cultivation beds for fungus mounted on the walls, ladders nailed to the sides. Once they managed to get out of the exchange, the scoundrels pulled glass orbs from under their layers, shaking them to activate the glowing algae inside.

A few minutes of walking took them to the point where the rails took a sharpish turn, and a dark corridor with no implanted lights loomed.

"These are the old beds, the ones that they don't use anymore," Scarecrow said.

"Yes," Uppercut nodded. Together, they entered the dark corridor.

A rattle hissed through the dark, and both scoundrels drew knives.

"Centipedes," Uppercut said. "If we don't bother them... they should be well fed enough to leave big prey like us alone."

"That's so very comforting," Scarecrow said through his teeth.

Penetrating the thick darkness, they tread on the deep mat of moss, water welling in their footprints as they squished along. Clumps and tangles of roots, vines, and webbing thickened as they went, until they were pressing through curtains of dank matter while bugs scurried out of their path.

"Here," Scarecrow said, relief clear in his tone. They discovered an old metal-lined shaft, too narrow for their shoulders to fit, stretching up into the ceiling. The bottom of the shaft was mounded up to the spout. It was overgrown with moss and fungus in weird twisting bundles.

"Looks like we weren't the first ones to have this idea," Uppercut said, wry.

"Lots of unclaimed packages, though," Scarecrow said as he tugged a clump of fungus loose, revealing a wet patch of leather on a backpack below.

"That old vent used to go to a mansion basement. It isn't very well guarded now that the mansion was cut up for apartments," Uppercut said. "The building fixer has quite a side racket of charging people to drop packages down into the Warren." He stooped to pick up the tough leather cases that rolled off the mound, and he brushed one off. "Here we go."

Uppercut unfolded the leather wrapping, revealing the chilly spirit bottle inside.

"There's Lumby," Scarecrow grinned. "He should be just as helpful now as he was when you chatted this over with him yesterday."

"Good thing you were lucky with the first worker you bought," Uppercut muttered. "We've got a bit of debt paying off this heist anyway, and it would have been rough to go back."

"Yeah, the Spirit Wardens apparently make the Sedeesy operation bottle the spirits of the dead workers they plant in the beds. Just to make sure. And I happen to know somebody who smuggles some of them out to auction off to weirdos like you." Scarecrow took the other leather pack, and nodded at the bottle. "You going to open that?"

"I think you mean weirdos like *us*," Uppercut said mildly.

"I really don't," Scarecrow squinted.

Uppercut smiled to himself. "We had better change. Now it gets sticky."

Scarecrow opened the other leather bundle, pulling out their tough work clothes. The scoundrels carefully removed their costumes and put them in the duffel bag, hanging them on a hook away from the damp. They strapped their boots tight. It was going to be dirty work from here.

"Look around for the third pack. The one with the tools," Scarecrow said. It only took a minute to locate the long bundle, unwrapping it to check that the sledge and prybar and such were intact.

"Sand's running through the hourglass. We had best get going," Uppercut muttered. He twirled the lid off the spirit jar. A plume of plasmic essence blossomed up into the thick air, taking shape, somehow more defined in the haze of spores and fog. Gaunt, starved, desperate features surrounded the pits of eyes.

"Lumby," Uppercut intoned.

Here we are, back again, back again, the spirit mouthed. *I can almost see*

"Would have been handy if he could have drawn us a map," Scarecrow groused, not looking at the apparition.

"But he can't," Uppercut replied softly. "It's confusing, when you look through the Mirror." He focused on Lumby's echo. "The foundation stones with the markings. Take us there. Can you feel them?"

I feel them, the spirit murmured, and it twisted, its ragged edges flaring in an invisible breeze.

The apparition drifted along, somehow visible but providing no light in the darkness. The scoundrels followed, climbing down among slick and filthy rocks, slogging through knee-deep mud, and clambering over broken and overgrown bracing materials in a collapsed section. They squeezed through a narrow gap, sliding down into a slurry of waste.

"Not to complain," Scarecrow said through gritted teeth as something meaty squirmed away under his boot.

"Then don't," Uppercut replied, sharp.

A brief climb later, and they stood in a pocket carved from the earth, where the digging had stopped. Where the digging had uncovered something it was not meant to uncover.

In the ghost-light, spidery glyphs glittered on the finished stone, carved on the outside of the buried foundation.

"But... there's no door," Scarecrow observed.

"And that's why we brought the sledge," Uppercut agreed.

"You think those runes are a problem?" Scarecrow asked, gesturing at the cold etching that stung the eye that crossed them.

"I think I can knock them out long enough to break through the stone," Uppercut said, something subdued in his tone. "Centuries have dimmed them some. A quick shock will likely do it."

"Like a ritual?" Scarecrow pressed.

Uppercut turned to the apparition. "Thank you, Lumby," he said quietly.

The spirit's rotten visage twisted. *Do it.*

Uppercut tightened his fist around the idea of the spirit, then threw a punch towards the stone foundation. Lumby was swept into it with a heart-stopping bang that was felt but not heard. Something crackled around the fringes of their sensations, and the glyph-light flickered.

Uppercut hefted the sledge, and slung the first of many hits into the foundation stone.

CHAPTER SEVEN

The Vans family prided themselves on their connections at the Imperial Court. The family culture focused that pride on their capacity to bestow aid rather than extract favors. For generation after generation, they were determined to run up a score of service that the Immortal Emperor could not repay. They were the most irrepressible of the three main loyalist families in the Weatherwatch District.

The Barrowcleft dissidents ruined the Vans family fortunes as part of their overall strategy to smash the political, economic, and social power of the Weatherwatch loyalists. The survivors in the Vans family faced destitution in a ravaged territory. When the Lightning Wall barricaded Doskvol, abandoning the Weatherwatch District and designating it as "Lost" in 562, the patriarch of the Vans family defiantly remained in the wreckage of the ancestral estate. He presided over a community of extended family and allies.

Undaunted, Kruse Vans was determined to keep illegal supply lines open so his people could survive. He founded the smuggling tradition that still distinguishes Doskvol rovers from other contraband cultures. A descendant of Kruse Vans ruled the Vans outlaw estate and criminal enterprise from the Lost District for five generations before unrelenting dissident efforts on both sides of the law finally scattered the survivors.

—From "Profiles of the Lost: Lingering in the Ruins"
By Tavisha Camber

With a spray of gravel, the paving stone broke loose.

Scarecrow grunted as he leaned his full weight on the prybar, and the rock shifted with a grinding hiss. He paused, leaning against the wall as the stone slid out and dropped to the earthy floor with a thud.

"Now remember," Uppercut said, pale in the shadows, breathless as he held the sledgehammer in still-tingling hands. "This basement is within the two outer rings of protections. We penetrated the basement, just the flooring glyphs. So we should be okay if we stick to the interior doors. Right?"

"Right." Scarecrow squinted at the Whisper. "You are sure about this plan?"

"I'm sure we don't have any more time or resources to go with a *better* plan," Uppercut retorted. "Here we go," he said under his breath. He clasped the edges of the socket where the paving stone had been, and pulled himself through the bottom corner of the basement chamber. Shaking his algae globe, he got enough dim shine to see the bulky outline of the furniture in the storage room.

Scarecrow panted as he hauled himself up into the gap, and Uppercut dragged him into the chamber.

"Now let's see if those plans were accurate," Uppercut muttered. He climbed up on a battered desk and stepped onto a sideboard, holding his globe up to the corner of the ceiling. A bleak smile crossed his face, and he brushed the cobwebs out of the way to reveal an iron ring hanging from an old trapdoor.

"Give it a tug," Scarecrow said.

"You know, I'm the mystic, and I'm supposed to be the brains of the outfit. *You* are supposed to be the muscle," Uppercut muttered.

"Good thing we're both so very capable," Scarecrow said through his teeth. "Less griping, more pulling."

Uppercut manipulated the bolt, drawing it out of the locked position. He reached into his pocket, retrieving a knotted cord with a hook. He snapped the hook through the ring, gripped the cord, and let his body weight pull the trap door. With a squeal, the wood tore loose of the nails holding it in place, dropping down. Uppercut listened for a breathless moment, then drew a knife and cut through the carpeting above.

The trapdoor had steps fashioned on its upper side, so when hanging down it formed a short ladder. Uppercut emerged into the cool dimness of the appraisal chamber as Scarecrow started climbing furniture below.

The portraits gave off a dim glow. Radiant pigments in the paintings created images of lamps and torches that released actual light. About a dozen frames were set on easels along the side of the gallery. The ceiling was out of range of the lights, a balcony above shrouded in darkness.

Uppercut sensed a simmering energy, a slick of consciousness like a dream. He narrowed his eyes, and reached out a hand towards the paintings, feeling the interleaved layers of energy folded through the texture of the Mirror. He tugged his mask out, fixing it in place, and felt the definition become crisp. There. He attuned to the layer emanating from one of the modestly sized portraits, about an armspan across.

Uppercut closed his eyes and concentrated, tuning out the rattle and clank of Scarecrow struggling up through the trapdoor. Relaxing his awareness, he re-oriented it to match the portrait rather than his surroundings.

Opening his eyes, Uppercut found his consciousness in the grainy swirling textures of the garden portrait. A petite woman with delicate features sat on the lip of the well, a steadily shining lamp at her side, radiant roses climbing the wall behind her and giving the scene a sanguine tint.

A visitor, the echo projected. *Aren't you bold.* Her expression drifted towards shrewdness, stiff and difficult to shift as her essence was fixed in the canvas image.

"Merrihel Vans," Uppercut murmured. "We can help each other."

Can we now.

"You want to possess people. It's what you do," Uppercut said. He took a moment to catch his breath, the constraints of the painting tight. "I want to get you and a few of your peers out of this place."

You do not have long before you get stuck, Merrihel pointed out diplomatically.

"My accomplice doesn't realize it, but he's primed to be a hollow," Uppercut said. "Easy for you to slip in and ride. You can jump over there and walk his body out with me. What say you."

She frowned. *What of my home?* she asked with an airy gesture that unfolded with a visual stutter.

"I have a plan to get the painting out. You will be reunited. And given opportunity for some exercise in your new home." Uppercut had to stop, concentrating to force motion through his ribs. He felt himself slowly drowning, flattening in the painting's protective constrictions.

For a long moment, Merrihel said nothing. *You focused on me and offered me a ride,* she mused. *So you must know something of my history.*

"Your needs," Uppercut agreed. "Your temper. I am here to ask."

Her visage shifted to a somewhat sunny smile. *Very well. But three of my companions come along.*

Uppercut blinked. "Three? You mean, of course, that we bring the paintings. We planned on that."

Three. There was triumph in her echo. *Riding in your hollow. With me. And you also bring their paintings.*

"Whatever. He'll be fine," Uppercut said. "How do we do this?"

Her smile widened to a grin, revealing wickedly sharp teeth.

*

Scarecrow peered at Uppercut's impassive mask, taking in the glaze and the fine cracks riddling its surface. "So... how are we doing?" he asked in what he intended to be a casual tone.

The Whisper shivered for a moment, and cleared his throat. "She agreed to our deal, and she'll bring along three others."

"Oh, you mean the paintings. Yeah, we planned on that."

"Riding your body," Uppercut clarified, looking away.

"All at once?" Scarecrow said, eyes wide.

"Look, we need to move fast," Uppercut muttered. The light from Merrihel's portrait flickered, and Scarecrow felt a certain magnetism from it; a fascination, a peculiar urge to stare into it. He shook it off, turning his back.

"Right over there," he said, pointing at the rack of barrels built into the room that had once been a cellar. "It'll take her a minute to, you know," he said with a gesture.

"She's gathering her strength. Let's not rely on her patience," Uppercut said through his teeth as he crossed the cellar and closed in on the barrels. "Now." He waved his hand, and nodded to himself. "It's in there. Asleep."

"It only wakes up if we trigger the defenses, the auctioneers didn't want some confused attack on actual guests or experts," Scarecrow said. He sucked air in his nose, and explosively blew it out his mouth. He clapped his hands together, rubbed them rapidly, then assumed a wide stance facing the barrels. "I'm ready."

"Then let's do this," Uppercut said under his breath. He returned to Scarecrow's side. Careful, he placed his hand on Scarecrow's face, a thumb on one temple and a fingertip on the other, his palm warm against the scoundrel's forehead and nose.

"Remember to do this quiet-like," Uppercut whispered. "You are sneaking in and borrowing, and if you wake up the owner of the house, you'll have a fight on your hands."

"Please," Scarecrow scoffed quietly, his eyes twitching slightly as he flexed them tight. "Have a little faith."

Uppercut let out a long, hissing breath, then his mouth chipped out a nasty Hadrathi phrase, triggering the ritual they had prepared hours before.

Scarecrow felt the jolt of his spirit unmooring from his flesh. He sensed the dull clatter of his body toppling over, and the room was washed in paleness, flickering between remembered states, none of them wholly real to him now.

An emerald glow suffused the barrels before him, and he slipped through them and into the shape on the other side.

Gently, he entered the armor. He felt the core, locked tight, where the animating spirit was quiescent. The bone skull inside the hull's helmet *was* real to him, and he slipped into it, condensing into its shape.

The skull was welded to delicate instrumentation, an array of glyph-work pins, acupuncture for the anatomy of a spirit inhabiting bone.

Here we go, Scarecrow's echo emoted. He focused in the skull. Through it, he felt the four legs and two arms. He felt the armored torso shape. The helm atop the mechanical marvel.

Concentrating on visual sight, he felt a flicker through the network of the hull, and the lamp-like eye sockets glowed to life. One arm was resting on the release lever, and Scarecrow tossed a thought down the arm. It shivered and moved, and with a clack, the mechanism disengaged and the fake wall behind the barrels smoothly pivoted open. His thoughts leaned forward, and Scarecrow piloted the hull a couple steps out of the hidden compartment. He felt the dim glow in his belly as the electroplasmic generator engaged, sending warmth through his newly-acquired limbs.

Uppercut took an involuntary step back as the hull unfolded to twice his height, arms flexing and clicking as the joints engaged.

"Scarecrow?" Uppercut said cautiously.

This is pretty great, Scarecrow replied, the bass register of his tone a palpable force.

"Will... will the rest of the plan work?" Uppercut demanded.

Scarecrow's smile was invisible as he concentrated, but he was already sensing the intuitive controls of the hull's body. He felt the chest compartment as though it was part of him, and with a thought, he unscrewed the reinforcing bolts so the chest opened to reveal a dusty compartment inside.

"Okay," Uppercut said. "Merrihel and her friends will take your body out with me, then you just wait for the opportune moment, sometime before close of business tomorrow, and walk those paintings out." He turned to the row of portraits. "The hollow is ready for you," he said.

Uppercut hefted Scarecrow's unresponsive body, gripping it under the arms and dragging it over to Merrihel's portrait. The massive hull behind him whined and sputtered for a moment, then clomped over to them.

The plume of force ejecting from Merrihel's portrait was only visible to one attuned to both sides of the Mirror. As a spirit entombed in steel, Scarecrow could viscerally sense the possessing spirit launching from her painted image, clawing her way into the senseless body with his face on it.

Watching his own eyes snap open was one more surreal experience to add to the day's collection.

"Ugh," Scarecrow's body grimaced. "This one is broken." Merrihel disdainfully shook the wrist on Scarecrow's body, eyeing his hand with disapproval. "Broken bones? Some sort of bowel upset?" She frowned. "You put me in a body that's *hungry*," she complained.

"I was sure you'd want the pleasure of eating," Uppercut said, thinking fast. "Most possessing spirits do."

"That's not *all* I want to do now that I'm in a body," Merrihel said with a coy tone that was jarring coming out of Scarecrow's mouth. "Now. Business first, then the rest of the business. Skyler, Escalan, and Tris; come on, let's go. Room for all of you," Scarecrow's body said with a crooked grin. His body limped over to the paintings and opened arms magnanimously.

Uppercut saw the low pressure dragged down by Merrihel's spirit, thinning the Mirror long enough for three other spirits to flow from their paintings into Scarecrow's body. The body staggered, and Uppercut could sense the bruises blooming through the meat and spirit mix as they violently rebalanced.

"Careful," Uppercut said through his teeth. "You still have a long walk to relocate, and you're stuck in that body until we get your painting out tomorrow."

"This thing is a mess," Merrihel said as Scarecrow's body grimaced. "A drunk. And—what, a cultist or something? There's massive scarring in here." She scoffed. "I'm surprised this thing walked *in* here, much less *out*."

"It's temporary," Uppercut growled. "You had best not press on any of that scarring. It's not good for spirits."

"Whatever, let's go," Merrihel said as Scarecrow's body waved off an airy gesture.

Uppercut carefully lifted the frame of Merrihel's picture, pivoting to carry it over to the hull. He leaned it inside; it was a near fit, but the painting could be inserted without damaging the frame or canvas. Moving quickly, he slotted three more into the compartment.

As he turned to get another painting, he felt a palpable reverberation in the Ghost Field.

Hey! projected the painting of a heavy-set man surrounded by spaniels. *Merry! Don't you dare leave me!*

"Gerald, darling, this is me leaving you. Again," Merrihel said with a wicked grin.

Oh yeah? Gerald snapped. *Maybe you don't get to leave either!*

"Be reasonable," Merrihel said, narrowing her eyes and crossing her arms.

Gerald released a gust of maniacal laughter as he focused, releasing a blast of energy that bathed the door to the chamber in etheric imbalance.

Just like that, a switch flipped, and the auction house defenses were galvanized. A distant bell mechanically hammered out a tinny stream of noise. The whole house creaked as its energy shifted.

Scarecrow felt the core of the hull snap open, and in a flash, he was no longer alone at the helm.

WHAT! roared the hull, and Uppercut pivoted with a gasp.

The skull inside the armor was keyed to its pilot. Two spirits were suddenly both in the same place, so a ghost door flicked, and the two of them were ejected to a pocket behind the Mirror. They faced off on a stony and wind-swept outcropping.

Scarecrow blinked, feeling his essence waver. His opponent looked like a big man with aggressive facial hair, dressed in military fashion a century out of date.

"Hello there," Scarecrow said experimentally.

"My home!" the spirit roared. "You cheeky fool, I'm going to rip your head off." He flexed, and his hands filled with a rapier and a parrying dagger. He saluted Scarecrow, and charged.

Scarecrow sprang to the side, but he still moved like he needed muscles and bones to adjust his position; he was no match for the warrior spirit that adjusted with the barest thought. The spirit's weapon leaped forward, embedding in his chest.

Scarecrow felt the same jolt of pain he got from bumping his broken leg; darkness flashed through him, and he let out a scream—the shriek of a raven. He felt shadow ripple through the ghostly space where they stood. The attacking spirit was blown off his feet, spattered with dark speckles, like a spray of ink.

The spirit dropped his weapons, scrambling away, hissing as his material corroded. His eyes widened with fear. Scarecrow felt himself waver; he sensed the shadow and resonance as though he was within the dark curve of one of the Bellweather Seminary's bells, slowly shifting in the wind, far above the world.

Darkness bloomed through his spirit form, as though an ink sac had ruptured within him and now flowed out towards his boundaries. He looked to the spirit, feeling his eyes glitter with Void.

"Alright, I won't fight this thing. Whatever you are," the other spirit said. "So you can just wait until I'm ready to *deal* with you." Frowning, he waved his arms, and then set into a strong, balanced stance. The image of stone that supported the two spirits shifted, then gaped beneath Scarecrow. With a yelp, the scoundrel fell, then clattered down through a defensive layer to land on something soft.

Above, a hatch of some sort snapped shut. The room glowed slightly, and Scarecrow looked around. He lay on a bunk in a narrow cabin, surrounded by riveted steel and the accommodations of a berth in a Leviathan hunting ship. There was no porthole, and a quick check confirmed that the door was bolted from the outside.

"This must be where he lairs when he's locked up," Scarecrow said to himself, glancing around his tidy prison, noticing the bookshelves lining the interior wall.

He straightened, ignoring the black ooze leaking out of his punctured spirit. Planting his fists on his hips, he frowned at the door.

"I'm not the reading type. I'll get out of here in no time."

*

"That can't be good," Merrihel observed dispassionately as she watched the hull drop to one knee with a loud grinding sound, internal machinery jamming.

"I don't think our guy is going to win this one," Uppercut agreed as he reached into a coat pocket. "He doesn't have experience as a spirit, much less a possessing spirit. Go in there and rescue him."

"I'm flattered, but drained," Merrihel sniffed. "Jumping in here, then making bridges for my family, was too much. I think your friend is lost."

"With your painting, let's not forget," Uppercut said. "You've got something to lose. And something to gain." He pulled a vial out of his pocket. Its interior glowed with an intense blue.

"That's wing essence," Merrihel said as Scarecrow's body cocked an eyebrow. "Where did you get it?"

"Made it myself," Uppercut said without an effort towards modesty. "I have been saving it for a special occasion, and I figured this might go wrong with Scarecrow inside the hull. I'll give you this elixir if you go in and rescue him. Put him back at the helm. If he loses this, we all lose."

"And if I don't come back? I could see the value of running the hull with my painting inside." Scarecrow's hand reached out for the vial.

"You wouldn't make it out," Uppercut said. "There are more hulls upstairs. And say you did make it to the street. Then what?" He paused. "I have a contact with the Reconciled who will take good care of you. Or, you know, you can take your chances." He held the vial out to her.

Merrihel was thoughtful as she took the vial and twisted it open, pouring it into Scarecrow's mouth. A grin revealed blue-stained glowing teeth.

"Good stuff," she gritted out. Scarecrow's body stiffened as though shocked by electricity, his head thrown back, and in the shine pouring up out of his mouth Uppercut saw the ascendance of Merrihel, limned in plasmic essence. She dove at the hull as it began to rise, its internal struggle over.

Moments later, the hull's lamps flashed. **And that's that,** boomed a coy voice. **Should buy you a couple days.** The frame shivered, and Merrihel dove back into Scarecrow's body as it bled from its eyes, ears, and nose.

"Scarecrow?" Uppercut prompted.

Yeah, I'm back. Scarecrow's voice was taut, and the hull shifted as though uncomfortable. **Not feeling so great.**

"Hang in there. We'll meet up tomorrow." Uppercut paused, but could not think of anything else to say.

The room trembled as other hulls stamped down from the upper levels, closing in on the gallery.

"Let's go," Uppercut said, refocusing.

"First, a little errand. I need fire," Merrihel said.

Uppercut handed over a sparker. "You can smoke when we get outside," he said.

"I won't *get* outside if we have a snitch," Merrihel responded. Turning, she flicked the sparker, and a scream wound through the Ghost Field as Gerald's painting caught fire. "*Now* let's go."

The security hulls fumbled with the gallery door as the scoundrels dropped through the trap door and pulled the carpet back in place. Uppercut strained to lift the door up, then rammed the bolt home to secure it from below as Scarecrow's body gingerly climbed down from the furniture.

"Exciting stuff," Merrihel said, droll.

"Through there," Uppercut said with a gesture at the hole in the cellar foundation. He spared a glance upward as dust drifted down, jarred loose by the hulls clomping about overhead.

Too late to worry about how that would unfold. Time to worry about his end of the escape.

He squeezed through the foundation after Scarecrow's body, vanishing into the darkness.

THE WARREN, SEDEESY PLAZA. BRIGHTSTONE
34ᵀᴴ MENDAR, 850. *OVER AN HOUR LATER*
HOUR OF WINE, 8TH HOUR PAST DUSK

"This thing is falling apart," Merrihel complained, and Scarecrow's body sagged against a wall.

"We're almost to the chute," Uppercut said, stiff. "Then we can change back into our disguises, infiltrate the restaurant, and get out the front door." He didn't have the heart to check his time-piece; they weren't moving very fast through the tunnels. Maybe the ceremony would go long.

"You can't find a way out besides the front door?" Merrihel said skeptically. "I thought you had some kind of plan."

"We do. And some backup plans. But this is how we're getting out of here," Uppercut said. He breathed a little freer as he saw the leather bags hanging from the hooks in the tunnel ceiling, and the axe propped up alongside them. "Now you'll need to change."

Merrihel paused, glancing around, forehead creased with puzzlement. "Did you ward this spot?" she demanded.

"What? No," Uppercut replied, and he concentrated—

Plasm jetted across his consciousness behind the Mirror, burning at his opening senses. It was blood—not the blood of the living, but instead, the life essence of a spirit.

As he gagged, staggering back, Merrihel let out an unearthly scream. The shadows rolled back from a spirit that smoldered with power.

You have something of mine, the Draper hissed. Merrihel pivoted to flee, but her clumsy meat body was no match for the spirit that pounced into it.

Uppercut managed to clear his vision in time to see Merrihel's head yanked back out of Scarecrow's meat, her hair embedded in the Draper's fist. Of all the weapons the Draper could have imagined, all he needed was a simple bone-handled knife. He slit her throat, his spirit blade cutting deep enough to simulate the rasp of blade on bone. Flexing, the slaughter spirit was sprayed in plasmic viscera, and he glittered with another layer of death. The Draper aligned with Scarecrow's body, filling it.

"Wait," Uppercut called out, hoarse. "Don't kill the other spirits in there." He cleared his throat. "Please."

Scarecrow's body squared off with him, eyes shining. "Hold on. Here it comes," he ground out in Skovic.

Uppercut sensed the rolling wave a moment before it arrived, but there was no way to brace against it. The soundless sensation flicked through the tunnel, and he grunted with pain as his guts squirmed within his torso. He dropped to one knee, and he heard a grim chuckle roll out of Scarecrow's mouth.

"Good thing I made it back," the Draper said, shifting to rough Akorosian. "That curse hit me too. Might have knocked me out to the Void. And I'm not ready to go," he said as his face creased into a savage grin, blood sliding down from where his battered skin opened from the strain of carrying so many ghosts.

Uppercut's mind raced. The Warren couldn't be as protected as the Plaza. That's why he smuggled a ghost in from outside, rather than trying to take it through the Plaza. So, if the Draper could somehow sense Scarecrow's body, he could... Uppercut sniffed, and brushed his cuff along his runny nose. Next steps. Gotta figure out next steps.

"So we're cursed. You know what that means?" Uppercut asked the Draper.

"Some idea," the Draper nodded. "Hm. Missed this." He rolled Scarecrow's shoulders, and breathed deep. "It stinks down here," he said with something close to delight.

"We need to go back through the Plaza," Uppercut said.

"No. Too warded. And now you're cursed anyway," the Draper replied. "Do what you want. I'll find my own way out."

"Keep those spirits alive. The other three," Uppercut said quickly. "They are haunting paintings that we're looking to sell. Kill the spirits, the paintings are just art. We lost the most expensive one already."

"Worth every notched penny," the Draper murmured, and he sensuously rubbed his arms along his torso. "Delicious."

"Scarecrow. He's in a hull, he will get out tomorrow as soon as there's an opportunity. He will need his body back." Uppercut watched the Draper closely.

"We both want him in here," the Draper murmured.

"Then maybe we should stick together," Uppercut said through his teeth.

"Suit yourself," the Draper shrugged. "Keep up if you can." He panted a laugh, then pivoted, light on the balls of his feet. He sprang off into the murk and shadows, running with fresh power.

"Rip the joints," Uppercut swore vehemently. He faced an instant choice; he could retrieve the costumes and try to find a way out, or he could attempt to keep up with the murderous possessing spirit. Huffing out a quick breath, he lengthened his stride and raced into the darkness after the Draper.

Like a nightmare, the run seemed to stretch on forever across punishing and uncertain footing, chasing something that couldn't be caught and fleeing something that couldn't be shaken. Darkness was a constant pressure on Uppercut's eyes, and the flashes of reflected water or hanging roots or fungal caps punctuated the mad dash with bits of context.

Was the Draper slowing to allow Uppercut to stay at the edge of his awareness? Did the Draper know, or care, that Uppercut pursued? Those questions quickly fell before the heaving bellows of Uppercut's overtaxed lungs, driven out of his mind by the rush of swirling blood trying to feed his body enough fuel to keep running.

At last, Uppercut staggered and fell. The Draper outran him. Rolling over, trying to coax air into his exhausted lungs as his heart tried to batter its way out of his chest, Uppercut felt the icy grip of surrender closing around him.

He blinked. The silhouette of the Draper was climbing a ladder above him. At the top of the ladder, the light of a moon-lit cloud glowed in the distant open air.

Shaking with weariness, Uppercut dragged himself to his feet and gripped the ladder, pulling himself up as quietly as he could. The climb seemed to take forever.

Trembling and completely spent, Uppercut managed to heft himself out of the narrow shaft. The shaft was cunningly stacked stone, at the end; it looked like a chimney, but it was a long-forgotten passage down into the Warren. Uppercut no longer had the energy to swear.

The haunting lilt of a tin whistle tune wound its way through the night. Uppercut risked a peek over the mossy roof that held him up.

Scarecrow's body was seated next to a boarded-up well, leaning against a pillar on a structure that was once a community gathering spot now overgrown with thorn bushes. The Draper played a strange tune, thin and light considering the weight of centuries and tradition underneath it.

"What are you doing here?" Shimmer snapped.

Uppercut flinched, staring around wildly, only to see the Tycherosian spy step out of an alley onto the street below. She squared off with the Draper in Scarecrow's body.

"Playing a song. I thought you were observant," the Draper chided, his soft voice soaked with malice.

"You are wearing Scarecrow," Shimmer glowered.

"I know," the Draper agreed.

"It's too soon," Shimmer continued. "Get out of there."

"Plans change," the Draper said. "There was a curse. It would have hit the body empty." He paused. "The body is no good to you empty. And you still need me. So I did what I had to do."

"It's too soon," Shimmer repeated, stern.

"Scarecrow is in a hull. He won't be available until tomorrow. And I'm not sure what that curse did," the Draper said, looking down at Scarecrow's body. "Even without it, he's in poor shape."

"If you derail this, I will visit suffering upon you that you cannot fathom," Shimmer murmured so quietly Uppercut could barely make out the words.

The Draper cocked Scarecrow's head to the side. "I'm going to go murder someone. Make a big, sloppy mess. Then I'll go get Scarecrow back. Then the plan goes on. Either you can live with that, or we have a problem we had better fix right here on the spot."

Shimmer stared into him for a long moment. "You get Scarecrow back in there. You let them drive you out. And you get back in position. No cryptic last words. No hints. No riddles."

"No riddles," the Draper smiled, his teeth rimed with blood.

Shimmer stepped back, then vanished into the alleyway.

Uppercut panted lightly through his mouth, his heart and mind both pounding as they processed his struggles.

The Draper? And Shimmer?

The world seemed to tilt as two elements that Uppercut considered separate turned out to share the fabric of conspiracy. Somehow, the discovery failed to thrill him.

CHAPTER EIGHT

*In news writing, lower cuts trim off less important informa-
tion at the end of the story, to fit it on the page. Then there are
upper cuts, shorthand for "cut because it would antagonize
someone we do not wish to antagonize." Upper cuts tend to
either omit the names of certain powerful people, or snip the
whole story.*

*Dalmore refused to learn from the numerous firings in his
short-lived journalism career, so he hired on to the Bluecoats
and caused the same problems with the same results.*

*From what I hear, Old Finstyle saw that Dalmore would
always insist on making decisions that any prudent supervi-
sor would undo, so he called Dalmore 'Uppercut' to rub it in.
Maybe he thought the poor bastard could be shamed out of
stubbornly chasing defeat.*

*Not me. I figure Dalmore will reach a point where no one will
hire him, so he'll be his own boss. Without a protective cen-
sor, he'll keep running headlong at freight trains until one of
them wipes him out. Frankly, that outcome will be a relief for
everyone involved.*

—From an interview of Haim Sleeth,
ink rake and former associate.
Conducted in a private follow-up
background investigation of Dalmore
for Lord Bennington, 848

Uppercut woke with a jolt.

The bay door slid open with a grinding squeal. A tinny alarm rattled to life inside, blaring a warning through the auction house.

Uppercut scrambled to his feet and snatched up the rope neatly coiled at his side on the gabled roof. A padded sleeve was rolled up with ties so it formed a cylindrical weight at the end of the rope. Flexing his shoulders, Uppercut doled a length of the rope out, the sleeve dangling at the end, then swung it hard so the rope sailed over the wall and dropped the bundle into the courtyard.

A massive hull ducked out through the bay door, slowly treading across the courtyard. In the weak light of day, the armor plating gleamed under a thin coat of dust, and the four-legged construct lurched as though at the brink of exhaustion. The upright torso's arms were crossed over the chest.

The hull bent over and picked up the bundle at the end of the rope, squeezing it slightly so the ties popped and the sleeve unfurled. The pounding bootfalls of guards signaled their approach from inside the house. The hull's chest trembled, and slid open. With what felt like agonizing slowness, the hull delicately pinched the frames out of the chest compartment and lined them up, sliding them down into the sleeve.

"Come on, come on," Uppercut growled as sweat beaded on his forehead. Two of the rooftop towers echoed the bang of opening trapdoors. Guards climbing into the shooting positions.

The first four House Guard raced through the bay door, brandishing rifles, closing in on the hull. The battering reverberations of multiple running hulls trembled all the way through the ground and building to shiver the roof under Uppercut's feet.

The hull slumped, and Uppercut hauled back on the rope with all his strength. Planting his feet and widening his stance over the roof peak, he dragged at the rope as fast as he could. The heavy sleeve shimmied up the wall, flopping over it between the spikes, swinging wide across the street between the barrier and Uppercut's position.

The House Guards in the courtyard cautiously surrounded the inert hull, rifles at the ready. One of the tower guards spotted Uppercut, and shouted a challenge.

"Right," Uppercut ground out, and he tossed the rope down into the street, pivoting to hang from the roof and drop to the cart he positioned below. He slapped down into the fodder, and rolled out. Unclipping the rope, he hefted the sleeve, and ran for it. Moments later he was racing down the cramped street, out of sight of the auction house walls.

A sharp hiss caught his attention. He tossed a glance over his shoulder, then skidded to a halt.

Rivulets of tacky blood formed a delta across Scarecrow's face, and his staring eyes gleamed with madness. He stood in the doorway to a tavern basement, a thin-lipped smile stretching his face. The Draper beckoned Uppercut with a crooked finger, and withdrew into the darkness.

"Drains and pains," Uppercut swore. He looked around once more, then followed the possessed Skov into the dark and closed the door behind himself.

Sliding his spirit mask on, Uppercut took a moment to focus, then turned to face the Draper.

"Did you hurt him?" Uppercut asked quietly.

The Draper did not reply, so Uppercut shifted his awareness towards the spirit instead of the body. In the reflection of the Mirror, there were lights glimmering in the basement that eyes could not see. The Draper was more visible than Scarecrow's body.

"Are you going to go peacefully?" Uppercut asked as his free hand closed into a fist.

The Draper smirked, then settled on a chair. Scarecrow's eyes closed, and his head bowed. The Draper stepped back out of him as though straightening from a shallow bow.

None of that dressing is his.

Questions jostled in Uppercut's mind, but each one risked trading information.

"What's your game," Uppercut demanded.

The Draper's fierce smile revealed teeth that glowed with fresh energy, and his outline glittered with death. The possessing spirit pivoted and slid away through the earth, leaving the basement.

Uppercut dug his sparker out of his coat pocket and lit a hand lamp, shifting his padded sleeve of paintings down to lean against a bench. He checked Scarecrow's wrist, relieved to find a slow pulse. Flipping the sleeve's flap open, he pulled out the paintings one at a time, tilting them against the rough basement wall.

Four. They would have to be enough.

Three of them featured their subjects against various backgrounds, but one was smeared with rotting plasmic discharge. The slick on the canvas was iridescent over tarry brown.

"That's not good," Uppercut said through his teeth.

Steeling himself, he focused, his mask cool against his face as it drained some of his life heat into the chilly gulf of the corrupted painting. Attuned with the painting's layer of reality, Uppercut leaned forward and put his fist against the canvas. He pushed, and his hand squished through the surface into the shallow edge of the Mirror on the other side. Uppercut opened his hand, and leaned further; he was elbow deep, almost shoulder deep. Concentrating, he reached out into the murk.

Something brushed his fingertips.

He felt a hand grasp his. Clamping down, he leaned back, dragging with all his physical and spiritual might.

With an intolerable sucking sensation, he freed his arm. Holding his breath, he focused on his grip; he did not topple backwards, still anchored to the spirit in the morass.

Breathing out in a steady stream, he concentrated on the wavering edges of the spirit he gripped, as though blowing a bubble with a film of soap. A sharp tug, and he freed the spirit from the painting's surface.

Scarecrow drifted in the air, flickering, barely cohering.

"Into your body," Uppercut said, hoarse. He gestured like an orchestral conductor, shaping a breeze behind the Mirror, and prodded at the spirit so it filtered into Scarecrow's body.

The body and spirit knew each other, and clicked into alignment. Scarecrow blinked, then gagged and spit.

Something wet and meaty slapped down on the floor.

Scarecrow and Uppercut stared at the eyeball on the floor between them.

"Why was that in my mouth?" Scarecrow demanded, hoarse and shaky.

"I... think you should know, things did not go wholly according to plan," Uppercut said.

Scarecrow stared at him and said nothing.

"Merrihel rode you out, along with her friends. Are they still in there?" Uppercut asked with a wince.

Scarecrow blinked twice, then doubled over and vomited a plasmic mass of impossible volume. Hesitant, Uppercut moved to his side and patted him on the back, hoping that was reassuring. He frowned, his palm now bloody from touching the gory Skov.

Wailing, three spirits rose from the ejected mess and twisted into their paintings.

Scarecrow blew out one nostril, then the other. He straightened his torso, wincing.

"So... how do you feel?" Uppercut asked.

"Grounded," Scarecrow whispered, eyes closed. "What Merrihel did to that spirit, in the hull... he withdrew. What was left of him. And he... he took the world with him. There was a great... emptiness." Words failed him.

"Well you're back now," Uppercut said, trying to mean the smile he wore. "Safe in your meat." He resisted the urge to clap the sticky Skov on the shoulder, and instead tugged a kerchief from his pocket and scrubbed at the blood on his hand. Turning, he frowned at the filmy swirl of putrescent plasm on the canvas that bore Scarecrow out of the hull.

"Merrihel must have been hiding some profound corruption in there. I'm sorry you had to dip in it."

"I... I don't think that was her," Scarecrow said. He swallowed hard. "I have... an internal injury." He frowned. "My spirit got, you know, punctured somehow." He looked to Uppercut. "Maybe you could check it out."

"Of course," Uppercut agreed. "But don't take all that onto your shoulders. The painting is not *that* shallow, you were only in there a few minutes tops." He extended his hand, tilting his perceptions slowly like a safe cracker sensing tumblers.

The spirit mask mostly concealed the scowl that saturated his features.

"This is not ideal," he said under his breath.

"I had an *eyeball* in my *mouth*," Scarecrow gritted out.

"One thing at a time," Uppercut said. He stood motionless.

"Well?"

"It's like an infection," Uppercut murmured. "Like a broken bone that didn't heal right. You've got... discharge. All through your energy. It's not just spirit, nor is it just physical, but it's... cracks run through both. Like taproots."

"Can you fix it?" Scarecrow demanded.

Uppercut eyed the Skov, weighing his words. "Maybe. Given time. There are rituals." He stopped, then shook his head. "For now I can bolster your essence. And we should bind up your wounds again," he said, noticing the Draper had stripped them off Scarecrow's body.

"Ugh, I'm covered in—in blood," Scarecrow said, holding his arms out to the side as he inspected himself. "What *happened* while I was gone? Where is Merrihel?"

"She walked you to where we stashed the costumes, but we were too late. The Resonant Chime cursed us."

"Yeah, I felt that, even in the hull," Scarecrow frowned.

"Well the Draper was caught up in it, but he got to your body before the curse hit. He destroyed Merrihel and subdued the other spirits. I told him I needed your body back today, and he showed up. I guess... he did some objectionable things while he was riding you."

Scarecrow jolted to his feet as the layers of shock sifted through him. "The Draper. And you let me out of your sight!"

"He runs faster in your body than you do," Uppercut protested. "I didn't have much choice unless it was to pick a fight, and I thought that would do more harm than good." He cocked his head to the side. "How's the leg?"

"Huh," Scarecrow said, looking down. He flexed his foot. Experimentally stamped. "I mean... way better than I left it." Pulling up his sleeve, he looked at the scars on his arm from where the fangstrider mauled him. They were puckered, pale under the clotted blood. "These closed up," he said, a note of wonder in his voice. "I know the Draper got more out of my body than I did, last time he rode me, but—can ghosts heal people?"

"Most can't," Scarecrow said, something reluctant in his tone. "Interesting."

"The Draper didn't strike me as the nurturing type," Scarecrow mused. "Maybe it was one of the other passengers."

"Maybe," Uppercut agreed. "They're too worn out to contact, for now. Anyway, let's stop the leaking from your punctured spirit caul. I've got a little bit of this wing essence left. I can mix up something that will swell your boundaries, give your spirit a chance to heal." He paused. "It comes with fever, and you'll need to rest for a bit."

"We can't do that now," Scarecrow said. "We've got to get paid, and figure out that damn errand Shimmer wants us to run, plus the zemi is still—"

Uppercut raised his hand to interrupt. "I can take care of all of that," he said. "For now, let's get you cleaned up, stashed somewhere safe, and on the road to recovery. With what we make on this sale we can get a leech to give you proper attention. These problems will wait until tomorrow. You've done your part, I'll take it from here."

Scarecrow chuckled. "That sounds really great," he agreed. "You should say that more often."

"Maybe save the mockery until *after* I've fed you the potion," Uppercut suggested. He turned to collect three of the paintings and put them back in the sleeve, leaving the corrupted frame leaning against the wall next to the plasmic vomit and eyeball.

Scarecrow grinned as he raised up to the balls of his feet, flexing his calves, then lowered.

Uppercut pretended not to notice. One thing at a time.

The hissing sizzle was a prolonged echo on both sides of the Mirror as a handful of dust crisped through the flame. Smoke plumed up to mingle with the haze drifting around the barrel vault ceiling. The trestle table was covered with glass, stone, wood, and paper.

Uppercut glanced around, cautious. He resisted the urge to adjust his hair, parted down the middle and slicked down to his boxy skull. The lab assistant escorted him in, then bowed and withdrew. Uppercut glanced around the alchemical workshop, waiting for the scholar to acknowledge him. He adjusted his grip on the bulk of the padded sleeve he carried.

Uppercut's host wore a leather apron and elbow-length rubberized gloves, and he was peering into the fire through tinted goggles.

"An extra half second!" he boomed. Straightening, he turned to face Uppercut. "Cross-cut grinding increased the surface area and added a full half of a second." He grinned, planting his fists on his hips.

"Excellent," Uppercut nodded. "I have brought you paintings, as we agreed."

"Straight to business then." The scholar carefully removed his goggles, then tossed them on the counter and tugged at his gloves.

"I know you are a busy man, Professor Wildthorn. I respect your time." Uppercut kept his voice even.

"How many were you able to get?"

"Three," Uppercut said. He glanced around for open counter space, but since there was none, he lowered himself to one knee and opened the flap. He carefully removed the paintings one by one, leaning them against a bench.

"I thought you were aiming for at least five," Wildthorn chided, his deep voice filling the room.

"We succeeded in getting three out," Uppercut said. "Nothing links us to you. The spirits are present and grounded, they consented to go."

"I don't see Merrihel," Wildthorn observed with a frown. "I specifically asked for her."

"You knew how temperamental she would be," Uppercut said. "I approached her first, as you said. She consented to go, but loaded three extra spirits in the hollow I brought. She also spurned one of the other ghosts and torched his painting; she got the alarm trigg—"

"Don't care," Wildthorn said abruptly. "She was always a whole lot of woman, more than anyone could handle, and that would be as true now as ever. You don't have to explain how she was too much for you. Is she still at the auction house?"

Uppercut watched him for a long moment, ordering his thoughts. Wildthorn listened to his silence, and his brows lowered as a grimace set in. He slowly turned, squaring off with Uppercut, waiting.

"Merrihel was destroyed by a more powerful spirit," Uppercut said quietly. "We were ambushed."

"Destroyed."

Uppercut nodded. "A powerful possessing spirit—"

"Merrihel Vans was important to me," Wildthorn said. "I wanted her protected, even if you could not retrieve her. I was specific, that she was not to be damaged."

Uppercut frowned at his tone. "You knew there were risks. I gave no guarantees."

Wildthorn was inscrutable. "I'm sure you did your best," he said in a flat voice. He heaved a sigh, and rubbed his eyes. "You just can't know what the world has lost, now that she is not in it." He looked at Uppercut sideways. "There's no chance she survived?"

"I am a Whisper," Uppercut replied. "I sensed her destruction." He paused. "I did get her frame out, if you want that."

"No," Wildthorn said. He chewed his lip. "I've got some difficult conversations ahead of me. I hope none of my friends are so disappointed they decide to express themselves to you."

"What, spirits?" Uppercut said, raising an eyebrow.

Wildthorn suppressed a smile. "Oh yes, Whisper, spirits. You've dealt with your share. But have you met one of the Reconciled? Interacted with them at all?" He paused. "What they can do to a Whisper is *far* worse than what they'd do to one of the Blind. You have vulnerabilities that you lack the training and awareness to *understand*, so safeguarding yourself is impossible."

"Interesting perspective," Uppercut growled. "Perhaps you can console them with the other spirits I did retrieve."

"Payment!" Wildthorn boomed. "Indeed. This way." He rounded the table, headed to the back desk, Uppercut close behind. "Thank you for meeting me here. This cozy little nook is well placed to supply the Devil's Tooth with some of their more esoteric ingredients, nice and fresh. And I do some consultation, appraisals, you know," he said with an airy wave. "I'm meeting Mistress Kember for drinks later. I don't suppose you can join us," he said dismissively.

"No, thank you," Uppercut said politely, playing along. "Much to do."

Wildthorn opened an iron box and dipped out six heavy gold Coins. "Two for each spirit, as agreed. When faced with a partial and complicated success... I prefer to focus on the success."

Uppercut took the Coins with a nod, feeling a certain weight of worry ease off his shoulders. "Thank you, sir. Happy to help out." He paused. "Could we perhaps arrange a time to meet to discuss the other matter?"

"The zemi?" Wildthorn said. "Not right now. I'm managing my disappointment. Not feeling particularly generous in the moment." A wry smile touched his features. "Though at least I know you can pay for a consultation."

"I understand," Uppercut said. "Well. Enjoy the paintings." He offered a shallow bow, and turned to go.

"Indeed," Wildthorn said, hefting his gloves and thrusting one arm in. "My best to Shimmer. I appreciate her loaning you boys out for my little errand."

"No problem," Uppercut replied with a too-bright smile.

"I sent her some fruit. Seemed the least I could do." Wildthorn worked the other glove on, eyes straying to his workbench.

Uppercut froze, mind racing.

"Just the fruit?" he said, trying to keep his tone light.

"Don't worry about a thing," Wildthorn replied, his mind already retrained on his project. "I mentioned you. Credit where credit is due."

Uppercut swallowed hard. Then he left.

He had to deal with Shimmer sooner or later. Might as well be sooner.

Scarecrow luxuriated in a rambling belch. Various flavors of thin stew and awful spirit concoction bubbled up with the release, flavoring his mouth.

He shrugged at the blanket hanging on his shoulders, and pressed the back of his hand to his forehead again.

"I thought I was supposed to get a fever," he said to no one in particular. So far the only side effects he could feel were strange skirling twitches in the corner of his vision, a fidgeting sensation in his blood, and the sense of caressing patterns all around him as though he passed through spiderwebs.

Turning, he resumed his pacing in the narrow hallway. He walked without a limp, without pain. It was a delicious feeling.

A grating croak brought him up short. Suddenly alert, he sifted his senses to figure out if his ears heard the noise or if he sensed it some other way, perhaps from a greater distance.

"Carc?"

The glass pane rattled with backdraft as the deathseeker crow landed on the windowbox. Scarecrow opened the window without hesitating, and the crow hopped in.

Scarecrow rubbed at his eyes again. The only thing in his field of vision that didn't swarm with shifting patterns and textures was the crow, a blank patch on a busy canvas.

Carc focused on Scarecrow with one eye. Expectant. Motionless. Present, ready to witness.

Scarecrow sensed something was about to happen. Unease twisted through him, and he tightened his grip on the blanket as he glanced around. Crossing the room, he picked up his crossbow. He let go of the blanket to cock the weapon and fit a quarrel in the groove.

His anticipation grew. Carc pinned him with a golden empty gaze, motionless.

"I sure don't like this," Scarecrow muttered under his breath.

Then he detected a high-pitched keen, a whine, just outside his hearing range. Frowning, he glanced around the narrow apartment. The kitchen area. The cupboard.

His heart sped up as he considered the hidden compartment where they stashed the zemi. Too late to pretend it wasn't calling him. Excitement threaded into his blood alongside anxiety.

His hand trembled slightly as he opened the compartment and touched the zemi. The stone was cool, and he briefly scoffed at the idea he would expect it to be anything else. He pulled out the chunk of carved rock, hefting it, and he examined the surface.

That pattern.

His blood froze for a moment, as though his body understood something his mind had not yet comprehended. He focused harder.

Right. That pattern, the interlinked spirals. It repeated all over the zemi, worked into every other pattern on it. He wondered if he saw the patterns differently in his altered state, with a punctured spirit caul and Whisper drugs unbalancing him. He saw it clearly, prominently. It would be impossible to unsee it.

He knew it, he recognized it, he felt it carved on his bones. He did not understand it, but he felt the pattern. He felt a kinship with skilled musicians looking at notes on the page and hearing music in their minds.

At last, his awareness caught up. He pictured Jafrain, and the wall with her designs, and the patterns inked on her skin. The pattern, once seen, became pervasive. A link. Between Jafrain, the zemi, and him.

A bleak triumph seemed to suffuse Carc. The deathseeker crow took a few steps, pivoted, and seemed to strut along the bed. Satisfied. Supremely satisfied.

Scarecrow stood lost in thought, feeling that pattern echo down to the Draper, to the curse of the Resonant Chime. He stared down at the rock in his hand.

"Huh."

Downstairs, the door creaked open. Scarecrow flinched, and squinted at the window. The light had shifted. How long had he been lost in the zemi?

Clearing his throat, he shook his head, then stuck the zemi back in its hiding place. He had time to cat-foot to the front room and pick up his shirt, then the door to the apartment drifted open. He pointed the crossbow at it.

"Now now," Shimmer soothed. "We're all friends here, right?"

"Sure," Scarecrow said quickly, setting the crossbow down on the table in easy reach. "Shimmer! I wasn't expecting you."

"Weren't you?" she retorted mildly. "You owe me a report."

"Oh, I thought—didn't Uppercut fill you in?" Scarecrow said. "I'm just now getting over a nasty relapse." He coughed into his hand unconvincingly.

"Uppercut filled me in on Chain Crossing. More or less," she said. "You had your own assignment."

"I know that," Scarecrow said defensively. "Check out the Honorable Guild of Fish Cleaners. And I did. Made some friends, uncovered some secrets. I thought Uppercut was going to tell you about how I've got some irons in the fire, I'll have some deep stuff to report in a few days. Don't want to rush it," he explained. "They would get suspicious. What's pushing the timeline?" he asked, innocent.

"Events are accelerating in a very satisfactory way," she replied. "I'd like to see the zemi now."

Scarecrow blinked. "What?"

"You are so good at playing stupid," Shimmer replied, pursing her lips with amusement. "It's an effective go-to move, you nailed it. Feels *right*. But I know better. I'd like to see the zemi," she repeated.

Scarecrow stood still, mind racing.

"I'm not angry," Shimmer clarified. "We are on the same side here. I just want to see it. My respect for you two went up a notch when I found out you had it. It was a boost you needed," she said, confiding in him.

"Okay," he said slowly. "Okay." He backed away from her, into the kitchen, and he retrieved the rock. His nerves hummed, and he felt violence at his fingertips as he returned to Shimmer, holding the stone.

"You want to touch it?" he demanded.

"No, I like seeing it in your hand," she said. "I think you were meant to have it."

"Yeah?" he said, cautious.

"Yeah," she confirmed, savoring the word. She stepped close, and his adrenaline spiked as he held very still. "Time for this whole thing to escalate, Scarecrow." She looked him in the eye, and he felt like he was high on a precarious ledge. "You've got a job to do."

"What—what job?" he managed.

She looked away, letting the tension ease. "Take another look at the Gutters. Actually do it this time. I'll be in touch."

"Be—be in touch," Scarecrow agreed with completely false aloofness.

Shimmer vanished through the door. But he didn't hear the outer door close.

PAPER STREET, STONEPARK. NIGHTMARKET
35ᵗʰ MENDAR, 850. *ABOUT THE SAME TIME, ELSEWHERE*
TENTH HOUR PAST DAWN

Uppercut strode along, mind swirling with contingency plans and speculation; was it time to run, or fight, or could the bluff be salvaged? He struggled to push up to the next level of strategizing, beyond the immediate next move.

"You must be Uppercut," said a roughly accented voice behind him. Uppercut stopped, turning slightly.

"I am."

"Hello!" A rangy broad-shouldered man stepped into his field of vision with a broad wave. He had long ringlets of hair and a narrow face with a trim moustache and goatee. His demeanor was uncomfortably energetic.

What caught Uppercut's eye was the man's splayed fingers and the ring upon one of them; a silver nail, fashioned into a circle, gleaming behind the Mirror.

"Have we met?" Uppercut asked evenly, hands in his pockets.

"Just now," the Severosian said with a dashing smile. "Though I understand you've been asking around. Your friend Dushnel. He is an idiot," the man explained.

"You aren't wrong," Uppercut muttered. "So what do you want?"

"Your motives," the Severosian said, blunt. "I asked around too. Your partner is a Skov." He raised his eyebrows. "We kill Skovs. You traffic in ghosts." His smile widened. "We kill ghosts too. Are we going to have a problem? This, here, is your chance to convince me we won't."

Uppercut glanced around, but the walkway beside the park was empty. "It's not about me, my partner, or ghosts. There's a Tycherosian checking you out. She wanted a profile. She may be targeting you, or looking to hire you. I frankly don't know, but I've been dragging my feet."

"And involving Dushnell."

"Clearly a mistake," Uppercut agreed. "Things are souring with my employer, so let's just walk away from each other."

The Severosian smirked. "I'm in a good position these days, so I can afford to be generous. Okay. This, here, is your chance to do just that. Walk away, we don't hear from each other anymore." He paused. "You only get one of these chances."

He walked away.

CHAPTER NINE

After the Cataclysm, commoners were reliant on their patrons for goods and services. Aristocrats did the matchmaking between needs and resources, redistributing goods and assigning work as they saw fit.

The Imperial treasury created a shorthand in the form of heavy gold coins that anchored big transactions between rulers. Inevitably, as markets stabilized and organized groups gained self-determining control of resources, more discrete incremental currency was developed and circulated. This "realm currency" is in denominations of scales and slugs.

Imperial Coin is still a dividing line between rulers and subjects. There are exchange rates that can break a Coin down into realm currency, but for prestige purchases, a Coin opens access to resources that money alone cannot buy.

—From "Transactional Leverage and Political Submission"
by Professor Ankelat

"I'm not thrilled about this meeting spot," Scarecrow muttered, glancing through the shadows.

"Perhaps you think I am here to thrill you, yeah?" said the leathery old man perched on a bench. "You look like the type that would insist a fancy lady go under a roof and behind a door to perform her service." He leered, his tobacco-stained beard bristling.

"Thin walls are better than curtains," Scarecrow agreed as he eyed the old man. "So that's the chit chat out of the way. I'm told you used to work for the Gutters. You keep up with former co-workers. But they aren't taking care of you in your retirement. That's a sad story, Carp."

"Lose a couple fingers and you find out who your friends are," the old man said, waggling the three remaining fingers on one hand. "Make no mistake, youngster, I can still flip 'em and slit 'em faster than you could chew 'em. You only need all them fingers if you don't know how to pinch the meat."

"Sounds like you 'retired' for other reasons, then. Forced out?" Scarecrow said, managing a smile as he struggled to be sympathetic.

"I've stripped a peeved hagfish whilst blindfolded. I've spearfished in a lightning storm. My granddaddy was a limmer, and it's in my blood to open and empty any damned thing that's touched the Void Sea." He paused. "But over time I've reached the conclusion that I overestimate my skill at playing cards." He glanced down at his hands. "These amputations didn't come to me because I let some slipper twist under my knife." He squinted at Scarecrow. "You got debts, boy? A debt is a heavy thing."

"I know it, sir," Scarecrow said with a sage nod. "But I brought you some relief for yours, if you can just give me some of your wisdom." He paused. "A little gossip. The good stuff. What the Gutters are up to these days."

"I may be old, but I have a lot to do before I take that last dive," Carp sniffed. "You are asking for sensitive insights on the leaders of people who can butcher meat, hot or cold, with all the ease and effort you put into dressing yourself. That's a mighty risk," he said, leaning in close. His queasy fish stink enveloped Scarecrow.

"Tell you what," Scarecrow said, looking him in the eye. "I'll take you to the tavern of your choice and you can have as much to eat and drink as you like, with companionship afterwards, all on me. And I'll cover this week's payment to your lender. Over supper, you'll fill me in."

Carp's stomach gurgled, and he gripped it with a splayed hand. "Well my gut instinct is to agree," he said. "Let's head over to the Flensed Mermaid. They've got a striper stew that's just the right kind of gluey."

"You got it, Carp," Scarecrow said. "We better get started, you've got a lot to tell me." He ran some quick calculations in his mind; the gourmet delicacy, surely dessert, rounds of drinks for them and for all the friends Carp would certainly involve, companionship. He had enough to cover it.

The distinctive ring of shod goat hooves clattered down the alley as a narrow cart approached. Scarecrow and Carp stepped into the entryway of a shop to let the cart squeeze past in the confined space. The cart halted in front of them.

"He wants the key back," the cowled driver said in a low voice, looking at Scarecrow.

"Basket?" Scarecrow said. "Is that you?"

"Yes," the driver said, pushing his hood back to reveal his face. The solemn teenager nodded to him. "You can send it or bring it."

Scarecrow turned to Carp. "I will take you up on that offer later," he said. "I have to go. Right now."

"What offer?" Carp replied, unreadable.

Scarecrow contained his frustration, and turned away, hauling himself over the wall of the cart and stepping up to the buckboard to sit next to Basket.

"Let's go," he said quietly. The teen flicked the reins, and the goat leaned into a smart trot so the cart rattled onward.

The door swung past the bell, and a silvery tinkle announced Uppercut's entry. The narrow shelves reeked of turpentine, and the only strong light in the shop was over the front counter. A lean man with fuzzy forearms that were as tough as cordwood glanced over as he polished his hands with a rag.

"How about that," he said under his breath. "Officer Dalmore."

"Not anymore," Uppercut said. "Not for a few years now. "

"Right, I hear you are Uppercut now," the man said. "How do you like it?"

"Pretty much the same as the Bluecoats," Uppercut said. "How about you, Chef?"

"Constantly interrupted," he smirked. "How about we get on with it. You want something."

"Yes, an expert, and you came to mind," Uppercut said. "I'm mixed up in some trouble and I need leverage. I've got information and I need to turn it into knowledge."

"Well I've got plenty of expertise. Glazes, matte, tar sealant; you need something covered and colored, I'm your man." He leaned back, crossing his arms over his chest.

"I'm looking for a different kind of paint, Chef," Uppercut said quietly. He dipped two fingers into his coat's inner pocket and produced a Coin. Wordless, he placed it on the counter between them.

"That is some serious weight."

"I have a serious question."

The moment lingered, both men waiting as some calculations hummed in the background.

"This way," Chef said abruptly. He turned, vanishing through the beaded curtain to the back room. Uppercut picked up the Coin and followed.

"I don't have to tell you that this is confidential," Uppercut said. "The subject of this conversation alone could be—"

"You don't," Chef replied sharply. They descended steep and shoddy stairs, and the first landing had a metal door with access to the alley. Chef reached between coats hanging on the rack behind the door, tugging a switch, and a hidden door soundlessly shifted on its pivot. Chef led Uppercut through, and the door settled behind them with a solid click.

The only paint smell here came from fumes they carried in with them. Instead, the air was thick with the stink of parchment, paper, leather, and mold. Chef hissed a phrase in Hadrathi, and rune-painted glass panes hanging from the ceiling glowed to life, splitting the murky room into light and shadow.

A round sand table dominated the center of the room, mounted on a potter's wheel. The walls were covered by shelves with locking gratings like cabinets. Chef positioned himself opposite Uppercut, and leaned forward with his fists on the table.

"Ask."

Uppercut pulled the folded paper from his pocket, briefly consulting it, then he bent and sketched out a symbol in the sand.

"Stop," Chef said quickly, and he trod on the pedal under the table as he pulled it to a slow spin. "Hands off my table," he said with indignation. "You come in here cursed and touch my tools?"

"I—I didn't think it would matter," Uppercut said, off guard. "I don't even know what the curse does."

Chef pulled bellows from a shelf and pumped a few gusts over the sand, scattering Uppercut's marks. "Whatever. Show me the markings."

Uppercut held out the paper, and Chef took it, frowning at the neat lines.

"Mixed up in another blood map, eh."

"Tyvissi," Uppercut nodded. "I think there are three targets left, to complete it."

"You'll give me that Coin, and also context, or you will get nothing from me," Chef said in a matter-of-fact tone.

"Fine," Uppercut said through his teeth. "I'm under the thumb of this Tycherosian fixer, Shimmer. She's been sending me on errands, but I need a bigger picture. A colleague consulted with Coinpurse, who insists we stop telling people he gave us information. Coinpurse said we could find out more about what Shimmer's up to if we looked at the Thickwrist tattoo shop. I checked it out and found a bloodmap that's mostly punched out, hidden upstairs. Jafrain is a tattoo master." He paused.

"Those three symbols are the last three in the bloodmap, and I need to know who they are. I think Shimmer is working with the Spirit Wardens. I think they are using each other, and she's after the Reliquary Scrip bounty on Tyvissi."

Chef did not look up from the paper. "What do you want. What outcome."

"I want to get out from under Shimmer. She has reason to be angry with me. I used her contact and suggested I was authorized by her, and I did a side job. Plus my partner and I scooped the treasure from her last score. She is likely to feel betrayed." He frowned. "I need some insurance. Prove I'm useful."

"That's short term," Chef observed. "How do you want it to turn out."

"I don't want the Reliquary Scrip, if that is what you mean," Uppercut said. "Spirit Warden gifts are poisonous. I don't much care whether the targets live or die, I don't have a stake in the Tyvissi outcome. Seems superstitious to me." He cocked his head to the side. "If you have questions, ask them."

"I think…" Chef mused, "you told me what I need to know." He turned his back on Uppercut and smoothed the paper on the counter jutting out from the shelves. "For one Coin I can tell you some generalities about each target. For an additional Coin each… I may be able to get you names. Whether or not I succeed, the attempt is worth a Coin. Per person." He squared his shoulders. "You owe me one Coin. Do you want generalities for them, so you owe me four? Or do you want names, for seven?"

Uppercut flexed his jaw. "Seven. But I only have six."

"Coin doesn't operate on credit," Chef said. "I thought Old Finstyle taught you better than this."

"He vouched for me with you," Uppercut replied. "He extended weight to me, gave me my credentials, so I can trade in Coin. When he did that, he shifted one favor you owed him, to me. Right? I'm calling it in. Please."

Chef leaned back, crossing his arms. "What you're asking me... even taking on this research and divination could be considered that favor. You are compounding this ask with a loan?"

"If I don't get this mess sorted out, I will probably be too dead to call in the favor at some future point," Uppercut said.

Chef considered that for a moment, then nodded to himself. "Twelve hours."

"I'll wait."

KELLEN'S PUB. CHARHOLLOW
35ᵀᴴ MENDAR, 850. *ABOUT AN HOUR LATER*
HOUR OF SONG, 2 HOURS PAST DUSK

The cart had not quite stopped as Scarecrow slung down from the buckboard, striding across the grimy courtyard. Pushing through the scullery door, he grinned broadly at the bustle of the kitchen.

"Scarecrow!" one of the cooks bellowed. "You must have smelled Kina's cooking!"

"No need," Scarecrow yelled over the din. "Just follow the Brigade and look for smoke!"

Rapid-fire pleasantries and banter swirled as he pressed through the kitchen, but he evaded any efforts to pin him down physically or socially. Ducking into the pantry, he crossed the dim room and kicked a section of scuffed trim along the floor. A rusty hinge groaned, and he dragged a section of shelving aside, pivoting and pulling it closed behind himself.

The confined space beyond hosted three men sitting around a squat iron stove that provided both heat and light. They watched him expressionlessly, and Scarecrow adjusted his sleeves.

"I brought a key for the boss."

"Then go on through," one of the men said.

"Thanks, Scul," Scarecrow said with a nod. He passed through the chamber and followed the rough planks of the hallway siding, stopping in front of the door. Composing himself.

"Come in," called out a rough voice inside. Scarecrow shouldered the door aside, all smiles.

"I thank the waves, the wind, the Circle that returns us one to the other," he said formally. He bowed deeply.

The elderly man seated before him allowed himself a moment of amusement. His face was seamed. A scarf was tied over his sparse hair. He leaned back in a chair, his feet up on a desk, gnarled fingers laced over his belly. He looked comfortable in draped fabrics, surrounded by sheaves of paper, ink pots, quills, needles, brushes, and paints.

"All that's a bit much," he said mildly in the Skov tongue. "What a treat, to hear that Ulthar was looking for little old me." He extended a hand, palm up. "I'll have that key back."

"Of course, thank you," Scarecrow said as he pulled an iron key from his vest pocket and gave it to the old man. "Someday maybe you'll tell me how Basket tracks those keys."

"It's possible, I suppose," the old man said. His smile was warmer than his words.

"I really appreciate this audience, Master Kinlay."

"You're going to have to knock this off or I'm going to strain myself rolling my eyes," Kinlay said. "Tone it down, kid. You're in the door. Have a seat. Something to drink." He wiggled his toes. "We're all just taking a break and having a chat. Can't wait to find out what we're chatting about," he added with raised eyebrows as he reached for a dark and dusty bottle.

Scarecrow picked up a cup from the sideboard and held it out, and Kinlay poured some pulpy wine into it. He waited for Kinlay to pour himself some, and the men sipped their drinks. Scarecrow cleared his throat, focusing.

"When I was a teenager you told me you'd give me truths if I knew how to ask for them."

"Here we go," Kinlay said with half a smile.

"Please tell me about Jafrain."

"Off to a terrible start," Kinlay retorted, amused. "That's not a question."

"Okay, alright," Scarecrow said. "I met Jafrain and things seemed to be fine, but then I got a pang from my broken leg, and she overreacted. She got—I don't know, angry. Kicked me out of her shop. I have no idea why." He paused. "Why is Jafrain upset with me? And—I mean, what's between you two? She wouldn't ink me because you did."

Kinlay regarded him fondly for a long moment, gathering his thoughts. "I remember that Following Day. Thirty candidates, every one lined up with fresh haircuts and scrubbed cheeks, these teenagers who all wanted prestige ink. Set to pursue honor, and glory, and responsibility. I picked you that year. Never once regretted it."

"I can't tell you what it has meant to me," Scarecrow said, his voice low. "The path it put me on."

"Yeah, the path. The path... that's the problem," Kinlay said, a distant look in his eye.

Scarecrow waited.

"Turns out, you were meant for Jafrain," Kinlay said quietly. He refocused on Scarecrow. "I'm going to tell you a secret, boy. You must keep this to yourself, but apparently it's time you knew."

Scarecrow swallowed hard, and continued saying nothing.

Kinlay nodded. "Right. So... I am a Radiant Master," he said. "I bear the mark of the Three Sisters. I have gained rank and title, penetrating the mysteries of one of the deepest and oldest of the Illustrator Traditions." He gestured. "Which you knew. People like me don't get through the trials and pass the tests without some customized adept training. Learning energy manipulation through various means." He studied Scarecrow. "And now you need to know more about what that means for you."

"I do," Scarecrow agreed.

"When I put the Isle of Storms on you, I marked you. Prepared you as a vessel. Doomed you, really," he said. He licked his lips, and took another swig from his cup. "From that moment on, you were going to burn brighter than you would have otherwise. And most likely explode faster. A shorter, more intense life."

"Are you talking about fate?" Scarecrow asked, not yet deciding to believe or disbelieve.

"That's a pretty vague question unless you can explain to me what you think fate is," Kinlay replied, eyebrows raised. "You don't have the background you would need to understand. Let me make this as simple as I can." He leaned forward and put his elbows on his knees.

"Your heart pushes your energy all around your body, all the time," he said. "Your head is like a tree with roots in a stream. All that blood rushing by feeds it, but the tree regulates how much comes in and where it goes, so it's a filtered experience. Right? So what the Radiant Masters can do is to adjust your roots. Adjust what comes in, and where it goes. Just a bit. But your energy changes, so your future changes." He rose to his feet.

"Once I put that mark on you, the one you wanted so badly, it was inevitable that you would become undead."

Scarecrow stared up at him. "Like a ghost?" he said.

Kinlay shook his head. "No, son. Not like a ghost. Spirits are leftover patterns. They are dead, and they echo back. You were fated to be undead. Neither fully alive, nor fully dead." He paused. "I can taste the deathseeker crow reeking on your breath, rustling in your shadows. Your life was cracked. Maybe years ago. And recently something made that crack wider."

"Yes," Scarecrow whispered, breathless.

Kinlay pursed his lips. "The deeper we go into mystery, the more we must surrender generally accepted facts in the face of a new truth. We live in a reality that most people will never see and would never understand. It's not often that we try to help people grasp this new world without following a long path to get there. Some things must be lived into, rather than explained. And you've been living into it," he said as his eyes traced across Scarecrow.

"Why would you put a mark on somebody if you think that mark will make them undead?" Scarecrow asked, trying not to make a demand.

"That's the trouble with a peek through the keyhole," Kinlay sighed. "I can't give you the whole view. The big picture. So when you ask me questions that half matter, you walk away with a skewed perspective. Still, I've come this far, so I'll try to explain." He paused. "I needed to make at least one undead as part of the price I pay to have the mastery I have." He turned away, gazing into the lamp. "Might as well tell you the next bit too."

"Please do," Scarecrow said, jaw locked.

"I will someday be killed by an undead. Probably one created by another Radiant Master," Kinlay said.

"I won't kill you," Scarecrow said, forceful, adrenaline searing his sinuses.

"No, you won't," Kinlay said as he turned to face Scarecrow. "I know the specific flavor of the undead that will come for me. I can taste it in my dreams, smell it on the breeze, feel it on the skin of my back when I am too long in the sun. It is layered through me. Each Radiant Master accepts that price; that they will create the undying, and that one of the undying will kill them in the end." He almost smiled. "And no. It isn't you. Not for me." He raised his eyebrows.

Scarecrow jolted to his feet. "You think I'm going to kill Jafrain?" he said, his blood cold.

"*Jafrain* thinks you will kill her, apparently," Kinlay corrected. "And I would trust her judgment. She would know. It's an unmistakable and unique energy, the undead that will bring your death. If she felt yours, and reacted, it's unlikely she's mistaken."

"I won't do it," Scarecrow snapped. "Fate is goat shit."

Kinlay smiled, broad and genuine. "That's my boy," he soothed. "Don't you worry about the superstitions of a bunch of crazy old mystics. Fate, indeed... But you asked me. Why is Jafrain upset with you? I could tell you 'She's not upset with *you*,' and I think that would be true. It can be very upsetting coming face to face with the prospect of your own death." He stopped, thoughtful. "I'm too tired to play coy." He gazed into the lamp again. "I put you into this game, the least I can do is give you a glimpse of the rules."

"I could go shoot myself right now. I could lose a fight with the people who are trying to control me. I almost died twice—"

"Stop," Kinlay said, his quiet voice made of immobile iron. Scarecrow abruptly sat down, fuming. "You asked me," Kinlay pointed out. "I gave you the answer, the *real* answer. Live with it for a while. If you get better questions, pick up a key from one of my people, and I'll send Basket around to collect you when I've got time to chat."

"That's good advice, and thank you for the opportunity," Scarecrow said as diplomatically as he could. "I need to hear your truth on the other question as well. Before I leave. If that's alright." He swallowed hard.

Kinlay smiled. "I like your tenacity." He resumed his seat. "What's between me and Jafrain, that she will not ink you because I did. That's easy enough. It's nothing personal," he continued, something dark and magnetic in his unwavering gaze. "I shifted you. Adjusted your fate. Changed your energy. Some of my life force is now in you. My blood is only one of the ingredients that distinguishes the ink I put in your skin. If she were to connect to you in the same way, then there would be overlap. Some of my death might unbalance hers, some of her fate might bleed into mine."

Scarecrow flexed his jaw, struggling.

Kinley heaved a deep sigh. "Here's a truth. You don't have to understand it, or agree with it, but you must listen. You must." He looked Scarecrow in the eye. "Radiant Masters do not try to escape their fates. Nor do we pursue them. We learn our fates as temptations, so we develop the discipline not to meddle. We do not try to game the system, or eliminate what threatens us. To do so is inevitably to make it worse in the end."

Silence hung heavy between them.

"I chose to burn brighter," Kinlay murmured. "I accept there is a cost to that. In the end. Knowing what you know now, tell me you would have refused that mark when I offered it to you."

"Of course not," Scarecrow hissed, tears brimming in his eyes.

Kinlay nodded to himself. "Of course not," he echoed. "You want to lead. You want to make a difference."

"Yes."

"Well... do it. This changes nothing. Not really. There were always going to be setbacks and obstacles. You were always going to have to face challenges. Death. Worse. And overcome." He extended his hand to Scarecrow. "This changes nothing," he said softly.

Scarecrow accepted his hand, they gripped each other's forearms.

"This changes nothing," Scarecrow agreed. His helplessness and vulnerability again mixed with his ambition and will. Something in Scarecrow deepened.

"I will see you soon," Kinlay said.

Scarecrow nodded. "Thank you." He turned, and left the way he had entered, his steps heavy with the weight of new secrets.

"You're welcome," Kinlay murmured to his departing shadow. He drained his cup to the dregs.

SOOTHER'S GATE, THE SANCTORIUM. BRIGHTSTONE
36TH MENDAR, 850. *ABOUT SIXTEEN HOURS LATER*
SIXTH HOUR PAST DAWN

As the solemn bells overhead tolled midday, Uppercut stood motionless in the shadows.

Members of a choir filed out along the rampart, then turned. They began to sing, crooning the harmonies of the hymn My Bones, Awash in Blood. Clanking and rattling, the back door's ponderous weight tilted open. The communion was over. The procession of the faithful began its dignified exit from the echoing halls within.

There were about thirty congregants. Uppercut spotted his quarry. He closed in, timing his arrival with the conclusion of the hymn and the end of the ritual, the worshippers once again back in the press of the world.

"My Lady," Uppercut murmured as he lined up his walk with hers.

Shimmer glanced over at him, startled. "This is hardly the place," she said, her tone flinty.

"I come bearing gifts," Uppercut replied. "Please grant me an audience."

Shimmer pointed a look at the other congregants, then nodded. "Follow me."

She crossed the broad avenue, entering an alleyway, and opening the back door to a distinguished restaurant. Ignoring the kitchen staff, she led Uppercut to the freezers. She hauled one open and stepped inside. He ducked in after her, and she snapped the door shut.

"You've got some courage," she said, her tone dangerously neutral.

"Initiative," he clarified. "I came to explain what happened, and why, and where we can go from here."

There were many things she did not say. "Go on." Her eyes almost vibrated with intensity.

"Gunnr Erling. Vidar Skau. Aric Tofte." Uppercut looked her in the eye. "That's what you're after. I can smooth your path to get them."

"What?" she demanded.

"Finishing out the Tyvissi bloodma—"

So fast. She attacked, driving a knuckle jab into his throat and shoving him through a spindly shelf, her forearm pinning his jaw to the unyielding wall of the freezer as her stiletto pricked through his skin, lined up between ribs.

He struggled to swallow as triumph kindled behind his eyes.

After all, he was still alive.

Four agonizing seconds later, she released him, stepping back with his gun in her hand. "You've got a couple breaths left to make your pitch," she said, somehow colder than the ice-rimed walls around them.

"You don't want thugs," Uppercut ground out, his voice hoarse from abuse. "You don't want lackeys. You can get that anywhere. I'm still alive because you need experts. Independent thinkers. Creative problem solvers. And that is what you've got." He cleared his throat, feeling his racing pulse throb in his eyes. "Silver Nails. They have a semi-retired veteran, Gunnr Erling. She fought on the wrong side of the Unity War. She's a trusted advisor to the leader of the Silver Nails based out of Gadavant Circle." He swallowed hard.

Shimmer's eyes glittered as she stared at him, motionless.

"You want her dead?" Uppercut grimaced, slowly rubbing his throat.

"I do," Shimmer said slowly. "Bring me proof you did it. Her head will do nicely. Do this for me in four days... and I will reconsider my plans. And our arrangement."

She tossed his pistol aside, and it clattered down on a slick of ice. Turning, she opened the freezer and stepped out, leaving it open.

Uppercut stood catching his breath for a long moment. The frozen rot lacing the air tasted sweet. He bent to collect his pistol, tucking it away, then he strolled out of the freezer.

His shadow was trailing chill, as though he had escaped the broken Gates of Death.

Uppercut rubbed his hands together, the friction spreading warmth across them with the hiss of skin on skin. His face stretched, somewhere between a grimace and a grin as he peered out the window and across the courtyard. "It will be dark soon," he said, taking in the lowering clouds. "Early. I think it will snow again."

Scarecrow leaned against the wall next to the squat iron stove and said nothing.

Uppercut listened to his silence for a moment. "Look... I'm sorry I spent Wildthorn's payment on secrets instead of getting you fixed up. We need to mollify Shimmer, then we can use her resources to make sure you're able to run her errands." He flexed his jaw. "All part of the plan."

"So you've said," Scarecrow agreed.

Uppercut turned to face him. "We can get past this little hurdle, then we'll finally be positioned to get clear of Shimmer and the tangle she's weaving. We may even come out of this with leverage on the Spirit Wardens. These dangers are going to give us victories, a foundation we can build on. They'll crush us or elevate us." He paused. "Are you with me?"

Scarecrow took a long pull from his cloudy bottle, and set it on the table with a thud. "Of course."

"We've got the zemi. We've got contacts. We're building a bigger picture. Making moves."

"Stop," Scarecrow said, closing his eyes. "I get it. Just... stop."

Uppercut turned to the window again, but his attention was still focused on Scarecrow. "I was concerned when you disappeared after I gave you the remedy. There are likely side effects to what you're dealing with. And you are probably a suspect for a gruesome murder that we don't know anything about."

"You *just said*," Scarecrow snapped, "we've got all these plans to get out from under Shimmer. Well she came by while you were out and reminded me to go after the Gutters. So I *did*. Meanwhile, you signed us up to be assassins, and I have worked my ass off to set up tonight's hit." He clamped his mouth shut in a scowl, staring at the table.

"I know you don't like being told what to do," Uppercut said carefully.

"So maybe stop doing it."

"Sure," Uppercut said with a tight nod. "Now that we have the three names, we should be able to wrap up this map and move on. Out of this shadow." He listened, but heard only the echoes of raucous food service in the tavern below, and snoring from the room next to theirs. Nothing from Scarecrow. He scowled as the cold continued filtering into him, blunted by his body heat but unrelenting in its push.

"Just... I would feel better," Uppercut said slowly, "if you would tell me the plan for tonight."

"You agitate Beamline, Erling's horse." Scarecrow's voice was flat, his delivery rapid. "She goes out to check and make sure everything is okay, and we jump her while she's separated from the others. Saw off her head with the wire and go to the cheese shop basement. From there into the sewers, and from there to the barge. If we get split up, meet back at Kettlebox."

"Right," Uppercut nodded. "You've got the wire."

Scarecrow touched his lumpy vest. "Over my heart."

"So, we're ready to go," Uppercut prompted.

"Good to hear," Scarecrow muttered unhelpfully.

Uppercut closed his eyes, digging deep for patience. "We have time. Before all this gets started. If there's anything you want to talk about."

Scarecrow stared at the ceiling. He could feel a numbness in the Isle of Storms ink. He tasted the briny gel of the eye that had been in his mouth when he returned to his body. Jafrain's shock simmered like an afterimage in his vision. His blood rustled with the echoes of the ghosts that packed into his body while he was away from it. The distant breeze that cradled the deathseeker crow slowly circling overhead was cold against his flesh, trickling along his skin under his clothes.

Twining through each image and sensation, the reverberating pattern. It hooked the zemi to his blood, to his ink, to Jafrain's designs, to the etchings on Carc's beak, to the flickering candle oozing light on the table in front of him.

He said nothing.

The rectangular establishment reared up into the night. The wooden tavern was built on a stone foundation that served as the stable. Hunched in the alleyway across the street, the scoundrels waited, their breath steaming.

"You sure that horse-bothering device will work?" Scarecrow asked.

"I'm sure. Zekel's uncle apparently raised horses in Skovlan, and Zekel has studied some of the legendary Skov warriors who rode with the Silver Nails. Membership in the Silver Nails is a Severosian tradition, but a number of Skov heroes are part of the lore. These horses are specially bred and trained, they are sensitive to reflections in the Mirror." He paused. "It's technical," he said apologetically. "Just toss that pebble in Beamline's stall and I'll do the rest."

Scarecrow shrugged at the weight of the crossbow strapped to his back, unable to get comfortable. "That's overstating it. Considering."

"Yes, I mean I'll agitate the horse," Uppercut said through his teeth. "And of course you're the one who has to deal with Erling when she shows up."

"And anyone she brings with her," Scarecrow added. "While I'm hiding in a *very* secure stable that's guarded by ghost-hunting mercenaries. And by 'deal with' you mean kill her from ambush and saw off her head. But you'll do the rest besides that."

"Exactly."

The moment soaked up the strains of a robust Severosian chorus, third time around the traditional drinking song, filtering from the tavern above the stable. Otherwise, the evening traffic was sporadic, and clouds covered the moon.

"Okay then," Scarecrow said. "Give me a five minute head start."

CHAPTER TEN

Skov battle medics are traditionally called "scarecrows." These warriors get enough training to bind up wounds, diagnose basic ailments, and triage casualties. They aren't proper healers—they know just enough to "scare the crows away" from the wounded and the dying.

The immigrant communities of Skov refugees cannot afford proper medical care, and they do not have enough healers to look after their population. The tradition of experimental medicine evolved and expanded. Any amateure Skov healer who is affordable and sympathetic is called a scarecrow.

As a kid, Ulthar was part of a family that was big, poor, and tragic. He grew up fast, responsible for managing his household before he reached puberty. He tried to cook and mend and keep the finances together while the adults were injured, missing, off at work, or in a drugged stupor. Family teased him, calling him the house scarecrow as he fixed up the busted people and bent over the bubbling pots of stew and laundry.

He kept the title as an honorific. He may never be able to heal his family or his people, but he seems desperate to fix them up enough to keep the crows away. He will never achieve the stature, training, and resources to make his people whole. It seems probable he will die trying.

—Sealed Case File, Ministry of Preservation, 848
Interior Intelligence Analysis of the Knotwork's Related Personas

Scarecrow crossed the street, reaching the same side as the Clubfoot. Lamps cast pools of light on the street, and he was a shadow among shadows. Stepping softly, he approached along the alleyway behind the carpentry shop next to the stable. Faint hammering sounds drifted through the wall. Apparently work continued into the darkness for more ordinary professions as well. Scarecrow stealthed towards the stable, close enough to hear the muffled chatter from guards posted near the entrance.

The Silver Nails only needed to be ready to respond to a disturbance. Nothing would sneak up on their horses.

Flexing his jaw, Scarecrow unfocused his eyes. "Okay," he whispered. "Let's get quiet."

He felt Carc slowly wheeling, riding the night. Some part of Scarecrow opened up. His heat, his blood, the thrashing of his hard-working organs, the air jetting in and out of his body... All that noisy life. It drifted up, its tether loosened, and he felt the cold and the night welling into him in the spaces left by his receding energy. The weight of all that meat and bone, cloth and metal, became somehow less real.

His eyes snapped open. Leaning forward, he slid through the shadow and the air, his step a whisper, hardly a ripple displacing his surroundings.

Up to the side door. His stiletto fit through the gap in the frame, and he flicked the latch, easing the door open. He drifted inside, past the guards and their game of knucklebones, unseen.

The architecture of Severos was reflected in the squat construction and rock walls, but Akorosian adaptation added a tall profile and extensive use of wood. Scarecrow felt like a fleeting thought, a resonant memory, and his boots noiselessly slid along the flagstones as he followed the wide corridor between the exercise yard and the stables.

Scarecrow stopped abruptly as he reached the doorway. A central aisle serviced twenty stalls, ten to a side. Over a dozen horses fixed him with an unwavering stare. Their eyes were chips of mirror reflecting a piercing and motionless flame. A sensation shivered through him, echoing their sharp teeth and hooves.

A couple of the horses grumbled a low neigh or tossed their manes, balking. Scarecrow knelt to stare at the floor, concentrating on blanking out his thoughts and feelings.

One of the horses let out a derisive snort, and the attention pinned on him weakened, drifting apart somewhat.

After a time, Scarecrow rose to his feet, light-headed with the banked spiral pattern unfolding above and suspending the weight of his life and death. He sensed Carc wearying of the burden. Pressing his rising desperation deeper, he crept forward.

The row ended with the largest stalls, and two were occupied. One of the horses was deep-chested, body and spirit patterned with scars, something savage and regal in her stance as her stare bored into Scarecrow. Her stall's glyph was unfamiliar, but she likely belonged to the leader.

The corner stall next to hers had the glyph Scarecrow was looking for, the Severosian mark for Beamline. The horse in the stall was milky white with bright black eyes, shining like the reflection of stars on the underside of the Void Sea's surface. She whickered slightly, revealing her teeth; fang strider canines had been planted in the mare's jaw long ago, and they were part of her. Scarecrow felt her stare as a mix of curiosity and contempt.

"Let's give you something else to look at," he whispered. He flicked a pebble into her stall, and melted back into the shadows.

Outside

Uppercut sat cross-legged in the alleyway, feeling the drift of the pebble he marked. It wormed its way across the Mirror's edge with a presence on both sides. Then, finally, it fell to the ground.

Without opening his eyes, Uppercut carefully unfolded and climbed to his feet. He held a stone with holes drilled in it, attached to a long cord. The roarer stone was part of Zekel's family inheritance, over a century old, used to provoke spirits to battle. In the hands of a Whisper, it could be far more focused.

Uppercut played out the cord, the stone dangling, then he rocked it back and forth to get some momentum. He got the rock spinning, and as it did, the air whistled through the holes in the stone. The whoosh and hum was almost inaudible in the alley, but a growing wail soared from the friction behind the Mirror.

Concentrating, Uppercut sensed the brightest life force near the pebble, and attuned through the conduit to align with the spirit of the horse. Flexing around the resonance of the inaudible shriek, he tightened it to match frequency with a single horse rather than pouring across everything sensitive in the area.

Uppercut felt the alarmed horse whinny, felt her muscles bunch as she reared and struck at the air with her hooves. A grim smile creased his features as he leaned into the swinging cable, and its pitch increased to an intolerable level for its target.

He got dim impressions through the pebble.

don't know

there there girl

i don't sense anything

better get erling

back off, everybody back off

He eased up on the cable and slowed the spin, still not opening his eyes; he could feel the cold burn on his face from the glare of the beacon he twirled behind the Mirror, but he kept it in motion as he felt the horse restlessly stalk around her relatively spacious berth, hackles up.

Sweat beaded on his face as his muscles whined with the ongoing tension, but he dared not release the beacon until the right target was present.

His legs were trembling by the time he felt a shift in the horse's energy. A certain relief, a fierce confidence; the horse shook her mane and fixed her beloved master with an indignant stare. Uppercut leaned into twirling the roarer faster, provoking a jolt of reaction from the furious horse. Then he gasped, breaking the momentum and letting the roarer spin down.

The stone was a deep and bitter cold, dangerous to touch. Dropping it into a thick leather satchel, Uppercut ducked through the strap, and straightened. The night seemed almost warm after that ordeal.

"You're all set, Scarecrow," Uppercut muttered. He glanced around, and nodded to himself. All going according to plan, and his partner had everything a competent scoundrel would need to finish up.

Pulling the brim of his hat low, Uppercut strode out of the alleyway and headed for the cheese shop.

Inside

Scarecrow squatted on a beam, his back to the roof joist, opposite the agitated horse's stall. Two of the Silver Nails were still in the stable, a respectful distance from the end. The rest pulled back.

Spreading his focus so he almost forgot he was there, the scoundrel rested his crossbow in position and relaxed everything he could relax. He ignored the sense that time was running out. The deathseeker crow overhead was barely able to circle higher than the building's roof, weighted down with his suspended essence.

Approaching steps. Passive, Scarecrow was vaguely aware of the crisp authority in the orders from the newcomer. His eyes drifted lazily to the stable entry, and he saw the tall woman in a Severosian drape, dismissing all but one other guard and ordering him to stay at the door. She approached, her cropped hair glinting silver in the lamplight.

She murmured soothing phrases in Severosian. Beamline responded, eager to see her partner—then her eyes rolled, she let out a piercing whinney, and her hooves lashed out as she reared.

Erling dropped to one knee, hands out, and did not retreat. Beamline stood shivering, head low, and Erling did not hesitate. Rising, she let herself into the stall with the anxious horse.

Scarecrow felt the slow and painful thud of his heartbeat. He lined up the shot, right between Erling's shoulderblades. Couldn't miss.

"There there," Erling murmured in Skovic, petting Beamline's wet nose. "What do you see. What do you see. Show me what you see."

Just pull the trigger. *Just pull the trigger.*

"Bang," Scarecrow said quietly.

Erling pivoted, and immediately spotted his shadowy perch in the rafters. She took in the crossbow, then looked him in the eye, and waited.

"I'm supposed to kill you, but I'm not going to," Scarecrow said quietly. His voice was rough as he broke the silence. "You are in a lot of danger."

She crossed her arms over her chest. "Go on."

The last of what Carc suspended slid back down into Scarecrow, and his legs immediately cramped as labored breathing worked his chest. He swallowed hard as he pointed the crossbow away.

"The Spirit Wardens want you dead. I don't. But if you walk out of here, my partner and I are probably going to get killed by our client." His voice wavered, and his mind raced as it tried to form some kind of new plan as the old one crumbled to dust.

"So why am I still breathing?" She was unreadable.

"Maybe I'd rather die than kill you," Scarecrow said through his teeth. "I guess."

Her eyes narrowed. "And why do you care? Have we met?"

"No," Scarecrow said. "No, we have not."

"Then you want something."

"*Everybody* wants something," Scarecrow agreed. "This is about memorial ink. *Your* memorial ink. You have a remembrance on your skin somewhere."

Erling frowned, and waited.

"You may not know this," Scarecrow said, his voice low, "but you're one of the last shadow carriers for Tyvissi's sigil. The Spirit Wardens want his memory erased from living flesh." He paused. "You got a tattoo at some point. From a master."

"You seem like a nice boy," she said in Skovic. "Raised in Dunslind Fields, or that area, from the sound of it. Am I right?"

Wordless, Scarecrow nodded.

"Did you hurt my horse?" she asked, her tone dangerously soft.

"Just annoyed her," Scarecrow replied in a small voice.

"That's good," Erling said. "What happens now?"

"I don't know," Scarecrow whispered. "I came here to kill you, then escape. That's the whole plan."

"How long do you have until your partner and client know you did not do so?" she asked, her voice level.

"Maybe an hour, for my partner. Maybe a day, for my client." Scarecrow closed his eyes, his heart racing and his palms sweating.

"You know I have to ask," she said.

"The client."

"Yes." Erling waited.

"Shimmer. Tycherosian fixer." Scarecrow let out a shaky breath.

"So your partner is Uppercut. Who swore he was walking away from us, wanted a truce."

"I guess so," Scarecrow said, wincing in the shadows.

Erling turned her attention to Beamline, soothing her and stroking the horse's broad neck.

Scarecrow painstakingly extricated himself from his minimizing crouch on the beam, lowering himself to drop to the floor in a pile.

"I suppose I should kill you," Erling said to Scarecrow, her attention still focused on the horse.

"You won't," Scarecrow replied.

"Oh?"

"Silver Nails. You walk into traps and murder your ambushers. If this isn't a physical trap, you're thinking about what other kind of trap it might be, what stakes might be higher." Scarecrow stretched out, flat on his back, aching with the noise of his heart and his rushing blood. "Because you are a commander. People live and die on your decisions. I hear you are a really clear thinker."

"Killing you is expedient," Erling pointed out calmly.

"Expedience is not the highest good," Scarecrow replied, almost dreamy. "And it is not my fate to die here, with you, like this. I have things to do." He wondered if he believed it, and he could not be sure.

"I know, queen, I know," Erling murmured to her horse. Then she slung a leg over the stile and stepped out of the stall, approaching Scarecrow. He lay still.

"Hands over your head please," she said quietly. Scarecrow winced as he shifted to oblige. Erling knelt next to him, and put her palm flat on his chest.

"Undead," she murmured, the word unfamiliar in Skovic. "I see."

"You see?"

"I can work with it," Erling said, crisp. "My second husband was undead. You poor sorry meatrag." She rose to her feet. "We'll need to pick up your partner. For everyone's safety. Tell me where to find him."

Scarecrow was too committed to balk now. "Look for the Glimmer, a Skov barge, moored by the Dextri Bridge base quay."

"I suspect things are going to move very fast now," Erling said. A smile crossed her face. "Just how I like it."

"Cavalry," Scarecrow said reflectively. "May I get up?"

"I think you'd better," Erling replied. "We have a lot to do."

THE GLIMMER, DEXTRI BRIDGE BASE QUAY. BRIGHTSTONE
39TH MENDAR, 850. *HALF AN HOUR LATER*
HOUR OF THREAD, 4 HOURS PAST DUSK

Uppercut frowned as the solemn tolling of the hour rolled out across the subdued district. The unflinching glare of the plasmic street torches simmered in his eyes, closing his pupil, choking out his night vision. He felt unsteady, and chose to believe the sensation came from the barge under his feet and not the noiseless seething of the Mirror.

Crossing his arms over his chest, he leaned back against the barge's cabin wall. He gazed above the row of buildings, backlit by the swirling curtain of plasmic energy generated by the lightning tower across the river.

"Come on, Scarecrow," he muttered as tension curled in his guts.

Alert, he spotted one of the barge's crew approaching the captain, who lounged by the helm. Uppercut watched their brief conversation. Both men looked at him, considering some new development. Uppercut flexed his jaw as the captain approached.

"Time's up. We are casting off," the captain growled.

"What's going on?" Uppercut asked quietly.

"The Silver Nails are on the prowl," the captain replied. "Something riled them up. Either you stay on board and go with us, or you disembark now and wait for your friend on shore. Decide now."

Uppercut narrowed his eyes, then nodded. "Cast off. Let's go."

The captain turned away from him and barked orders in Skovic. The heavy mooring cables were cast off the pilings, and the barge drifted away from the docks as Uppercut scanned the quay and the upper level of the street.

The wide canal felt claustrophobic as the barge drifted with the current, only minimal running lights lit. Uppercut hugged himself, rubbing his arms, feeling the shift behind the Mirror. His discomfort intensified as he saw the curling mist ahead.

Turning to follow the captain to the helm, Uppercut pointed to the mist. "I suppose that's normal in these parts, this time of night," he said.

"We are headed out to the river. She breathes," the captain said. "Normal? It happens sometimes. I don't know about *normal*." He shut his mouth, and examined the waterway ahead. "You there," he said to the crewman at his side. "Get to the bow. Sound off." He turned back to Uppercut as the sailor darted off to carry out the order. "A precaution, see, to make sure we don't drift into anyone. In the murk."

"Sensible," Uppercut said, disliking the taste of the word. He stepped back, then re-oriented and headed towards the prow.

The clatter of horses echoed along the faces of the buildings flanking the canal. Uppercut looked back to see two riders post trotting up to the quay where the Glimmer cast off, staring towards them as they followed the current into the mist.

"Just barely too late," Uppercut mused, paying attention to how wrong the idea felt. Or maybe it was a little bit of theater. Drawing the eye, like an illusionist's trick. Turning away from the rear view, he spotted the bridge as the barge drifted towards it. The bridge that would be overhead for a minute or so as they passed under it.

His heartbeat accelerated as he hauled his pistol out, cocking it, crouching beside a bale of dry kelp. He breathed out, centering his focus, and he shrugged the sensations in the mist out of the way. Squinting, he studied the bridge. His mouth went dry as he waited for riders of the Silver Nails to clear the guard rail and drop to the barge.

"Calm down," said a clear voice behind him. Uppercut froze, then tilted his head to the side. He heard the click of the hammer drawn back on the pistol aimed at his back.

Uppercut put his gun down on the bale of kelp beside him. Hands out to the side, he slowly turned to see the sailor who had approached the captain. Up close, it was clear; hardly a sailor, after all. The cavalry soldier was dressed down, but he was obviously a soldier all the same.

Behind him, ropes unfurled down from the bridge railing, and four more Silver Nails slid down to land on the barge. The five of them surrounded Uppercut as the barge angled to the quay on the other side of the bridge.

"Taking me alive?" Uppercut said.

"Oh yes," the soldier nodded. "No need to be concerned. Just relax and cooperate and all this stays friendly." His eyes were steady and bright. "Act out, and your friend won't take it well. He won't appreciate it at all."

Uppercut reluctantly let go of the half-dozen partial plans swarming through his mind. "All right," he said through his teeth.

One of the soldiers behind him picked up his gun, another stepped forward and patted him down, removing another pistol and a couple knives.

"Not that," Uppercut said, sharp, as the soldier touched on his spirit mask.

"Let him keep it," the leader agreed. "Professional courtesy. The man is a Whisper."

Uppercut looked him over carefully, but could not read his tone.

The barge captain and his crew kept their distance from the soldiers and the Whisper. The barge leaned over by the quay, but did not throw casting lines. The soldiers quickly disembarked with Uppercut at gunpoint. Several of the cavalry were waiting, holding the reins of the other soldiers' horses. They swung up into the saddles, and the plainclothes soldier faced Uppercut.

"You can call me Jimson," he said. He thrust out his hand. "Come on up."

Uppercut gripped his arm, and Jimson helped swing him up to ride behind the saddle. It was an awkward mounting, but Uppercut managed. He gripped Jimson, distressed by the horse's long legs and barrel body. They rode into the mist.

"Where are we going?" Uppercut demanded.

"Not far," Jimson replied.

They crossed the bridge and followed a straight road past dimly lit houses, closing in on another barge. Now they were beyond the canals. This barge was moored on the river itself.

Dismounting, they crossed the gangplank, leading the horses. The gangplank rattled up behind them, dragged aboard, and the barge rumbled as its steam engine was stoked up. The paddlewheel at the back began to churn, shoving the barge into the river current.

The side door to the barge cabin opened, and Erling ducked out. She offered Uppercut a cool smile. "There you are. Glad you could join us."

"Is Scarecrow still alive?" Uppercut asked evenly.

"Oh yes," Erling replied. "He has been catching me up on your predicament with Shimmer. Come on in." Turning, she stepped down into the barge interior.

Scowling, Uppercut followed, with Jimson at his heels.

Padded benches surrounded a small iron stove built into the barge wall. Scarecrow sat with his elbows on his knees, pale, staring at the floor. Two other soldiers stood guard at a distance in the comfortably appointed cabin. Erling stepped over a bench and seated herself across from Scarecrow, gesturing for Uppercut to sit as well.

"All together, it seems," Uppercut said as he settled on the bench.

"Let me answer some of your questions," Erling said, crisp. "Would an outside observer presume me dead? Unclear. My duties have been reassigned, security greatly increased at the Clubfoot, and we're spreading some currency around with questions about unfamiliar faces in the area. So your attempted assassination is not easily *disproven* with the available facts at hand."

"Are you alright?" Uppercut asked Scarecrow, studying his face.

"I told her about Shimmer and the Tyvissi bloodmap," Scarecrow said. "It's all been real friendly so far." He could not make eye contact with Uppercut.

"We are headed to the Fourth Camp, a cozy little spot in the Lost District," Erling continued. "We should have plenty of privacy for our discussion there. We must plan our next moves. A spider painting a target on my head is not something I care to ignore. Before we get to our plans, I must know how much you understand about what you're trying to do," she said to Uppercut. "This one is either very good at feigning ignorance, or he really doesn't know. You?"

"Shimmer wants your head," Uppercut said through his teeth. "Something about getting everybody with a certain tattoo. Some reward from the Spirit Wardens."

"You are a *terrible* liar," Erling observed. "Once more. With feeling."

"Hey," Uppercut said quietly, focused on Scarecrow. The Skov looked up, eyes bloodshot, and sniffed. Uppercut considered what he saw in Scarecrow's eyes, and he nodded.

"Shimmer is a Tycherosian fixer," Uppercut said. "She's in league with the Spirit Wardens. Scarecrow and I spoiled a heist she ran, stole their prize. Instead of killing us, she was impressed enough to force us to work for her. We haven't been model employees," he growled. "So, she was considering having us killed. We're trying to get out from under her influence, but keep her happy enough in the meantime that she doesn't tie us up like loose ends. So I tried to figure out what she's after." He paused. "The Tyvissi Bloodmap. Considering her ties to the Spirit Wardens, best I can figure, she's after the Reliquary Scrip the Spirit Wardens offer as a reward for wiping a bloodmap out. She has three deaths in her way. You're number one." He cocked his head to the side. "May I see the memorial ink?"

"Why not," Erling said. She loosened her shirt, and pulled it open. Below her bra, a dense and complicated tattoo like a stained glass window was painted over her upper abdomen.

"That's fine work," Scarecrow blurted, raising his eyebrows as he glanced over the intricate brushwork and spidery glyph lettering. "It has aged amazingly well."

"There's more going on there than the memorial ink," Uppercut said. "I think it's likely you *do* understand better than we do."

"Why do you think the Spirit Wardens want me dead?" Erling asked directly.

"I don't know," Uppercut confessed. "I know they want the memorial ink wiped out. Everyone wearing it must die. I do not know why. Superstition, I guess. Legacy."

"Self defense," Erling clarified. "This here is a guy wire that supports a tower of pain for the Spirit Wardens." She patted her torso. "They snap all three cables, and the tower gets unsteady fast. This ink I wear is... sacrificial, I suppose. But it's for a good cause." Her smile was tight, her eyes glittered.

"I gotta know more," Scarecrow said, unable to tear his eyes from the bold patterns on her flesh.

Erling shrugged her shirt off altogether, and pivoted to aim her shoulder at Scarecrow. "Take a look at that," she said, showcasing a knotwork design that covered her upper arm.

Scarecrow flinched back. "What—" he said. "I—I can't."

Uppercut's eyes opened wide as he felt the resonance of the design on her arm, emitting a faint tactile hiss on the back of the Mirror. "I've never seen anything like it," he said.

"This ink protects me from undead," Erling said, matter-of-fact. "Makes it harder for them to see me. They struggle to fight me. Don't be too hard on your buddy," she said to Uppercut. "He almost pushed through the resistance, but he couldn't manage it. He didn't even know it was there. I bet that was confusing," she mused, looking Scarecrow over.

Uppercut's mind was racing. "How?" he breathed. He scowled. "Why?"

Erling chuckled, and rose from the bench. She turned to a set of bottles strapped in a wall cabinet. The scoundrels saw more ink across her back, her ribs, her neck. "I've got a history with the undead. Hell, half my soldiers have dealt with their share. Tragic stories, most of them. All that is beside the point." Erling handed each of them a bottle of wine. "Need glasses?"

"Nah," Scarecrow said, working the cork out.

"The point," Erling said, "is that we need to decide what we're going to do about Shimmer."

"Wait, undead?" Uppercut demanded, alarmed as he stared at Scarecrow.

Erling paused, looking him over. "You *are* a Whisper," she said. "Right?"

"I—yes, I am," Uppercut said as his face flushed. "My training focused on hauntings, ghost wrangling. There is—I know there is a lot of lore out there," he gritted out.

"You used to be a Bluecoat," Erling said. "I can tell. So, I'm guessing something went wrong on the job, you dipped your meat into this whole other world behind the Mirror, some traumatic event. You come to this late. Crash course, enough to get work on the wet side of the Mirror. You must have a lot of raw power, to own the title with so little background."

"I get by," Uppercut muttered through his scowl.

"When things got weird, you went one of three places. Either you knew of a cult and you checked with them, or you went to the College of Immortal Studies with Doskvol Academy... Or maybe you went to the Morlan Hall of Unnatural Philosophy at Charterhall University." Her eyes narrowed as she read his reaction. "Morlan it is. Nobody there would initiate you as a Whisper on such a short timeline, and there's no way you could afford the tuition, so you asked around until you found some disgraced scholar, adept, or Whisper to... right," she smiled. "You went to Old Finstyle. He gave you the basics and a reading list, broke you in hard and fast, and turned you loose. You gave him a pile of cash, and he vouched for you. Gave you those street credentials. Gave you the weight to deal in Coin."

"As you said," Uppercut growled, "this is beside the point."

Erling shook her head. "Whatever happened to send you spiraling into the Voidsenses, it's still unfolding, because you're on a much deeper level with this path you're on. You aren't ready for this. Which is why you're here, I suppose," she mused. "You really don't know any better."

"Sounds like we are caught up in some kind of shadow war," Scarecrow said. "Right?"

"Something like that," Erling agreed. "There are no uniforms, though. Nothing so clear-cut. And most of the people involved in the conflict, like yourselves, don't even know what they are doing. I've been fighting in this war for nearly two decades and I still don't really understand it."

"We can get back to that," Uppercut said. "You said Scarecrow is undead."

"Right," Erling nodded. "He's not alive. He's not dead. He didn't come back from the dead, and he didn't die. But he's got life and death all mixed up in there." She handed a bottle to Uppercut, who took it and set it aside.

"Is it from the crow?" Uppercut asked Scarecrow.

"No," Scarecrow said. "The crow, Carc, came later. I just found out about the undead thing, I wasn't keeping a secret," he said earnestly to Uppercut. "There is a tattoo master, Kinlay. He gave me prestige ink, the Isle of Storms. I just went to see him, he said—he said that something about the tattoo changed me. Like a crack in my life force."

"A crack that got bigger," Erling said. "You don't get a mix like yours overnight."

"It's been a rough time lately," Scarecrow said, looking away.

"So, is Scarecrow in danger?" Uppercut demanded of Erling.

"Oh yes," she said with a nod. "Very much so."

"How do we fix it?" Uppercut said after a moment. "How do we protect him?"

"We don't. That's danger inside your skin," Erling said to Scarecrow, a trace of pity in her eyes as she regarded the young Skov. "No way to know how your story will play out, but it won't have a happy ending."

"I don't accept that," Uppercut said, grim.

"Okay," Erling sighed. "Maybe I'm wrong. For now, his undeath is not the most pressing issue."

"Shimmer," Scarecrow agreed.

"And the Spirit Wardens behind her," Uppercut said, "and whatever's behind *them*."

"Now you're talking sense," Erling smiled, and she took a long drink from the bottle.

CHAPTER ELEVEN

The dissidents scoff at the Gifting that convicts offer to the communities they have wronged. These "moralists" would prefer wasting those lives with executions that only take, and give nothing in return. They reductively label our rich Heritage traditions as "limmer magic" and seem unaware of the irony as they put their faith in the fumbling experimentation of their scholars on energies extracted from Leviathans.

If these "innovators" had their way, they would shift the foundation of our protections away from human life force, settling wholly on the fickle ichor of demons. Think, for a moment, of the hubris this represents. The arrogance, to think that we both deserve (and can trust) the essence of Leviathans to protect us from death storms.

We must be true to the Immortal Emperor's civilizing gift of the Warding Ceremony and our traditions. There is a holistic interconnection in human life force. We take from present life to shield us from those who came before, in defense of those yet to come. To pollute the purity of this cycle with stolen ichor is blasphemous.

—From "The Folly of Stealing from Demons"
by Lord Anserra Teevan, published 553

The thick doors clanged shut behind them once they left the tunnel. Several soldiers dragged netted masses of crates and other debris over the doors, concealing them. They worked in the light of the magnificent lightning wall.

A tower rose five storeys above them, its emitters flaring and crackling as they projected a wavering sheet of energy from the ground to the top of the tower. The field flexed in the winds on both sides of the Mirror.

"D'you suppose the Spirit Wardens know about that tunnel?" Scarecrow said to Erling, eyeing the way they came. The entry had vanished, blended with the shadows.

"The smugglers who built it have an arrangement with the Spirit Wardens," Erling replied. "We have an arrangement with the smugglers. It's all been arranged."

"Sounds tidy," Uppercut growled.

They turned away from the light that marked the edge of relative safety. Before them sprawled the desiccated corpse of a once-proud district.

Their eyes watered in the smoldering red glow that crowned each of the poles set at intervals along the crumbling road. The horses walked slowly, heads down, as though pulling a heavy load. Their riders accompanied them alongside, hands on the weirdly massive necks of the horses, soothing them. As the riders came in view of another upright pole, it began glowing, and one behind them faded.

"Is it... is it the horses?" Scarecrow asked as he squinted at the lights.

"Somehow," Uppercut nodded, unsettled. "Apparently the Silver Nails can attune the life energy of these horses to the beacons. Repel ghosts." He paused. "I have never even heard of anything like this."

"We don't advertise," Erling said. "You'll kill a horse trying to keep it up over a great distance, but from the river to the camp isn't bad. Especially with a number of horses."

"The horses have a scarification, a brand," Uppercut frowned, concentrating. "Under the saddle. Some sort of connection, a pre-set ritual."

"More of a technique," Erling said. "Now hush until we reach the camp. We don't want to draw attention."

They scanned their surroundings as they followed the uneven street, irradiated with the eerie red light. The buildings were motionless except for the wavering line of shadows blocking the glow. Some structures had collapsed altogether, others were stubbornly intact even after centuries of neglect.

"I don't feel like we are alone," Scarecrow murmured, adjusting the strap on his crossbow.

"We absolutely are not," Uppercut hissed back, subdued. His skin crawled with the reverberations through the thinness of the Mirror, beyond the lightning wall. It felt like the stirring of a breeze at the leading edge of a fast-moving storm that could roll in at any moment.

The procession reached a gate with heavy posts flanking the road. Banded doors were open, with guards standing alongside them, watching the horses and soldiers approach. The stone wall surrounding the courtyard was pitted and scarred by years, but it was kept clear of plant growth. Nearby buildings had been demolished to open up sightlines to all approaches. Red lights were mounted along the wall, their glow somehow more penetrating than what shone from the poles.

"Now we can breathe easier," Erling said with a genuine smile as they passed through the gates. The guards set their shoulders to the doors, heaving them shut, and massive crossbars shot into position. Several horses tossed their manes and whinnied, and their riders led them towards the stable barracks.

Uppercut stared at the menhir in the center of the courtyard. It was twice his height, a rough and crooked stone with lines of carved sigils delineating its meridians. He felt the stone's energy in his skull, his blood trembled with the overlapping echo of heartbeats compressing through the sigils somehow.

"Uppercut," Erling said, firm. "I take it you've never been outside the lightning walls before."

"No," he said, his face slack as he stared at the menhir. "No I have not."

"This is how they used to do it," Erling said. "The limmers. Back before the electroplasm. You put your ritual together, mix up a concoction with some Leviathan blood, drag your sacrifice out here. Take the limmer knife. Feed the stone, charge it up so it continues pushing the ghosts away." She paused. "We have to recharge this stone once a year. In return, we've got this cozy little home away from home." She looked around the grim mercenary camp, regarding the three story tavern fort at the far end of the courtyard. "We've killed for less."

"That... that stone," Uppercut said.

"A gift from the emperor," Erling said reflectively. "This particular stone was carved in the second century after the Gates broke. There have been some lapses here and there, but it has been charged and operational for the better part of six centuries. That's craftsmanship."

"That's a lot of human sacrifice," Scarecrow observed.

"Don't try to do the math," Erling smirked. "When this area was populated, the stone was a lot thirstier, providing protection for more people." She looked to one of the soldiers, who took the reins, guiding Beamline towards the stable. Erling led the scoundrels into the tavern, passing through the surprisingly cozy common room to step into the snug tucked in beside the bar. Benches flanked a narrow table. The window to outside had been boarded up long ago, so the only entries were the door and a window to the barkeep's area.

"Welcome to the Mustang," Erling said with a gesture around the tavern. "Now we can speak freely. More or less. Have a seat." She leaned back against the wall.

"You said your ink was a 'guy wire,'" Uppercut said. "One of three. Something about a tower of pain for the Spirit Wardens."

"What do you know about the Reconciled?" Erling asked quietly.

"Powerful ghosts. Spirits, more specifically. Specters. They don't go insane with the passage of time," Uppercut said. "I guess they have some unique abilities."

"Right," Erling nodded. "There aren't many. They do love their puzzles and riddles. I don't have to tell you that you were on the wrong side of this thing. I don't exactly work for the Reconciled, but I am a supporter. Sympathetic to their interests. And the faction I deal with is opposed to the Spirit Wardens. Pretty fiercely," she said reflectively. "The Reconciled have discovered the secret to avoiding insanity or fixation on vengeance." She paused. "Some of them can possess someone indefinitely, keeping the host alive and not twisting into vampirism. They all know how to siphon arcane energy from spirit wells to bolster their powers. Almost all of them are in a collaborative network, each one working a long game. These plots knit and braid together. Eventually the modular pieces fit in place and their master plan comes to pass."

"Okay," Uppercut said after a brief pause. "What's the master plan?"

"No idea," Erling mused. "But I know Tyvissi is determined to drive the Spirit Wardens out of Doskvol, for a start."

"That's bold," Scarecrow observed.

"Indeed," Erling nodded.

"Guy wire," Uppercut prompted.

"Patience," Erling said. "I'm getting to that. The Reconciled, first. This term can mean several things. There's a network of powerful spirits that are the Reconciled, but the term has also generalized to any spirit that persists and remains sane. For the faction, specifically, they developed a method to sustain their sanity. This method is a pretty closely guarded secret, but I'm going to trust you with it since you're already pretty deep in the thicket." She paused, and frowned slightly. "It's the flow of blood. The flow of living blood, that's what gives the spirit an anchor so they are not driven away from their minds by the winds behind the Mirror."

"The glyphs in the ink," Uppercut said. "They serve as some sort of connection between you and the spirit?"

"Yes," Erling agreed. "My blood smooths along underneath. Like with the horses, as we were coming in, sipping a little energy for the defense is a bit tiring on a short stretch. For a long haul, you want to spread out the impact. That's why there is a bloodmap, why the Tyvissi sigil is inked on several hosts at a time. Together, we can hold Tyvissi's sanity close enough for him to reach it. For him to stay in contact with our world."

"Let me get this straight," Scarecrow said, an edge in his voice. "The Spirit Wardens want the bloodmap wiped out, killing all the living people with the Tyvissi sigil inked on. Because, if all of you die, a Reconciled spirit goes insane."

"That's right." Erling looked him over. "Sane, Tyvissi will keep working on his master plan to undermine them. Insane, he's a powerful nuisance—but he doesn't have the staying power to pose a threat to the Spirit Wardens."

"Are you in touch with Tyvissi right now?" Uppercut asked. "I don't see a connection behind the Mirror."

"It is subtle stuff," Erling explained. "He has a way to signal me if he wants me to go to a pre-arranged meeting point to have a face-to-face. If there was anything more direct, we would both be a lot more vulnerable. Speaking of which, you said Shimmer has three deaths in her way. Do you know who the other two are?"

"You don't?" Uppercut retorted.

"It's safer if I don't know," Erling said. "Compartmentalize all this."

"We're way past safe," Uppercut said. "Aric Tofte and Vidar Skau. Both Skovs. Shimmer will be targeting them. And you, if she thinks you survived."

"Of course we're all Skov," Erling said, amused. "Sounds like Tyvissi."

"Hang on," Scarecrow said, still behind in the conversation. "You said flowing blood, life energy, can keep the Reconciled sane. But they can possess people, right? So why do they need the tattoo? Why not just possess people to stay grounded?"

"The spirits have to feel the rushing blood with mortal senses," Erling said. "The tattoo creates an approximation of a 'mortal sense' for them, part of the life force of the bearer. Otherwise possession is basically a spirit sense overlaying the fleshy machinery of a living body, that's not the same because they can't really *feel* the life in the body the same way."

"But why don't the Spirit Wardens go after Tyvissi directly?" Uppercut asked.

"He is elusive, for one, and powerful, for another," Erling replied. "Plus this is kind of a wheels-within-wheels contingency plan. The Spirit Wardens and Tyvissi play these elaborate games with back-ups and feints and so on. There's no way to know what's really at stake in any given power struggle. Don't just accept any of this uncritically. I am not totally sure I believe everything I'm telling you."

"Great," Uppercut grunted. "Well, it seems pretty straightforward, now that we have some more context. Tyvissi is keeping himself sane by tethering to the life force of three Skovs through tattoos. The Spirit Wardens want Tyvissi dealt with, and will reward Shimmer with Reliquary Scrip if she manages to track down and kill all the shadow bearers with Tyvissi's ink. Because killing all the shadow bearers will unmoor Tyvissi and he'll go insane, abandoning his long-term plots."

"That's one level," Erling said.

"Don't get him started," Scarecrow said, rolling his eyes. "This guy is all about conspiracies and hidden forces operating all around us."

"But they are." Erling looked Scarecrow in the eye.

"Shimmer needs to be dealt with, that's the priority," Uppercut said, thinking fast. "Then we have an artifact we need to recover from our previous lodgings. We must put together a plan of action, going forward. We are running out of time. Can I assume you will give us some tactical support and a refuge?" he asked Erling.

"Yes," Erling said. "We will need to isolate Shimmer and put her out of the equation. Take her alive so she can explain some details."

"And after that," Scarecrow said, "we need to have a long chat about your history. Your ink. Experience with undead. I gotta know more."

"We can work that out," Erling said with half a grin. "What's this 'artifact' you need to acquire?"

A knock rattled the door. Erling opened it, one hand casually resting on her gun.

"Captain," the soldier said. "Calfas and Bynum have disappeared."

"Stay here," Erling said to the scoundrels, striding out the door.

"Maybe not," Scarecrow retorted, awkwardly levering himself up to his feet and following Uppercut out of the snug.

A handful of soldiers were in the common room of the tavern, tersely checking in. One of them opened a cabinet and handed out short rifles to the other grim soldiers.

"Something is up, and it isn't spirits," one of the soldiers said to Erling. "We have company."

"You reinforced the waterside wall where Calfas and Bynum disappeared?" Erling demanded.

"Yes captain," the soldier replied. "We are waking the next shift. All hands."

"Erling!" Scarecrow yelled, eyes wide as he pointed at the menhir in the courtyard.

As the others in the room turned to look at the shadowed menhir, a shape stepped aside, separating from the dark outline.

Soldiers raised their guns. Some got a shot off, but the silhouetted figure sprang away and dove behind the baggage wagon. The meridians on the menhir glowed a sickly green, the image wavering in the eye. Most of the soldiers raced out into the courtyard to pursue the intruder.

"Oh no!" Uppercut shouted, grasping at the bar and turning his face away.

With a bone-jouncing crack, the menhir split from top to bottom. The slabs of the shattered monolith slid away, thudding down and breaking cobblestones.

"Time to go!" Erling shouted, stepping towards the tavern's rear exit. "Get the horses, meet at the back gate," she said to one soldier, and she pivoted right past Scarecrow. "No time. Let's move." She shouldered through the doordoor, the scoundrels at her heels.

A gunshot thundered, and Erling slammed against the doorframe and rebounded. Another blast from the shadows by the back door, and a mass of her chest sprayed across the window.

Uppercut had the presence of mind to head for the gun cabinet where the last soldier in the room was lining up his rifle on the back door. A gunshot rang out from the other side of the courtyard somewhere. A bullet caught the soldier in the ribs and knocked him into the wall. Unarmed, Scarecrow scrambled to the wall under the window, out of sight, as Uppercut rolled over the bar and glanced around for the firearm that would surely be stashed there.

Snatching the pistol tucked out of sight for the barkeep's use, Uppercut peered over the bar, weapon at the ready.

"Hold your fire," called out a gruff voice from the back door. "There's no time for this. A deathstorm is rolling in right now, and you've got a choice to make. Stay here and take your chances with the Silver Nails, or come with me."

"You have *got* to be kidding," Uppercut growled.

"Am I?" the voice retorted. "The Nails trusted you. Brought you here. Minutes later, an attack. Far as they know, we're working together."

"Who are you?" Scarecrow demanded.

"We work for Shimmer, so we're on the same team," the gruff voice replied. "You can call me Crumbs. Now we need to get going; we've got seconds before the first ghosts show up."

A dramatic rush of flame spilled across the roof of the stable, and unsettled horses neighed loudly inside. Most of the soldiers closed in on the stable, letting the horses out, emerging with armloads of lances, saddles, or supplies.

Uppercut and Scarecrow exchanged a glance, then headed for the back door.

"Don't get any clever ideas," said the tall, broad-shouldered man in a greatcoat, looming in the corner an arm-span from the back door. "We are on the same side until you prove otherwise, get me? I want this to work out." His broad face was inflected with a cruel amusement. He lashed out with his heavy chopper and cut through the dead woman's neck. Erling's head rolled free, and he snatched it up by the hair. "Come on." He turned, glancing around the back alleyway, then heading away from the horses.

Not sure what else to do, Uppercut and Scarecrow ran after Erling's killer, trying to ignore the head jouncing from the handful of hair gripped by Crumbs' fist.

A thin screech reverberated behind them, then amplified and spread like the flame from a match dropped in a pool of oil. The scoundrels did not look back as they raced along in the near-darkness, following a trail of dimly glowing algae orbs tucked here and there along the broken paving stones of the street. Uppercut scooped one up and shook it vigorously, provoking a brighter light.

Scarecrow stumbled and crashed down on his elbows and knees, pain jolting through him. Uppercut was at his side, hauling him up.

Crumbs turned to check on them. "Almost to the first marker," he hissed. "Keep moving."

Somewhere back in the firelight, horses screamed. Uppercut staggered as the shockwave behind the Mirror hit, rolling through the world as the mass of starving ghosts collided with living things back in the Mustang courtyard.

Ahead, they saw a concentration of algae globes around a signpost that was snapped off at waist height. A bleeding man was securely chained to the post, groggy and battered. A ritual circle was laid out around him. Sticky black streaks lined out shapes and glyphs, and candles flickered at key points. In the background, the upper reach of the lightning wall was now visible. Its rippling glory pushed pupils tight, darkening the world. It was still too far away.

One shadow separated from the others. A man in all black, face covered by a mask and hood, was a moving emptiness only suggesting solidity and form.

"What about Pops," Crumbs demanded, closing in, hardly winded.

"She's coming," the shadow replied. "Good work," he said, looking over the head and the two scoundrels in tow.

"Slippers, meet Uppercut and Scarecrow. Now we gotta hope Pops shows up." Crumbs peered into the shadows. He ignored the display of the lightning wall ahead, and the death storm's billows of pale colors behind them.

"Here dammit here," called out a voice further back on the road. They shifted, looking towards the figure that jogged towards them gasping for breath. She wore a loose hood and carried a rifle. "Hate—plans—running—" she managed, pressing the heel of her hand to the stitch in her side.

"We are about out of time," Crumbs muttered as he squinted at the pulse and swirl of ethereal lights over the Fourth Camp. "The storm." He kept his tone neutral.

"All set," Slippers breathed, gesturing at a pitcher and a couple jars set off to the side by the ritual. The captive chained to the post roused slightly.

"Oh, you better let me go," he slurred.

Limping with the strain of recovering, Pops rounded the edge of the ritual and picked up the pitcher. She stepped over behind the captive.

"Buy us some time," she said to the sacrifice. Then she carefully tilted the pitcher, the iridescent clear liquid spattering down on him.

The man screamed, intense and frantic, thrashing against the chains as his flesh and hair melted down off bone and ran down his jaws and neck in runnels of sagging meat. Glowing smoke gusted up from the boiling corpse.

"That repels the ghosts," Crumbs said to Scarecrow. "Covers our exit. Right Pops?"

"Buys us a few minutes," Pops nodded. "Lit up his life force." She tossed the pitcher to the side and planted her hands on her knees, struggling to catch her breath.

"Let's use 'em," Crumbs said through a fierce and unamused baring of teeth. He spared a moment to consider Uppercut, who stared with profound horror, seeing both sides of the Mirror as the ritual's victim disintegrated. A massive plasmic reaction was invisible to the naked eye, blaring a devastating shockwave through the ether. Leaving the ritual trappings, the scoundrels pushed on, following the spaced trail of orbs.

Staggered, Uppercut heaved and flexed, retching hard, dropping to one knee as his torso tried to empty itself. Scarecrow dragged at his arm, pulling him along; the other scoundrels kept a relentless pace, and even so, the temperature was dropping fast and they could all feel the plasmic traces driven before a gale behind the Mirror.

The deathstorm loomed behind. Before them, the lightning wall.

Inaudible shrieks reverberated in the bone marrow of the scoundrels, draining the heat from their blood and distorting their balance.

"Not gonna make it!" Pops cried out as they rounded a corner and saw the post further down the street, the captive struggling against her chains. Slipper pulled a package off his back and flung it down the street. Glass broke inside, and another burst of alchemic reaction splintered out behind the Mirror, leaving a column of rotten fire burning in the street.

Crumbs sprinted, snatching Pops on his way by and dragging her along. Slippers reached the site first. Uppercut and Scarecrow did not dare to look back over their shoulders as they staggered as fast as they could.

Uppercut let out a hysterical noise, snatching Scarecrow; both scoundrels fell flat, almost driven down by the swell of the leading edge of the death storm.Then the stone pitcher tilted, another screaming victim was burned apart in an alchemical explosion behind the Mirror, and a shockwave drove the storm back.

The nearest section of the lightning wall flickered and dimmed, then winked out with a ear-splitting crackle as its field was pulled into the vacuum of the sacrificial ritual. Something inside the lightning tower clicked and clacked, resetting to power up again.

"Now! Now!" They dimly registered Crumbs shouting, and they scrambled up and pushed onward, barely able to breathe, unable to glance backward.

Through a building, then past the humming base of the giant lightning tower. The burning fog behind the Mirror was so intense Uppercut felt blood welling out of his eyes as he stumbled through it. The scoundrels managed a drunken stumble down a flight of stairs. They saw the steam launch, tucked in as close as possible to the broken quay.

"Come on! Jump!" shouted a wild-eyed woman as she stared past the scoundrels to what pursued them.

The next moments were unbearable as Uppercut and Scarecrow dug deep into their reserves and pushed as hard as they could, racing across the last stretch to hurl themselves at the launch. The other scoundrels dragged them up into the launch as its rear paddlewheel churned, spraying water and pushing the boat out away from land.

Pops was weeping with relief and strain. Crumbs leaned on the cabin, chest heaving, staring into the cascading menace of the death storm.

"Come on," Crumbs ground out. "Reset. Reset, damn you."

A snap hiss burned the night, then another; a cable of energy twisted from one tower to the next, caught, and flared with a thrum that made the water dance. The vibration shook the launch. The curtain of energy jerked and twitched as it began to fill out once more.

The death storm had momentum. It tore into the restored lightning wall, and a horrific screech and hiss sprayed out into the night as the death-shaped plasm flared like droplets of water poured on a hot skillet.

Half delirious with overstimulation, Uppercut heaved and vomited, emptying himself over the side of the launch over and over again.

"And we're clear," Crumbs announced, louder than he meant to, eyes locked on the curl of the death storm that managed to clear the lightning wall, scattering and adrift above Dosk River.

"Okay then," sighed the woman at the helm, daintily pushing a strand of hair out of her face with the back of her wrist. She picked up a cloth-sided case, and snapped it open. Grimacing, Crumbs hefted Erling's severed head, and jammed it down into the interior. The case shut, and the woman stowed it under the counter.

"You must be Uppercut, and you are Scarecrow. Welcome to the Mazy. I'm Sendoff." She dropped a sarcastic little curtsy with courtly manners that didn't match her overalls.

"We had—the situation—under control," Uppercut rasped out at Crumbs, still trying to slow his heart and catch his breath.

"I'm sure you did," Crumbs replied, mild. "That's what I'll tell Shimmer. 'They had the situation under control.' Still. I helped it along. We joined our resources to yours. Carried the day. Together. Right?"

Uppercut stared at him.

"Right," Scarecrow said. "Right, of course. Yes. Thank you." He pointed a look at Uppercut, who did not meet his eyes.

"How about it, buddy?" Crumbs said directly to Uppercut, his voice soft.

"We carried the day together," Uppercut muttered, staring at the floorboards.

"Our stories gotta match," Sendoff said. "So help us out. You were at the Clubfoot stable, Gadavant Circle. Something happened there."

Scarecrow and Uppercut exchanged a furtive glance.

"I got caught," Scarecrow blurted out. "So I spun this story about the Spirit Wardens, and a conspiracy. He's always talking about conspiracy theories," he said with a nod to Uppercut, "I told the Silver Nails a whopper, that the Spirit Wardens were getting ready to move on the base Erling uses in the Lost District."

"Kind of strange that the Nails transported you out there, then," Sendoff sighed, rolling her eyes.

"Yeah, so, I told them I could stop the attack if I gave a certain signal. Because the Spirit Wardens were watching their place," Scarecrow said, eyes darting side to side as he thought fast. "I pretended to be working for them directly. The Spirit Wardens."

"Clever," Sendoff said with an approving nod. "How about you?" she said to Uppercut.

"Me? Uh, I handled the distraction to lure Erling in," Uppercut said. "Then, according to plan, I went to the meetup point. That's where the Silver Nails ambushed me. Took me prisoner."

"They wanted leverage," Scarecrow said. "He was a hostage, to make sure I behaved myself. They didn't want anybody carrying a message out about what went down." He paused. "You were there for the rest."

"You sure pulled that operation together fast," Uppercut said through his teeth, locking eyes with Crumbs.

"We operate in the Lost District from time to time," Crumbs replied. "We had some ritual materials prepared. As soon as Slippers saw you loaded onto the barge, we got our own preparations underway."

"You seem awfully helpful," Scarecrow said. "I'd like to know a little more about why that is."

"Shimmer comes on strong," Crumbs said. "She can be a real handful. We all get frustrated from time to time. I get it." He paused. "But it's smoother when we come to our senses. Right? Realize what's best for everybody. Stay on task. Push through!" he barked.

The other scoundrels echoed, "Push through!" All except Scarecrow and Uppercut, who were startled.

"Nobody likes a snitch," Crumbs continued. "So you are on board with the plan, right? We'll knock off these other two targets and get paid."

"You bet," Scarecrow nodded. "Push through! That's great." He looked at Uppercut. "We need a catch phrase."

Uppercut ignored him, eyeing Pops. "You must be a Leech."

"Certified," she said. In the ruddy light of the launch, her Iruvian features were almost smug. "I'm a spellbreaker. Confirmed kills for six major rituals, from Heritage times. Counting the one that just went down."

"What did you do to that menhir?" Uppercut asked.

"I have a special alcahest formula," she said, her tone airy. "Cuts a seam down the blood groove residue, the meridians of the rock. Cracks the ritual seal. Lets out the whole charge at once. For a node that old, with that much energy in it, I knew it would give. Still pretty satisfying." She grinned. "Precious rare materials for the breaker, though. Took five Coin to pull it together."

"Lucky thing you were prepared."

"Going after the Mustang tavern, that 'Fourth Camp,' was inevitable," Pops said.

"Enough," Sendoff said with a sharp look.

"Plus," Scarecrow said, "you're a handy shot with a long rifle." He smiled at Pops.

"I get by. I like to have a good look at my handiwork, once Slippers gets it in place." Pops turned to Sendoff. "Steer the boat. Don't you worry about me."

"Crumbs," Uppercut said. "About our story. I'm concerned that there might be survivors. People who have a different accounting of what happened." He gestured back at the storm that churned over the Lost District. "Do you think we need to factor in possible survivors?"

"Maybe," Crumbs mused. "Some of them might have gotten to underground shelters, or through ghost doors. There are a number of emergency measures like that all through the district. Still. The story doesn't have to last forever. Just for now. Right?"

"Right," Uppercut agreed. He leaned back into the shuddering corner of the hull, against the mount for the paddle wheel.

Gazing back towards the indistinct turbulence of the death storm, he saw a mass of ghosts suck together, a bright flicker like lightning. His mortality lay across his tongue, bitter.

Chapter Twelve

Cultists worshiping "Forgotten Gods" call their divine patrons "forgotten" for a reason. They suggest these secret gods used to be established and prestigious, but people no longer remember. In truth, as far as our research can determine, these cults were all invented after the Cataclysm. Even generations after they are founded, their leaders make up rituals, history, and traditions when it is convenient to do so.

Who can argue? The leaders of the cult are initiated into secrets that others cannot be expected to know, and what thin "proof" may be offered is embedded in initiations to authority within the cult. Given the choice between profiting from a con, and exposing it to dupes who wish to remain fooled, these mystics choose power. Or, less cynically, they choose to suspend their disbelief and steer the faithful in useful directions.

Cults provide quite enough predation on desperate or deviant people without involving any supernatural power. Our findings conclude there is plentiful pursuit of escapism, yearning for authority, and desperation to belong. The Forgotten Gods would be well supplied with worshipers even without magical signs and miracles.

—From the introduction of
"Choosing Our Shackles: A Study of Mystery Cults"
By Dr. Grinter Malyn, Head Dean of Immortal Studies,
published 823

THE WELTERWASH HOUSE OF COMFORT. THE DOCKS
39TH MENDAR, 850. *ABOUT AN HOUR AND A HALF LATER*
HOUR OF PEARLS, 7 HOURS PAST DUSK

The launch turned towards the long dock, wallowing in the surf as it angled in towards the pilings. Slippers expertly leaped from the tilting deck to the dock, kneeling to wind a mooring cable around a cleat. Crumbs muscled a gangplank into place and secured it. Pops led the scoundrels off the boat. The cloth case containing Erling's head was tucked under her arm. Sendoff stayed behind.

Even in the dead of night, light poured from the rear windows of the converted warehouse at the end of the dock. Wrought iron gates attempted to add some class to the building's defenses. Strains of music floated out into the night, and silhouettes moved across the lowered shades.

"Nice," Scarecrow said through his teeth. "I suppose Shimmer is bringing us to a fancy house to make a point about how she's the client, so she gets the pleasure she wants."

Crumbs chuckled. "There are lots of ways to get screwed, and lots of ways to get paid."

"And lots of ways to punish unruly contractors," Pops muttered to Scarecrow. "You better not mess this up for us."

"It's cold," Uppercut growled, shrugging to settle his coat. "Let's get inside."

Crumbs hauled the back door open and led the way into the chilly common room. Several languid workers were draped across couches, covered in heavy blankets that were artfully arranged to offer inviting curves of flesh and lace. A couple stone-faced guards stood in shadowed alcoves, watching the handful of drunken patrons that fondled the attractions and emptied the bottles. The air was thick with incense, smoke, sweat, and perfume.

"So pleased everyone made it," said the gaunt man behind the counter, the lantern light glittering on the scales that flanked his face like reptilian mutton-chops. "She is waiting for you in the Garnet Suite upstairs."

"Thank you, Tink," said Crumb with a deferential nod. The scoundrels followed him up the curved stairs and down the hall, the floor creaking under their boots. Crumbs leaned on the door to the Garnet Suite, opening it into the room.

Shimmer stood with her back to them, gripping the railing, gazing out over the river. Scarecrow blew on his hands and rubbed them together to ward off the chil flowing in from the ; the open balcony door.

"I don't suppose we could stick around after the briefing," Pops said with a crooked smile. "I could use some warming up."

"Not tonight," said Crumbs as he watched Shimmer. "We're still on the clock."

Shimmer turned away from the view and stepped inside the room, pulling the door shut with a rattling clack. "Well. It's the Bitters, alongside Scarecrow and Uppercut. How lovely."

"We are glad to return," Crumbs said with a polite nod. "Have you taken precautions?"

"Yes, speak freely," Shimmer said with a gesture towards the side table. A thick black candle burned, its flame motionless in the drafty room. Ritual lines were painted around the candle's base.

"We succeeded, working together," Crumbs said. He took the case from Pops, and clicked the catch, opening it and placing the case on the end table by the sofa. Shimmer peered into it with interest, allowing herself a thin smile.

"That is good news," Shimmer said. "Now that we have begun, we have to move fast. Is anyone badly hurt?"

"My crew is in good shape," Crumbs said. "We are ready to act." He looked over to Scarecrow and Uppercut.

"We are fine," Uppercut rasped. "Perky." His smile was a grimace.

"Right then," Shimmer nodded. "Crumbs, take the Bitters. Go kill Aric Tofte. I want his head too. I'll pay double for this one, since it's a double header. So to speak." Her smile was unamused.

"You got it," Crumbs said. "Where can we find him?"

"Chain Crossing," Shimmer replied. "He is the alchemist that supplies the arms dealers that sell illegal plasmic ammunition out of the basement market." She looked Crumbs in the eye. "I want his head by noon tomorrow. Can you do it?"

"For double pay? Yeah, we'll bring you his head," Crumbs said with grim confidence.

"I will swing by your place to pick it up," Shimmer said dismissively. "You two, stay," she said to Uppercut and Scarecrow.

Crumbs and his crew turned and left. The door clicked shut behind them.

For a long moment, the quiet and the severed head separated Shimmer from Uppercut and Scarecrow.

"We cannot risk Vidar Skau hearing about the others dying, and going into hiding," Shimmer said. "I am sending the two of you after him. Too many people may be able to piece together what we are up to, so I need him dead and his head in my hands before tomorrow midnight."

Uppercut's face felt numb. "That's a lot to figure out, with no time to plan," he said.

"I've done some of the background for you," Shimmer said. "I have my contacts, after all, and once I knew names it was easier to uncover what we need to know. Skau is a priest of the Pillars of Night, he serves the leaders of the Gutters. Meets their spiritual needs," she grimaced. "He is an old man, with a bushy stained beard and dramatic eyebrows," she said, waving at her face. "He lives in a rusty train car in the Old Rail Yard, in Coalridge. You know it?"

"I know about the rail yard," Uppercut said. He clamped his mouth shut.

"We'll find the site," Scarecrow said.

"From what I hear," Shimmer continued, "he is presiding over some ugly ritual, scheduled for tomorrow at midnight. His preparation is supposed to start at noon tomorrow. That's where you'll find him, and when," she said, cocking her head to the side. "I want you to get him before the leaders of the Gutters show up with their security."

"Where do we meet?" Scarecrow asked. "You know. After."

"Kettlebox Court," Shimmer replied. "It's too bad you don't have more information on the Gutters. I was really hoping you would find out some useful details," she said with an arch look at Scarecrow.

"I guess I didn't get around to it," he murmured.

Shimmer watched the two scoundrels for a long moment.

"I know your loyalty is... unsteady. Just now. So I think we need to have a little chat. Add some context," she said. "First off, Scarecrow. I want you to keep the zemi with you at all times until this is over."

Uppercut's eyes widened, and he looked over at Scarecrow, who flushed red.

"Wait," Uppercut said. "What?"

"I know you stole it. I dropped in on Scarecrow and got a good look at it about four days ago. I want you to hang on to it. We may need it," Shimmer said, watching Scarecrow.

Uppercut narrowed his eyes, unsettled by his pounding heartbeat as adrenaline jetted through his system and his mind raced.

"Check the box on the mantle," Shimmer said, nodding toward it. Scarecrow opened the box and lifted the zemi out. "It wasn't very secure where you left it."

"Got it," Scarecrow said. He slid the stone into his coat's inner pocket.

"I am constrained," Shimmer said, looking to Uppercut. "As I tamper with fate itself, I have to have a light touch or else fate pushes back. Dealing with prophecies and such, you use the direct approach sparingly."

"What are you trying to do?" Uppercut asked, blunt.

"I have reasons to extend more patience to both of you," Shimmer said quietly. "I want to tell you some of those reasons, so you understand your value. So you can see my motives for keeping you alive. So if you were tempted by thoughts of betrayal, you would perhaps reconsider."

Scarecrow swallowed hard.

"Again," Uppercut said. "What are you trying to do?"

"I like bold sometimes," Shimmer replied, her tone dangerously neutral. "Not while I'm giving you a gift. Maybe you can let me take the lead for this dance. Yes?"

Uppercut's nostril twitched. "Yes."

Shimmer glanced at the candle, assuring herself it still burned and protected the room from spies. "I will destroy Tyvissi," she said quietly. "I have accessed a number of divinatory resources through Spirit Warden contacts. These divinations suggest Tyvissi's weak point, in the array of fate and forces that surrounds him, is the Draper. Turning those same divinations on the Draper, I am told his greatest vulnerability is connected to Scarecrow. Ideally, we can get the Draper to ride Scarecrow and battle Tyvissi, armored by flesh where Tyvissi is spirit only. Once Tyvissi wins, and the Draper is weakened, Scarecrow can lend a hand in finishing the troublesome spirit off. Rather than forming an independent plan, I am leaning into the winds of fate with this overall scheme." She watched Scarecrow, studying his reaction.

Scarecrow tried to shrug off the scrutiny. "I bear no love for either ghost," he said. "I don't mind taking them both down. As long as the plan involves me walking out the other side."

"Of course," Shimmer said. "I have further plans for you beyond that confrontation. Your particular abilities will be a tremendous asset. I do not lightly give up my resources."

"Quite a relief," Uppercut growled.

"And you," Shimmer said, regarding the scowling Whisper. "I was impressed by how you copied the Clavalian Ghost Key, on the fly, and held the pattern until you could use it. I've only heard of a handful of mystics that could detect, much less copy, a ghost key. You did so, and then deployed it. Made it work. That's rare," she said. "The closest talent I could find was Riposte. And he is no longer an option."

"What do you need to open?" Uppercut asked, eyebrows raised.

"In Six Towers, the Path of Echoes built a fortification over the Torrent Spirit Well, on the other side of the Mirror. They called it the Porcelain Crossroads." She paused, ordering her thoughts. "Two centuries ago, the Spirit Wardens focused their resources on hunting down the leadership for the Path of Echoes in Six Towers. The ghost sympathizers were ferreted out. Their leaders and heroes were imprisoned or executed. Before the Spirit Wardens could take control of the Crossroads, the Reconciled launched a coordinated counterattack. They took the ephemeral fortification, then they sealed it with complex locks the Spirit Wardens could not defeat. At least, the Spirit Wardens could not break in before the defenses annihilated them."

Uppercut's brow was gnarled in a scowl. "We'll just add that to the list of things I've never heard of before," he muttered.

"Tyvissi took the Crossroads over as his own fortress," Shimmer continued. "From there, he can scheme until he's ready to slip through the

Mirror and affect the business of the living. When challenged, he can withdraw into the Crossroads, beyond reach. Before this is over, I suspect we will have to pursue Tyvissi into his fortress. If we are to manage that, we must have the resources at hand to breach his defenses."

Uppercut waited for a moment. "There's no way that's the whole story," he growled.

"Of course not," Shimmer agreed. "But it's more than you had. Now you understand some of your value. Why I have not killed you out of hand." Her eyes narrowed. "And perhaps you have a better sense of how it would be inconvenient, but by no means impossible, to replace you in my plans."

"Nice," Scarecrow said. "So... how does the zemi fit into all this?"

"The zemi," Shimmer echoed. She cocked her head, sending light glancing from the scales along the side of her face. "It brought us together. And when I saw you holding that rock, it seemed... right. I think it's part of how you fit with the Draper."

Scarecrow blinked. "That's it?"

"Just because *some* things are complex and interlinked, doesn't mean *everything* is," she replied, smirking.

"Speaking of complex," Uppercut said abruptly. "Why do you need the Reliquary Scrip?"

"Really," Shimmer mused, sparing him a glance. "That's not part of this discussion."

"You mentioned a lot of divination, and the Spirit Wardens don't loan out their prophecies and seers cheap," Uppercut pressed. "So you need to pay them off. But using their resources so you can get a rare favor to pay off the debts you pick up in the process—that's worse than a closed loop. There's got to be something else."

Shimmer crossed her arms over her chest. "That's enough for now. Stop kicking." She looked Uppercut in the eye. "I mean it. I gave you some more context as a gesture of good faith, so you could go about our business with an easier mind. Show me my generosity was well placed. Handle this assassination, and make it slick. Then we can talk some more."

Uppercut slowly nodded. "Sure. Okay." He looked at Scarecrow. "I guess that's our cue to head out."

"This assassination," Scarecrow said. "It seems pretty straightforward, but we need it to go smoothly. Right? A lot rides on it. So just in case, we need some resources. Some currency, some Coin. To handle the unexpected."

Shimmer slowly smiled.

"We put a lot of Coin into digging up those secret names," Uppercut added.

Shimmer rolled her hand on her wrist, and opened her fist to reveal five heavy Coin. "Here you go," she said, offering them to the scoundrels.

Scarecrow stepped forward and lifted them from her palm, tucking them into his coat. "Thank you," he said.

"Better get moving," she replied, turning her back on them.

The scoundrels left the soundproofed suite. As they followed the creaking floorboards of the hallway towards the stairs, they ignored the moans of passion from a room to the side, and the more distant screams and cries.

They were halfway down the stairs when the gaunt man behind the counter cleared his throat. "Do you wish to rent a carriage? Several wait."

"Yes. Charge the Garnet Suite, thank you," Scarecrow replied.

Then the scoundrels were back out in the frozen night, swinging up into a carriage as its springs creaked and the draft goat hitched up in harness snorted a cloud of breath.

"Coalridge," Uppercut called out.

"Whereabouts?" replied the driver.

"The Old Rail Yard," Uppercut yelled.

The whip cracked, the goat bawled, and the carriage jolted along the dock road.

Scarecrow leaned back against the seat, the street lamps sliding light and shadow along his features. "You were thinking about shooting her right there, weren't you? Can't be just me."

"Of course I was," Uppercut growled. "But she knows we are too deep to strike out on our own." He stopped.

"And she knows we're curious," Scarecrow admitted. "We want to see where this is going."

"Yeah," Uppercut grunted. "Speaking of curious. Why the hell didn't you mention that Shimmer knew we had the zemi?" He kept his voice as even as possible as several emotions surged in his chest.

"It's been a weird week," Scarecrow said, evasive. "There... there's more. That we might need to talk about."

"By all means," Uppercut muttered, scowling, his eyebrows bristling. He bit back all the other things he wanted to say.

"I have secrets," Scarecrow said. "I want to trust you with them. With things I said I wouldn't tell anybody." He paused, studying Uppercut's craggy face. "Can I trust you?" he asked quietly.

"I think you had better," Uppercut retorted.

"This isn't funny," Scarecrow snapped. "Just—come on. Tell me you will keep my secrets."

Uppercut took a deep breath, let it out, and looked Scarecrow in the eye. "I will keep your secrets."

"Okay. Okay." Scarecrow snorted, cleared his throat, and settled himself on the swaying bench of the coach. "So... I might know some more about what Shimmer is up to."

Uppercut waited, stoic.

"I wasn't keeping this a secret on purpose. It's just—a lot happened right afterwards, so I kind of forgot I might not have told you. But after that little speech—it might be...relevant." Scarecrow cleared his throat again. "So, Jafrain. While you were looking for what was going on there, I was chatting with her about tattoos, and... I asked her about Shimmer. You know, the direct approach. See if she would just tell me what was going on. And she said she wasn't going to get involved, because... Shimmer is her sister."

"Oh," Uppercut said, nostrils flared, voice flat.

"Yeah, I know, but I'm telling you now," Scarecrow said quickly. "That information may be *sensitive*, but Jafrain just told me flat out. So it's not really *secret*." He paused. "I went to ask Master Kinlay why Jafrain would not ink me. And he told me some more about this prestige ink I got from him, all those years ago." He paused again.

Uppercut watched him.

"Kinlay told me I am undead, and I got... cracked somehow. By the ink. Recently it has gotten worse. So that's why I'm not alive or dead. It was the Isle of Storms. I was just a kid when I got it. But then... then there was the time I ran up against some bullies, about ten years ago. They kicked me around, then hauled me up to the crow's nest of a ship, and tied me to the mast. They knew I didn't like heights. So I was half-conscious, way too high, busted up. And that's when Carc... I opened my eyes when I got hit in the forehead. Felt like a hammer. There was this deathseeker crow. Crazy. I wasn't dead, and I yelled, but... couldn't... so the crow didn't leave. Pecked me on the head, a bunch of times." Scarecrow pulled off the silk headband he habitually wore, and frowned. His forehead puckered around a wad of scar tissue. "When the weather is just right, you can see a kind of symbol in this mess," he said, touching it.

"And the deathseeker has been following you around ever since," Uppercut clarified.

"More or less," Scarecrow agreed. "I mean, weird, but... no big deal, just kind of cool. Made me feel special I guess. I figured out how we could communicate. I could mark targets using our...connection. Track them without seeing them."

"Yeah," Uppercut said, offering no opinion.

"Then there was that whole Clavalian thing," Scarecrow mused. "The bites. And the Draper." He looked Uppercut in the eye. "I almost died."

"And you were full of a ghost. Not just any ghost, a specter. Forceful." Uppercut looked away, out the window. "So you got more death in your undead mix."

"Yeah, and started to... you know, intuitively know things. Like Grainger was about to die. Like..." He swallowed hard. "Like somehow I knew Riposte was dead. Just by thinking about it. Concentrating."

"Well it's not unique, if Erling was right about the undead," Uppercut said.

"Right, not unique. Because Kinlay told me that these tattoo masters, I mean the Illuminated Masters, they have to make an undead. And they can recognize the undead that is 'fated' to kill them. If they meet," Scarecrow said with a significant look at Uppercut.

The Whisper frowned.

"That's why Kinlay got mad," Scarecrow said. "When my bones twinged, *she* felt it. I guess she thinks I'm the undead that is going to kill her."

"Hang on," Uppercut said, his frown intensifying to a scowl.

"There's more," Scarecrow said. "Kinlay—he said that the reason the Illuminated Masters can feel the undead that's going to kill them is because that's their temptation! Their lesson not to screw around with fate! To try and cheat death!" he said, words piling out as excitement lit up his face. "And you heard Shimmer!"

"She said she was trying to do something with fate," Uppercut agreed. "What are you thinking?"

"Well if Shimmer and Jafrain are sisters, maybe they were talking. Maybe Jafrain let it slip, right? That she was going to be killed by an undead?" Scarecrow's eyes were wide. "If you were a twisted control freak, and you found out your sister was going to die—"

"So then," Uppercut said, "Shimmer goes to the Spirit Wardens, to try to cheat fate, to try and sabotage the pre-ordained death of her sister," he said, unable to resist the Skov's enthusiasm. "That's the payoff she wouldn't tell us about, the reason she got involved in the Tyvissi bloodmap at all!"

"She's trying to save Jafrain! She must be!" Scarecrow said in a strangled mix of whispering and shouting.

Uppercut paused to think about it for a minute, and his scowl returned. "That doesn't make any sense," he said, shaking his head.

"Or maybe it does and we're just missing a few pieces still," Scarecrow retorted.

"What was Shimmer doing in the Clavalian Estate?" Uppercut said. "How could it be anything but chance that the zemi is involved, that we were there going after the same prize? And don't say fate, that's not good enough," he glowered.

"Okay, we don't know everything," Scarecrow said. "But—this fits too well to ignore it. I mean, especially you!"

"What's that supposed to mean?" Uppercut snapped.

Scarecrow took a deep breath, and blew it out. "Okay. Okay, so I was looking at the zemi. Right before Shimmer showed up and demanded to see it. And... and Carc was there. Looking at me. All expectant. I could... I heard the zemi. It was calling to me somehow."

"Four days ago," Uppercut said. His eyelid twitched.

"Right," Scarecrow said, looking out the window. "So then I picked it up, and looked at the patterns. It's covered in patterns, right?" he said, pulling the zemi from his coat pocket, studying it in the wavering light drifting around the coach interior as it rolled past lamps. "For the first time, I saw—really *saw*—this spiral pattern. Interlinked spirals. Here, here, here. I saw them on the stone, and I saw them on my skin, in my tattoos, in Jafrain's tattoos—everywhere but on Carc. It's like my blood moved in that pattern. Suddenly it was *everywhere*." He looked directly at Uppercut. "And I think that's what it is like for you. When you get going on your conspiracies. Suddenly it looks like everything is connected, even if it doesn't make sense. You can't stop seeing these links and patterns, and they are on everything. I mean, I can't really trust it because it doesn't make sense, but it's so *real* that the only other answer is maybe I'm going insane. I'm betting you know what that feels like," Scarecrow said, leaning back.

Uppercut looked him over. "Rude, but I'll allow it," he said with a faint smile on his craggy features.

"It's... probably because of that wing essence. I was full of it. Trying to recover from all that damage, from the spirit fighting," Scarecrow said. He could feel the manic energy starting to fade. "Changed how I saw things."

"Maybe it was real, maybe not. Do you see the patterns now? Did the effect persist?"

"Yeah," Scarecrow nodded. "Sometimes more, sometimes less, but... I feel like I was changed forever. It was always there and I never noticed. But now, I can't unsee it."

Uppercut let out a sigh. "Too bad we can't talk to Erling about this."

Scarecrow tightened his jaw and stared down at the zemi.

"It's been a long day," Uppercut mused.

Scarecrow felt his eyes tracing over and around the patterns in the zemi as his thoughts followed a different circuit. He felt his pupils widen.

"Uppercut," he said. "You didn't know about the undead. How they are different than ghosts."

"Right," Uppercut said, a note of warning in his tone.

Scarecrow looked him in the eye. "If that kind of detail is part of the lore of the Illuminated Masters, and the Silver Nails, but not necessarily all Whispers... What if Shimmer doesn't know the difference either?" he breathed.

"What?"

"Shimmer said she wanted to get Tyvissi—and the Draper. But I could walk away. Now maybe she was just saying that," Scarecrow said, raising his eyebrows.

Uppercut waited, thinking.

"Maybe Shimmer thinks the *Draper* is undead," Scarecrow said. "Maybe, somehow, she got a cryptic message, and she thinks the *Draper* is going to kill Jafrain."

Uppercut frowned.

"Hang on, hang on, Shimmer was asking questions of these mystics and adepts and—and seers," Scarecrow said with a wild gesture. "But she wouldn't tell them what she was looking for exactly, or why. So maybe she didn't really understand the signs they discovered."

"And maybe it was too convenient to ignore, when the Draper and Tyvissi could be turned against each other," Uppercut joined in. "The one she paid to discover, and the one who could discharge her debt."

"And she didn't see me after all," Scarecrow said, eyes wide. "She might not be taking a broad enough view of the pattern!"

"And maybe we aren't either," Uppercut said quickly. "This is all—this *guesswork*—we can't assume this is true. Not yet."

"Well, keep an eye out," Scarecrow said. He slid the zemi back into his coat, and crossed his arms. "This is the first time things have seemed to make any sense at all."

"I've chased theories enough to be very suspicious of that moment," Uppercut said with a faint smile.

"Yeah... and in the meantime, we've got somebody to kill," Scarecrow said, his heart sinking as he felt the somber weight of the task.

"The way I see it," Uppercut said, "we don't dare strike out on our own. Too many heavy hitters are involved here. But if we can find someone else, another faction, and we can *defect* in this shadow war... that has possibilities."

"But who? I'm not on board for joining up with a priest of the Pillars of Night. Have you heard about their rituals?" Scarecrow said, uneasy. "I'm not sure we should go after the other one, either. We just don't know enough to risk crossing the Bitters and Shimmer and everything else on their side."

"Well... there's Tyvissi," Uppercut said, eyes bright.

"How though? How would we find the Crossroads, or get a message to the Reconciled, or..." Scarecrow threw up his hands.

"You got us some Coin," Uppercut replied. "I've got some contacts." His smile grew. "We go after Skau, sure. But first we send out some messages. And we keep an eye out for the response."

"You think Tyvissi would be fine with us killing his shadow bearers?" Scarecrow said, skeptical.

"I think if the Reconciled are playing out a layered and multi-generational scheme, they will understand that sometimes your actions seem contradictory to your purpose," Uppercut mused. "I think it's our best chance. Unless we want to trust to Shimmer's mercy."

"Ancient ghosts it is," Scarecrow said promptly.

"We don't have to reach the Reconciled directly," Uppercut said. "Shimmer said so herself; the Path of Echoes paves the way for Reconciled plans. And I happen to know how to reach the Path of Echoes."

"Really?" Scarecrow said.

"Oh yes," Uppercut replied. "In the meantime, we need to figure out what we're going to do about Skau."

Something dark flickered in Scarecrow's eyes, quick as a wingbeat. He scented the air, high above the city, and felt the peculiar spiraling flight path of Carc's weightless drift.

"I've got an idea," he murmured.

CHAPTER THIRTEEN

The "spider sight" is an art form rising from limmer traditions. String or sinew winds around a rounded rim and crosses its interior. Patterns are formed by the intersection of these strands. They pull each other into new alignment as they are wrapped and tugged. There are both symmetrical and asymmetrical designs. Some are primitive, some are elaborate. Sometimes beads, ribbons, bones, or other decorations are incorporated. Authentic samples of the form are unsettling to human senses.

This art form began as limmer seers pushed their damaged sanity in a desperate attempt to communicate insights the human mind cannot process. The limmers received glimpses of the Leviathan consciousness, beyond linear time, as they were exposed to the Dark Baptism of touching demon blood. Not only are there patterns shaped by an intersection of the past, the present, and the future, but those patterns are in motion somehow.

What is malleable and what is immovable? What images are curling surf, and which images are the rocks upon which the waves shatter to foam and slither away? What truths are the rim, and what truths may be pulled into different alignment as the strings are manipulated?

—From "The Art of Unquiet Blood"
By Ceevia Talels, Curatorial Dean of the Sadavath Collective

The ember of the midday sun was muffled in cloudbanks. Snow fluttered down, silently gathering on the cold roof and along the window pane. Inside the dilapidated ruin, a single lantern glowed.

"You're okay with not having Carc along, right?" Uppercut muttered, his breath wisping out in the chill air as he squinted down at the dimly glowing parchment. His hand was splayed on the counter, pinning the strip of paper in place. His writing was steady, the rock and sweep of the pen's nib leaving a trail of glittering ink.

"I have to be," Scarecrow replied, arms crossed over his chest as he watched the big deathseeker crow. Carc perched on the back of a chair, micro-movements of his head tilting his vision between Uppercut and Scarecrow. "We've done our shopping, and I was scouting with him while you got the ink ready. How long do you think this will take?" he asked with a gesture to the note.

"Old Finstyle is many things," Uppercut mused. "He is neither predictable, nor punctual." Straightening, Uppercut regarded his handiwork. "That should get their attention," he said as he reviewed the cryptic note. He looked over at Scarecrow. "Ready?"

Scarecrow puffed out steam, then approached Carc, looking the deathseeker crow in the eye. "This isn't about loyalty to me," he said. "It's about pulling a fast one on these creeps. Misbehavior. Entropy. You like that, yeah?" he said, cocking his head to the side in an unconscious imitation of the crow.

Carc met his gaze, unmoving.

Uppercut rolled the note strip into a tight little scroll, and slid it into the metal canister with his fingertip. He handed it to Scarecrow, who approached the deathseeker crow.

Scarecrow bent his attention to the crow's black scaled leg. He was acutely aware that his ear, jaw hinge, and neck were all exposed to the crow's iron-hard beak as he delicately twisted the wire to fix the canister in place.

"How do we tell him to go to the Light and Times Tea Shop?" Uppercut asked.

"He's smarter than half the partners I've ever had," Scarecrow replied. He leaned back, regarding Carc. "You heard the man. Go make some trouble."

Carc bobbed his head, as though adjusting his balance or agreeing, then sprang from the back of the chair. He propelled himself across the room with a couple lightning-fast downstrokes of his wings, flying out the open window as the gusts flared across the scoundrels.

"That's done," Uppercut said, his expression souring as he clapped his hands together and rubbed them vigorously for warmth. "Sending Carc was a good idea. I don't know how he always knows where you are, but in this case it's damn handy. He should be able to lead Tyvissi right to you, wherever we end up. Maybe Carc will get the message through to Tyvissi quickly, and maybe Tyvissi will come find us before we get to Skau."

"Maybe, but we can't count on it," Scarecrow agreed.

"So let's kill this bastard," Uppercut growled. "Time to review the plan."

"It is pretty basic," Scarecrow said as he turned to the table, where charcoal lines sketched out a diagram. "There's Skau's shrine boxcar, rusted to the track." He tapped on the rectangle with a grungy "x" through it. "There's the watertower, where the local muscle has look-outs."

"Plus there are patrols, and some key areas have watchers on higher points. They have whistles," Uppercut said.

"Yeah, I spotted four of them. Here, here, here, and here. Plus two patrols, in pairs," Scarecrow added as he continued pointing out locations on the diagram. "If everything goes right, we won't have much to do with them anyway. In and out, fast."

"Yeah," Uppercut agreed without much enthusiasm. "So while you are comfortable here," he said, looking at an empty tin of fishmix marking a lookout position on the table map, "I'm drawing him out from here." He pointed to where the two-tined fork was wedged between the table planks, standing upright.

"I shoot him," Scarecrow nodded. "You cut off his head. Then we run for it. To the back gate here," he said, rounding the table. "If we get split up, we meet back at the depot. If that doesn't work for whatever reason, Kettlebox Court."

"And if *that* doesn't work," Uppercut frowned, "we meet at the tavern across from the mine entrance."

"Let's hope it doesn't come to that," Scarecrow said absently. "This should be pretty smooth. I'm using Talon, instead of a rifle," he said as he patted the crossbow. "We might manage to bring Skau down, get his head, and pull out before anyone realizes we're there."

"Can you imagine?" Uppercut said with a weary smile.

Scarecrow chuckled. "Let's not borrow trouble."

"About that crossbow," Uppercut said, again serious as he studied the layout. "You can reload pretty fast, right?"

"Fast enough," Scarecrow said. "Why?"

"If this goes wrong... if it looks like I might be taken prisoner... " Uppercut paused. "I don't want that. I'd rather get a clean death. So if it comes down to it, shoot me." He looked Scarecrow in the eye. "You got that?"

"I mean, I hear what you're saying," Scarecrow said.

"These lookouts," Uppercut said. "They work for Kru Dornas."

"Yeah, I know about Dornas," Scarecrow said, not meeting Uppercut's eyes.

"Do you?" Uppercut pressed. "You have contacts with the Gutters, and they use him for security. But have you seen his work? Up close?"

"I've heard stories," Scarecrow said.

"When I was with the Bluecoats, I was assigned to Coalridge for six months," Uppercut said. "The Old Rail Yard was part of my beat. We used to clean up after some of the rituals these cults conducted. Pack up the bodies, rinse off the leavings. Shovel up the organ piles. Chip corpses out of mortar." He let the moment breathe. "Plenty of those horror shows were attributed to Dornas and his people. He is dug into the Old Rail Yard shoulder deep, like a tick; cults who do business here understand he is involved for security. Something went very wrong with Dornas while he was in Ironhook. He went in a thug and came out an artist."

"And you don't want to be his canvas," Scarecrow said, finishing the thought.

"Right," Uppercut nodded. "The man is a sadist. He attracts like-minded followers. Then he puts them at the service of cults. Plus, there's Skau himself. The goddamn Pillars of Night." He shrugged uncomfortably.

"Yeah," Scarecrow winced.

A moment passed. "You know," Uppercut said reflectively, "I'm a decent shot."

"No way," Scarecrow said with half a grin, playing along. "I went in close last time. It's your turn to get your hands dirty."

"I guess you're right," Uppercut said with a smile that felt out of place. "You couldn't finish the job. Better do it myself."

"That's enough rubberbone banter," Scarecrow said, rolling his eyes. "Let's get this done."

The two scoundrels packed up their gear and prepared to depart. Uppercut rinsed off the bowls and beakers he used to prepare the magical ink, tucking them into a sling bag, and Scarecrow settled his backpack and tested the tensile pull on his crossbow. They headed out.

The shadows were all wrong. Fresh snow soaked up darkness, pale in the corners and crevices of the Old Rail Yard. The sun was diffused through heavy clouds, so the thinner streaks in the clouds glowed silver, painting glitter on the falling snowflakes. The bustle of the city seemed distant and muted as the scoundrels left the ruined depot, following a side path to the rear of the old warehouses that used to service the trains.

They reached the decrepit ladder bolted to the back of a warehouse. Scarecrow squinted up the ladder, hesitating.

"I can't believe you're a sniper," Uppercut muttered, shaking his head.

"Shut up," Scarecrow retorted, a reflex with no feeling. Gritting his teeth, he put his hands on the ladder and gave it a test shake. Then he gingerly started to climb, eyes fixed on the upcoming edge of the roof.

Uppercut followed the side of the building, cautious. He reached the edge of the shadow, and knelt as he looked across the treacherous expanse separating the warehouses from the parked boxcars. Snow was filling in the gaps, covering over the rails and trestles. The ankle-turning landscape was difficult to navigate at the best of times. Crossing the open stretch when it was daylight and the ground was half-hidden in snow was going to be a challenge. On this patch, it was difficult to run or hide.

The target boxcar was a dozen paces from the nearest scrap of cover. Thick black vines draped the whole rectangle, laying across the top and down the sides. Snow gathered on the vines, and banked around the base of the car, drifting up around the metal plates that had been welded over the wheels and the undercarriage gap for security reasons.

Uppercut considered the vines. Something... He pulled his spirit mask out of its pocket at the small of his back, sliding the warm plate over his face as he closed his eyes and breathed out. He felt the mask simmer in his consciousness, and he opened his eyes.

Behind the Mirror, energy trickled along the sides of the vines. They were radiant material, connected to ritual somehow. Not surprising. There was a distortion, like a mirage, so the boxcar and its surroundings seemed to ripple slightly.

"Of course," Uppercut muttered. "He's preparing a ritual there after all." Defenses, protections, precautions; a clear view would be more suspicious than a mirage. Squaring his shoulders, Uppercut mastered his misgivings. Still. Might as well give Scarecrow another minute or two to get into position.

The glowing sky turned the water tower into a silhouette, but Uppercut spotted two lookouts on the tower's side gantries. From his current angle, he could only see one of the lonely sentries standing atop a boxcar, keeping an eye on the area.

Light flicked on inside the shrine, filtering out between the vines through windows that were only visible when backlit.

"I guess Skau has showed up for work," Uppercut growled, straightening and brushing at the snow on his coat. A thread of adrenaline wove into his blood as his guts sank. He frowned, and started walking out into the open. He moved slowly, his steps deliberate, ignoring the itch of his imagination sensing weapons aimed at his exposed body. If he was very lucky, Skau would step out to greet him but the guards would not spot his approach.

Above, on the rooftop, Scarecrow's heart beat faster as he saw Uppercut drift out of cover towards the box car. The biting cold had seeped through most of Scarecrow's body, numbing him. He was laid out in the shadow of a roofline, with a clear view of the boxcar, Talon propped up and loaded. Scarecrow hoped the shadows blurred his out-lines enough to protect him from detection. He flexed his grip on the haft of the crossbow, breathing out a slow steady breath as he peered down the sight.

A silhouette shaded the lit window, and a panel snapped open. Scowl-ing, Scarecrow tried to line up a sure shot, but his mind raced with all the misdirections that might be in place to baffle a sniper. Missing his shot while Uppercut was in the open would be a disastrous move. Scarecrow felt a bead of sweat form at his hairline as he blinked the snow out of his lashes, frantic in his concentration.

"We're closed," snarled a reedy voice from inside the boxcar.

"That's why I'm here now. You'll be busy later," Uppercut said. He raised his hands out to the side. "Can we talk?'

"What do you want?" demanded the figure in the boxcar.

"I have some information that might interest you," Uppercut said. "I'm not going to yell it out here in the open."

A few seconds of silence were nearly unendurable.

"Well then," the voice in the boxcar said, oddly coy, "we should talk."

Uppercut gasped as a sudden jolt of energy squirmed out from under the boxcar, twisting under the snow. The vines were on the ground too! Uppercut quickly stepped back, but he was too slow. The vines spasmed, bursting out of the snow and slapping against his calves.

Stooping to clutch at the vines in an attempt to free himself, Upper-cut was off balance as the vines yanked on him. Carried off his feet, he banged down on a rail, and before he could grab at his surroundings, he was dragged a half dozen paces through a spray of snow as a trap-door clattered open.

Uppercut slammed against the edge of the pit and rebounded, un-able to get a grip as he was sucked underground. The vines flexed up, swinging him to pivot on his shins so he hung upside down, his hat flying off. He bounced back against a curtain of vines, and sev-eral curled around his arms and torso and legs. A sudden tightening bunched the vines, gripping him securely, and he heard the hatch slam shut above.

Forcing himself to remain calm and resist the impulse to squirm, Up-percut breathed as deeply as his racing heart and upside-down lungs allowed. The shock of energy that infused the vines was still slithering through the plant matter, letting off a glittery cold sensation where the plant tightened on his flesh.

Uppercut saw a shaft of light drop down a ladder as the man inside the boxcar opened a trapdoor. Clanking footfalls and a swaying shadow followed, and the man climbed down to the underground chamber where Uppercut was captive.

The man turned, and Uppercut saw his thick eyebrows and massive beard.

Vider Skau, Priest of the Pillars of Night.

"Well hello there," the old man said, sardonic. He tossed a handful of powder to one side, then the other, and where the powder touched the vines it glowed. The overall effect was as bright as candles, lighting up a thickly overgrown underground chamber three times the size of the boxcar above. "You have information for me."

"Sure do," Uppercut said, struggling to keep his tone neutral. "I won't share it like this, though. Let me down."

The old Skov's chuckle was more chilling than the snow above. "No." Taking his time, the priest pulled on a gauntlet made of black and green plates. "Why are you here."

"You have an enemy who is about to make a move," Uppercut said. "You will never guess who it is. You don't know what angle they are planning. If you don't heed my warning, you'll get blindsided."

"And just how do you know what my preparations and guesses involve?" the priest asked, eyes glittering in the radiance. He flexed the gauntlet, and Uppercut felt an answering flex in the vines that held him. His heart beat even faster.

"What I heard, your foe researched you deep. Knows you, from before, too," Uppercut said quickly. "That's all you get, unless you release me."

"Let's have a look at you," Skau said, almost grandfatherly. His eyes drifted half closed as he raised a hand, questing in the air, as though trying to concentrate on a flavor. He frowned, opening his eyes. "Well, I had better get rid of you fast. That curse of yours; I don't want it to taint my ritual." His eyes narrowed. "That's why you're here, isn't it.

So I'll kill you, and your curse will move into my ritual. Did Drabarn send you?" he demanded.

"What? No!" Uppercut protested. "The curse—that's unrelated. I got it from a priest of the Resonant Chime, he was unhappy with my—my punctuality," Uppercut grated out as the vines squeezed him gently.

"I suppose that could be true," Skau said reflectively. "Do you even know what the curse is doing to you?"

"I really don't," Uppercut wheezed.

"This curse infects one single thing. It just sits there in your energy," he said as he gestured with his free hand. "Then one day you will attempt something really important. And that one thing... will fail. No matter what." Skau smiled. "Maybe that happens today. Since you're so near the end of your life." His frown returned. "No matter. I'll get you out of here, there is no call to get that mess in my ritual." He shrugged. "I'll have to kill you elsewhere."

"Missed—opportunity," Uppercut grated out. "Warning—"

"Weak," Skau retorted. "Quiet now. You can wait until Dornas arrives. He'll be *delighted* to have you all to himself," he said, his teeth glinting in the dim light.

Uppercut fought against panic, sipping air like a drowning man.

Outside

Scarecrow clenched his eyes shut, pressing his forehead against his forearm as he lay on the roof. He trembled. What now. What now.

Opening his eyes, he glanced around the field below. Half a dozen predatory cultists had stalked out of cover, summoned by the disturbance, looking all around. They saw the trail where Uppercut was dragged underground, and their eyes probed the shadows. Four of them followed the tracks back towards where Uppercut entered the open area.

Quick math flashed through his mind. Six below, probably another six to ten nearby, they knew the area better than he did but he could maybe hit and run, use ambushes. The odds were not ideal, but maybe he could do it. Lead them off. Circle back. Rescue Uppercut. His guts were a block of ice.

Squinting, he lined up on the shoulder of one of the cultists, furthest from him. Aim for the shoulder to spin the target around, confuse the question of where the shot came from. Then there's wounded, and that's more complicated than corpses; the defenders have to do something with them. Breathing out into the snow to hide the steam, he narrowed his shaky energy into a single column.

Ice rimed across his crossbow, crisped along his skin. His heart skipped a beat. Instinctively, he knew he was not alone. He forced his head to turn, slowly.

Crouched beside him on the roof, the Draper's outline glimmered in the mid-day sun, like the snow was hallucinating about murder. Insane eyes locked on his, pouring cold into the marrow of his bones.

Hello there Scarecrow, the Draper grinned.

Inside

Skau gestured, languid, and the vines writhed back out of the way like a stage's curtain pulled to reveal the scene. Four people hung by their ankles, restrained and gagged by a mat of vines. They were swooning and terrified.

"Today is the day," Skau said to them, condescending. "Our fate becomes your fate." He chuckled. Turning, he regarded Uppercut. "You see, we are benevolent at our heart," he said with a dramatic gesture. "These dock workers will survive the ritual. But it binds their well-being to the Gutters' well-being. So if they act against us, they act against themselves. Our pleasure is theirs, and so too is our suffering." His smile grew. "We are all about unity. Just ask the dozens who have already survived their visit when the stars are right."

"Can... you reach... Tyvissi," Uppercut gasped, on the edge of passing out from the pressure on his chest.

Skau pivoted to face him, beard and eyebrows bristling. "Say that again," he said, opening the gauntlet's grip slightly.

"Tyvissi... can you reach him?" Uppercut managed.

"Interesting," Skau breathed, brow furrowed. "No. I cannot, nor would I. How do you know about Tyvissi?"

"Blood map," Uppercut wheezed. "You—last one." He drew in the deepest breath he could. "Warn him."

"That's not how it works," Skau said, cocking an eyebrow. "Heh. Like we're friends." He shrugged, dropping the pale vestments covering his torso, so he stood before Uppercut wearing high-waisted pants and the gauntlet. "I bear the shadow of Tyvissi as a *cost*."

Uppercut blinked. In the surreal light of the underground shrine, he could see the extensive tattoos covering Skau's arms, torso, and neck. The old man's flesh sagged, but under his skin was muscle and bone as tough as tree roots. Articulated like plates of armor, the tattoo designs were modular but interconnected. A complex wheel under Skau's sternum was the size of a palm, and the center of the pattern bore Tyvissi's design.

"Now you're in danger," Uppercut managed, daring to shift a little in the grip of the vines. They did not give.

"Just now?" the priest scoffed. "You really have no idea. I am a Prelate of the Path of Echoes. I support three of the Reconciled, and two Wards. In my youth I accepted a Binding that yet holds neath the throb of my blood. My pulse is woven into the fabric of this city's secrets," he said with uncomfortable intensity, his eyes glittering. "I have survived two centuries and I will survive two more. I hope you enjoyed your little decades, because we are done here. I will use these vines to break your hands and feet, your arms and legs, then I will vomit you back up to the surface. Dornas and his people can take their time with the rest."

"Wait," Uppercut faltered.

"No." Skau's gauntlet began to tighten, and Uppercut's wrists began twisting past what sinew could bear.

Outside

"H-how did you f-find—" Scarecrow managed.

Our curse makes it easy. I always know where you are, the Draper echoed. *Looks like you have a problem.*

"Right," Scarecrow whispered. "But... why are you... you know, helpful?" His eyes were narrow with suspicion. "What am I to you?" They both knew gratitude wasn't worth considering as the Draper's motivation.

You are my armor, my toy, and maybe my heir, the Draper replied.

"I don't want to be *any* of those things," Scarecrow bristled.

But you do want to rescue your friend, the Draper pointed out. The slick of plasmic blood shone as it oozed down his face, arms, and torso. Sprays and streams of gore drifted around his head, as though he was underwater. The pinpoints of intense light in his eye sockets were deeply unsettling. *I get you what you want, and you pay me in blood.*

Scarecrow didn't try to restrain his trembling any longer. His jaw shivered, chattering his teeth. "We g-gotta talk-k about Tyvissi," he hissed.

Yeah, the Draper said, the light in his eyes intensifying as he tilted the image of his head back. *Tyvissi. Shimmer wants him dead. Wants us to do the deed.* Teeth seemed to push his lips and cheeks out of the way so the grin could shine out.

"So who—how," Scarecrow began.

No time for that now. Later.

"So are you R-Reconciled-d?" Scarecrow chattered.

Yes and no. I'm not part of their stuffy club. But I use blood to stay grounded too—since before I died. I come from limmers. Never had both feet stuck in this world anyway. And I learned something they don't know, the Draper echoed.

"W-what-t's that."

I know how to pull stability out of ghost blood, the maniac murmured as the temperature dropped again. Those eyes. The gravity at their center dragged at Scarecrow.

"So I l-let you in," Scarecrow whispered, "and we g-get Upp-pper-cut-t, and you l-leave."

For now, the Draper nodded.

Scarecrow flexed his jaw. "D-do it." He closed his eyes, leaning his head back.

Like sliding on a comfortable shoe, the essence of the mad specter flowed into Scarecrow's undying body and soul.

All the math went away.

When Scarecrow's eyes snapped open, nothing sane stared out.

Scarecrow rose, then slid down the roof, springing off to sail through open space as the cultists spotted the incoming threat. Midair, Scarecrow snapped off a shot from the crossbow. The bolt punched through a cultist's face. When Scarecrow's body hit the ground, his legs and torso absorbed the impact. He dropped to one knee, feeling no pain, then straightened as the cultists closed in. He tossed the crossbow aside as a spectral bell tolled.

A smile twisted the front of Scarecrow's head. He was unrecognizable.

Then the killing started.

Too eager for weapons, the Draper snatched the guard's fist that held the blade as it slashed down at Scarecrow's body. He drove his head forward, smashing into the hapless guard's face and snapping his head back on his neck. A circular twist ended with Scarecrow holding the guard's blade, whipping it out to knock another incoming attack aside as the Draper stepped Scarecrow inside the attacker's reach, deftly plucking a dagger from the victim and twirling it around to jam into the man's throat.

Ripping it out sideways, the Draper tore open the neck, and the pressurized blood sprayed out as he darted forward through it, throwing both blades at an incoming defender. One hit each shoulder, the force of the attack reversing the charge and flooring the guard. Another peal of a distant bell, reverberating into audible perception.

"Yes!" Scarecrow screamed as a big man lunged at him, swinging a two-handed cudgel. Easily ducking the attack, Scarecrow snatched the man's hair and yanked him forward into a brutal elbow strike to his jaw hinge. The big man choked on a gurgle as Scarecrow hopped up to pound a heel strike down into the side of his knee, then used his own falling momentum to drive his victim to the ground hard.

Scarecrow tossed the cudgel up and snatched it, pivoting to fling the weighted club at a guard who was lining up with a pistol. The club banged into the man's chest, sending him hurling back as the gun spun out of his hand.

So *fast*. One of the attackers backpedaled, desperately blowing his ear-splitting whistle. He tripped on a rail and tumbled back, winded. Two other attackers turned to flee, and the Draper pounced on one, leaping up to kick her in the small of the back. Propelled forward, she stumbled and fell. Scarecrow was on her, gripping a handful of hair and hauling up as he stamped hard on the base of her neck. Bone snapped.

Two defenders fired from the tower, their shots pounding into the snow near Scarecrow. He ran, scooping up the heavy cudgel and a knife, racing towards the boxcar. Another somber tone reverberated behind the Mirror.

Vines coiled up out of the snow, and the Draper made no effort to resist as they snatched Scarecrow's body and dragged it forward, a trap door clanking open. Tugged through, the body was swathed in eager vines, twining around his limbs and holding him immobile.

"So who are—" Skau began, then his eyes widened and he took a step back.

Scarecrow's body flexed hard, and a screaming whine filled the underground chamber as energy was forcibly dragged out of the vines, into the rampant specter. The vines dehydrated, crispy and shrunken, their brittle touch snapping off as the Draper strode towards the priest.

Almost hysterical with agony and relief, Uppercut began thrashing against the loosening vines as the defenses refocused on a new threat.

"I bind you," Skau snarled in Hadrathi, "you may n—"

The cudgel slashed into his torso with a two-handed blow, snapping ribs and sending the priest battering through the ladder as debris sprayed. Scarecrow's body was right behind, jabbing another hit into the side of his head as the priest struggled to rise, knocking him flat.

Twisting gracefully, Scarecrow's body dropped a hard knee strike into the prone man's chest, robbing him of air. Discarding the cudgel, he snatched a handful of the priest's beard and jerked his chin up, exposing his neck. The other hand held a knife, and it plunged down in a series of rapid chops as the priest's horrible choking filled with blood that gushed out of its bounds, down his throat and into the air and all over the wall and floor. The knife rasped against bone, driven into a joint in the spine with unnatural strength.

The sodden butchery continued as Uppercut staggered out of the recoiling vines, unsteady, his hands tucked against his torso by his crossed arms. "Draper!" he shouted, fear swarming through his blood.

Scarecrow's body paused, then sighed, standing straight. He turned, the blaze of spectral light eerie in his shadowed eye sockets.

"*The* Draper."

"Right," Uppercut said carefully. He looked down at Scarecrow's hand, holding a fistful of the priest's beard as long strands of blood oozed out of the neck stump from the ragged decapitation. Runnels and spatters filled the beard and decorated the face. "So... what happens now?"

"I get paid, we escape, and you keep this," the Draper said casually, hefting the head.

"You won't find it so easy!" shouted Skau's head.

Both scoundrels took a step back, staring at the disembodied head.

"You think decapitation is enough to do *me* in? You *amateurs*! You have *no idea* the forces you're dealing with!" Skau's head screamed. Blood and spittle sprayed.

"Neat," the Draper grinned.

CHAPTER FOURTEEN

Imagine the world as a pile of sticks and logs. Then, imagine the activity of the living as flame, rooted in the wood and consuming it. Activity reshapes the physical world, and transforms its material. Lifeless trees lose their shapes to become ashes, light, heat, and motion. Time and change grind away at everything.

Above fire's destructive activity you will find smoke and a rippling mirage. So too you will find echoes, memories of the real world, printed in the ghost field, unblemished by the changes occurring in the tangible world. Life and memory fixed some images behind the Mirror and beyond the reach of time.

Mystics have used different occult traditions to create stable "ghost doors" to connect a point in the solid world to a point behind the Mirror for centuries. The keys to these doors are sometimes arcane devices of incredible flexibility and complexity, and sometimes simple objects tuned to a specific connecting point. Even though the practice of creating and manipulating these connections is ancient, the theories about how and why they work are still disputed.

Beware any technique where our ability has far outrun our understanding.

—From "Fugitive Adepts and Their Evasive Methods"
By Inspector Drin Seevol, published 714

The severed head released a clotted shriek that trembled the air and the vines, pulling loose energy behind the Mirror towards dormant forms.

"Gag that thing!" Uppercut shouted. Wincing, he almost doubled over, holding his arms tight against his body as pain seared through his twisted forearms and wrists. "We only have a few seconds!" Ghosts were coalescing behind the Mirror, gathering strength.

The Draper swung the head by its beard, bopping its face against the ladder, but that didn't faze Skau. The Draper tugged at Scarecrow's sleeve, ripping the forearm off his shirt to slither out of his coat's cuff. Kneeling, he wadded the cloth up and jammed it in the screaming mouth, muffling the sound and disrupting Skau's concentration.

One of the hanging dock workers caught Uppercut's eye. The victim released a strangled cry. The Draper glanced up.

"No time for that, leave them," he said.

"Got to cut one free," Uppercut gritted out. "Move the choice—to free the others or not—from my conscience to his." He struggled to draw a knife from his belt sheath.

Exasperated, the Draper rose and snatched one of the thick vines. Concentrating, he drained the radiant energy out of it, and as the vine crisped and withered, more of them twisted away from the attack. One of the dock workers slid to the ground as the others struggled with renewed vigor in the loosening grip of the vines.

"We aren't going to make it past the guards up above. Not without a tough fight," Uppercut said, hoarse. "Any ideas?"

"Of course," the Draper said. "First I get paid. I told Scarecrow I needed blood."

"You leave them alone," Uppercut said. Mastering his fear, he stepped between the entrapped workers and the mad spirit.

"Not them," the Draper said, dismissive. He tossed Skau's head aside, and scrambled halfway up the ladder. A couple quick jabs with the knife broke the clasp holding a ceiling plate in place. It swung open, and masses of coiled and ropy vines flopped down. Gleaming as pale as bone, the wet pulp of the vines' heart mass was exposed.

"That must fill half the undercarriage space of the train car," Uppercut frowned as the hideous stink of rotten vinegar and meat washed over him.

The Draper jammed his knife hand up into the mass, wrist deep, and he let out a maniacal peal of laughter as he flexed all his muscles, draining the swollen life energy from the vines' heart.

"Excellent!" he barked as convulsions swept through the traumatized masses of greenery. He tore his hand loose, and a gloppy splat of plant viscera slapped down on the flooring. The Draper was unbearably bright on the other side of the Mirror, so Uppercut winced away. Scarecrow's body tore the dangling plate loose and jammed it across the trapdoor up into the car, severing the ladder poles and blocking the way. He dropped to the floor of the chamber, and shrugged to settle his coat. Then he stooped to pick up Skau's head by the beard.

"I hope you have another idea for a way out," Uppercut said through his teeth.

"The vines hide an escape tunnel. These people always have escape tunnels." The Draper pivoted, leaning forward as though scenting and preparing to pounce, and stopped. "There." Confident, he walked into the vines, and they writhed back to reveal a narrow brick tunnel.

With a dull groan that creaked against the seam between solid matter and plasmic echoes, a ghost slid through the wall. Its mouth yawned with a slack howl of agony, and chips of intense hate glittered in its empty eye sockets.

Uppercut pivoted, confronting the ghost. He concentrated, and his surroundings flickered in his consciousness as he aligned with the ghost.

"Leave," he snarled, his teeth glinting.

Caught up in the command, the ghost shimmered, then was forced back through the wall.

"Help us!" cried out one of the panicking dock workers, half free of the vines.

"Don't leave us here!" another managed in a breathless plea.

Uppercut turned away from them, loping into the darkness of the brick tunnel. Behind him, the sadistic guards started pounding on the plate barrier.

A couple workers started screaming, their suffering reverberating through the narrow corridor as Uppercut stepped out into a bigger space. Still underground, this tunnel had narrow gauge rails. The only light was a nimbus glowing around Scarecrow's body, excess energy bleeding out of the Draper.

"I've healed up this body and reinforced Scarecrow's caul," the Draper said without looking at Uppercut. "This is good preparation. We are getting close now, to the big fight." His smile had no amusement in it.

"Can you do something about Skau?" Uppercut asked with an apprehensive glance back the way he came.

"No, he has some weird armor. Figure it out on your own, or let Shimmer handle it," the Draper said. "I was never here." He fixed his intense gaze on Uppercut. "Got it? You never saw me."

"Got it," Uppercut said, his face numb.

"Exit is that way," the Draper said, pointing down the dark tunnel passage. Then he flinched and shuddered, as though shot, and Scarecrow sagged as the Draper flickered out of him and whisked away.

As Uppercut put his hand on Scarecrow's shoulder, the hideous chewing of Skau's head managed to clear most of the cloth.

"For this—summon—I call upon—" Skau managed, and Scarecrow dropped the head. Kneeling, he struggled to jam the gag back in without losing a finger to the gnashing teeth. He whacked the skull against the rail a couple times, but the priest didn't react, continuing to sputter blasphemies until Uppercut got involved. The Whisper filled Skau's mouth with a glove and wrapped his belt around the head as a makeshift gag and tether.

"I think somebody's coming," Scarecrow slurred, facing the brick corridor. Uppercut did not answer, instead grabbing his elbow and pulling him along the tunnel at an unsafe speed in the dimness, Skau's head dangling from his other fist. Traces of light filtered down from snow-covered vents in the ceiling. It had to be enough.

"Wait," Scarecrow said, freeing his arm and stopping. "Talon. My crossbow."

"We can't go back for it," Uppercut said through his teeth. "We'll be lucky to escape as it is."

Scarecrow hesitated for just a moment, then scowled and trudged on.

They approached a grating across the tunnel entrance, relieved to see the cold paleness beyond under the weak sun's light.

"Hey!" shouted a voice in the darkness behind them. "You there! Stop!"

Scarecrow grimaced as he hauled a pistol out of his belt and fired at the lock, point-blank. The sturdy lock was jarred by the impact. "Come on!" Scarecrow shouted, rearing back and unloading a kick. The damaged grating shuddered and clacked, the bent mechanism knocked out of alignment enough for the grating to open. The footfalls of running boots echoed towards them as the scoundrels shoved their way through the grating and sprinted across the street, orienting on an idling carriage.

They piled into the carriage, both yelling "Nightmarket!" The cabbie lashed the draft goat, who jolted forward and dragged the carriage at a brisk pace as Scarecrow broke his pistol open, discarding the spent shell and reloading.

"I hope the cabbie didn't see the head," Uppercut scowled, peering out the back window of the carriage. He saw their pursuers run out through the grating, pointing after the scoundrels and shouting as they raced up to another carriage. "Looks like we might have a chase."

"No we don't," Scarecrow scoffed. "Cabbie!" he yelled. "Take the next left!"

The carriage veered to the left moments later. "Slow down!" Scarecrow hollered. The carriage slowed, and Scarecrow opened the carriage door and took a long step down to the curb. Uppercut was right behind him, and the forward motion of the carriage slammed the door as the scoundrels jogged into an alleyway. They caught their breath as the pursuing carriage rattled past.

"That's only likely to fool them for a minute," Scarecrow panted. "Let's get another cab."

Fortunately it was midday, and several cabs waited for customers along the curb on a nearby cross-street. They casually rented one, assuring that Skau's head was completely wrapped up before venturing out into the public's line of sight.

"What are we going to do to shut that thing up?" Scarecrow demanded, unsettled as he watched Skau's jaw working to chew at the leather gag. "I don't want to shatter the head too much, it has to be recognizable."

"We give it to Shimmer," Uppercut muttered. "Make it her problem." He watched the road behind the carriage, restless and wary.

"How are your arms? Legs? I guess those vines twisted you up pretty good," Scarecrow said carefully.

Uppercut frowned. "I wasn't sure how much you were following, with the Draper running things," he said. "I have a lot of pain, but I don't think there's much damage. How about you?"

"I don't know what the Draper did in here, but I feel great," Scarecrow confessed. He flexed his legs. "I haven't felt this good since before we hit the Clavalian place."

"Well let's not sniff a gift goat's cud," Uppercut sighed. "Take a win for once. We have to go to Kettlebox Court. Change clothes, swap out gear. Wait for Shimmer."

Scarecrow banged on the carriage roof. "Driver! Kettlebox Court!"

KETTLEBOX COURT. NIGHTMARKET
40TH MENDAR, 850. *ABOUT AN HOUR LATER*
SIXTH HOUR PAST DAWN

Scarecrow secured his currency wallet in his jacket as the coach rattled off down the cobbled road. "Here we are. I still feel like somebody is going to jump out at me any minute."

"Let's just get inside," Uppercut growled, squeezing the head in the bag between his elbow and ribs to try and muffle its squirming.

The scoundrels entered the courtyard at the center of the massive stack of apartments, heading for the stairs. The loud clack of a cane against a paving stone caught their attention.

"Scarecrow, you had a visitor," said a gangly young man seated in the corner. "Said his name was Getch. He wanted you to go to the Tumble

Trout. It's on Ink Lane, you know, the Docks. Said someone would let him know when you show up, just be sure to wear that red headband."

"Thank you, Quarrel," Scarecrow sighed as he hauled his currency wallet out again.

"Always a pleasure to be of service," Quarrel grinned, showing off several gaps in his smile.

"You go take a look," Uppercut said. "I'll stay here. Look after our package, keep an eye out for visitors."

"Are you sure?" Scarecrow said, forehead creased. "This is a pretty pivotal day."

"You're right, it is, so you need to find out what Getch knows. Don't worry about me, I'll be fine," Uppercut said as his features tightened. He could feel Skau working his way through the last of the leather restraints. "I have to get this upstairs." He turned, heading for the staircase.

"We don't get bored," Scarecrow said reflectively, fishing out a handful of currency and tossing it to Quarrel. " And you. Keep up the good work."

"Yes sir," Quarrel said, neatly pinching up the coins that missed his begging apron. Scarecrow was already headed back out to the street.

Meanwhile, Uppercut worked his way through three locks and a tripwire, his impatience with security peaking as he struggled to just get inside. He slammed the door, kicked a trunk open, dropped Skau's head inside, stuffed a heavy blanket on top, and snapped the chest shut. Then he heaved a deep, deep sigh, and sat on the chest.

"What a day," he muttered.

Rising, he limped over to the makeshift kitchen, shooing beetles off the countertop as he considered the tins and the unappetizing leftovers inside.

A strange pressure rose around him, and he narrowed his eyes. Careful, he pulled his spirit mask out and slipped it onto his face, concentrating until he felt its coolness merge with his Voidsenses. Opening his perceptions, he felt the flickering presence in the street outside.

Uppercut crossed to the window, leaning against the frame as he looked down into the street. There. Clearly visible even from the fourth floor. The coach, and the man standing next to it—the man who was possessed by a spirit. The spirit overflowed with power and stared directly into his eyes.

The spirit beckoned to him, then mounted the buckboard and waited expectantly.

Uppercut only thought it over for a moment. Frowning, he rifled the cupboard in the kitchen until he found his heavy leather bag. He opened the trunk, retrieving Skau's head, and he tilted it into the bag. Then he returned to the kitchen, hefting a pail half full of murky water. He poured the water into the water-proof bag as Skau sputtered.

"That should encourage you to keep it down," he growled, and he cinched the bag shut and buckled the flap. He ignored the unsettling squelches from the bag as he slowly treaded down the stairs once more, leaving through a different exit. He crossed the street, facing the coach.

"What's this," he demanded quietly.

"Your idea," the possessed coachman replied, polite.

"Right." Uppercut let himself into the coach, and pulled the door shut. "Let's go."

THE TUMBLE TROUT, INK LANE. THE DOCKS
40TH MENDAR, 850. *ABOUT AN HOUR LATER*
SEVENTH HOUR PAST DAWN

Leaning against the bar, Scarecrow surveyed the late lunch crowd packed into the tavern. He spotted a kid standing by an alcove, squinting at him. He offered a mock salute, tapping his red headband, and something like recognition crossed the teen's features. Turning, the teen hustled out of the tavern.

"That ought to bring Getch here," Scarecrow muttered. He ordered an ale, but by the time he got it he was thinking. Looking over the exits. Considering various possibilities.

Leaving his ale untouched, on the off chance it had been tampered with, Scarecrow headed for the rear of the tavern. Slipping out the back door by the scullery, he considered the alleyway, then chose an intersecting alley. He stepped out of sight behind a stack of broken crates. In spite of the brittle stink of the freezing corridor, he was more comfortable here than he was inside, in the crowd, easily visible and somewhat cornered.

Some time later, he stamped his feet then blew on his hands. He stopped, listening carefully, and crouched to reduce his visibility. Stealthy steps crunched through the debris and ice in the adjacent alleyway as Getch approached the back of the tavern, looking over his shoulder.

"Fresh meat," Scarecrow said quietly.

Getch froze. "Still kicking," he said, rueful. He turned, spotting Scarecrow. In the weak sunlight, Getch's many tattoos were faded. Outside the shadows of the tattoo shop, he seemed smaller. "You can't make anything easy."

"Easy costs extra," Scarecrow said, but there was no smile in his banter. "Are you alone?"

"I am. No trap here," Getch said. "I need your help."

"Tell me about it."

Getch glanced around the squalid mess behind the tavern, and scanned the rooflines quickly. He frowned. "Three days ago Jafrain was drinking. She's been doing a lot of that. Snarling at people. It's not like her. After she met you, she was really struggling with something."

"Was?"

"Yeah. She figured something out, put some facts together or got some news. First she was thoughtful, then... really angry. I mean, pissed off. Cold and quiet mad, you know? So the night before last, she headed out, didn't tell anybody where she was going. I gave her twelve hours of privacy before I started asking questions." Getch rubbed his scalp, his features creased with distaste.

"Is she okay," Scarecrow asked, feeling his heart beating higher up in his chest than usual.

"I tracked down people she was talking to in the days before," Getch said, evading the question. "I found out she was looking for Shimmer. How to find her at home, not working. I got the information she got, and tracked her down to this fancy house, you know, for comfort."

"Right," Scarecrow nodded. "Then?"

"I asked around real quiet like. Turns out Jafrain met with Shimmer, night before last. They had an argument—a loud one. The fancy lady in the room next door said Jafrain was yelling at Shimmer. Seemed like a bad move, because Shimmer is known to disappear people. And Shimmer, I guess, captured Jafrain. Something about keeping her safe until 'this' is all over."

"You have to have more than that," Scarecrow breathed.

"Yeah, I do. Shimmer was overheard saying something about taking Jafrain to White Corners. I was going to find out more, but Shimmer's people found out I was asking questions." He tilted his head, showcasing sullen bruises on his cheekbone, a slightly swollen nose. "They discouraged me. If I keep at it, they'll see me coming."

"What were they arguing about?" Scarecrow demanded. "Any detail helps."

Getch thought for a minute. "The fancy lady said something about... arrogance. Danger. A broken promise."

Scarecrow swallowed hard. "White Corners. That's, what, a place?"

"I think it's in Charterhall," Getch nodded.

Scarecrow considered him for a long moment. "Okay, this is what we are going to do. You stick close to the shop, so if I need to call you in for backup, you're around. I'll mount a rescue."

"Thank you," Getch said, sincere. "That means a lot to me. To us."

"I guess we'll see," Scarecrow muttered. "Okay, get out of here. I'll be in touch."

Getch nodded, then he turned and followed the filth-choked alley back the way he came.

Scarecrow leaned back against the wall, pressing the heels of his hands into his eye sockets, thinking fast. "White Corners," he murmured, fixing the name in his mind.

Wood scraped on stone, somewhere nearby. Scarecrow was instantly alert, casting around for the source of the noise. A couple pebbles slid off the edge of the roof above his position. Alarmed, Scarecrow stepped up on a crate and jumped, gripping the extended eave and pulling himself up so he could scramble to the adjacent roof.

"I wondered if you'd come up here," the giant Skov said, massive arms crossed over his chest.

"Granite."

"I figure if you want to cause trouble, I'll toss you off the roof," Granite mused. "Should be easy, you're still gimpy and missing your crossbow."

Scarecrow instinctively knelt, feeling more steady and balanced. "You sure do move quietly for a big guy."

"Oh yeah," Granite nodded. "I was in the Crestmount nautical assault division in the war. Managed the rigging, night raids. I'm real quiet. A third of the people I killed never even knew I was there." His tone was the only amused part of his demeanor. "My people and I have been following Getch all day. Wondering who he would try to recruit. Since it's you, I have a problem."

"What's your problem?" Scarecrow asked cautiously.

"Well Getch didn't heed his warning, so he dies, that's straightforward," Granite said reflectively. "But you... I'm supposed to also kill whoever he talks to. That's an order. *But,* Shimmer *also* told all her contractors *not* to kill you and Uppercut. Just, you know, stop you if need be, and report to her, and she'll handle you. So I've got orders to kill you, and also not to kill you. It's a puzzle," he observed. "What to do. What to do."

"I can't believe you're working for her again," Scarecrow said. "That didn't end up too well last time. I've heard about how she speaks to you."

"I'm taking this job at a pay cut, just for the chance to get back in her good graces," Granite said. "Her, and the people in her network. When she's cranky with one of us, word gets out. So you can see this is not the perfect time to repeat the mistakes I made with Grear. Listening to you, letting some rotten cud escape, lying about it." He stroked his chin. "I guess I'll split the difference and let gravity decide. I'm really liking this idea of tossing you off the roof."

"Come on now, I don't believe you want to do that," Scarecrow said with careful charm. "You had the drop on me. Could have hit me before I knew you were there. But you wanted to chat." He paused. "I think you still want to chat."

"Less and less with every passing moment," Granite replied, brow furrowing as he flexed. "Let's get this done."

"Wait," Scarecrow said, quiet but intense. "Wait a minute. This is the third time I've crossed your path. Maybe I'm your last railing. Maybe I keep popping up because you're going the wrong way, and I'm the last thing between you and the drop."

"What is this nonsense," Granite mused, shaking his head as his fists tightened.

"Push through me at your peril," Scarecrow continued. "Push through me and see what's on the other side for you. We can do better, Granite. Better than Shimmer and her crooked plots. You were in the Crestmount division. Everybody has heard of that division. You were a warrior, not a soldier."

"I can't believe you think this fast-talking sales pitch will work," Granite said, rolling his eyes. But he did not take a swing.

"Shimmer and I see the same thing in you," Scarecrow pressed on. "You know Uppercut and I crossed her more than once, but she didn't kill us. She *has* thugs, Granite. All she needs. But what she's really looking for is people with *initiative*. You have management potential, just like we do. If she can get you to settle for less, she will. Like this situation, right? Look at the bigger picture. She is trying to protect Jafrain. This tattoo artist. Works in the same shop as Getch."

"So?"

"She's trying to protect Jafrain from a ghost. That's what all of this is about. What if you show up and report that you found and killed the ghost she's worried about?" Scarecrow raised his eyebrows, simmering with contagious excitement.

"What are you even talking about?" Granite demanded, patience dangerously thin.

"There's a murderous Skov specter that busted out during the Clavalian heist. Uppercut and I have worked out a way to summon him, then take him out. We'll cut you in." Scarecrow locked eyes with the big Skov.

Granite's words came slowly, struggling to emerge. "Let's take a look."

Uppercut jogged the leather bag so it sloshed, dislodging Skau's head from chewing on a seam inside. The Whisper watched the coach rattle away down the street, and he turned to squint up at the blazing electroplasmic torch on the uppermost tower of the tea shop. Taking a deep breath, he refocused down the stairs to the basement entry below street level.

"I am made of patience, sturdy and rich, not easily worn to threadbare sheen," he murmured to himself. The quote soothed him. He reached the door, seeing that it was equipped with an attunement lock. He paused, wondering if it was appropriate to attempt it himself. Before he made a decision, the gears twirled and the bolt rasped back. A trim man opened the door.

"Welcome to you, Uppercut," said his host. "Do please come inside."

Uppercut eyed the man's expensive suit, and he stepped in as he wrestled down his sense of unease. "Thank you ever so much," he growled. "What's this about?"

A grating croak from across the room startled Uppercut, and he spotted a deathseeker crow perched on the sideboard.

"Carc?" he said. The bird bobbed its head for balance.

"Master Vans will be with you shortly," the host said, almost gracious.

"Wait, *Vans*?" Uppercut said sharply.

"Indeed; Sir Adric Vans, the famed scholar and musician," the host clarified. "He tends to be overindulgent when asked to autograph things for fans." His smile was barely polite. "Please excuse me." The host offered a shallow bow, then pivoted and vanished through one of the parlor's exits.

At a loss, Uppercut looked around the understated luxury of the room. He took in the details; the deep pile carpet underfoot, the furniture carved from hardwoods and upholstered with rare leather, the velveteen walls, the chandelier.

Then the bag under his arm flexed as Skau's head managed to draw enough breath to let out a horrid moan. Uppercut frowned, and squeezed the bag between his elbow and ribs.

"Thank you for waiting." A smooth voice preceded the slender man who strolled into the room. "I do appreciate your flexibility, combined with the intriguing missive you sent to us." He smiled, and the delicate accents of his makeup emphasized his eyes and the angles of his narrow cheekbones and jaw. "I expect you are looking forward to this meeting. Much to everyone's surprise, Tyvissi has agreed to see you."

Uppercut's eyebrows raised. "Tyvissi himself. I do look forward to that," he said experimentally, unsure whether it was true or not. "Time is of the essence."

"Agreed," Vans said diplomatically. He focused on the bag. "Oh dear. That must be Prelate Skau."

"Uh, yes, his head," Uppercut clarified. "Sort of... soggy now." Uppercut was horrified by the sudden idea that he might blush.

"If it's all the same to you, I can take that for safekeeping during your meeting," Vans said with a disarming smile. "I will give it back to you when you are ready to go."

"Could you make him, you know, quieter?" Uppercut asked.

"We can talk about that later," Vans said. "May I?"

Uppercut handed over the bag, and Vans led the way through one of the side doors, down a curving spiral staircase, and through two ornate arched doors. Vans put the head bag on a countertop, and turned to a circular pool, the central feature of the room. It was lit from below, and its ripples shone on the dome above.

"Please remove your clothes," Vans said, matter-of-fact.

"All of them?" Uppercut protested faintly.

"Please," Vans nodded.

After a moment of hesitation, Uppercut shrugged out of his heavy coat, his vest, his long shirt, several belts, boots, pants, socks, and knee brace. Scowling, he crossed his arms.

Vans circled him once. "Interesting. Not a single tattoo."

"You might be expecting my partner. The man wears a book all stretched out on his skin."

Vans smiled. "Very well. Please step into the pool."

Too late to hesitate now. Uppercut lowered himself to sit on the rim of the pool, and he was surprised that the water was an ideal temperature, and the pool was only knee deep.

"Plays tricks on the eye," he said, gruff. "Now what?"

Vans arched an eyebrow. "You are the Whisper. You tell me."

Uppercut looked down into the pool, his brow knotted. He concentrated, letting his eyes drift in their focus to see what wasn't visible. A pale energy, glowing, stable, up to the center of the pool.

"Is—is that a conduit?" Uppercut muttered.

"Yes, this pool connects to a spirit well some distance from here," Vans confirmed. "You may follow it to where Tyvissi awaits."

Uppercut swallowed hard, then let his focus drift to match the conduit before him. A hissing sound filled the chamber as half the water shifted to steam, obscuring and filling the room.

Most excellent, echoed a powerful spirit, the clarity of the tone penetrating Uppercut's bones. He whirled, and his coat swirled around him. Startled, he looked down to see himself dressed in a stylish black interpretation of a Bluecoat uniform. He stood in a marble hall, with windows along one side and tapestries on the other. The windows overlooked a seething and shifting radiant forest, gently stirred by a breeze.

Seated on a throne at the end of the room was Tyvissi himself. The spirit wore a lion mask with a feather mane over a trim and dashing formal suit, centuries out of date.

"Greetings, Honorable Spirit," Uppercut said with a deep bow.

Greetings to you, esteemed troublemaker, Tyvissi responded with some amusement. He rose, and blurred, standing face to face with the Whisper. *Here we are at last.*

"Are we in the... the Porcelain Towers?" Uppercut asked, looking around at the elaborate architecture.

Alas no, I am not yet so trusting, Tyvissi echoed.

"Sure, that's completely reasonable, considering... you know, what we've been up to. Cutting you loose." Uppercut felt adrenaline simmering in his blood, his heart accelerating.

Don't give it another thought. No hard feelings, Tyvissi replied with an airy wave. *All part of the game.*

"Did we miss a tether?" Uppercut asked cautiously.

No, very thorough job, you got them all, Tyvissi mused. *I built up some reserves, I saw this little challenge coming. I've got a reservoir mask to extend my time. And I do plan to make the most of this interval. Much to do.* He paused.

"Everything okay?"

Your curse, Tyvissi responded. *The Resonant Chime. Let me tidy that up for you.* Tyvissi focused on Uppercut, and nudged him as a Whisper would attune with a spirit bane charm. Just like that, something shifted, like a bone popping back into place, restoring range of motion. Uppercut grunted with unexpected relief. *There you go.*

"Just like that?" Uppercut said, awed. "Just—you wanted the curse gone, so..." he found his hands imitating a "poof" gesture.

That curse was truly a modest effort, more of an afterthought, Tyvissi echoed. *Easy.*

"What about Scarecrow? Can you correct his?"

No, Scarecrow's curse is part of my plan, Tyvissi replied.

"Wait, you're saying that your plan was so intricate it involved us getting cursed by the Resonant Chime?" Uppercut frowned.

Don't be silly, Tyvissi soothed. *Of course I plan, with layers and intricacies. But I never put my planning above the opportunities of the moment. I braid my preparation with emerging possibilities,* he said, gesturing with one hand for each. He aligned his hands. *This interweaving changes both and makes something stronger than either.*

"So the curse *became* part of your plan," Uppercut clarified.

The moment I learned of it. Now. Tyvissi leaned back, and reappeared at the window, gazing over the forest below. *Do you know what that curse does?*

"Maybe," Uppercut muttered. "Prelate Skau explained it to me. I would be honored if you'd share your expertise on the matter."

The curse lodges in one thing. A single task that you will attempt. No matter what, no matter how hard you prepare or what measures you take to assure success... that one task will fail. The spirit regarded Uppercut. *I have freed you of that certainty.*

Gratitude didn't feel like the right response. "Why?"

You are part of my overall plot now. Rather than trust events unfolding randomly, I have chosen to shape your role and refocus it. Some of what is ahead requires your consent. Some does not. Even if you choose perversity, there are still ways for you to be useful.

"That's ominous," Uppercut observed.

Indeed. But the stakes are high, Tyvissi agreed.

"What *are* the stakes?" Uppercut asked.

The lion mask seemed to smile. *I think it's time you knew.*

CHAPTER FIFTEEN

Dr. Eylisach first coined the term "reconciled" to refer to the vanishingly rare plasmic consciousnesses that did not quickly succumb to obsession and confusion once they were discrete entities operating in the ghost field. This morphological distinction was generally applied to a sub-set of specters, as a prerequisite power level seemed intrinsic to a sustainable equilibrium. Her conceptualization of the term focused on establishing harmonious relations between the specter's past and present states, or "making peace" with an physiological and paradigmatic rebirth and eschewing vulnerability through establishing yet-unrevealed methodology to regulate the inevitable and unbalancing impulses of debilitating focal concepts that are inherent to the transformative process of prolonging consciousness beyond physical death.

The technical and taxonometric term "reconciled" is distinct from the factional designation "The Reconciled" as there are some specters who are not aligned with the faction even as they meet the criteria to be classified as "reconciled" spirits. A clarifying statement from the specter of Lord Wilmiat in 532 reinterpreted the usage of the term "reconciled" to illuminate the faction's aims.

Where Dr. Eylisarch considered the specters to be reconciling their previous and current states of being, Wilmiat suggested the faction was in pursuit of reconciliation in the sense of a fiscal ledger; these specters sought to establish a balance akin to settling financial accounts by paying back what they owed and collecting on outstanding debts. Tragically, this conceptual framework reinvigorated controversy in what morphological and psychological traits delineated the classification, as Wilmiat recontextualized their balance as a refinement of vengeance and obsession rather than a transcendence of same.

—From "A History of Taxonometric Endeavors
in Spectrological Studies"
By Anicia Breece, DPA, CnT, KlE. Fifth Edition published 612

Scarecrow frowned at the floor, on his hands and knees, dragging the wax block over the uneven floorboards. He paused to look over at the diagram on the parchment, then resumed scrubbing a circle design.

"How long is this going to take?" Granite rumbled, uneasy. He looked around the narrow loft again.

"I figured Uppercut would have started before I got back," Scarecrow said, "but he's not here. So it's a good thing I know how to read the ritual, and you're here to back me up." He straightened, shifting back to sit on his heels. "Did you check the plasmic ammo?"

"Yeah, it's real basic but it will do the job," Granite frowned. He gestured at the four pistols laid out on the table by the box of plasmic rounds. "How long."

"Oh, probably about an hour. You've got some time, you can take it easy while I finish this up." Scarecrow leaned forward again, planting a hand for support, and resumed scribbling quick jerky symbols with the wax block.

Granite planted his fists on his hips, looking up and taking a deep breath. "This ghost have a name?"

"Yeah, the Draper. He gets really cranky if you leave out 'the' and just call him 'Draper' but that's the least of his problems. He thinks he stays sane by tearing other ghosts apart and wearing their wet bits." Scarecrow shifted position, squinting at the parchment.

"I knew a few guys like that, during the war," Granite said, subdued. "It's an old tradition, among the warriors of our people. Real old." His eye settled on the sideboard, and he stepped over to examine a bottle of cheap wine. Shaking his head, he used the corkscrew to open the bottle, and he took a long swallow.

"This stuff is gross," he said reflectively as he held the bottle up to the light.

"It gets the job done though," Scarecrow smiled, focusing on his work.

"I could stomp you a couple times and be done with this. Get you back to Shimmer. That would be a damn sight faster than whatever nonsense you're doing," Granite muttered.

"That's probably true," Scarecrow agreed.

Granite took another pull from the bottle and made a face at the sour flavor, then stood by the window, watching the street.

"You might want to stay away from the window," Scarecrow said without looking.

"I would love to," Granite replied. "Get this ghost in here so we can shoot it up and go back to Shimmer. Wrap all this up."

"We always want these things to work faster than they do," Scarecrow said under his breath. "At least have a seat."

"What, am I making you uncomfortable?" Granite rumbled, scowling at the smaller man.

"Suit yourself," Scarecrow said, not looking up.

Granite downed more of the bottle, and slammed it on the table. "Did you piss in this?" he demanded.

"Now there's a thought," Scarecrow smiled. He straightened, rocked back on his heels, and stood, facing Granite.

"Your leg sure got better," Granite observed, clenching his brows. He blinked, sensing the slur in his voice.

"It did," Scarecrow agreed. "Arm, too," he said, holding it out so Granite could see the weirdly pale puckers of scarring from the fangstrider bite.

Granite let out a ragged grunt, widening his stance, blinking rapidly. "Oh, what did you do," he snarled.

"We never drink the sideboard wine," Scarecrow explained. Granite staggered back and fell into a chair, scrabbling at the guns on the table. He got one, and as he swung it around to line up his aim, Scarecrow blocked his wrist and tugged the pistol out of his numb grip. "It's just for show. Because of all the sedatives in it." He shook his head. "Uppercut's idea. He said drinking somebody's wine without asking was a power move, something that a cocky enemy might do if they catch you at home. Just to prove they are in charge."

Granite wrenched out an unintelligible oath, and slid out of the chair, struggling against the drug. Frustrated, he banged his head on the floor.

"Oh, don't do that," Scarecrow said with some concern. "Your headache is already going to be pretty legendary."

"Th'sz... not ovr," Granite panted through his teeth as his eyes unfocused.

"It's kind of impressive you got half the bottle down," Scarecrow said, picking it up with a speculative look.

With a last wheeze, Granite lay back, unconscious.

"At least it wasn't poison," Scarecrow said reflectively. He crossed to the cabinet and pulled out some rope. Kneeling by Granite, Scarecrow twisted the rope around his wrists and secured a few knots with practiced ease. "I guess I'll drag you into the bedroom. Ugh. Don't like how *that* sounds."

Scarecrow looked out the window at the nearby clocktower.

"Ten hours." He clenched his jaw, trying not to think about Shimmer. If everything went smoothly, she already had a trophy head from the Bitters. "I guess I get to search the place. Because you might have stowed the head here for me to find." He closed his eyes and rubbed his face. "Where the hell are you."

Granite snored.

TYVISSI'S AUDIENCE HALL BEHIND THE MIRROR
40TH MENDAR, 850. *TIME IS UNSTEADY HERE*
PROBABLY ABOUT EIGHTH HOUR PAST DAWN

I suppose you read up on me, Tyvissi emoted. *Checked into my context.*

"That would have been useful," Uppercut said slowly, "but I have not had the time. I mean, the Spirit Wardens are hunting you, and it's all part of this elaborate game, so I figured any inquiries into you might draw attention to me. My focus has been on Shimmer and getting out from under all this mess."

Wheels within wheels, Tyvissi agreed. *Yes, all of us keep tabs on who access certain books, ask certain questions, pursue witnesses to certain events, and seek out keepers of family stories. There are many self-serving versions of the narrative out there. Perhaps it would be useful for you to know mine.*

"I am listening," Uppercut nodded.

I died in 548, Tyvissi echoed, *a casualty of the shadow war between the loyalists of Weatherwatch and the dissidents of Barrowcleft. I was a prominent loyalist in those days, and I remain in the service of the Immortal Emperor in my own way. Even in life I was a spider, engaged in subverting the Church of Ecstasy in Doskvol. I was opening pathways into Church leadership for agents and sympathizers working for the interests of the Path of Echoes.*

"Does that line up with serving the Emperor?" Uppercut asked.

I forget how counterintuitive our work appears to those not immersed in it. The Church was controlled by the dissidents as an instrument of maintaining hegemonic control in concert with the Ministry. In order to break the dissident grip on power, we needed to insert loyalists. The Path of Echoes was motivated to weaken or redirect the Church's attention for ideological reasons, so we sought loyalists with ties to the Path who could leverage those alliances to assist us in our mutual aims.

"Blood and bones," Uppercut muttered. "Please continue."

To make a long story short, Tyvissi smiled, *the dissidents brought in the Draper to unstitch loyalist efforts as a terrorist, using mayhem and violence. He was unpredictable and savage, disrupting the rhythm of operation. The Draper forced us to divert our attention to dealing with him. Part of that disruption was assassinating key leaders, including me,* Tyvissi observed, hand on his chest. *He caught up to me in Jayan Park.*

Uppercut shifted, uncomfortable. "And vengeance doesn't drive you."

Vengeance? No. Tyvissi flickered over to the window, clasping his hands behind his back as he took in the unreal view. *My faithful entourage spirited me away and submerged me in a concentrating solution for a decade, until I rose a specter. By then the conflict was decisively won by the dissidents, so I have been engaged in a long-form resistance ever since.*

"Resistance, right. The Spirit Wardens are keen to destroy you," Uppercut observed. "What is it you want? I mean, what are you trying to accomplish?"

I will see to it that the lightning walls are shut down. Together with my allies, I will restore the warding rituals to protect the city.

Uppercut's eyes were round with shock. Tyvissi continued without turning.

Please, no platitudes about the horrors of human sacrifice or the advances of science. Any apologist who can walk through the tenement next to a textile mill, or one of our packed orphanages, or the workings of the coal mines, then tell me about precious human life... these people are not to be taken seriously. They destroy lives and crush people for wealth. That is not any nobler than sacrificing people to shield civilization from death storms.

Tyvissi flickered back to his throne. *Leviathans have too much power over humanity as it is. Mortals do not understand the patience of their plans. As knowledge of Heritage ritual fades among the young people, and as the elders die, human reliance on Leviathan plasmics increases. You cannot for a moment think that humans surprise the Leviathans on the open sea and steal from them without some level of acquiescence from the Elder Demons.*

Noiseless and fluid, the image of Tyvissi leaned forward. *What would happen, do you think, if a year went by with no successful hunts? Let's choose one of many possible outcomes, and speculate on how simple it would be for a faction to seize control if that faction offered the only reliable source of Leviathan blood. What if it was a charismatic individual who seemed to have influence with the Leviathans?* Tyvissi relaxed.

I know of one charismatic individual, and one faction, who have laid the foundation and worked on contingencies to take advantage of just such a situation. There is a fine line between speculation and opportunity, and those who have prepared can trigger both.

"So do you have, what, a supply of menhirs? I thought only the Immortal Emperor knew how to lay the foundation for city-wide protection through the old ways," Uppercut said.

We have experimented for centuries. We have solved the problems, Tyvissi emoted. *Still, there is only one meaningful obstacle to the implementation of this objective. Before I can accomplish a transition of protective methodology, I must first drive the Spirit Wardens from Doskvol as part of a larger scheme to destroy the order utterly.*

"Wow," Uppercut said, otherwise speechless.

A liquid ripple of amusement flowed from Tyvissi. *Delightful. My friend, you do not know what the Spirit Wardens aim to do. You do not understand why they pursue their research with such fervor, why they accept some alliances and reject others.*

"I am fully prepared to take your version with a grain of salt," Uppercut said with a wry grin, his mind reeling. "This feels too much like the sort of conspiracy theorizing I used to get pulled into, late at night in the back rooms of taverns on Ink Lane."

I expect nothing less than skepticism, Tyvissi replied. *Some truth is too painful to bear without seasoning and preparation. Still, I will plant this seed of knowledge, and it is up to you whether you nurture it or dig it out. And while skepticism is useful, I trust I will not encounter unreasoning disbelief.*

"Please go on," Uppercut said, a glint in his eye.

The Spirit Wardens have long term plans to subjugate demons and open up a multi-realm empire. They intend to conquer and fortify other worlds so they can extract resources for human use. What's more, they believe that the shattering of the Gates of Death put humanity on a necessary path to redefine what humanity means, expanding our capacities of sense, spirit, body, and communication. When they look to steal from demons and alien intellects, they want resources to transform themselves to become a new kind of human.

Tyvissi paused, considering Uppercut. The Whisper stood motionless, thinking fast, an expression of vague horror shaping his features.

I think these pursuits are unwise, Tyvissi echoed, mild. *Our current flawed limits are for the best. We should aim to develop safe areas here, where the Mirror is at arm's length. We must bend our efforts towards restoring the wholeness of the world, rather than conquering through the breach in it.*

"But there you're working against your own interests again," Uppercut said, blinking. "What role would you have in such a world?"

Do not confuse my fate with my objectives, Tyvissi chided. *I am... a corrective measure. I exist because we have fallen too far out of balance. If that balance is restored, I am no longer needed. If my choice was genuinely between rest and eternal life, the choice would be simple. However, as I said, I serve the Immortal Emperor. Whether he has embraced the madness of the Spirit Wardens or not, their destruction is in His best interest.*

"So... pushing back the Spirit Wardens... that's the main objective of the Reconciled?" Uppercut asked as he struggled to wrap his mind around this new perspective. "I mean, it's common knowledge there's a long feud there, because Spirit Wardens are protection against ghosts."

The escalation of the conflict, and its motives, twisted as they were mirrored against Uppercut's previous understanding.

It is not so simple as that, but I think you could accurately say it is an objective we all support. To this end, we ally with other corrective measures. Such as Whispers. The Spirit Wardens may feud with some sects of Whispers, but they believe these expanded senses and abilities, this power to manipulate the Mirror and its creatures, is the future for all of us. Tyvissi paused. *I prefer a future where Whispers are few, defending the portals between, but otherwise of little use.* The specter's head tilted. *Which would you prefer?*

"What I have experienced is not what I would choose for everyone," Uppercut said through his teeth.

Including you?

Uppercut hesitated only a moment, then nodded.

But if someone offered you peace. Rest. The easy way out. And all you had to do was let them have their way.

Uppercut looked the lion mask in the eye and said nothing.

I knew we would understand each other, Tyvissi rippled, satisfied.

"I mean, as far as it goes, this is all... it's a lot. And maybe it makes too much sense. Feels too tidy," Uppercut frowned. "Even if all this is true, can the Reconciled trust their own motives? I mean, what if there is something behind all this that is weaponizing the Reconciled to neutralize a threat posed by the Spirit Wardens?"

Indeed, Tyvissi echoed. *There is certainly some of that going on. And there are other factions as well, especially if you widen your consideration to involve the Forgotten Gods.*

"Yes, Forgotten Gods, I have questions," Uppercut said quickly.

This is not the time, Tyvissi replied. *Shimmer will be looking for Skau's head. We approach the defining confrontation of our little drama. I am to die, after all.*

"Right, about that," Uppercut said as he made a determined effort to refocus. "What do you want from me? And why won't you involve Scarecrow?"

We will have a showdown with the Draper, Tyvissi mused. *We don't want to complicate that unduly by contaminating Scarecrow with traces of my presence. After all, the Draper is going to defeat me, and I am going to kill him, to wrap it all up for Shimmer.*

"You seem pretty calm about all this," Uppercut said, eyeing Tyvissi with some suspicion.

Of course. I have been getting too much attention lately. It is time for me to disappear again, to throw my foes off the scent and give me more freedom to work.

"I can feel your power," Uppercut said. "You have resources, allies, connections... all that in addition to your experience and your personal..." he waved vaguely. "What do you need me for? I mean, if the rest of the Reconciled are like you, why not move against the Spirit Wardens more directly and give up all this cloak and dagger? Do they really constrain you?"

We do not have time right now to get into more secrets of the Spirit Wardens. They have developed secret weapons over the centuries, and they have borrowed, traded, and stolen objects and techniques from worlds beyond this one. For example, their life force is warped to connect back to an other-dimensional access point. Spectral combat with Spirit Wardens carries the risk of being caught up in that connection and dragged out of the world. They have other... weapons. Deterrents. Things they may release if they are pressed. Tyvissi paused. *Like me, they are willing to die to win.*

Tyvissi flicked to Uppercut once more, looking down on him, his lion mask inscrutable. *We must go gently. We must be subtle and patient. We must force them out over time, building support as we go, so humanity is ready to survive without them. You will not understand, but for now, that must be enough.*

"More than enough," Uppercut said, ignoring the sour taste in his mouth.

I have questions of my own, Tyvissi continued. *The most pressing is, what are you willing to do, to stand against the Spirit Wardens and their forces? Understanding some of the dangers, are you willing to pit your life force against their threat?*

Uppercut's eyes were clear. "Yes."

Good. We haven't got much time.

The pool stirred, then rippled. A glow from deeper than the pool's stone floor lit the chamber, then Uppercut rose through the surface, eyes closed, his face slack. He shivered, then his eyes snapped open.

"Welcome back," Vans said, polite.

Uppercut looked down at himself, surprised to see he still wore the black coat and suit he imagined during his conversation with Tyvissi. Water beaded on the fabric, he felt it soaking into the pants. Uppercut sloshed over to the side of the pool and stepped up out of it.

"New clothes I guess," he muttered.

"A gift from Lord Tyvissi," Vans agreed. "It's a little consideration he likes to offer his guests."

"Just when you think he's done giving you things," Uppercut frowned, his thoughts distant.

"It's best not to think about it," Vans smiled.

"If only," Uppercut said to himself. He reoriented on Vans. "I'm going to need that head."

"Of course," Vans said. "I have it packaged by the door. You may leave when you are ready." His smile widened. "Visitors often need a moment to collect themselves after a chat with Lord Tyvissi."

"Packaged, that sounds promising," Uppercut said. "Were you able to, you know, shut him up?"

"Not entirely. It's a little too complicated," Vans replied.

"How is it complicated?" Uppercut asked. "I mean, I know it's weird, that he's still talking. I'm not asking how it's complicated to shut up a severed head. I mean, how is it complicated generally, in the sense that death usually simplifies things and shuts people up. At least their bodies get real quiet. How is that bastard still aware and talking?" He paused. "Without lungs, too."

"Skau made many... commitments," Vans said delicately. "He was not supporting Lord Tyvissi so much as he was anchoring him. The difference is subtle, but it matters. The connection he had to Lord Tyvissi is severed, but he was also connected to other patrons." Vans hesitated.

"Past the bone, you see. Deeper than flesh, or blood. He is tied to something further out in the Void than Leviathans." His features shifted with distaste. "What matters here," he continued, refocusing, "is that Shimmer will be satisfied because the memorial ink is disconnected. Still. It is best not to let her chat with Skau overmuch."

"In and out, that's what I would prefer," Uppercut growled. "I'm ready to get clear of this mess."

"I hope you mean clear of Shimmer," Vans said. "There are other associations that could result from this unfortunate episode that could be to our mutual benefit." He cocked his head to the side. "You already have a contact or two in the Path of Echoes."

"True," Uppercut nodded, brushing water off his coat. "I think it's safe to say I'm committing to the cause of the Reconciled, at some level." He looked Vans in the eye. "I don't know about the Path of Echoes."

"There are shades and complexities to the motivations that drive loyalty for all of us," Vans said. "Our interests overlap in some places, but not others. It is to be expected. We are a consortium, after all, rather than a cult. A consortium with resources. Oh, that reminds me," he said, dipping into his pocket and pulling out a neatly folded card. "Here is an address."

"Alright," Uppercut said, taking the card and reading the printed address. "And?"

"Our people at this address will give you and Scarecrow some House Guard uniforms and passwords. No need to tell anyone else we were involved."

"What, you think we're doing a heist or something for you?" Uppercut growled, eyebrows bristling. "That wasn't part of any deal we talked about."

"It's not for us," Vans clarified. "It's for you. For the heist you're trying to do, on short notice. Scarecrow will explain. Consider it a gesture of goodwill." His smile was broad and gleaming.

"I'll do that," Uppercut said cautiously. "What time is it?"

Vans checked his intricate pocket watch. "Quarter past nine. Midafternoon." He looked to Uppercut. "You have over eight hours until Shimmer's deadline." Vans snapped the watch shut.

"I don't suppose you could give us a sense of where she is so we could turn the head in early," Uppercut asked without optimism.

"No need. She'll find you long before the deadline, I suspect," Vans observed. "We are watching the coming confrontation with great interest, and we are invested in your success," he said seriously.

"Who is 'we' and how are you watching us?" Uppercut asked.

"The Path of Echoes," Vans clarified. "You know about picket ghosts, echoes tasked with reporting activity from their perches behind the Mirror. The Path of Echoes has more elaborate surveillance options. We have already interfered in the confrontation as much as we dare. The rest is up to you." He paused. "The Path of Echoes and the Reconciled have shared resources and covered for each other as a matter of course through the centuries. Lord Tyvissi occupies a fortress built by the Path of Echoes, and our mortal contacts assist the designs of the Reconciled just as our designs require their knowledge and power. We are aiming to craft a different world than the one reinforced by the Spirit Wardens and their allies in the Ministry and the Church." Vans looked Uppercut in the eye. "I think you'd like our world better."

"I am already going to bleed for the current plan," Uppercut said, mild. "Let's get through this next bit before we map out the future."

"Of course." Vans gestured gallantly towards the exit, and followed Uppercut into the adjacent room. Carc perched on a heavy carrying case, eyeing the Whisper.

"Let's get this done," Uppercut muttered. Carc sprang from the case, sailing out the open door and up the stairs to the alley beyond. Uppercut hefted the case, ignoring the tremble of something thrashing inside, and followed.

KETTLEBOX COURT. NIGHTMARKET
40ᵀᴴ MENDAR, 850. *ABOUT HALF AN HOUR LATER*
TENTH HOUR PAST DAWN

The door handle shifted, and Scarecrow stopped pacing to line up a pistol on the entry.

"It's just me, Zekel," came a muffled voice from the other side. "I'm opening the door."

"Oh yeah?" Scarecrow retorted. "Best drink in Holloway."

"Goatsnout Stout," Zekel replied. "Okay?"

"Come on in," Scarecrow said, easing the hammer back on the pistol and lowering it to his side. He felt a pang, missing his crossbow, but he scowled the thought away.

Zekel closed the door behind himself. "I got your message, and came as quickly as I could," he said.

"Have you heard from Uppercut," Scarecrow demanded, his jaw locked as he tried to keep his voice low.

"No."

"Damn." Scarecrow pivoted, staring out the window, struggling with his frustration. "Okay. Do you know where White Corners is?"

"White Corners?" Zekel echoed, surprised. "I mean... there's a posh and high security area in Charterhall, in the shadow of the Spark Tower of the University, called White Corners. Does that sound like what you're looking for?"

"What, you don't think that's my style?" Scarecrow said, wry. "Well you're right. I need to know where someone is, in the White Corners. Who has rooms there. Which ones."

"That's all pretty confidential," Zekel cautioned. "People pay extra for privacy. But if you're willing to spend for it," he continued thoughtfully, "I know of a university register that tracks contracts and leases. The University is the landlord for the whole block."

"And you know a clerk or something," Scarecrow prompted.

"I might know someone who could take a look for us," Zekel nodded. "How much time do we have to handle this with some delicacy?"

"We need to set up, carry out the heist, and be back here by midnight," Scarecrow growled, not looking Zekel in the eye.

"Huh." Zekel blinked. "Tonight?"

"Yes tonight," Scarecrow snapped. "*This* midnight. Eight hours." He thrust the pistol into his belt, struggling to contain his reaction. "We are rescuing someone. It's not ideal. I know that. We don't have the resources or the time." He scowled. "Or the people."

"I'll do what I can," Zekel said, hesitant.

"There's no way the two of us pull this off, I know that," Scarecrow said, sharp. "So we need more. Damn. Dammit." He kicked a chair, and stood still, thinking hard about who he dared include. Then he shook his head, and barked a laugh. "Okay. Here we go." He looked Zekel in the eye. "Desperate times." He picked up two pitchers from the sideboard, and stepped into the bedroom.

Kneeling by Granite, he put the pitchers on the floor and drew his knife. Scarecrow sawed at the ropes binding the big Skov. Once the snoring giant's hands were freed, Scarecrow tilted a pitcher of cold water over his head.

Granite snorted, and sprayed water from his beard. He shifted, his face bunching up as the headache rode his blood all the way through his skull.

"I need your help," Scarecrow said, fierce. "You and me, we are going to mount a rescue."

"Wut," Granite managed, disoriented.

"Listen to me," Scarecrow demanded, rising to his feet. "You are more than a soldier. You are a warrior. The war isn't over. It just looks different here."

Granite squinted up at him, pushing through his confusion and pain, then frowned hard and struggled to rise.

"It's been a long time since you did more than grease the way for criminals," Scarecrow said, switching to Skovic. "Your people still need you, and you are no deserter."

"I'm gonna kick your ass," Granite snapped, then he blinked and steadied himself.

"Shimmer captured an Illustrated Master," Scarecrow continued, undaunted. "I am not going to let that disrespect stand. Shimmer has been in Akoros long enough to believe she can do whatever she wants as long as she is rich. As long as she can hire people to hurt her enemies. She has the protection of powerful people. What about you?" he demanded. "Is Akoros in your blood now? Do you think connections and money are what make you powerful? Do you think these people should be able to do anything they want if they buy your service first?" He leaned towards Granite, staring him in the eye. "Specifically *your* service?"

"You are *such* an *idiot*," Granite snarled. "You dress up your stupid crimes in some sort of loyalty to Skovlan, like you're a waterblooded folk hero in some story. You want to talk about Skovlan? You want to talk about *my people?*" he roared, pounding his chest. "*My people* don't want anything to do with me!" he shouted. "Ask your precious Knotwork. They shut me out!"

Scarecrow blinked. "They did?"

"Guess you didn't hear," Granite ground out, leaning over the smaller man. "When I first got here, I did some quiet work for the Ministry. The Knotwork found out, won't let it go. They don't trust me," he sneered. "They don't have *fine words* about how I'm a *warrior* in the tradition of *Skov heroes*." The sarcasm was painful.

"Well they're wrong," Scarecrow said, chin jutting out. "They don't see what I see. They may not trust you. But I do." He stared right into the furious Skov's eye, unafraid. "You do this with me, and I'll get you into the Knotwork."

"You think if I betray Shimmer I'll be trustworthy for you?" Granite scoffed, dumbfounded. "That's beyond naive, you moron. The Knotwork will never listen to you anyway."

"The Knotwork doesn't get to tell me who you are," Scarecrow replied, his voice level. "Shimmer doesn't get to tell me who you are." He nodded to Granite. "Under all that I can feel the Skov blood in your veins, right beside the sea salt and the old songs. I know a lot of turncoats. Weak and petty men. That's not you." His brow furrowed. "Is it." He held the knife out to Granite, hilt first.

Granite took the knife, staring down at his captor.

A croak sounded from the next room, and the window rattled in its frame with a gust from the downbeat of wings. Zekel quickly opened the window, and Carc hopped on the table.

Scarecrow turned his back on Granite, who blinked and struggled against the painful fog of the drug's aftereffects and the indecision that rooted him in place.

Peering out the now-open window, Scarecrow saw Uppercut carrying a heavy case as he crossed the street, incoming.

"Well," Scarecrow muttered, "things are looking up." He allowed himself a bleak smile.

CHAPTER SIXTEEN

The Lord Governor had publicly stated that Skovs were only good for work. If they could not or would not labor, they drained the state's resources and stirred up unrest. In the winter of 812, hundreds of Skovic refugees were charged with wartime espionage and held in Ironhook's Sifting Square. The courtyard was converted to a deadly holding pen. Prisoners were exposed to the elements without adequate food, shelter, or medicine.

A Skov spy, Selray, knew the atrocity in Sifting Square was designed to provoke the resistance to attack. The prison fortifications were defended by two hardened companies of Akrosian troops. Mounting a rescue would be suicide.

So, Selray led a suicide mission. Posing as a work crew, Selray and four agents smuggled in electroplasmic bombs disguised as large paving blocks. The spies "made repairs" to Ironhook's outer wall, hauling out massive cracked stones and replacing them with explosives as soldiers watched.

The bombs were mostly in place before Selray was recognized and the "work crew" was caught. According to legend, a guard questioned Selray: "What are you up to?" His reply: "Not work!" And with that, the spies detonated the blocks. The explosion cracked windows as far away as Nightmarket.

The east wall's defenses were in disarray. The Skov resistance breached Sifting Square and fought a high-casualty holding action as the prisoners escaped.

Many escapees joined the Skov resistance. They honored the Sifting Square Martyrs by continuing Selray's "not work," draining the state's resources and stirring up unrest. This subversive organization came to be known as the Knotwork.

—From "Legends of Resistance: Tales of Scovic Provocations"
By Canar Roluvian

Scarecrow jogged down the creaking stairs, rounding the bannister. He intercepted Uppercut, who glanced up with alarm as he heard rapid movement closing in.

"So tell me where you've been," Scarecrow said with false lightness as he squared off with the Whisper.

Uppercut was pale. "We had best discuss that later. What did Getch have to say."

"You've got the head, right?" Scarecrow countered, pointing at the case.

"Yes. Contained. Quiet, for now," Uppercut said. "Our plan worked."

"Ah. That's... good. Right?" Scarecrow raised his eyebrows, trying not to wince.

"It's good." Uppercut glanced around. "Let's talk upstairs."

"Or outside," Scarecrow suggested. "We are out of food. I need some supper. Figure we could get a foldable from the corner cart."

"Alright, but I had best put this away upstairs first. You can bring me something. We aren't leaving it unattended and I want to keep it off the street," Uppercut said, hefting the case.

"Upstairs is no good. Let's walk and talk," Scarecrow said, passing Uppercut and pushing the door open. Glancing both ways, he stepped out to the street, the Whisper following him.

"What's going on upstairs," Uppercut muttered, not really wanting to know.

"Granite," Scarecrow replied under his breath, jamming his fists in his coat pockets and setting a brisk pace. "Let me start further back, with Getch."

"Please do," Uppercut growled.

"Jafrain came out of her binge drinking with some kind of clarity. Maybe she figured out what Shimmer is up to, trying to save her," Scarecrow explained. "Sounds like she tracked down Shimmer and confronted her, so Shimmer basically captured her. Getch tried to locate Jafrain when she didn't come back to the shop. Shimmer's people beat him, but he wouldn't drop it. He contacted me, and for that, Granite put a death mark on him. Getch was warned to leave it alone, but he didn't. We have to get Shimmer out."

"Only half of what you're telling me is making sense," Uppercut frowned.

"Right, stick with me," Scarecrow nodded. "Granite ambushed me after Getch left, told me he was supposed to kill anyone who was going to make a move on Jafrain. But, Shimmer *also* told him to keep you and me alive. So he was trying to figure out what to do."

Scarecrow scratched his beard. "I did some fast talking. Told Granite a story, that Shimmer was really trying to stop the Draper, and Granite could get around this conundrum by helping us destroy the Draper. That was a victory he could report to Shimmer, to get on her good side."

"And he *agreed*?" Uppercut said, dumbfounded.

"I can be very persuasive," Scarecrow sniffed. "I brought him back here, planning to involve you in my misdirection. But you were gone."

"Yeah, I got an audience with the big guy," Uppercut rumbled, glancing around the street.

"So I stalled with a fake ritual," Scarecrow continued. "Marked up the floor. You know."

"Granite thinks you're taking a break from summoning a ghost?"

"No, he got bored. Helped himself to the sideboard wine," Scarecrow said.

"I told you that would work," Uppercut grinned.

"Sure did. He went down," Scarecrow agreed. "Problem is, we have to rescue Jafrain. We don't have the time, resources, planning, nothing," he said, his amusement cooling fast.

"Did Getch get anything? We can't start from nothing," Uppercut scowled.

"Yeah, Getch tracked her down to White Corners, it's a posh setup in Charterhall," Scarecrow explained. "I called Zekel in, he's heard of it. Says the University is the landlord. Zekel thinks he can figure out which apartment Shimmer leases if we can dig up some resources for bribes." He hesitated. "That's as far as I got. We have less than eight hours to pull this off."

"House Guard," Uppercut said reflectively.

"They'll be all over it," Scarecrow agreed. "Security is going to be tight."

The scoundrels reached the pushcart that was tucked up against the alcove of a shuttered corner store, the vendor huddled in the doorway for warmth. They bought a box of foldables, the meat and mushroom pockets still warm in the milled kelpflour wraps.

"Likely to snow tonight," the vendor wheezed, sullen behind his smile.

"Stay warm," Scarecrow nodded absently, tossing some currency on the cart's lid. The scoundrels turned away, and got some distance before resuming their conversation.

"So you have an unconscious killer upstairs," Uppercut prompted.

"Not anymore," Scarecrow said around a mouthful of food. "I woke him up and told him he was going to help us out."

Uppercut stopped, staring at the Skov.

"I appealed to his warrior breeding and patriotism," Scarecrow said, grinning.

"What."

Scarecrow swallowed. "Yeah, he doesn't like Shimmer. And once I talked him out of the confrontation in the alley, he knew in the back of his mind he'd have to explain *that* to Shimmer. Once he didn't get the win, nailing the Draper, he'd have to explain how I got the drop on him. Or at least hope she didn't find out. He's moved outside his orders, he's followed my lead, and every time he does that I get a little more leverage. I'm making the most of it." His eyes narrowed. "Dammit Uppercut, I can't rescue Jafrain alone. I don't think the two of us can pull it off without help. We need him, and I got him, and we'll have to make it work."

"You think he's still up there?" Uppercut growled. "You think he didn't take off as soon as his hypnotist ran an errand? If he *is* still there, then we're walking into an ambush!"

"I got Granite to trust me," Scarecrow retorted, "and now I need my partner to trust me too. Right now. We have a lot to figure out and we're running out of time."

"Okay, trust," Uppercut nodded curtly. "I need the zemi."

Scarecrow blinked. "Uh... Shimmer told me to keep it with me at all times until this is over."

"We aren't very obedient, are we," Uppercut observed.

Scarecrow slowly reached into his jacket, and pulled the zemi out of the inner pocket. Hesitating, he frowned, then offered the stone to Uppercut.

"Thank you," Uppercut said, taking it. "I'll keep it safe." He slid the zemi into his coat, patting the pocket.

"You went shopping for clothes at a time like this?" Scarecrow said, looking over Uppercut's imposing outfit as he tried to deal with his discomfort.

"A gift from our new friend," Uppercut muttered. "Are you sure it's a good idea for you, particularly, to be in a dangerous situation with Jafrain? Considering? I mean... accidents happen."

"I don't like it," Scarecrow said. "I thought about leaving it alone until after all this is over. But if we do that, Getch will be dead. I can't predict what Shimmer will do next. This feels like our best chance."

"You know nothing will kill Jafrain but you, right?" Uppercut said, something curious in his tone. "Because of fate."

"Don't tease me," Scarecrow said, brow furrowed. "Not about this. I don't know." He took another big bite of his foldable. "You wanna try it without me?" he demanded around a mouthful of mushroom.

"I don't want to try it at all. You could focus on protecting Getch instead. That seems like it would make more sense. But that's not accounting for *destiny*," Uppercut mused. "I am troubled," he said quietly. "I think Tyvissi already knew you were going to rescue Jafrain. He didn't tell me that, in so many words, but she is part of his plan."

Scarecrow stopped chewing, then swallowed hard. "What... what's he like?" Scarecrow murmured, leaning in closer.

"Like nothing I've ever seen," Uppercut replied quietly. "This is all going to get very strange."

"Just now?" Scarecrow retorted.

"We need Jafrain, and we need to get to her quickly. Then I've got some work to do. You'll have to handle the last stretch without me," Uppercut said, unsettlingly focused. "A lot will change tonight. For all of us."

"Okay, you gotta tell me more about this meet," Scarecrow insisted.

"No, I can't," Uppercut said. "You are going to be with Shimmer. With Spirit Wardens. So you must not know the plan."

"I guess that makes sense," Scarecrow agreed reluctantly. "How about the plan to get to Jafrain?"

"That we work out together, right now," Uppercut said as he glanced around the street. More people were moving about now, as the early shift was trudging home before dusk. "Let's go."

The scoundrels crossed the street and pushed into Kettlebox Court, mounting the stairs and approaching their door with some caution.

Scarecrow stepped in. He concealed his relief to see Granite sitting stoically at the table, fists planted, red-rimmed eyes glaring at him. Zekel leaned against the wall on the other side of the room, trying to look casual.

"Look who's back," Granite said, his jaw locked.

"I got us a Whisper," Scarecrow said.

"I guess that's not nothing," Granite growled, and his nostrils flared.

"Zekel," said Uppercut, "we need you to move fast. Work with your contact. Figure out what suite Shimmer is renting in White Corners. We can't plan out the rest until we know where Jafrain is held."

Scarecrow pried up the counter with a screech of stressed nails. Reaching into the dim cavity below, he disarmed a trap, and pulled out a box. "This is the *emergency* emergency fund," he said, turning to Zekel. He jogged the box, and it rattled with currency. "Should be enough here to bribe your clerk friend." He handed it to Zekel.

Zekel nodded, and scurried out.

"We can make *some* plans," Granite said. "We'll have to get into the building, unless you think we'll hit her place from outside." He paused. "Which I would not recommend."

"I have a source for current House Guard uniforms and passwords," Uppercut said. "What other supplies will we need?"

"I figure it's time for bad news," Scarecrow grinned.

"Yes," Uppercut agreed, thoughtful. "Bad news, indeed."

Granite closed his eyes, rubbed his forehead, and struggled to make peace with the decisions that brought him to this point.

WHITE CORNERS. CHARTERHALL
40TH MENDAR, 850. *FIVE HOURS LATER*
HOUR OF SILVER, 3 HOURS PAST DUSK

"Quit fussing with it," Uppercut said under his breath. "We're almost there."

"I don't think I got the fold right," Granite frowned, tugging at the sash of his House Guard uniform. His was tighter than Uppercut's. Their contact was fortunate to have anything close to big enough for Granite's wide shoulders.

"We'll cover it over with confidence," Uppercut said. "Get ready."

The coach rolled to a halt, and Uppercut exited first. Granite followed, ducking under the strap of his sling bag. The coach rattled off as they approached the guards flanking the entryway to a courtyard.

"Evening," Uppercut said, mild. "Figure it will snow?"

"Password," the guard said, eyeing him.

"Sunset Ridge," Uppercut replied, something tense in his tone.

"No," the guard frowned, planting his hand on the butt of his pistol. Two other guards noticed, focusing on the newcomers.

"Really? Must be a roster mixup. That's a shame," Uppercut said with something like relief. "Here, you can deliver this for us." He offered a black scrollcase to the guard. "Message for the Gazelle Suite."

"Hang on," the guard protested, recoiling from the scrollcase. "Is that from the Church?"

"I didn't ask and I don't want to know," Uppercut said loudly, taking a step forward. "Now take this and deliver it. I forgot the password, so I can't go in. It's as simple as that," he insisted.

"That's yesterday's password, and you know it," the other guard chimed in. "Who sent you?"

"I can't tell you that," Uppercut said through his teeth. "It doesn't matter. There's a message. It's for the Gazelle Suite. That's all we need to know. Right?" He waggled the scrollcase. The glare of the plasmic lamps shone on the pressed black wax of the seal.

"You think you can come here from Brightstone," the guard retorted, frowning at the insignia on Uppercut's collar, "and make us do your dirty work? Not likely. Did you bring a recipient waiver so you can drop it off?"

Uppercut gritted his teeth. "It's hand delivery only," he admitted grudgingly. "But I can hand it to you, and you can hand it to the recipient—who could be anyone," he said too quickly.

The other guard scowled at the scoundrels. "I guess we could send notice to Gazelle Suite to come collect a priority message," he said.

"Yeah," the first guard said sarcastically, "let's go ahead and have that scene here at the gate."

"We can't do that anyway," the third guard protested. "Gazelle Suite? There's the *special order* on that one," he said, raising his eyebrows, reminding the others. "She can't come down here."

"Fellas," Granite interrupted, "I was supposed to be off duty an hour ago. But you know the protocols. Nobody carries one of these alone. Gotta make sure it arrives. So here I am. Can we wrap this up please?" he said, almost petulant.

"What's that you've got there," the guard demanded, noticing Granite's bag.

"I'm overnighting somewhere," Granite said suggestively. "And this is cutting into my *overnight time.*"

The gate guards exchanged an amused glance. Uppercut rolled his eyes.

"Okay you know what, I messed up, I forgot the password," Uppercut said. "So let's do this. Let's get an exception form, and we can all sign it, so we document every person who was here. Right down to the date and time. A tidy list of *everybody involved*, and you can submit it to the head office. I think that's the best thing!"

Two gate guards stepped back and looked away, to the chagrin of the one who challenged Uppercut in the first place. "A tidy list," he echoed, grim.

"I think that's best," Uppercut repeated, looking him in the eye, his heart pounding. "In case anybody has questions later. Wants to know more." He still held out the scrollcase. "Or you could just take this and deliver it."

"I have a better idea," the guard scowled. "Fackrell. Check the roster. The code. Are we still in the overlap to acknowledge it?"

"Turns out we are," Fackrell lied, not bothering to check the roster.

"I guess we're all in luck," the guard said, staring Uppercut in the eye. "How about you deliver that message."

"I thought you said this was gonna work," Grante muttered under his breath, glaring at Uppercut.

Uppercut studied the guard for a calculated moment, then lowered his arm. "Okay fine," he said. "Thank you for your cooperation." He straightened. "Duty is my satisfaction; service, my pleasure," he quoted.

"Oh, same," the gate guard grinned. "You know the way to the Gazelle Suite?"

"No," Uppercut said, rubbing his eyes.

"Fackrell!" the guard said.

"Dammit," Fackrell sighed.

The guard gallantly waved Uppercut and Granite in, and the scoundrels followed Fackrell past the elegant topiary around the entry to White Corners. The gate clanged shut behind them.

The compact foyer and staircases had an understated luxury and high security. Climbing three flights of stairs, they passed guards posted in the stairwell at each level. Fackrell led them down a hallway, their footfalls absorbed in the carpeting. A radiant vine plant was cultivated on a shelf at eye level, fancifully curling along the hall's length and providing a delicate light that blended with the plasmic lamps shining through frosted shades.

Two House Guard stood flanking the doorway to the Gazelle Suite. They eyed the approaching guards with curiosity. One stepped forward.

"What's this then," he demanded.

"Coldcuts," Fackrell said. The password did little to relax the guards at the door. "They have a message, hand delivery only."

"Alright then," the door guard nodded. He turned and slotted his key in the lock, turning it so the latch retracted—

Uppercut jabbed a blow into Fackrell's face, staggering the startled man. Granite snatched one door guard and slung him into the other; both targets were carried off their feet by the force of the attack, and as they clattered down, Granite rushed over and stamped down at their heads. Uppercut whipped a punch and backhand strike across Fackrell's head, stunning him as the plasmic light glinted on the iron knuckles reinforcing Uppercut's fist.

Relentless, the scoundrels shoved or dragged the battered guards through the unlocked door. Jafrain stood in the center of the plushly appointed suite, a dagger in her hand and surprise in her eyes.

"It's a rescue," Uppercut gritted out as Granite slugged a struggling guard, knocking the rest of the fight out of him. Uppercut shoved Fackrell, who sprawled headfirst into a pillar and rebounded with a meaty crack.

"Who are you people?" Jafrain demanded.

"Getch. Figured out where Shimmer put you. Hired us," Uppercut said. "We have to go. Now," he insisted.

"Getch is a nosy bastard," Jafrain said through her teeth. "Alright, let's go."

Granite was already back in the doorway, peering out. "Looks like the stairwell guard didn't hear us," he muttered.

"Back stairs," Uppercut nodded.

The scoundrels escorted the Illuminated Master out of the suite, closing the door. They followed the hall to the servant staircase, tastefully out of the way and screened from view. Moving fast, they clattered up the spiral twist.

"Not downstairs?" Jafrain called out, trying to keep her voice down.

"No," Uppercut said.

They reached the door to the roof. It was fitted with heavy locks. Uppercut also felt a trickle of chill winding from it; an etheric switch that would be flicked if the door opened, notifying an adept somewhere downstairs.

Uppercut leaned against the door, quickly dragging the bolts open. From the inside, it was simple. He concentrated on the switch, trying to still his pumping blood so he could feel its nuance.

Then he swore. "Well, we were going fast anyway." He shoved the door open.

"Triggered it, didn't you," Granite said.

"Whatever," Uppercut said over his shoulder. "Come on."

The scoundrels spilled out onto the roof, and Granite slammed the door behind them. As Uppercut looked around for potential defenses, Granite ducked out of the shoulder strap of his bag, tugging it open.

"What now?" Jafrain demanded.

"The fun part," Granite said through his teeth. He lifted the pulley assembly out of the bag.

"Oh dear," Jafrain said faintly.

"Jam the door," Uppercut said. "Jafrain. Take the bar. Wedge it." He gestured towards the door. She ran over to it, cast about for the defensive bar, then set it in place to slow the defenders.

A hiss, then a crossbow bolt slammed into the brick of the chimney a few paces from the scoundrels. Matter-of-fact, Granite rose to his feet, his hands full with a hammer, piton with a ring end, and the pulley. The thin rope tied to the crossbow bolt still slithered in the wake of its momentum.

Uppercut snapped the bolt so the thin rope fell, then scooped it up and knotted it around the shaft of another crossbow bolt. He freed a collapsible crossbow from Granite's bag, folding the crossbow's body open and mounting the bow on the stock.

Working quickly, Granite slugged the stakes into the chimney and mounted the pulley, threading the light cable through. "Maybe post lookout," he growled to Jafrain without pausing.

Jafrain stared across the street to the brick building across the way. She saw a Skov on the roof, standing up from the shooting position with a heavy crossbow, gesturing an invitation.

"There," Uppercut muttered. "Clear my line."

Granite was already winding the thin cable around his palm and elbow. He shrugged out of the neat coil and set it at Uppercut's feet as the scoundrel balanced the crossbow on the roof ledge, squinting. He picked up the bolt with the cable, and slotted it into the crossbow groove.

"Aim high," Granite said, sharp. "Higher. *Higher.*"

"I've got it," Uppercut gritted out.

The door to the roof banged as guards found it barred. They began battering on the door with concerted blows.

Uppercut triggered the weaker crossbow, and the shaft whizzed up into the dimness, the cable's drag pulling it down as it sailed across the street.

Scarecrow ran to where the quarrel clattered on the roof then slithered towards the edge. Diving, he caught it. He scrambled to his feet and raced over to the pulley mounted on his side of the street, threading the cable through then tying it to the heavy crossbow. He ran to the edge of the roof and tossed the crossbow down on a cart.

Zekel looked up, Scarecrow waved the go-ahead, and Zekel flicked the reins. The goat trotted ahead, pulling the cart away, the crossbow in the back wedging itself against the back grating like an anchor as the cable slithered along through the pulleys.

The end of the cable was fixed to a heavier cable, which was dragged towards the pulley across the street, slowly bounding up and down with the friction as it was hauled towards the White Corners rooftop.

"Come on, hurry," Uppercut said, straining as he heard the hinges begin to splinter on the rooftop entry.

"I don't like this plan," Jafrain said, eyes wide as she stared down four storeys to unforgiving cobbles below.

"Nobody likes this plan," Granite agreed, pulling gaff hooks from his belt and twisting each hook to be perpendicular to the grip. "But here we are."

The cart dragged the cable to a comical overextension as it was forced to round a corner, following the street. The cable rasped along the facades of the buildings along its trail. Granite's quick hands made sure the heavier cable made it through the pulley, following the lighter cable back towards Scarecrow.

"Couldn't do a zip line," Uppercut explained, terse. "No good positions for it. Climbing across would be too slow. This is our way out."

"Shimmer will have you killed if this goes wrong," Jafrain said. Her tone had more worry than threat.

Uppercut barked a laugh. "She'll try to kill us if this goes *right*."

"Get the flask," Granite said.

Uppercut pulled the last object out of Granite's bag, a glass bottle with a complex metal cap. "Think they are coming through?"

"You used to be a Bluecoat," Granite growled. "What do you think."

A wrenching creak followed the bang as the House Guard knocked the door loose. One more push would do it.

Uppercut yanked the metal cable in the teeth of the mechanism on the lid, and a shower of sparks poured up from it. He hurled the glass bottle, and it shattered on the breaking door, sloshing fuel all over the scene as the spark fountain lit it up. Guards screamed and swore, falling back down the stairs in a tumble.

"Get on it," Granite gritted out, pulling Jafrain over to the cable and pressing a gaff hook in her hand. "No time to think." He clacked the hook over the cable and pushed her. She screamed as she swung over the edge of the roof, two hands gripping the hook.

On the other rooftop, Scarecrow had taken the end of the heavy cable and fixed it to a net full of crates that was perched on the edge of the roof. He pulled a block out from under the support, and the whole stack slid off, hurtling down to shatter on the street below, spraying rocks everywhere.

The forceful pull of the plummeting crates dragged the cable, and Jafrain zoomed across the street as the first House Guards ran out of White Corners brandishing rifles.

Uppercut snapped off a couple shots with his pistol, startling the guards and pulling their attention to the White Corners roof. Across the street, Scarecrow opened his arms wide, catching Jafrain as she slid over the lip of the roof to relative safety.

The Illuminated Master was winded and dazed by her flight, but her eyes widened as she recognized Scarecrow. "You!" she gasped. "Are you here for me now?"

"No," Scarecrow said firmly. "I understand. I get it. Neither towards, nor away from. We will follow our paths. And it won't be today." He looked her in the eye.

"Okay," she managed. "What now?"

"We have a coach downstairs. Come on." Turning away, he ran to the open door leading into the building. Jafrain followed.

Uppercut grimaced as he reloaded, the pistol's metal hot. "We'll never make it across if they are shooting at us," he said.

"Right," Granite nodded. "We go with the backup plan."

"Cracks and knobs," Uppercut swore. "Let's do it."

Granite grinned, his blood flowing true and hot. Just like the old days. He wrapped the cable around his wrist, then slid over the edge of the roof. The friction of the cable rattling through pulleys slowed him enough as he sailed down, firing at the surprised guards. Granite landed hard and rolled, dispersing the impact. Leaping to his feet, he raced down an alleyway, the House Guard in pursuit.

Meanwhile, on the rooftop, Uppercut circled back around the roof access that jutted up like a shed. Climbing on top of it, he crouched out of sight. Guards crashed through the smoldering door, guns drawn, fanning out to cover the roof. Uppercut slid down the back and stepped boldly into the search pattern, still wearing his House Guard uniform.

"You!" called out one of the guards. "I don't recognize you!"

"Today's code is coldcut," Uppercut said. "Transfer. First day."

A cry went up as the guards found the pulley, and attention refocused. Uppercut crossed to the stairwell. "We found something!" he yelled, then he trotted down the stairs to carry the message to the captain who would be coordinating below.

From there, it was simple enough to join a search party and march out into the streets.

Granite stubbornly ignored the stitch in his side as he ran up to the goat cart and swung into the back. "Go already," he growled to Zekel, who snapped the reins and pulled away, melting into the traffic of the city streets as the House Guards rounded the corner at the end of the block.

"Did we win?" Zekel demanded.

"Yeah," Granite said, a grin stubbornly pushing to the fore. "We won."

"What is this," Jafrain demanded, seated across from Scarecrow in the jouncing coach as it rattled along.

"Getch came to me," Scarecrow said, eyes averted. "Your reaction to me scared him. We agreed to work together to figure out what set you off. When I checked with Kinlay, he explained it to me. You think I'm the undead that will kill you."

"Kinlay needs to keep his mouth shut," Jafrain said, mild.

"I didn't tell Getch. Anyway, Getch couldn't leave it alone when you disappeared. He tracked you to Shimmer, to White Corners. Contacted me. I couldn't leave you there." Scarecrow looked her in the eye. "I might not be alive this time tomorrow. If I was going to do something to free you, it had to be now."

Jafrain said nothing, her brow furrowed.

"My partner, Uppercut, says you're part of a plan. That there's a Reconciled who is waiting for you. Once we get you back in circulation," Scarecrow said.

"Let me guess," Jafrain said quietly. "Tyvissi."

"That's the one. We are headed to a drop point. Uppercut can take over from there. Get you to safety until this is over one way or another."

"What do you think is going on? What do you think 'this' is?" Jafrain asked.

"Our working theory: you told Shimmer that an undead would kill you, but you made her promise to leave it alone. She couldn't. So she's done all these divinations to find the one that threatens you... and she guessed wrong. She thinks the Draper, this murder specter, is 'undead' who will kill you. She plans to take him out." Scarecrow paused. "We don't think she realizes it's me. Or she would have killed me weeks ago."

Silent, Jafrain studied Scarecrow. She seemed to be a motionless point in a swirl of activity as the coach rolled through the streets, lights and shadows chasing each other across every surface.

"So... are we right?" Scarecrow asked in a small voice.

"I think maybe you are," Jafrain said at last. "Certain things make more sense from that point of view. Of course Shimmer won't discuss it with me directly."

"She's in trouble," Scarecrow said. "I think she's out of her depth. Will you help us wrap this mess up?"

"I will," Jafrain nodded. "Hm. Looks like it's just as well nobody's killed you yet, after all."

"I'm going to take that as a compliment," Scarecrow said with a wry smile. "Now. What else don't I know?"

Jafrain's hearty laugh trailed off into the night.

CHAPTER SEVENTEEN

Jayan Park is famed for trees that are deadly artwork, poisonous to the touch and surreal to the senses. Many of the trees date back to when the park was re-purposed for radiants at the dawn of the eighth century, somehow eluding the erosive damage of time.

Most people think this Charterhall landmark was Dr. Jayan's testing ground for botanical exploration. They picture an elderly scholar and his assistants dutifully tilling the soil, brushing fertility treatments on tree buds, and pruning the radiant shrubbery.

The park was the showcase for Dr. Jayan's successes, a storefront window displaying their finest goods. History tends to glide past Dr. Jayan's massive 200 acre plantation abutting the Weatherwatch District. That is where he spent the better part of his eighty years wrenching secrets from the earth, demons, and his rivals. Hundreds of people died for his work, their spirits and bodies feeding his grotesque experiments. If Jayan Park is the storefront, you may imagine Jayan's plantation as three stories of water-damaged warehousing above the shop.

Upon his death, his enemies made sure the whole acreage was burned, hacked apart, or plowed up. The horrors he created were not so easily destroyed.

Now only assassins and their suppliers dare to visit the nightmare jungle that sprang up from the plantation's ruin. The secrets in that lethal tangle are best left undisturbed.

—From "The Undisclosed Price of Progress"
By Servitor Kaleen, published 818

Scarecrow sat at the table, deliberately slowing his breathing. He relaxed his hands, splayed out and pressed on the tabletop. He waited.

The door burst open. Crumbs pounced in with a gun in one hand and a knife in the other as Slipper darted to Scarecrow's flank, covering the room. Scarecrow did not need to see Pops to know there was a sniper on the opposite roof.

"Where's the head," Crumbs growled.

"Sideboard," Scarecrow said, unmoving.

"Down," Slippers said. "Feet spread. Hands behind your back."

Scarecrow carefully slid out of the chair, down to his knees then face down, keenly aware of Slippers behind him with a pistol trained on his head.

The latches on the case snapped open, and Crumbs tilted it open. A clotted screech tore out of Skau's head, startling the cutter. He jerked back, the case fell on its side, and Skau's head rolled out to thud down to the floorboards, still pushing out an inarticulate roar.

Scarecrow was almost face to face with the severed head, just a couple paces away. Some distant part of his mind noted the purple and white mottling on the corpse-meat, the bloated eyes swollen with the pressure of Skau's screaming, the caked blood scabbing along the ruined head. Crumbs swore explosively in the background as he staggered back.

"Put it back in the case," Slippers snapped.

Crumbs only hesitated for a moment. Scowling, he snatched Skau's beard, hoisting the head up and jamming it back into the case. He worked the latches, sealing the horrible sounds inside.

Then Crumbs sidled to the window, peering out for a long moment. He nodded, then turned to the doorway. "Clear," he said.

Shimmer stepped in, wearing a close-fitting silver suit with a long coat. She rested her hand on the pommel of the rapier that hung from her baldric, and she glanced around the apartment.

"Where is Uppercut," she demanded quietly, her tone glacial.

"I'm not sure exactly," Scarecrow replied, eyes on her boots as he lay still.

"You have the zemi?" she asked.

"He borrowed it."

Shimmer's frown was audible. "I told you to keep it with you until this is over."

"Right, I remember," Scarecrow murmured.

"Get him up." Shimmer crossed the narrow room and stood in the corner, out of view from the windows. Scarecrow was hefted into the chair, Crumbs standing behind him. "Now. Scarecrow. Where is Jafrain."

"I really don't know," Scarecrow said, looking Shimmer in the eye. "Dropped her off about fifteen minutes ago on the Nightmarket side of the bridge, same as Uppercut. But we got Skau's head," he pressed on, "ahead of schedule. Careful. He bites, and swears, and he can summon ghosts. But we got him."

"You sure did," Shimmer agreed, expressionless. "For weeks you don't have the capacity to do your assignments, and here at the end you have an abundance of energy and planning. Enough to dig into my business."

"It's the adrenaline," Scarecrow said, deadpan.

Shimmer studied him for a long moment. "Sendoff. Signal our mutual friend," she said.

"On it," said the slide in the hallway. She pattered down the stairs.

"I don't have time for this right now," Shimmer said distinctly, looking Scarecrow in the eye. "You and me, we'll settle up later."

Scarecrow swallowed hard, and said nothing.

The shadows of the room seemed to shiver for a moment as a Spirit Warden stepped through the doorway. The weak lamplight glowed on the burnished copper of his mask. The matte black uniform beneath the glitter of his buckles and charms reflected no light. He shrugged his half-cloak back, then reached for the case, opening it. Skau was wary, silent.

"Very good," the Spirit Warden said in an accented baritone. Unsheathing clippers, he snipped a couple times, removing most of Skau's beard with the frictionless edges. He beckoned without looking, and Sendoff was at his side with a metallic cylinder. The Spirit Warden slotted Skau's head into the cylinder, and screwed it shut, popping up a handle on top.

"That is the last of them, Captain," Shimmer said with respect in her tone. "Are you satisfied?"

"We will need to conduct a ritual to confirm," the Spirit Warden mused, an ethereal resonance in his tone. "Come along." Turning, he swept out of the room carrying the cylinder.

"Bring him," Shimmer muttered, pointing at Scarecrow as she left with the Spirit Warden. The Bitters made no move to tie Scarecrow up or restrain him, and he followed Slippers obediently with Crumbs at his back.

They descended the stairs, crossed the street, and headed for the church at the end of the block. Along the way, Pops fell in with them. No one spoke.

They turned into an alley beside the sweeping stone wall of the church. Near the far end, the Spirit Warden led them down a staircase to a basement entrance, opening the way with a gesture. The underground corridor was stuffy, and it smelled of mold. The paving stones under the foundation were visibly older than the construction above.

They entered a dimly-lit archive, the congregation's records slotted into pigeonholes and locked shelving. The Spirit Warden did not slow down, crossing the room and pivoting a wall to enter a concealed space beyond.

"You wait here with your people," Shimmer said to Crumbs in a low voice. "Come with me," she said to Scarecrow. Turning, she passed through the secret door. Scarecrow did not look at the Bitters. He followed along, and the wall clicked shut.

More stairs down, curving, until they reached a heavy iron gate. The Spirit Warden acolytes on the other side unlocked it, opening the way for the Spirit Warden and his guests. The gate clanged into place behind them, and locked.

Two other Spirit Wardens stood in the glowing chamber, underlit by a pool. Scarecrow saw cylinders, like the one containing Skau's head, lining the bottom of the pool. The eye was easily tricked by the distortion of light moving through the surface, so it was difficult to gauge how many were in the pool or how deep it was. Scarecrow did not try.

"Is the ritual prepared?" the Spirit Warden asked.

"All is ready," one of the others intoned.

The Spirit Warden slotted Skau's cylinder down into the pool, then stepped back, clearing all water from his arm with a single flick. "Proceed."

One of the other Spirit Wardens gestured across the surface, broadcasting a fine powder that sifted down to prickle across the water's surface. The light dimmed slightly, obscured by the particles. Nothing else happened.

After what felt like an eternity, the Spirit Warden nodded. "Tyvissi is unmoored. We have confirmed it. No flesh shadows remain." He turned to Shimmer. "Kneel."

She sank to her knees before him, head down. The Spirit Warden placed his hand on the crown of her head, appearing to concentrate as he gazed down at her. He said a phrase in a liquid language that seemed to have the resonance of Hadrathi, but was unrecognizable to Scarecrow. The Spirit Warden nodded.

"All your debts are discharged," he murmured to Shimmer. "You bear the mark of the Reliquary Scrip. The Spirit Wardens are in your debt."

"You have my gratitude," Shimmer said, her tone careful. She rose to her feet in a smooth flex. "Yet our business is not concluded. I have a proposal."

The three Spirit Wardens regarded her. "Do you," said the one that brought her in.

"Yes, Captain," she nodded. "Tyvissi may be unmoored, but he still poses a threat. I can lure him out. I have built a trap for him, with bait he cannot refuse."

She had their undivided attention. "Continue," said the Captain.

"This one," she said with a gesture to Scarecrow, "shares a curse with a specter known as the Draper. Using the bond of the curse, you may summon the Draper to him. He is called Scarecrow," she said with a sidelong glance. "Tyvissi is no longer protected from his mania for vengeance by the memorial ink. A challenge from the rival who vexed him in life, then murdered him, is likely to be irresistible. We can choose the time and place of the confrontation, and assure its outcome."

"Interesting," the Captain murmured.

"Tyvissi was slain in Jayan Park," Shimmer continued. "I have made arrangements to secure privacy at the site of the murder tonight. If you summon the Draper and amplify a challenge behind the Mirror, I believe Tyvissi will come. He has lost three connections in quick succession, and he must be off balance. Vulnerable." She paused. "We have all the pieces we need in hand to make a bold move. Delay will only weaken our position."

"You make this offer even as you secure the Reliquary Scrip for yourself," one of the Spirit Wardens rumbled. "What is it you ask in return?"

Shimmer focused on the Captain. "You know what I desire."

"Immunity and protection," the Captain explained, bemused. "For an Illustrated Master."

"Those who ply their trade in corrupt ink must be destroyed," a Spirit Warden sniffed.

"Exceptions have been made," Shimmer replied, her tone even.

"We must consult," one of the Spirit Wardens intoned. "You may await our answer in the archive."

Shimmer bowed deeply, then turned and mounted the stairs, Scarecrow at her heels. The pivoting wall opened, releasing them back into the archive. Crumbs stood at the ready.

"Everything alright?" the cutter asked carefully.

"Yes," Shimmer nodded, the scales along her jaw glittering in the lamplight. "You may go. Your payment has already been released, with a bonus." Her eyes were hard. "Good job."

There was only a trace of reluctance as Crumbs straightened. "Thank you. As always, you know where to find us." He glanced over his crew. "Let's move."

They filed out of the archive, and the door closed. Scarecrow eased down into a chair at the table, watching Shimmer.

"Plans within plans, with contingency plans," he murmured. He was almost sympathetic.

Shimmer heaved a sigh. "That's how it goes. All your plots won't land, so you have to have enough of them to get what you're after." She was oddly reflective. "The Spirit Wardens will go for my offer to shut down Tyvissi. I'm sure of it."

"You just assume I'll cooperate," Scarecrow observed.

"Of course you will," Shimmer agreed. "The Draper is out of Upper-cut's league. Your best chance of getting free of the Draper is through this battle. If you don't wipe out the Draper, then you know sooner or later he'll take you over. You are no match for him either."

"That may be true," Scarecrow said. "This is dangerous, though. I could die. What's your thought on that?" He cocked his head to the side. "Do you plan to make sure I die either way? Or if I live through this, do I get to walk?"

Shimmer watched him for a moment, silent.

"Maybe I know too much," Scarecrow murmured. "Maybe I'm a threat to you now. Is that it?"

"No," Shimmer said slowly. "You are no threat. Not really. You are just caught up in something bigger." She sat opposite him at the table. "Like a storm. If your roof leaks, then yes, patch that up. The damage will just worsen. But sometimes, there's a wind off the violent sea. A wind that tears up the coast and hurls walls of water into the streets. Rain flows up under the eaves, through the panes, down the chimney. You don't restructure your house because of a little seepage when the whole sky comes down. And all this?" she said with an airy gesture. "This is the biggest storm I've ever survived."

"It's raining sideways out there," Scarecrow nodded, leaning back. "Once in a lifetime winds."

"So if you do survive, I'll ignore you. This time," Shimmer said. "And you'll stay out of my way in the future." Her eyes narrowed. "No more seepage into my business."

"That seems reasonable," Scarecrow said with a bleak smile. "In the meantime, how about some hazard pay. Some kind of compensation for my key role in all this. You've got Reliquary Scrip. Maybe do something for me."

"What would you ask for?" Shimmer wondered.

The door to the hallway rasped open. A Spirit Warden with a different crest on his helmet stepped into the room. "You," he said, looking at Scarecrow. "Come with me."

Shimmer rose to her feet. "He is part of my plan," she said. "We do not have time for this right now. We must be ready to—"

The Spirit Warden raised his palm, silencing her. "I know of your plan. We have questions that must be answered to settle deliberations." The Spirit Warden refocused on Scarecrow, who meekly rose and followed him out of the room.

Scarecrow asked no questions of the Spirit Warden, following the broad and armored shoulders as the mystic strode along the corridor and turned, passing through a reinforced door to a circular open shaft with stairs spiraling along its edge. The stink of suffering and stagnant water suffused the humid air. Halfway down the staircase, the Spirit Warden opened the door to a side chamber, waving Scarecrow through.

Reluctant, Scarecrow entered the darkened room. A handful of candles lit the space, painting light across confusing surfaces and twitching through the thick shadows. Bottles, parchment, and mummified animal parts were jumbled along the side cupboards and shelves. The table in the center of the room was cleared, revealing glyphwork burned into the surface in ritual patterns. The smell was powerful and ambiguous, and it was difficult for Scarecrow to breathe the air.

A haggard figure in a white mask stepped out of the shadows, crossing to the table. She hissed out a phrase in Hadrathi.

"See and be seen," Scarecrow guessed, replying in Akorosian with a traditional answer to occult greeting.

The masked woman chuckled. "How about that. Hello there little Skov," she said in Akorosian.

"You must be a Whisper," Scarecrow said, very aware of the Spirit Warden behind him. "Approved, I hope."

"Oh, I'm licensed, as is Sleet," the Whisper agreed with a gesture. Another Whisper joined her at the table. She sat down. "I am Blossom. We have questions for you."

"Ask away," Scarecrow said, attempting a smile as sweat began to bead along his ribs and on his scalp. Something about the room was too warm, the walls were too close.

"What do you know about Tyvissi?" Sleet asked, her voice grating.

"Very little," Scarecrow said. "He's Reconciled. We've been severing all connections on his bloodmap. He's got some kind of Mirror fort. I guess he's sneaky."

"What do you know about the Draper?" Blossom said, almost dismissive of the Tyvissi answer.

"Uh... he killed a lot of people while he was alive, and now that he's dead he kills people *and* ghosts," Scarecrow said. He was leaning into his Skov accent, knowing how Akorosians tended to stereotype dumb Skovs. "We let him out of the Clavalian Manor because he helped us escape. Kind of." He cleared his throat. "So he has been wandering the city killing folks. He got cursed by the Rapturous Chord. Me, too." He jabbed his thumb with his chest, eyes wide.

"I see," Blossom said. "You are undead."

Scarecrow blinked, thinking fast. "Undead?"

"Undead." Blossom stared at him, waiting.

"I... guess... so," Scarecrow said. "Is there a question?"

"The prestige ink that cracked you," Sleet whispered. "Give us the name of the Illustrated Master who broke your skin."

"I'm not sure," Scarecrow apologized. "That was a long time ago. He went by many aliases. I think he shared some nicknames with other tattoo artists. I never got a good look at him."

"You lie," Sleet said with palpable satisfaction. "Now—"

Sudden wind gusted through the chamber, laying the candle flames sideways as they flickered. Several blew out. Claws clicked on the wood of the table as Carc neatly landed between Scarecrow and the Whispers.

"Seeker," Blossom said, startled. She said something in the archaic dialect of Hadrathi, but Carc cut her off with an aggressive croak.

The Whispers and Spirit Warden stared at the deathseeker crow, and Scarecrow, for a long moment.

The Spirit Warden rounded on Scarecrow, his jaw clenched. "*Do not interfere with the holy work of the Seekers. What have you done.*"

"Wasn't my idea," Scarecrow said, taking a step sideways so his back was to the wall. "Carc sought *me* out."

"You lie—" Sleet shouted, but Carc interrupted with a screech.

Scarecrow tugged his headband off and scowled, bunching up the scar tissue in the center of his forehead. "This deathseeker crow marked me. Here," he said, pointing at the scar. "Came out of nowhere. Claimed me. You think *I* tell *him* what to do? No," he said, shaking his head. "That's not how it works with us. We're partners. We are *connected*. And it was his idea. Carc let the Draper ride me out of Clavalian Manor. Carc deepened my undeath. Carc revealed my connection to the Merenkaynti Zemi."

The deathseeker crow sprang from the table, wings spread, and landed on Scarecrow's shoulder. He walked around the back of Scarecrow's neck with delicate gripping claws, peering out past him, a darker shadow than the one Scarecrow cast. The bird released a grinding sound, almost like purring. Or growling.

"So tell me," Scarecrow said, reading the room. "Do you want to cross the deathseekers?"

Blossom hissed through her teeth, an unsettling noise. "If the Seekers are playing this one out... we let them," she said reluctantly.

"Are you satisfied?" the Spirit Warden asked, something cold in his tone. "Any further questions?"

"No further questions," Sleet said with a note of reverence. "Just one thing." The Whisper rounded the table, approaching Scarecrow. She slowly reached out, and touched the side of his face. Her fingertips were cold. "You have heard the Leviathan Song," she breathed, her exhalation rotten. "You are now part of the Pyressant Order. You are chosen," she enunciated, barely audible. "Not by the Elders, but instead, by the Seekers." She leaned in close, and the whole world seemed to shrink around Scarecrow. "You will know your title ere long."

"That will do," the Spirit Warden said, and the Whispers stepped back. "Come with me."

The Spirit Warden turned and left the chamber. Scarecrow followed, not looking back over his shoulder. Carc launched off of him, gliding out into the central shaft and wheeling.

"How did he get down here?" Scarecrow wondered aloud.

"Why don't you ask him," the Spirit Warden replied, subdued as he led the way up the staircase.

"What now?" Scarecrow asked, feeling the slithering breeze that coated Carc as the deathseeker circled.

"Now we wait," the Spirit Warden said. "The Sixth Coven will make a decision. And then... we will see."

THE IMMORTAL EMPEROR MONUMENT SQUARE, JAYAN PARK. CHARTERHALL
41ˢᵀ MENDAR, 850. *ABOUT FOUR HOURS LATER*
HOUR OF WINE, 8 HOURS PAST DUSK

Scarecrow shivered in the cold. "You are sure that thing will work?"

"Yes," the Spirit Warden adept said shortly. He squinted at the syringe he held, glinting in the pale light of the grove of trees. "When you tap this twice, the Draper will be expelled from your body. If you can get enough control to manage two taps, you'll be free." The adept injected the particle into the back of Scarecrow's hand.

"Ow," Scarecrow said, plaintive. Ignoring him, the adept clapped his hand over the back of Scarecrow's hand, concentrating for a few seconds.

The Captain strode over to where Scarecrow and the adept stood in the glowshade. "We are nearly set. Is the host prepared?"

"Yes, master," the adept said. "The particulate ejector is placed and attuned."

Scarecrow swept the plaza with his gaze. "Hell of a spot for a fight," he murmured.

Behind him, the obsidian column dominated the scene. It was topped by a massive statue of the Immortal Emperor. Scarecrow stood on an apron of close-fit bricks bearing inscriptions of loyalists who made donations to build and maintain the plaza centuries ago. Bushes screened half of the circumference of the plaza, and massive trees pinned down the eight cardinal points, separating the paths that led to this monument at the center of the park.

The ancient trees seemed to slowly twist as the eye attempted to lock on to them. Strands of color and texture wove across their bark, and the spread of their branches was an improbable pattern that seemed too orderly to be organic, and also somehow alien in design. Their leaves let out a variety of lights, some glowing and some shining. On other trees, the leaves seemed to drink in light while the bark glimmered.

Rustling and hissing bushes seethed all around the plaza, caught in a crosswind between breezes on both sides of the Mirror. On one side of the plaza, a path followed the shoreline and the river glittered beyond. A couple dozen serious adepts finished the preparations around the plaza, supervised by three Spirit Wardens and two Whispers. Off to the side, Shimmer watched.

"The slayer circle is complete," an adept said as he jogged over to join them. "Just as you instructed, it has been assembled there." He pointed to the other side of the monument.

"The Whispers are prepared?" the Captain demanded.

"Attuned and enhanced," the adept nodded. "They will peak shortly, then be heightened for about ten minutes."

The Captain took a deep breath, then let it out. Turning to a concentration of adepts, he frowned, and they were instantly attentive.

"Begin the drums."

The adepts arranged themselves, and began rapping out an arrhythmic pattern on small drums tucked in their laps.

The Captain carefully opened a velvet pouch, pulling out two crystals. "Open your mouth," he said to Scarecrow.

Reluctant, Scarecrow opened his mouth. The Captain slid one of the crystals inside.

"Close."

Scarecrow closed his mouth, the chilly crystal strange on his tongue. The Captain breathed out, a plume of warmer air billowing steam from his mask. Raising the other crystal, the Captain let his senses drift, then focused them. He slowly stepped around to Scarecrow's other side, then raised the crystal and repeated the process. Combined with the tasteless chill of the crystal in his mouth, and the odd drumming, and the shifting trees, and the cold, Scarecrow felt light-headed. There was a dream-like quality to the deep of night as it tilted towards a distant dawn. Scarecrow realized he had not slept for a very long time. The Spirit Warden raised the crystal again. Then again.

Scarecrow yelped, spitting out the crystal in his mouth before his mind registered the shock that coursed through him.

"Incoming!" the Captain shouted as he bounded away from Scarecrow.

Time was strangely compressed as Scarecrow felt the velocity behind the Mirror, the pressure built up before an impossibly fast-moving presence. There was an instant flash of one insane eye, then Scarecrow was hurled back off his feet as the Draper barreled into his body.

"The curse," Scarecrow felt his body growl as the Draper immediately adapted to his new situation. "What is this." Rising, the feral specter pivoted Scarecrow's body to take in the plaza. He saw the adepts, and spotted a couple Spirit Wardens. Impossible rage boiled through his blood.

Then hundreds of wingbeats caught his attention. A flock of deathseeker crows wheeled overhead, summoned from the nearby Bellweather Seminary tower by the patterned drumming the adepts unreeled into the night. Like a cloud of spectators, the crows descended to perch in the trees surrounding the plaza, shadows boldly intruding into lit spaces.

Scarecrow pressed into the Draper's control, exerting himself. The mad specter regarded him somehow as they shared the space in Scarecrow's body.

I know what's going on, Scarecrow projected with some effort.

Spirit Wardens, the Draper echoed. *Used our curse. Summoned me here. Where I slew Tyvissi.* The Draper's teeth twitched with gleeful fury as his image flickered. *At last. Time to slay him again.*

The deathseeker crows, Scarecrow managed. *They will carry your challenge.*

Scarecrow's body threw his head back and let loose a peal of insane laughter. As though that cackle wrung out all the sane air in his body, he drew in a profound breath that was tainted by his rage. Flexing his whole existence, the body-mounted specter screamed.

TYVISSI

The force of the scream shocked across the deathseeker crows, who reeled up into the sky like drunken shrapnel. They scattered, filling the night sky with chips of that scream spraying out behind the Mirror, as though each crow recoiled with a pealing bell tolling out for a death.

The forceful expulsion of all that energy left the Draper somewhat spent. Scarecrow felt himself fill out, becoming more real, and he looked around in awe. The Draper's summons created a haunted space behind the Mirror, adjacent to the breathing world, but recolored with ancient memory.

The plaza looked different now, from inside the Draper's possession. Weedy trees clung to life, their thin foliage hanging limp. Small fountains and rock formations filled in between the half-dead bushes. The patina of centuries marred this image, a powerful memory of the plaza in a bygone age.

There is my call, the Draper smirked. He crossed his arms, sending runnels of ethereal gore sliding down his shoulders and ribs, his resonant image overlaying Scarecrow's body. The specter took in his handiwork, part of the memory. A woman and two teens sprawled on the pavement where Scarecrow's body stood. They were just barely alive, their torsos slit open and their guts intermingled in a pile as they struggled to breathe. Their whimpering was the sound of misery dragged out past where inevitable death should silence it. *Tyvissi's family enjoyed a special closeness at the end. They were almost a part of each other, you might say.*

Scarecrow's consciousness teetered at the edge of the plaza, looking on.

Let's add the man himself to our fond memory, the Draper sneered. *Yes, that's how I remember it.* He turned to gaze up at the statue of the Immortal Emperor. A thin aristocrat was suspended, toes jerking with involuntary reflex, his body cavity emptied. He hung from the unbending arm of the statue, his guts looped over the metal several times, then wrapped around his chest to support his weight. The Draper stood under the corpse, grinning, spattered in red rain.

A kind of pain seemed to spasm through the scene, refocusing it. Then something clattered down on the paving. It was a lion mask, cracked down the middle.

Yes. A cold voice slithered through the plaza. *That's how I remember it too.*

The Draper and Scarecrow looked up to see Tyvissi standing on the statue's arm, reconstituted. The thin man dropped with ease, face to face with the Draper. His outline was indistinct with a vibration of power. Pinpoints of deadly focus hung in blackened eye sockets.

You turned away from this pain, the Draper echoed. He sidled to the corpses on the plaza, stepping into the pile of guts with a nauseating squish. *Buried it deep. But I dug it up. Here we are. Tell me you don't care. Tell me you're over it.* The Draper reached out to the side, and a knife solidified in his grip. *I'm wearing your legacy.*

This was the beginning of the end for you, Tyvissi observed. *You were a terrorist, and... you certainly did spread fear. What you did here made a real difference. Terrified previously staunch loyalists.* His tone hardened. *Pity you didn't live to see it.*

That's the difference between us, the Draper taunted. *You ended. Your cause, failed. Your family, dust. You had to start over after death. Me? I'm still doing what I did. When I open you up today, I'll wash myself in you again. What's in you will keep me going for years.* Cruelty stained his features. *Tell me you can care about your cause when I'm standing in your children.*

Tyvissi flicked his wrist, and he held a rapier. *I care about my cause.* Half the light fell out of the world as a pulse of hardened fury rolled out of the specter.

Get away from my family.

At last, Tyvissi's balance tilted too far to recover.

CHAPTER EIGHTEEN

My father can make an entrance. He can sustain thoughtful and erudite discourse in both academic and social settings. He focuses on the elegance of posture, fashion, and comportment. He believes it is incumbent upon him to embody the aristocratic ideal of accomplishment and grace. The expectation he inherited was to curate the family reputation, perhaps embroider it with fresh accomplishment, and pass on those expectations to another generation.

This is, on its face, ridiculous. We do not build up an army so we can admire their parade ground drills. We do not quarry stone so we may contemplate a re-arranged mountain. We do not build ships to decorate the skyline of the sea.

When I finish school, you will not find me responding to the Immortal Emperor's grace and gifts by preening my glorious plumage. There is work to be done. Our wealth is an armory, our reputation a rampart wall. The Barrow King dissidents were driven to the sea, and it is past time to drive them off the coast altogether.

—From Sulzer Tyvissi's journal at the age of fifteen

Tyvissi snatched at the Draper from across the square, and a blast of something like wind stripped all the ooze from the Draper's remembered flesh. *Meet me where I am, savage,* Tyvissi echoed.

I think I will hold my balance a while longer, the Draper replied, mocking. *I am grounded. Not just with life and flesh.*

Tyvissi blinked across the intervening space, but his rapier did not plunge into the Draper's torso; the agile specter twisted Scarecrow's body away, across the illusion of a dozen paces.

Let's make this quick, the Draper taunted. *We could be locked in struggle for years, ruining the weather. So I brought a weapon.*

That flesh? Tyvissi scoffed. *No.*

Tyvissi pulled the world in close around the Draper and drove at him. This time, the Draper opened wide, refusing to dodge.

Scarecrow spasmed, knocked deep into his own spirit, where two blazing specters focused the intensity of their battle as blood sprayed from his body's nose and mouth.

Of course it's a trap, the Draper growled, his thoughts reverberating through the cartilage and blisters of Scarecrow's twisted soul.

Tyvissi let out a cry of dismay as he slapped down in knee-deep filth. He was mired in something like putrid tar. The corruption pooled on the uneven flesh-like floor, discharge trickling down the walls. Like a foundation after an earthquake, the walls were riven and seeping. Scarecrow stared around in dismay.

The stench and the texture were too familiar. He shuddered as he flashed back to his escape from the picture frame of Merrihel Vans. A dim red glow filtered around them, like light passing through flesh. Somehow, they were standing in a stylized nightmare of his torso.

Just like that, our battle is over, the Draper mused.

Tyvissi squirmed and flexed, a burst of power illuminating the carrion chamber. He subsided, now waist deep. *And yet you lose as well,* Tyvissi snarled. *For you cannot open me up if this swallows me whole. If I die in this mess, all that I am feeds the blight. Not you.* A cruel smile twisted his features. *And you may find you have ventured too deep in this trap to escape.*

Scarecrow is on my side, the Draper replied, clapping the image of the man on the shoulder. *He will release me.* His features hardened. *And I **will** have you.*

The Draper knelt at the edge of the slowly churning rot, and he reached out his hand. *Let us do battle in here. The victor may feast, or deliver the conquered to this,* he added with an airy wave at the horrific surroundings.

Tyvissi reached out, and the specters touched.

Quicker than thought, the Draper lashed out to slit Tyvissi open. The killing stroke deflected with a chime.

As the Draper staggered, Tyvissi hauled at him. The Draper belly-flopped into the corrupt pool with a splat as Tyvissi launched clear.

The Draper screamed, his rage and sudden terror vibrating the walls and unbalancing Scarecrow. Tyvissi steadied Scarecrow, refocusing, the rage covered over with balance.

This next part is crucial, Tyvissi concentrated, locking eyes with Scarecrow.

The Draper shrieked. *NO! NO! YOU WILL NOT ESCAPE!* His insane visage flowed and twisted as he burned through his essence, struggling against the rotten sludge. He rolled over to glare at them, nothing sane in his eyes, and the filth clung to him so he was deeper in its grip.

You— Scarecrow stammered. *You triggered the curse!* His eyes widened. *You made him fail!*

Right, Tyvissi nodded. *Listen carefully. You must tell the Spirit Wardens that we both fell in. That we both are locked in place. They will take you to the slayer circle. Acquiesce.*

What about you? Scarecrow demanded.

Tyvissi's smile was almost sad. *You are about to make a mess behind the Mirror, and I'll slip out in the confusion. Ready?*

Scarecrow hugged himself with sudden alarm. *I—I*

STAY! Roaring, the Draper clawed up a mass of the corruption and flung it, a snotty stream connecting him to the wad as it flew at Scarecrow. Tyvissi gestured at it dismissively, deflecting the attack. He took Scarecrow by the hand.

Suddenly Scarecrow could feel his actual flesh hands. He spasmed, staring into Tyvissi's eyes.

Scarecrow tapped the back of his hand twice.

The ritual flexed in him, but could not free the Draper, so it misfired. Scarecrow found himself dazed, floating behind the Mirror, looking down at the scene.

His body was on its knees in front of the obsidian column. Ropes of corruption had curled out of his flesh to anchor it in place. As his ethereal essence swarmed, Scarecrow could not tell if the corruption was visible on the other side of the Mirror or not. He heard muffled orders. He saw a blur of activity around the plaza.

After only a moment, the world snapped into focus and he found himself face to face with Blossom, unable to move. The Whisper was painfully crisp and real as he was pulled into attunement, and he was able to think and speak.

"What happened," Blossom demanded.

The specters, both pulled inside, wrestling in a tarpit, Scarecrow responded with a rustling murmur.

The Whisper nodded, and turned away. "Quick. Put the body in the slayer circle. The native spirit is clear."

Sleet hustled up to Scarecrow's body with half a dozen acolytes. The Whisper rasped out searing phrases and made quick gestures, slashing the corrupt cords that held Scarecrow in place, and the acolytes hefted his body. Blossom and Scarecrow's spirit rounded the plaza to see the slayer circle.

"Stay put," Blossom snapped at Scarecrow. She stood on one side of the circle, Sleet stood on the other, and the acolytes lay Scarecrow's body in the center and backed away as fast as they could. The Whispers concentrated, and the burning circle flared up like a beacon in the twilight landscape behind the Mirror.

Painless tremors rippled through Scarecrow, and he drifted.

Blossom refocused on him. "Sleet. Can you confirm? Is the body clear?"

"There is no spirit within. The slayer circle has done its work. The flesh is hollow."

Blossom nodded, then gestured. Scarecrow was flung toward his body.

He felt himself twitch, boot scraping on the pavement, the flagstone cold under his head, his whole weight on a shoulder and a hip. Coughing, he struggled to flop over on his back, his breath steaming out.

For a moment, the only sensation he felt was the burning in the back of his hand, where the ejector blasted free.

Blossom loomed over him. "Are you intact?"

"M-mostly." He let out a gust of hot air that felt like his last breath. His chest ached.

The Captain approached. "Well?" he demanded.

"It was a lot," Sleet said, sour, her hands trembling as she pulled off her glove. "Definitely a specter level threat. Destroyed."

"Two of them?" the Captain clarified.

"Possibly," Blossom nodded. "They were weakened and intermingled with their battle. And something else. Something inside this one." She lowered her tone. "Shimmer chose her battleground well. He is undead." She prodded Scarecrow's shoulder. "They battled within him."

"Ah." The Captain leaned back. "Well then, more to the point, did anything escape?"

"J-just me," Scarecrow gasped. He clutched his chest, freshly out of breath. A whine slid into his struggle as he fought for air. As he winced, he felt his skin crease the blood deltas that flowed from his eyes and clotted his mustache.

"Clean him up," the Captain said.

"Then what?" Blossom asked.

"Give him to Shimmer." The Captain walked away.

Snow drifted down, as though the world wanted to cover up what happened in the plaza. Scarecrow unsteadily walked over to where Shimmer sat on a bench under the glowshade of a twisting tree. She looked up as he approached, oddly quiet.

"They said they were done with me," Scarecrow said. "I've been poked and prodded. They made sure I'm alone in here," he said with an expansive gesture. Wincing, he lowered his arms. "So it's over."

"The Draper."

"He's finished, nothing left," Scarecrow nodded. "I saw it myself."

Shimmer almost smiled. "That's what the Spirit Wardens said."

"You have doubts?" Scarecrow asked.

"No." She paused. "No," she repeated, shaking off the feeling. "Looks like you survived too."

"More or less," he agreed. "Now that you got what you wanted, are we done? Are you going to leave me alone, and Uppercut?"

"You don't want to pursue more work under me?" she retorted, raising an eyebrow.

"I don't think we trust each other," he said diplomatically.

"You're right," she said.

"There is the matter of what you owe me. For going through this *insane* venture just now," Scarecrow said with a slight tremor in his voice. "Like I said, we don't trust each other, so I want my favor and my payment now. Leave Uppercut alone, and me. And for payment, pay us five Coin." He paused. "Each."

"Ten Coin. How very bold," Shimmer said, mild. "I can afford to be generous just now. I'll give you six Coin, total, and you'll go away. You and your partner are more trouble than you're worth. I am done with you. Cross me again and you'll see what happens." Perhaps her smile was meant to soften the words. It did not.

"Heh. Same," Scarecrow replied. Turning away, he took his time leaving the plaza.

Scarecrow leaned heavily on the makeshift door, and it reluctantly groaned open. "Hey," he called out. "Fresh meat."

"Still kicking," Getch growled. He was seated on a bench opposite the door, a pistol on his lap. "We're closed."

"Except to me," Scarecrow disagreed. "I'm expected."

"Are you?" Getch retorted. "If you are expected, you brought me something."

"This," Scarecrow agreed, lifting his hand. He held a porcelain knob. "Doesn't look like much. Took some doing to find it, even with Jafrain's directions."

Getch scowled. "That's the point. Anybody follow you? See any spies outside?"

"No," Scarecrow said, feeling the weariness in his bones rising. "I've been searching for lookouts out there for twenty minutes. And before that, leading a merry chase across town."

"Alright," Getch said reluctantly, rising to his feet. "Follow me."

Scarecrow fell in behind the big man, rounding to the back of the counter and entering a narrow side gallery that smelled of metallic ink. The back wall was covered with brush strokes and artwork, and there was an adjustable padded bench and some stools. Getch screwed the porcelain knob onto a drawer, then adjusted its angle and concentrated. Slowly, he pulled it open.

The ink on the back wall twitched, then flared, forming a doorway.

"Maybe one person in five years gets to go to Jafrain's basement," Getch said in a low voice. "All this traffic makes me uneasy."

"It's alright," Scarecrow said. "We got her back for you. We'll keep her safe." He nodded to Getch, then stepped past him, ducking through the swirling doorway.

The heat was palpable. A slow grind of machinery, almost like a pulse, rumbled nearby. Scarecrow cautiously stepped forward, looking around the narrow stone hallway lit only by red lamps.

"Hello?"

"In here," Jafrain called out.

Scarecrow followed the corridor to where it opened up to a room with an industrial fan idly swirling on the side wall. A beam of bright light centered on a padded bench, where Uppercut sprawled with his shirt off, Jafrain seated on a stool and hunched over him.

"How did it go," Uppercut demanded weakly, his face deathly pale.

"We sort of won," Scarecrow said as he approached. "Hey, it's looking good."

Uppercut clenched again as Jafrain jabbed her needle stick forward in a quick rocking rhythm, working at the black line on his chest as blood oozed from the emerging shape.

"Feels... like I've been at this... all night," Uppercut clenched out, the veins standing out on his forehead as he suffered.

"Just finishing up the linework now," Jafrain said soothingly. "Then the color." She touched the needle stick to the pool of ink that surrounded the zemi in the bowl at her side. "Rest up while you can, we're almost ready to activate it."

"Oh—*such* good news," Uppercut growled. "That's me. Rested."

Fascinated, Scarecrow looked at the zemi. "So that's how it works," he said softly. To his undead eyes, the patterns of the stone interlocked with the swirls in the ink, and the pulse that pushed through Uppercut's body, bridged by the echo of pain from the needles.

Jafrain spared him an amused glance. "Yes. Uppercut told me he was trying to feed it his blood. Turn it on. Not sure what you were trying to make it do."

"Well it's secret lore," Scarecrow pointed out. He put his hand on Uppercut's shoulder reassuringly. "You're doing a great job. Besides, you said you'd unlock the zemi, and I guess you did."

Uppercut glared at him. "You have no idea how much your approval means to me," he said through his teeth. "I mean, look. I know I got it wrong. But I studied up. The passage for using the zemi says I speak to my blood, my blood speaks to stone. The stone hears the deep. Through surface and surface we meet."

"Yeah," Jafrain said with half a grin, "but that explanation, it's not for *you.* The zemi is for Illuminated Masters. What you found, that's just a little reminder note to refresh you when you already know what's up."

"It's the best lead my research uncovered," Uppercut gritted out, staring at the light overhead, flinching with pain.

"Our lore is an oral tradition for a reason, you weren't *supposed* to figure it out," Jafrain sighed. "You have to work the mix," Jafrain mused as her needles dug their way across the arch of a circle, closing it in Uppercut's flesh. "A little Leviathan ink, a little undead blood, some of mine of course, and then a few little extras."

"I guess it's your turn to wear my blood," Scarecrow faltered, unable to commit to the quip.

"Did the Spirit Wardens notice we bled you?" Jafrain asked absently.

"I don't know how they'd tell one injury from another. It's been a rough week," Scarecrow answered.

"How *is* the Draper doing?" Uppercut asked.

"He's gone. Trapped, then blown away by a Spirit Warden ritual run by their pet Whispers." Scarecrow shivered. "I guess Tyvissi escaped."

"Oh, he escaped alright," Jafrain said. "He dropped by a couple hours ago to donate some plasm to my mix. I put it in the red ink. Fill in the lamp, turn this thing on," she said with a gesture at Uppercut's chest.

The palm-sized circle centered around a stylized lamp surrounded by a texture of runes, contained in a thick black circle. The tattoo leaked a little blood, but Jafrain wiped as she shifted, working the needle stick into his flesh in a steady rhythm.

"Thank you for doing this," Scarecrow said quietly. "I know the circumstances are...unusual."

"You would think that," Jafrain said. "These are born out of necessity, and only rarely do the masters have the luxury of planning it out. Ideally, we would spend weeks on reliquary ink rather than hours. In real life," she sighed, "this art works more like emergency surgery. Which is why it is so expensive," she grinned.

"She's keeping the zemi," Uppercut said through his teeth.

"That's good," Scarecrow nodded. "You should have it." He paused. "Don't you already have one? I mean, you are an Illuminated Master."

"This is my first reliquary ink," she murmured, concentrating on the work. "I know how it is done, but I have not been bound to a blood map before."

"Well," Scarecrow said, unsettled. "Don't write it down. That's what got us all into this mess."

She smiled at that, but did not look up. "The zemi can unlock a lot more techniques than reliquary ink."

"Yeah, to be honest, I wanted the zemi so I could get the local Skovs to take me seriously as a leader. I'd rather have contacts with Illuminated Masters than a magic rock." He paused. "You are with us, right? Allies?"

"To a point," she murmured. With swift efficiency, she rinsed her stick and switched it out for another one. She turned the bowl, revealing the dividers set in it. Red ink gleamed along one flank of the stone, and she touched the needles to the pool's surface.

Pausing, Jafrain studied Uppercut's face. "This is going to burn," she said quietly.

"That's great," Uppercut growled. "Do it."

"Through surface and surface," Jafrain murmured in Hadrathi, the needles tucking red ink under the skin, past Uppercut's blood. He clenched his jaw, tendons standing out in his neck. He winced his eyes shut, and tears trickled out the corners. His fists locked on the arms of the padded chair bench.

Time passed. Scarecrow was hypnotized by Jafrain's unfolding art. Uppercut endured. Jafrain concentrated, the flow of her work instinctive as she filled in the red lamp.

Uppercut roused as the needle clattered down on the side table, and Jafrain wiped a cloth slowly across his new tattoo. "Are... are we done?" he slurred.

"You tell me," she murmured. "Can you feel it? The echo past the pain?"

Uppercut closed his eyes. "Hm. I think... yes."

"If you can attune to it, then it will activate," she said quietly. "Be ready. You will be the only anchor. You will... feel some things."

Uppercut raised one hand, open. Scarecrow stepped forward and clasped it, then settled into a wide stance.

"Okay," Uppercut said, his eyes clear. He raised his spirit mask and slipped it on as Jafrain gathered up her tools and moved to the side.

Almost dizzy with the prolonged pain of the tattoo, Uppercut concentrated on the aetheric puzzle that had been stitched into his flesh. Then he attuned to it.

With a disorienting lurch, he found himself on the deck of a ship at sea, lashed by a storm. A hysterical peal of laughter twisted down from the crow's nest, the lookout on the mast high above. Lightning forked down out of the sky, searing through him—

Excellent, Tyvissi smiled. The specter was visible to Uppercut, Scarecrow, and Jafrain as he stepped out of the shadows in the corner of the room. *You have brought me back. Anchored me once more.*

"A new lifeline," Jafrain said with a bow. "Fresh ink on a willing soul."

"Oh," Uppercut breathed.

The flash seemed to have sealed the tattoo wound, but it carried into him a depth of rage and pain. He shook with the force of it, struggling to keep himself in check. Muscles jumped into definition on Scarecrow's arm and neck as he tightened his grip on Uppercut's hand.

"Did we complete the tether in time?" Jafrain asked, subdued.

Just, Tyvissi nodded. *We will need to add a couple more.* He trembled, repressing the madness that pushed on every specter. As he pressed it back, some rolled into Uppercut.

"This—will take—some getting used—to," Uppercut gasped.

I will make it easier, Tyvissi promised. *I must seal up my house and go dormant for a while. Let the Spirit Wardens believe I am gone.* He paused. *Thank you. Both of you.*

"Happy—to be useful," Uppercut gritted out.

Tyvissi focused on Scarecrow for a moment. With a subtle smile, he winked. Scarecrow let out a grunt as he felt his energy flex. He was no longer under the Gaze of the Resonant Chime.

The room flickered, and Tyvissi was gone.

"Right," Jafrain said. "Let's get you back on the breathing side of the Mirror, that will help. Get you both a good sleep."

"That's the best idea I've heard in a long time," Scarecrow agreed, his hand aching. Uppercut violently twitched, and said nothing.

BASEMENT, KLEGGA SCORE SWEET SHOP, SIX TOWERS
43ᴿᴰ MENDAR, 850. *ABOUT TWO DAYS LATER*
EIGHTH HOUR PAST DAWN

The basement only had chairs on one end, at a long table. Six Skov elders sat in the shadows, out of easy reach of lamplight. A dozen other Skovs stood in the room. There were three exits, a handful of lamps, and a small arsenal of weaponry in the meeting space.

"Alright, that concludes our deliberations on the staffing changes at the Sorting Point." One of the elders took hold of the small cage on the table, and shifted it so the rocks inside rattled. "Now. What's next."

"We granted an audience to Scarecrow," the elder at the end of the table said, consulting the page in the record book.

"Great. Send for him."

A runner mounted the stairs, and a grumble spread through the room. The elder shook the cage again, the rocks clattering, and the others quieted down.

The stairs creaked as Scarecrow descended into the basement. He wore a new coat, and Carc gripped his shoulder, shiny black eyes darting around the room as the crow rode the man into the room. Granite followed behind, ducking through the low beamed doorway. Granite's hair was braided, his beard combed, his face washed, and his clothes respectable.

"Scarecrow, you have been granted an audience with the Knotwork," the elder said. "You have paid your allegiance. What is your business."

"I vouch for Granite, and sponsor his request to join the Knotwork as an agent to execute your will," Scarecrow said, skipping pleasantries. "I trust him. My honor will serve as a shield for his." He raised his chin. "What say you."

The elder frowned. "This is, what, the sixth time? No." He shifted. "Granite cannot be trusted. He worked for the Ministry. Various spiders. Spirit Wardens. He is not a risk we will accept, and you overestimate how much we trust *you*." The elder snorted. "Your *honor*."

Scarecrow narrowed his eyes, but before he could respond, one of the elders stood.

"Wait."

She walked around the table, into the lamplight. She was dressed in lace, knotted with fragments of bone, and her mask was wired together out of fingerbones.

"You wish to address the council, Mistress of Keys?" the elder said with forced politeness. A murmur raced through those assembled, and the elder shot them a warning look as he grasped the edge of the cage.

"Addressing the council is my right," the Whisper said. "I tell you we must honor this man's word," she said, pointing at Scarecrow. She turned, looking him in the eye. "He is the Minister of Crows."

The elder's frown was visible in the shadows. "Mistress, we—"

"*You must.*" The Mistress of Keys stood resolute, motionless.

The room was silent for a long, tense moment. Then the elder sighed.

"Mistress of Keys," he said patiently, "do *you* sponsor this request—"

Carc interrupted with a gutteral croak, startling the elders. The Mistress of Keys took a step forward.

"You. Must."

Uneasy, the elder exchanged a look with the other elders still behind the table. Then he scowled.

"Very well. We will make an exception in this case, and... reverse our previous rulings on Granite. He will be instated as an agent of the Knotwork." His frown deepened. "Watch your step, recruit."

"Yes sir. Thank you sir," Granite said, solemn.

"Alright then," the elder groused. He jogged the cage, and the stones rattled. "What's next on the agenda."

Scarecrow backed into the crowd, eyes fixed on the Mistress of Keys. He could not see her face, but he could feel her smile like a cold breeze. "Tolja I could do it," Scarecrow muttered to Granite, who was grinning. "Let's go get drunk."

THE PICKLED EEL. CROW'S FOOT
45ᴿᴰ MENDAR, 850. *ABOUT TWO DAYS LATER*
TENTH HOUR PAST DAWN

Uppercut grunted as he pounded the hanging bag. It jounced on the chain that suspended it from a crossbeam. Sweat beaded on his pale arms and chest as he battered the target, driving his intolerable feelings through his fists.

A knock hit the door, so he steadied the bag and turned, breathing hard. "Come in."

"If it's safe," Scarecrow smiled, stepping in. "I hate to interrupt. But you said you wanted to meet here." He looked around the open loft.

"Welcome to our new base," Uppercut said with a grin, gesturing around.

Scarecrow blinked. "What?"

"It's a gift from our contacts with the Path of Echoes. They are impressed with our recent efforts, and wanted to reward us for destroying the Draper. Apparently he's a threat to a number of Reconciled, not just his poor victim Tyvissi." Uppercut took a deep breath. "We own the whole tavern."

"Well that's something," Scarecrow said, thinking it over. "Good news, indeed. But, uh, if we own the whole thing maybe we don't need to set up in the attic. Maybe somewhere on the ground floor, or the basement."

"I'm sure we can work out something closer to the ground for you," Uppercut chuckled. He put his hand on the swinging bag to still it, and his smile faded. "Now we can start a proper crew."

"Interesting," Scarecrow said. "You still up for it? All things considered?"

Uppercut laughed, almost a snarl. "I think I need it," he said. "Who are we thinking about for recruits?"

"Granite, sure," Scarecrow said. "Also, a decent Red Sash. I know some contenders."

"How about this," Uppercut said. "We only accept members into our crew if they've been inked by an Illuminated Master." He barked a laugh. "Raise the bar."

"Well that gives Granite some work to do," Scarecrow grinned. "Sweet-talking an Illuminated Master into giving you ink is no simple task."

"Sometimes it involves a ridiculous amount of running around," Uppercut agreed. "Maybe we should put together a gang or two, you know, to handle errands and odd jobs for us."

"Getch could keep an eye out, maybe even lead a gang," Scarecrow said. "Maybe we could recruit some Skov runners looking to make a name for themselves, from the Knotwork's pool of hopefuls. What kind of work are you thinking about taking on, for this new crew?"

"We can be flexible. Talented fellows like us," Uppercut said, clapping Scarecrow's shoulder. He took a deep breath. "But whatever it is, I think it's going to make life difficult for the Spirit Wardens and their allies." He looked Scarecrow in the eye. "You in?"

Scarecrow felt the smile growing across his face.

"Yeah. I'm in."

SAVERSLICK CANAL DELTA THIRD ARM. THE DOCKS
47ᵀᴴ MENDAR, 850. *ABOUT TWO DAYS LATER*
HOUR OF THREAD, 4TH HOUR PAST DAWN

Uppercut leaned against the low wall, feeling a certain peaceful kinship to the falling snow. He squinted at the yacht. His eyes wandered over the silhouettes moving inside, the festive decorations. The Ripple Dame hosted a small, intimate party for a powerful nobleman and his friends, while the snow curtained their luxurious retreat away from the world.

Uppercut pulled a spirit bottle from his inner coat pocket. He hefted it, his finger tracing the engraved stopper.

"The yacht is shielded," he murmured to the bottle. "Still, its protections are far less effective than those around his great house. So here we are. It is time to reward your patience."

More snow fell, yet nothing seemed to change.

"I want you to send him a message for me," Uppercut murmured, almost to himself. "You can put it into your own words." He looked down at the bottle. "Every now and then, the victims... must have their satisfaction. Every now and then, we must remember that powerful people are not as far out of reach as they think. Sometimes, a man keeps his word, and gives you revenge." He twisted the stopper, pulling it out of the way.

The ghost of Giselle plumed up into the frozen night air, jaw working in a shriek that resounded on the other side of the Mirror. Uppercut snapped her into focus, and she fixed her eyes on him.

"The past so seldom stays dead," he breathed. "Now, you go tell him. Give my regards to Colsarch." He tucked the empty bottle into his coat. Turning his back, he walked away.

Uppercut's new ink burned as the screaming started.

━━ CONTRIBUTOR'S POST SCRIPT ━━

Searching the internet, I found Blades in the Dark fiction written by Andrew Shields. I offered my support on his Patreon. He asked his patrons if they would like to participate in an experiment where we would be creating, molding, and making the decisions for characters in a story.

In April of 2020 I embarked on a literary adventure. Logan and I joined the project, and thus Scarecrow and Uppercut were born.

None of us had a clue as to what would come from this project. I could ramble on for hours about our adventures as the three of us created the story itself, Andrew doing the lion's share while Logan and I plotted and schemed on what we wanted to see in the story and how we wanted Uppercut and Scarecrow to react to their challenges. It was a blast. It was epic.

Halfway through the writing, Logan passed away. He had shared with us a health issue he was dealing with, and it sounded like he was making a recovery. It sounds cliche, yes, but life truly is precious. Remember to enjoy it. In a dark world, dare to be a light.

I am grateful to have been a part of this story. I can say without doubt or hesitation that this experiment will live on in my mind.

Brett Casto
September 2021

Raining Sideways was an experiment. At first, I was looking for player engagement in writing a short story.

THE IDEA

I planned to use Storium, a website designed to let collaborators write fiction together. I had attempted a number of different Storium projects with different narrative structures, but ultimately I was frustrated at the limits of this kind of collaborative writing. The breakdown of shared understanding, the dissonance between authorial voices, the lag in writing time, and the artificial barriers created when characters were not comfortably shared between writers all combined to sour my enthusiasm. Eventually, every Storium shifted from engagement to grumbling because the experience of the writers transitioned from a hobby to a chore.

Still, the gamification of Storium held my interest. The narrating player posts an opening, and challenges. The players assign strong, weak, or neutral cards through their characters with narrative "moves" explaining how the cards they play address the challenges. With a strong outcome, the player's writing "move" should reflect the player controlling the outcome. With a weak outcome, the player points towards failure and leaves it open for the narrator to conclude. With a neutral outcome, the writing move should describe something in between. Of course, this is a flexible and ambiguous system, which is its weakness and also its strength. The player's hand must be emptied of both strong and weak cards before refreshing. Past strong and weak cards can be recycled, and wild cards mean new strengths and weaknesses can enter the story as play continues.

I was ready to try again, but this time I would do all the writing myself. I created shell accounts for the two players who volunteered to participate, Brett Casto and Logan Waterman. Play would be informed by Storium mechanics, and also reflect the mechanics of *Blades in the Dark*. We would not roll dice or make character sheets, but the shared assumptions underlying the game would inform the narrative and action in our story (just like it does in my other *Blades in the Dark* fiction.)

As narrator, I would create an opening for the scene, with challenges that describe strong, neutral, and weak outcomes for each. Then Brett, Logan, and myself would talk it over on our private Discord for the project. The players decided how the character cards would be spent in Storium, shaping the outcome of each challenge.

I took the overall discussion, and their decisions for spending cards, and ruminated on how I could craft "moves" in Storium to reflect the card-to-challenge relationship, the overall thrust the players wanted for the story, and my own sense of how things could fit together. Then I wrote the moves out, logging in as each player to put in the actual text and assign the cards.

The players were not "playing characters" in this structure. They were muses for their characters. They indicated direction, they spent a mechanical resource to put influences in the game, and they picked the elements they wanted to introduce and emphasize. Weak outcomes for challenges really reflected the partial successes and outright failures that would plague actual characters in the *Blades in the Dark* game, as well as reflecting the noir roots of the fiction. Since all the weak cards had to be spent, we had to pick their battles and interpret failures as well as successes in propelling the action forward.

THE STORY

I planned to write a series of short stories based on the three act structure built into Storium. For the first one, I chose an evocative name (Raining Sideways) and introduced a man in an alleyway, along with some general challenges. I deliberately avoided planning ahead. The way the players influenced the action was the direction I would take. As they chose objectives, I would lay track so our story train could reach those objectives.

It took some time and practice to get the mindset worked out for this writing experiment. It's not playing and it's not writing, but the project had elements of both. One distinctive flavor of the process was freedom for us to discuss plot elements the characters didn't know about, and make decisions about longer term outcomes and overall directions. The players didn't have direct control of the characters, and they didn't need to be kept in the dark regarding plot elements that had not yet emerged. Any background plan that had not explicitly emerged in the story was still flexible, and could still be changed.

I didn't take fiction written by the players. I also encouraged them not to micromanage. Assigning cards and picking overall flavors and decisions was their purview, and as the author I interpreted those elements and wrote up a version that fit in my concept of Doskvol, and in the story. My goal was to make a piece of fiction that would read just like my other fiction, with the divisions between moves and scenes sanded smooth and the mechanics suggested but invisible.

Logan wanted a deathseeker crow as his Hound's animal companion. I explained the deathseekers aren't really tameable and aren't totally animals in my version of the setting, and countered with some other suggestions. He really wanted that deathseeker crow, so I agreed he could have it... but Scarecrow would be pretty damaged, and part of a bigger malignant scheme that would likely kill Scarecrow off. Logan was delighted with both the victory and the price. Because of this, I developed the idea of undead as a separate supernatural affliction.

Brett wanted a Whisper who was a former Bluecoat. I didn't really see that being a normal progression, as Whispers would manifest at a younger age and not really pursue becoming a Bluecoat even if they did want to go into law enforcement. Still, I figured we could work out a way this happened, and we did. I used the unusual background experiences to shape a unique character that deepens the flavor of the overall story.

As Logan and Brett got the hang of it, they developed Scarecrow and Uppercut through their decisions and the discussion involved in reaching those decisions. They reacted to what I wrote, and spent both strong and weak cards to shape the future for their characters. In turn, I took their discussions and the elements they wanted to see emerge, and I applied my own creativity on a move-by-move and scene-by-scene basis. The process was a complex literary puzzle, and it was satisfying to succeed in telling stories through it.

The aftermath of the Clavalian Heist concluded the first short story. That story ended up being the first four chapters of the book. We had a pretty good rhythm worked out. I discovered Storium doesn't allow moving a character's cards to a new story, so instead I unlocked the long-form in Storium, and we continued.

THE NOVEL

I decided to make a novel instead of a series of short stories. I started dividing the Storium scenes into chapters with about 5,000 words each, and developing the headers.

The characters came into focus for me, and I pitched proposals for how they got their nicknames. The muses liked what I came up with, so I tucked those ideas in my planning notes. We had our establishing adventure, so I concentrated on the elements the muses liked best, and wrapped a longer story around their continuing themes.

Logan brought in the zemi. Brett was all about conspiracy theories in the Dusk, as both strength and weakness. Logan wanted Scarecrow to pursue respect in the Skov community. Brett pursued Uppercut's back stage pass to join the machinery of the power brokers behind the scenes in the haunted city. They both had a pretty cavalier attitude about the threat Shimmer posed, and they wanted to know more about tattoos in Doskvol.

By the time we wrapped up the auction house heist at the end of chapter 8, I was sussing out the end game for the novel. We had pulled out enough toys that it would take the rest of the book to get them all put away, to deliver on enough of what we planted.

I pitched the ideas that formed the foundation for the last chapters, so we would all know the direction we were working towards as we addressed various scenes and challenges along the way. Sure, these elements would change if the story went a different way, but knowing where I was headed helped me craft the necessary elements to get there while working within and around the constraints of the muse input and the card responses to challenges.

THE BREAK

I shelved *Raining Sideways* in the fall of 2020, because I was planning *Breath and Burns* in October and writing it for National Novel Writing Month in November. I succeeded in that effort, and I needed some time to recover, then edit the book and prepare it for publication.

After *Breath and Burns* came out, the muses wanted a reference document for *Raining Sideways* before continuing work, as there were a lot of people, places, plot devices, and plans to track. It took me time to pull that together. By the time I had everything ready to go and a new scene posted on Storium, we got word that Logan had passed away.

I talked to Brett about the possible next moves. I felt I could finish the story on my own and do justice to the process we used for the first ten chapters. I had already discussed the overall end with both of the muses. Brett agreed, and I dropped Storium, finishing the writing using my more familiar methods.

THE CONCLUSION

The last eight chapters are still driven by contributions from Brett and Logan. They set up directions and responded to what I wrote, locking in focal points. They approved the general origins of their characters' nicknames. They workshopped the last conflict resolutions with me. I think they would both really like the outcome.

The idea of using Storium came out of my desire to increase engagement with my Patreon supporters. At every stage, my patrons supported this work.

I enjoy both generative and interpretive creativity. I made up context, and interpreted the muse response to it. I pulled inspiration from Storium mechanics and *Blades in the Dark* structures (stylistic, fictional, and mechanical), as well as from my previous fiction and games played at my table.

The book you have should be fully accessible even if the reader has no familiarity with any of that background. Part of my creative task is to mix up all the ingredients so smoothly that the reader can enjoy the dish without knowing anything about the recipe or the kitchen.

Enjoy your meal.

Andrew Shields
September 2021

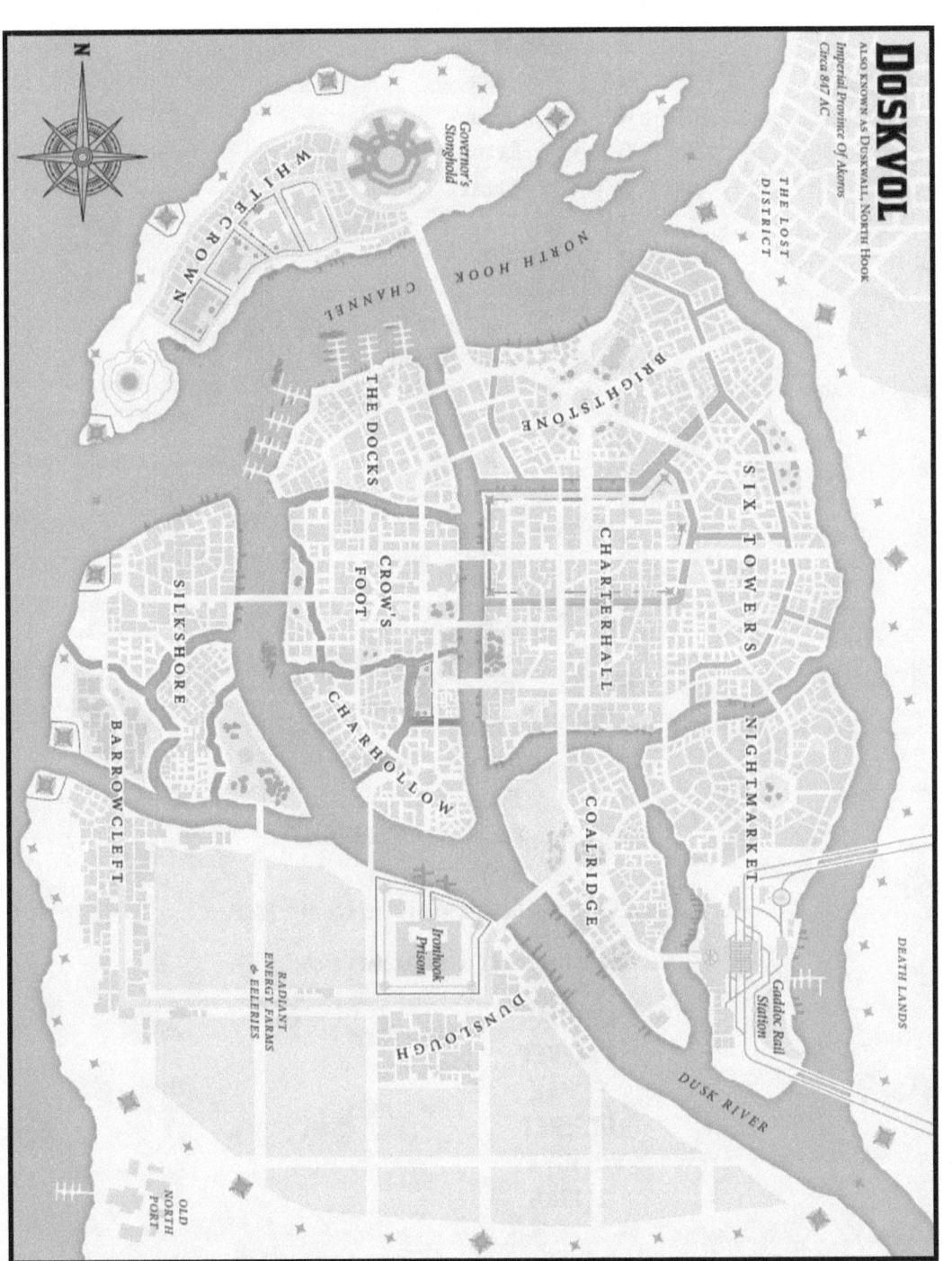

TIME	HOUR	
1 AM	SILK	
2	WINE	
3	ASH	
4	COAL	
5	CHAINS	
6	SMOKE	
7	1	DAWN
8	2	
9	3	
10	4	
11	5	
12	6	NOON
1 PM	7	
2	8	
3	9	
4	10	
5	11	
6	12	
7	HONOR	DUSK
8	SONG	
9	SILVER	
10	THREAD	
11	FLAME	
12	PEARLS	MIDNIGHT

THE IMPERIAL CALENDAR HAS SIX MONTHS, SIXTY DAYS EACH.

A MONTH IS TEN WEEKS WITH SIX DAYS EACH.

MENDAR	
KALIVET	WINTER
SURAN	
ULSIVET	SPRING
VOLNIVET	
ELISAR	FALL

PATREON SPONSORS

Phyllis Hurshman

David Brock

Mark Robison

RavenRavel

René Lößner

B. Bredthauer

Brett Casto

Dixie G Burns

Edward J. Cunningham

Elizabeth Parmeter

John Harper

Jonathan Shields

Joshua Louderback

Petri Wessman

R. A. Clark

Tom Hofmeister

James Robertson

Kevin Tompos

Michael Liebhart

Edchuk

PATREON